SEDUCING
THE HEIRESS

SEDUCING
THE HEIRESS

OLIVIA DRAKE

St. Martin's Paperbacks

This is a work of fiction. All of the characters, organizations, and events portrayed in this novel are either products of the author's imagination or are used fictitiously.

SEDUCING THE HEIRESS

For information address St. Martin's Press, 175 Fifth Avenue, New York, NY 10010.

ISBN: 978-0-312-94345-5

Printed in the United States of America

St. Martin's Paperbacks edition / December 2009

St. Martin's Paperbacks are published by St. Martin's Press, 175 Fifth Avenue, New York, NY 10010.

10 9 8 7 6 5 4 3 2 1

CHAPTER I

Colin Byrd, Viscount Ratcliffe, was on the prowl for a wife. He intended to snare the richest heiress of the London Season.

Halting his mount in the night-darkened alleyway, he glanced at the mansion beyond the trees. The faint lilt of a waltz drifted from the open windows, the squares of golden light glowing against the black monolith of the house. How ironic that he would make his conquest right under the nose of the Duke of Albright.

An unholy zeal gripped Colin. He would like nothing better than to come face-to-face with the longtime enemy of his family. It would give him great pleasure to fell the bastard with one blow.

But not tonight.

Tonight, Colin was on the hunt. His quarry was female—one girl in particular. She was young and vulnerable, and her low status as a commoner would make her all the more susceptible to a nobleman's calculated charm.

His charm.

He dismounted, his booted feet landing on the narrow lane that led to the stables. As he fastened the reins to a post, the nag whiffed softly in the darkness, nudging his hands for a lump of sugar.

Colin rubbed her nose. It was past time to put the ancient mare out to pasture. But he couldn't afford to replace her. Yet.

"Hang on, old girl," he murmured. "If all goes well, you'll have plenty of oats in your future."

Leaving the horse tethered in the shadows, he paced to the stone wall and peered into the gloom of the garden. The mews was quiet, in contrast to the front of the mansion where a long line of vehicles circled the square and coachmen gathered around makeshift fires to ward off the April chill. Albright's ball marked the opening of the Season. Every member of the ton was here, and that would work to his advantage. It should be simple to blend in with the hordes of aristocrats. He was one of them himself—even if his blackened reputation had barred him from their gatherings.

Because of that, he lacked the requisite invitation to enter by the front door. But he wouldn't let such a minor complication stop him.

At the rear gate, he lifted the latch and slipped into the formal garden with its dim paths arranged in geometric shapes. As he started toward the house, a clear sense of purpose fueled him: find his prey and isolate her. And in the doing, avoid Albright. Colin knew that if he encountered the duke, he'd be thrown out into the street. His plans would be ruined. But he could not—would not—fail.

Too much depended upon his success tonight.

Miss Portia Crompton knew she'd said the wrong thing the instant the words left her lips. The shocked stares of the aristocrats sitting at the supper table proved the rashness of her comment.

Lady Whittingham arched a thin gray eyebrow. Mrs. Beardsley scowled, a forkful of roast partridge clutched in her plump fingers. Her daughter, Miss Frances Beardsley, a blond china doll clad in pale pink, uttered a breathy squeak of horror.

Bite your tongue. In her head, Portia could hear her mother's scolding voice. Similar rebukes had been directed at Portia many times over the past year while she had been preparing for this, her grand entry into London society at the Duke of Albright's ball. She was to engage in polite chitchat about the weather, the splendor of the ballroom, and other dull topics.

She was *not* to mention any of her experiences growing up in India.

"*You've* bagged a tiger?" asked the Marquess of Dunn, straightening his gangly form in his chair. "How extraordinary."

Lord Wrayford's pale blue eyes goggled in his florid face. "By gad, Miss Crompton, you must be a crack shot. You make our fox hunting tales sound tame by comparison."

"If only I'd been there," the Honorable Henry Hockenhull said fervently. The third son of an earl, he had auburn hair and a youthful freckled face above an elaborate cravat. "I vow I would have protected you with my life!"

For the first time, Portia noticed it was only the ladies who looked disapproving. The three gentlemen at the small round table cast admiring looks at her. But she refused to be flattered by their fawning attention. Although the mirror in her bedchamber this evening had reflected a pleasing transformation, she knew it was her outrageously large dowry that fascinated them the most. If not for her father's riches—earned in trade overseas—she would never have been admitted to their exalted circle. These aristocrats were willing to overlook common blood for one reason alone: wealth.

Little did they know, Portia had no intention of marrying an English nobleman. Absently, she fingered the tiny gold key that dangled from her bracelet. She had a plan for her future. A risky plan she had kept secret even from her beloved younger sisters.

"Do tell us about this hunt," commanded Lord Dunn. "You must have suffered a terrible fright."

Just like that, Portia was transported back to the humid heat of the jungle, seeing the tiger burst out of the thick underbrush, hearing its guttural snarl, smelling the pungent reek of musk and gunpowder. She had fired on instinct, her senses honed by the long hours of instruction from Arun. Only afterward had she become aware of her pounding heart and weak knees. She had stood over the magnificent carcass, shaken yet exultant at having killed the man-eater that had terrorized several villages.

"There was no time to be afraid," she said. "It all happened rather quickly. It was a long time ago." Two years. A lifetime. A world away from this gilded dining chamber with its high vaulted ceiling and elegantly attired guests. Nostalgia vanished as she spied her mother at a corner table, glaring in her direction. "Er, the weather is rather chilly this evening, is it not?"

Her attempt to change the subject failed miserably.

"Hunting tigers," huffed Mrs. Beardsley. Her rotund form encased in brown silk, she resembled the sausage on her overloaded plate. "It's a wonder your parents would allow such behavior."

"It wasn't their fault," Portia felt obliged to say. "They didn't know where I'd gone."

"Indeed! Were you permitted to roam at will through the countryside?"

"And in such a heathen land!" old Lady Whittingham said in a quavering tone.

"*I* would never dream of behaving in so improper a manner," Frances Beardsley added. "Of course, *I* had a genteel upbringing." She batted her pale lashes at the men, but their attention remained fixed on Portia.

"India sounds dashed exciting," Henry Hockenhull said wistfully. "Were I not destined to enter the clergy, I should have liked to have gone there myself, as an officer in the cavalry, perhaps. I believe I would have made a first-rate commander."

The Marquess of Dunn leaned forward to block the young man from Portia's view. "The exotic locale only seems to have nurtured the delicate flower of your beauty, Miss Crompton. Perhaps after supper you would consent to another dance with me—"

"Have you ever seen a cobra, Miss Crompton?" Lord Wrayford interrupted in a bid to forestall his rivals. "I've heard there are magicians who can coax a snake out of a basket by playing a flute."

Portia had witnessed much more than that. She could regale them for hours with stories of mad dogs running wild, of holy men in turbans and women in colorful saris, of riding through the jungle on the back of an elephant. With all her heart, she yearned to return there. "Yes, I often saw snake charmers perform in the bazaar. They would sit cross-legged on the ground and play a tune on a *pungi*—a flute fashioned from a gourd. As if by magic, the viper would rise slowly from the basket and perform a dance, swaying back and forth."

"How very barbaric!" Mrs. Beardsley declared. "Pray consider our delicate sensibilities."

"Yes," said Miss Frances Beardsley, mimicking her mother's shudder. "If I hear any more, I shall swoon!"

Tickled by the image of the girl pitching facefirst into her plate of lobster salad and roasted capon, Portia suppressed a smile. She would never understand the tendency of these English-bred ladies toward silly histrionics.

Mrs. Beardsley patted her daughter's hand. "There, there, my darling. One must make allowances for Miss Crompton, since her parents never saw fit to send her and her sisters back to England for their schooling."

"We had the advantage of excellent tutors," Portia said in defense of her two siblings. "Ask me any question about geometry or astronomy or literature. If you like, I can provide the answers in Greek and French, as well as in Hindi."

Mrs. Beardsley glowered. "Cleverness is most unbecoming in a lady. My Frances learned the skills of the pianoforte and singing, not mathematics and shooting."

"I fear we are doomed to differ on the quality of my education," Portia said, smiling to take the sting out of her words. "For I shall never regret the tigerskin rug that lies on the floor of my bedchamber."

As one, the gentlemen leaned forward, their eyes avid. "Your bedchamber?" said the Marquess of Dunn.

"That must be quite a sight to behold," added Lord Wrayford.

"I should like to see—" Henry Hockenhull broke off, blushing to the tips of his big ears.

Belatedly, Portia remembered that ladies didn't mention their bedchambers in public. It was another of the many ridiculous rules of the highbrow British society that she had never aspired to join.

Mrs. Beardsley fanned herself with a white lace handkerchief. "This is too much. Close your ears, my darling Frances, lest you hear any more unseemly remarks."

"Yes, Mama." Miss Beardsley obediently lifted her hands to frame her face, although it was obvious from her alert expression that she had no intention of missing a single word of the conversation. Undoubtedly, she would take glee in repeating it to all of her friends. Portia would become the object of malicious gossip.

And then she would be in grave trouble with her parents. They wanted desperately for her to make an excellent match and establish the Crompton family as full-fledged members of society. At present, they were accepted solely on the basis of their immense wealth. It wasn't for her own prospects that she feared. Rather, her parents had warned Portia that failure would mean the ruin of her sisters, too.

And that she could never abide.

She forced a contrite smile. "I spoke out of turn. Pray forgive me if I've offended anyone."

The three gentlemen spoke all at once.

"You've done no wrong."

"No offense taken."

"You're utterly blameless."

Mrs. Beardsley's lips pinched into a thin line. "Spoken very prettily, Miss Crompton. However, I am reminded of the old saying: One cannot make a silk purse out of a sow's ear."

The insult slapped Portia. Although she had expected intolerance from the nobility, she had never anticipated such unbridled spite. To make matters worse, Mrs. Beardsley had projected her voice, and some of the guests at neighboring tables had cocked their heads to eavesdrop.

You're the nasty sow.

The retort sprang to the tip of Portia's tongue. It remained unspoken, for at that moment a tiny missile soared through the air.

It struck Mrs. Beardsley just above the décolletage of her gown, splattering red droplets over the pasty mounds of exposed skin.

Portia blinked. Was that . . . a *strawberry*?

Mrs. Beardsley released an unearthly howl. She reared back in her chair, her tight curls bouncing around her pudgy face. For the space of a heartbeat, the juicy morsel perched on the mountain of flesh. Then the strawberry skied down the white slope into the deep valley of her bosom and vanished from sight.

She screeched again. Throughout the supper room, gentlemen sprang to their feet. A flock of ladies flew to the rescue. Frances proved useless, half swooning into the arms of the hapless Lord Dunn. Lord Wrayford attempted to fish out the fruit with his silver spoon, which only made Mrs. Beardsley yell louder and beat at his hand.

Portia swallowed another untimely gurgle of laughter. Now *that* was judgment from the heavens.

But the strawberry hadn't fallen from the sky. Nor had it been dropped accidentally. Someone must have thrown it. Who would have dared?

She turned to scan the gathering. Throngs of people clustered around the table, making it difficult to see past them. Rising from her chair, Portia squeezed her way out of the crush. Her gaze stopped on an extraordinarily handsome, dark-haired man leaning against one of the pillars near the buffet table. His burgundy coat and crisp white cravat enhanced his powerful male physique.

She guessed at once that he was the culprit. Perhaps it was the way he stood watching her, his eyes a startling green against the tanned skin of his face. Perhaps it was the wicked smile that quirked one corner of his mouth. Or perhaps it was just that he looked like the sort of rascal who would enjoy playing a prank on one of the grande dames of society.

His next action affirmed his guilt. His gaze holding hers, he plucked another strawberry from a dish on the buffet and proceeded to eat it with relish, licking his fingers clean afterward.

A flush radiated from the core of her body. The warmth made Portia long for the fan she had left lying on the table. She couldn't quite fathom her spontaneous reaction to him. It rattled her composure and awakened irrepressible questions.

She had strict orders to avoid the company of any gentleman to whom she had not been properly introduced. But curiosity overwhelmed her. Seizing advantage of the hubbub, she marched straight to the stranger.

He was tall, forcing her to lift her chin to meet his gaze. Despite his casual pose, he radiated confidence and something else, something that made her pulse beat faster. Oddly, it robbed the breath from her lungs as well.

Unwilling to be intimidated, Portia resisted the impulse to take a step backward. "Sir," she said, keeping her voice low. "You threw that strawberry. Why?"

"It seemed an effective way to distract the woman."

Had Mrs. Beardsley's abuse been so loud? "You couldn't possibly have heard our conversation from halfway across the room."

"Shall I claim to be blessed by acute hearing?" He paused, considering her with those remarkable eyes. "No, I can see you're too clever a girl to trust such a boast. So let's just say I know the old baggage and the poison she spews."

He smiled, and her heart gave an irksome lurch. Of course, the involuntary effect didn't signify anything. He had done her a favor—even if in an indecent manner. "Well," she said, allowing a trace of hauteur to enter her voice, "I appreciate the diversion. You saved me from insulting her in public."

"Hypocrites deserve to be insulted." He picked up the

dish of plump red fruit and offered it to her. "Would you care for a strawberry?"

Eyes widening, she glanced over her shoulder. Thankfully, most of the guests still gathered around Mrs. Beardsley, who was being helped to her feet by a crimson-faced Henry Hockenhull.

Portia snatched the dish out of the stranger's hand and replaced it on the table. "Have you gone mad? Everyone will guess you're the cause of this uproar."

"You're quite right. I shouldn't wish to be tossed out on my ear when I've only just met the loveliest female present."

The tribute was too outrageous to be genuine. Yet he had a smooth sincerity that warmed her nonetheless. "Thank you, but we *haven't* met. I shouldn't even be speaking to you. If you'll excuse me."

He took a quick step to block her departure. "Viscount Ratcliffe, at your service. Otherwise known to my friends as Colin Byrd. There, I am no stranger to you now."

It was hardly a proper introduction. But he was a peer, so surely her mother wouldn't object to her bending the rules. And Portia did so want to loiter in his company. There was a compelling aura about Viscount Ratcliffe that drew her interest like a lodestone. "It's a pleasure to make your acquaintance, my lord."

She offered him her hand, intending for him to shake it. Instead, he bent down and the brush of his lips on her bare skin stirred a flurry of goose bumps. Once again, she found herself breathless.

"It's *my* pleasure," he said. "And you are . . . ?"

She hesitated, reluctant to surrender anonymity. "Miss Portia Crompton."

"Ah, the new arrival from India. I'm happy to discover the rumors of your beauty are no exaggeration." He playfully fingered the dainty gold bracelet on her wrist. "Is this the key to your heart?"

Startled, she jerked her hand free. If only he knew.

His silky tone and warm smile betrayed no surprise that he was conversing with the wealthiest heiress on the marriage mart. Had he known her identity all along? Had he lobbed that strawberry in order to draw her attention from his rivals?

The thought stirred a sharp disappointment in her. Lord Ratcliffe must be just another gentleman who lavished compliments in the hopes of claiming her rich dowry. She ought to take her leave, yet perversely she lingered. "Why did you call Mrs. Beardsley a hypocrite?"

"Because she was looking down her nose at you. It's rather ironic considering the dark secret in her past."

"Secret?"

"Not gossip, but an irrefutable fact." Lord Ratcliffe aimed a roguish wink at her. "Come closer and I'll tell you."

Without thinking, Portia found herself taking a step toward him, rising slightly on tiptoes, inhaling the spicy scent of his cologne. Eagerness tingled in her. It was absurd to react as if he were a snake charmer playing his *pungi*. But he made her so . . . so curious. "What is it?"

He bent down to whisper in her ear, his breath warm on her skin. "Mrs. Beardsley isn't the blue blood she would have you believe. Her grandfather was a fishmonger at Billingsgate Market."

The amusement Portia had been repressing all evening bubbled forth. "Truly? Oh, I shouldn't laugh. My father is a merchant, too."

"So he is. And I can only think highly of a man who has raised so lively a daughter." Taking hold of her arm, Lord Ratcliffe said, "It's far too noisy in here, don't you agree? Come, let's find a quiet corner and you can tell me all about yourself."

Just like that, he steered her toward the arched doorway. His nearness invigorated her, and she felt a burning desire to talk about *him*. What were his favorite pursuits? Where was his home? Who were his family? How swiftly a sense of camaraderie had formed between them, yet Portia knew next to nothing about him.

Certainly she liked his sense of humor. He was clever and charming and handsome. If she had to endure a Season in London society, she might as well pass the time with amusing companions. The prospect filled her with giddy anticipation.

From the ballroom came the inharmonious sounds of the orchestra tuning their instruments. The high drama of Mrs. Beardsley's mishap had passed, and streams of guests were leaving the supper room to join the next set.

As the viscount guided her to the edge of the throng, Portia noticed people staring at them, gentlemen frowning and women whispering behind their fans. Lord Ratcliffe nodded at a few without stopping to talk. Somehow, she had the distinct impression it was he who had drawn their interest, not she.

Or was it just her imagination?

His hand firmed around her upper arm. Pulling her to an abrupt halt, he muttered under his breath, *"Blast."*

"I beg your pardon?"

Then Portia spied her mother sailing toward them against the tidal flow of the crowd. A petite woman with a girlish figure untouched by time, Mrs. Edith Crompton wore a fashionable gown in a rich royal blue with a low-cut neck and short sleeves. A peacock feather bobbed and swayed in her upswept russet hair. She ruled the house with relentless vigor. Portia's father fondly referred to her as his little tigress, and at the moment, Portia could tell by the set expression on her face that she was perturbed. *Very* perturbed.

"It's my mother," she said, bracing herself for battle. "She'll want to meet you."

"Not if Albright has any say in the matter."

Only then did Portia notice the man at her mother's side. The sea of guests parted to allow him passage. A middle-aged man with silver at his temples, the duke was the epitome of sophistication in a gray silk coat, black waistcoat and breeches, with a diamond stickpin glinting in his white cravat. He strode forward with the authority of one who has known since birth of his exalted stature.

His alliance with her mother confused Portia. Upon her arrival in the vast entrance hall, she had made the obligatory curtsy to the duke in the long receiving line, a chore for her and a triumph for her parents. He had uttered a perfunctory greeting, hardly seeming even to notice the obeisance of yet another debutante.

Why did he look so intent on her now?

Lord Ratcliffe bent to whisper in her ear. The warmth of his breath sent a delicious shiver over her skin. "Meet me in Hyde Park at ten tomorrow morning," he said. "I'll be waiting in the small temple near the Serpentine. Do you know the place?"

"Yes, but—"

"Please, I must see you again. At least promise you'll try."

His urgent manner mystified her. "All right."

Then the duke and her mother stopped before them. The other guests gave them wide berth, while casting inquisitive glances their way.

Lord Ratcliffe seemed oblivious to any watchers. He radiated cool charisma as he inclined his head. "Albright. And Mrs. Crompton, I understand. May I say you have a most charming daughter."

"That's enough, Ratcliffe," Albright snapped. "I don't recall seeing your name on the list of invitations."

"An oversight, I'm sure."

"Hardly. You aren't wanted here. I won't have my guests consorting with murderers."

The breath seared Portia's throat. Try as she might, she couldn't draw air into her lungs. Several gasps and excited murmurs came from the onlookers. But her gaze remained fixed on Lord Ratcliffe. He was still smiling, though his lips now formed a tight line.

He arched an eyebrow. "You always knew how to spoil a party, Albright. I'll see myself to the door."

After bowing to the ladies, the viscount walked away, as casually as if he were going for a stroll in the park. Portia stood frozen, stunned that he had made no attempt to deny the duke's outrageous statement.

A murderer?

It couldn't possibly be true.

Edith Crompton looped her arm through Portia's, her manner sweetly conciliatory. "Pray forgive my daughter, Your Grace. She had no notion of the man's scandalous reputation."

Albright gave a crisp nod. "She wouldn't be the first to be taken in by that scoundrel. He's a notorious philanderer." He addressed Portia directly. "As your host, I must apologize for Ratcliffe's intrusion here. I would advise that in the future you stay far away from him."

"I'll make certain she does," Mrs. Crompton said swiftly. "May I add, we are most grateful for your intervention. Aren't we, my dear?"

Her mother applied subtle pressure to her arm, but Portia needed no prompting to speak. She craved answers to her burning questions. "If Lord Ratcliffe is guilty of murder, why is he not in prison?"

"The coward convinced the courts it was an accident—even though he had a powerful motive."

"Who did he kill?"

"Shush, darling, we mustn't upset His Grace any further—"

The duke silenced Mrs. Crompton with a wave of his beringed fingers. "It's quite all right. It would benefit her to know." He regarded Portia, his elegant features grave and unforgiving. "Ratcliffe had ruinous gaming debts. And to gain his inheritance, he shot his own father."

CHAPTER 2

Colin stood near the rear of the lending library. From his position behind a bookshelf, he had a clear view of the door. The place reeked of ink and leather bindings and perfume. Ladies strolled here and there, browsing the shelves, murmuring to one another or signing out their choices at the front desk. He plucked out a volume at random and opened it while furtively monitoring the arrival and departure of the patrons.

Under normal circumstances, he wouldn't be caught dead in a lending library. It was the domain of ladies—and the few gentlemen prissy enough to accompany them. But Miss Portia Crompton had a habit of coming here every other afternoon. And he had been reduced to spying on her from a distance as she went about her daily activities.

In the fortnight since they had met, he had been frustrated in his every effort to court her again. He had gone to her house several times, only to be turned away by a stone-faced butler. He had finagled his way into several more social gatherings, but always her mastiff of a mother was lurking nearby, along with the usual horde of suitors. On the few occasions when he had managed to approach Portia, she had frozen him with a glance and walked away.

Obviously, she believed all the nasty tales about him that the ton delighted in circulating. By his own design, she and everyone else had no way of distinguishing truth from falsehood. Damn it, he needed the chance to charm her—and her money—into marriage.

"Rat? I say, is that you?"

Colin bit back a curse. Beside him stood a man in a putrid yellow waistcoat, olive-green coat, and dirt-brown knee breeches. His sandy hair showed signs of receding and his body was stouter than when they had attended Eton more than a decade ago. They had been fast friends back then, comrades in tomfoolery. But damned if he hadn't chosen an inconvenient time to pop up again.

"Turnbuckle. Always the epitome of bad fashion, I see."

"And you, Ratcliffe, are looking as ratty as ever." Clapping Colin on the shoulder, the Earl of Turnbuckle laughed at his own lame jest. "Odd place to find you, old fellow. No dice or cards or"—he lowered his voice—"beautiful hussies."

Colin kept half his attention on the door. "I enjoy a good book every now and then."

"What's that you're reading?" Turnbuckle stooped to examine the title, then chortled. "*The Mysteries of Udolpho*? Since when have you taken an interest in gothic romances?"

"I was curious to see what all the ladies were reading. As I suspected, it's worthless drivel." Colin clapped the book shut and shoved it back onto the shelf. "How about yourself? What are you doing here?"

"I'm escorting my wife, Marianne. There, in the straw bonnet." He nodded to the elfin brunette who leaned against a column a short distance away. Obviously increasing beneath her maroon gown, she had her nose stuck in a book. "Ever since I succumbed to the leg shackle last autumn, she's delighted in dragging me hither and yon. At least the lending library is better than the dress-makers and milliners."

Despite the complaint, Turnbuckle wore an idiotic grin when he gazed at his wife. The change in him confounded Colin. Was that what marriage did to a man, turned him from a freewheeling bachelor into a panting dog? He himself had no intention of ever being led around on a leash by any female.

But he did intend to wed. He must do so soon out of necessity to pay his crushing debts. For that reason, he had chosen Portia Crompton as his bride. She had proven to be a delightful surprise with her sparkling manner and luscious beauty. And although he intended to coax her into falling in love with him, he had no interest in romantic delusions himself—except when it served his purpose.

Given half a chance, he was confident he could keep her very happy without surrendering his own autonomy. She had fire beneath all that ice. He needed only the opportunity to fan the flames, and then she *would* be his.

He entertained a vivid fantasy of them naked in bed, of suckling her breasts while she rode him with unbridled lust. Yes, it would be quite enjoyable to teach such an innocent all the wicked ways a woman could please a man.

"I say, is that the famous Miss Crompton?"

For one disconcerting moment, Colin thought Turnbuckle had read his private thoughts. Then a movement near the front door caught his attention. A new arrival had just entered the library.

Portia Crompton.

The coffee-colored pelisse over a rich amber gown accentuated her feminine curves. She was tall and slender, and he feverishly speculated on the long legs beneath the layers of petticoats. A stylish hat adorned with a spray of quail feathers drew attention to her fine features and upswept brown hair. How he would love to unpin that prim bun, to undress her bit by bit, kissing all the soft places he uncovered—

A man stepped in behind her. An older man in a dark tailored coat. *Albright.* He was handing a black umbrella to a hovering attendant.

Disbelieving anger struck Colin. He had seen the duke dance with Portia at several parties. But fulfilling a polite obligation was a far cry from escorting the woman about her daily routine.

What the devil was his purpose?

The answer hit Colin in a white-hot flash. Albright was courting Portia on purpose. Because he had witnessed Colin's interest in her. And he had guessed how desperately Colin needed her dowry.

His fingers locked into fists. By God, he would throttle that bastard with his bare hands.

He started to surge out from behind the bookcase, but Turnbuckle stepped squarely to block his passage. "Don't do it."

Colin glared in fury. "Get out of my way."

"Keep your voice down, man." Turnbuckle's expression took on a shrewd look. "I heard about the altercation at Albright's ball. That he stopped you from luring Miss Crompton away and ravishing her."

"You shouldn't believe everything you hear."

"Right. Well, believe this: If you start a brawl in a library, you'll never win her hand."

A glimmer of sanity forced its way into Colin's brain. He raked his fingers through his hair. He didn't want to admit it, but Turnbuckle had a point. "Damn him. He's more than twice her age."

The earl chuckled. "Since when has that mattered in

noble alliances? Albright needs an heir. Her parents wish to buy her a title and they could scarcely do better."

The lady in question was gazing straight at the bookcase behind which Colin stood. He stared back through the narrow opening, almost certain that the shelves concealed his identity from her view.

He didn't understand what Turnbuckle found so amusing. Maybe that was another way marriage spoiled a man; it made him gloat to see his single friends forced into the thorny brambles of courtship.

Albright was opening a thick tome and showing it to Portia. She listened to him attentively, nodding her head now and then. The duke had the air of a courteous, obliging suitor who had her best interests at heart.

Like hell. She had no notion of his conniving nature. Only Colin—and his mother—knew the truth about Albright.

Turnbuckle planted a commiserating hand on Colin's shoulder. "Never fear, all is not lost. There's another factor that influences the marriage game."

"Lust."

The earl laughed. "There is that. But I was referring to the lady's wishes. It seems you'll just have to find a clever way to steal her heart."

"So sorry, no letter," Kasi said, spreading her hands wide to show her withered brown palms.

Portia frowned at her old *ayah,* who stood in the doorway of the bedchamber. The short, leathery-skinned woman wore a brilliant orange sari beneath a drab cloak, from which wafted the damp scent of rain. A peacock blue scarf covered the knob of gray hair on her head. Behind her, candlelight flickered in wall sconces along the opulent passageway. It was past ten in the evening, and Kasi had just returned from her half-day off.

Portia should have been dancing tonight at Lady Mortimer's soiree. It had taken considerable persuasion to convince Mama to let her remain at home. She'd had to pretend a scratchy throat and a fit of coughing that was certain to repel all of her suitors. In reality, Portia had wanted to be here when Kasi returned. The letter she was expecting from India was much too important to miss.

But her scheming had been for naught.

"Nothing?" she asked in dismay. "Did you check directly with Mr. Brindley, not one of his underlings?"

Kasi nodded. "I ride in cab, go to docks like always. But no letter." Her brown eyes somber, she shook a finger as she'd done countless times during Portia's childhood. "I know what happen, missy."

"What?"

"You not do as I say, you not pray to Rama and Sita. That is why Maharaj Arun forsake you."

"Arun hasn't forsaken me." Lips compressed, Portia fished in her pocket for a coin, which she handed to the servant. "And you know full well I can't pray to your gods. Mama would have a fit. Now, thank you and good night."

As the door closed behind the muttering servant, Portia paced the length of her bedchamber, taking little notice of the plush carpet beneath her bare feet or the luxurious blue and gilt furnishings. She fretted over what Kasi had said. Had she really faded from Arun's mind? Had he forgotten the vow they had made to each other on the night before she had set sail for England a year ago?

Impossible. Or was it?

After all, she herself had been guilty of forgetting him, if only momentarily. It had happened a fortnight ago at the Duke of Albright's ball when she had fallen under the spell of Viscount Ratcliffe.

The memory made Portia blush with shame. She had been on the brink of going off with him, of letting him lure her away from the other guests. Heaven only knew what might have happened if fate had not intervened in the form of the Duke of Albright and her mother. Beneath his polished exterior, Ratcliffe was a ruthless, unprincipled scoundrel. Whether by accident or deliberate malice, he had caused the death of his own father.

The knowledge filled her with revulsion.

She had not gone to their rendezvous in Hyde Park. Rather, she had spent the following morning at the shops with her mother and two sisters, purchasing hats and gloves and other trivialities. She had chatted and smiled, all the while wondering how long Ratcliffe would wait for her, or if he was angered by her absence.

Not that his reaction mattered. He had deceived her into believing him to be an honorable man. But he was just another greedy fortune hunter, a man who would stop at nothing to take what he wanted.

In the past week, she had glimpsed him several times from a distance, once on the street as she was exiting her carriage. Ratcliffe had attempted to approach her, but she had turned a cold shoulder and hurried into the house. Then this afternoon, she was almost certain she had seen him watching her from behind a bookshelf at the lending library. If the Duke of Albright had not been present, she would have marched straight to Ratcliffe and ordered him to mind his own business.

Lately, the duke had become her self-appointed protector, much to her mother's delight. It rather suited Portia, too, for he was an easy companion, well versed in polite conversation and a formidable deterrent to Lord Ratcliffe's advances.

Nevertheless, the viscount unnerved her. He was too bold, too corrupt, too seductive. He was like a cobra, beautiful but deadly. And in character he was the precise opposite of Arun.

Arun.

Arun was the man she loved. They had become fast friends as children. While her father conducted business with Arun's father, the maharajah of Mumbai, she and Arun had played together. She vividly remembered the first time she had met him, a grave little boy in a long white robe, flying a kite in the gardens of the palace. He had given her the string to hold; it was attached to a brilliant butterfly made of colored paper and fine bamboo. The kite had felt alive in her hands, and the delight of seeing it ride the currents of wind still glowed in her memory.

If all went according to her plan, she would return to India at the end of the Season to be with Arun again. This time forever.

She paced to the bedside table and opened the top drawer. From beneath the jumble of handkerchiefs and notecards and books, she drew out a small gold box, the lid encrusted with emeralds, sapphires, and diamonds in the form of a peacock. Using the tiny gold key on her bracelet, she opened the box.

A single item lay nestled inside on a bed of blue velvet. It was an oval miniature of Arun. Cradling the painting in the palm of her hand, she held it beneath the light of a candle and studied his familiar features: the smooth dusky skin, the warm brown eyes, the noble bearing. Well educated by a series of English tutors, he had grown up in a magnificent white palace near the Crompton family home in Bombay.

She had always been aware theirs was a forbidden love, although by tacit agreement they had seldom spoken of it. Rather, they had spent their days in the innocent pleasures of reading to each other in the shade of the banyan trees or sitting on the banks of Mahim Bay to watch the boats pass by and the women doing their laundry.

She remembered the gentleness of their first kiss and then the shock of her mother's discovery of them in the shadows of the verandah. Livid, Mrs. Crompton had banished Arun from their property and lectured Portia on the impropriety of her actions.

"It's disgraceful enough that you would allow such liberties," she had ranted. *"But with a native boy—!"*

"I love Arun," Portia countered. *"He loves me, too."*

"Love! Have you no thought for your father's good name? And what about your sisters? You'll ruin all of us with your rash behavior."

"No, it won't be that way. Arun is a prince. When we marry, people will have to accept us."

Her mother's face turned white with fury. "I knew it was a mistake for your father to allow you such freedom. But enough is enough. You will not be permitted to dishonor this family."

No amount of impassioned arguments could sway her mother's judgment. The incident had caused an explosive quarrel between her parents. Portia had cringed to hear them shouting at each other behind closed doors. The following day, Mrs. Crompton had directed an army of natives to pack the family's belongings. To Portia's horror, they were moving to England to take their rightful place in society.

She had begged Arun to run away with her. But *his* father had been appalled by the notion of the high-caste prince marrying a foreigner. He, too, had prohibited the alliance, and Arun could not renounce his own principles by disobeying. He had assured her that, in time, he could persuade the maharajah to accept the match. The British community would be scandalized, of course, but Portia didn't care if she was shunned. She only wanted to be with the man who made her feel safe and loved, the man who had been her friend forever.

She clasped the miniature to the bodice of her nightgown. Arun always had written to her without fail; this was the first time since her departure for England a year ago that his regular letter had not arrived.

Struck by an awful fear, she groped for the bedpost and clung tightly to the cool mahogany. What if something dreadful had happened to Arun? What if he had fallen ill—or died?

So many dangers abounded in India. Poisonous vipers. Vicious tigers. Rampaging elephants. And then there were the fatal diseases. It was not uncommon for a person to be healthy one day and dead of a fever the next.

Shuddering, she placed the miniature on her pillow, unwilling to lock it away just yet. It would serve no purpose to worry. The missing correspondence was likely due to the vagaries of the mail system—a ship run aground, a voyage delayed. Surely there would be a letter next time, probably two at once.

The trouble was, she would have to wait for an entire month until Kasi's next half-day off. It was impossible for Portia to escape her mother's watchful eye long enough to travel clear across London to the shipping office at the docks. And she dared not have the letters delivered to this house lest her parents discover her scheme to return to India.

She went to the window and looked out into the night. It was damp and cold and gloomy. Here, there were no jackals skulking through the shadows, no buzz of crickets in the hot darkness. Had the moon been shining, she might have stepped out onto the balcony to gaze up at the stars. She and Arun had done so many times in India, finding the constellations and making up new ones to amuse themselves.

On a whim, she went into her dressing room and stripped off her pale nightdress, leaving it in a puddle on the floor. The spacious chamber had built-in cabinetry that held an impressive collection of morning gowns and walking dresses, ball gowns and riding clothes. Undoubtedly her mother thought the sky would fall down if the premier heiress of the Season were to be seen in the same attire more than once.

From the depths of a drawer, behind an assortment of corsets and petticoats, Portia pulled out a sari. A deep marigold hue spangled with tiny gold beads, the garment had been a going-away gift from Arun. When she held it to her nose, the faint scent of sandalwood clung to the fabric. She had seldom—never—worn a sari, but often enough had watched Kasi put one on.

Relying on memory, she looped and draped the length of silk around herself, finally tucking the end into her waist. The dressing table had a wide variety of cosmetics, and she used a pot of rouge to apply a tiny ruby dot to her forehead. Going to her jewelry box, she added an array of gold bangles to her arms. Then she stood before the long pier glass and blinked in amazement. Had her skin been darker, she might have been mistaken for a native woman.

How strange she looked, yet how familiar. A curious tug-of-war waged inside her, as if she had one foot planted in England and the other in India. Closing her eyes, she let herself wallow in memories of her childhood home. She remembered days so hot it took her breath away, a sky so bright blue it hurt the eyes, the raucous whistle of mynah birds in the trees. How she longed to feel the sun-baked earth beneath her bare feet again . . .

A draft of cold air snapped her back to reality. It had come from her bedchamber; the fire must need tending. Shivering, she rubbed her bare arms. The sari was ill suited to the climate of England, and her mother would have an apoplectic fit if she caught Portia wearing it.

But Mama and Papa were out for the night, and her sisters lay abed in their chambers at the end of the passageway. There was no one to stop Portia from indulging in a bit of fantasy. So she imagined herself a bride on her wedding night. Arun would be waiting in the next room, ensconced in her bed. She knew a little about intimate relations, having eavesdropped on the frank talk between native servants, although when she tried to envision herself doing *that* with her childhood friend, the image failed to materialize.

No matter. She would sit by the fire and dream about Arun holding her close again, gently kissing her . . .

Smiling, she floated into her bedchamber. Shock brought her to an abrupt halt. A strangled gasp choked her throat.

In the chair by the fire, his boots propped on a footstool, sat Viscount Ratcliffe.

CHAPTER 3

Watching her intently, he held up his hand. "Don't scream—please. I mean you no harm."

Portia didn't scream, not because he had said so but because she was horrifyingly aware that no one would hear her. Her parents would be out until the wee hours, her sisters were asleep in their rooms far down the corridor, and the servants were either in their attic bedchambers or in the basement workrooms.

But a footman remained on duty downstairs in the entrance hall.

Heart pounding, she made a dash for the door, prepared to cry out for help. The knob refused to turn. She frantically rattled it, shoving at the white-painted panel.

"It's locked," Ratcliffe said, holding up the skeleton key that usually rested in the keyhole. "A mere precaution."

Frightened and furious, she spun to face him. "How dare you!"

"I'd dare quite a lot to see you, Miss Crompton. When you didn't attend Lady Mortimer's soiree tonight, I had to resort to drastic measures."

What was he doing here? Had he gone mad?

Portia considered lunging at him, wresting the key out of his hand. Then she bitterly acknowledged his superior strength. If she gave him half a chance, he could easily grab her.

Her only hope was to summon a maid by tugging on the bellpull. But the gold cord hung near the fireplace. It was impossible to reach it without risking capture. Nor were there any handy weapons in the bedchamber—except for the fireplace poker which was propped beside him against the mantel.

"How did you get past the footman?" she demanded.

"I climbed up the trellis."

He waved to the balcony doors. Portia flicked a glance there to see the doors slightly ajar. No wonder she'd felt a draft of cold air . . . although she hadn't heard a sound. How had he even known which bedchamber belonged to her? He must have spied her as she'd stood at the window a short while ago. Under different circumstances, she might have marveled at his resourcefulness.

But not tonight, not when she was alone, not when he had her at a deadly disadvantage.

In her iciest tone, she stated, "Get out."

"I mean you no harm," he repeated in a soothing tone, dropping the key into an inner pocket of his dark green coat. "If it makes you feel better, I'll remain right here in this chair."

"I don't want you here at all. Now go."

He made no move to obey. "I only wish to talk. You have my word."

"*Your word.* You, a man who would sneak into my house in the middle of the night. But I don't suppose *that* is anything unusual to someone of your wicked character."

"I vow I've never before entered a lady's bedchamber without her permission."

The gleam in his green eyes unnerved her. He lounged in the chair as if he were a friend come to share a cozy chat. He was smiling, his manner disarming, his black hair tousled and damp with mist. His skin was swarthy against the stark white of his cravat, and a trace of whiskers shadowed his lean cheeks. Under the force of his scrutiny, she grew aware of her nakedness beneath the silk sari.

Deep within her, something dark and disturbing stirred to life.

She smothered it viciously. Colin Byrd was a rogue who seduced women. Worse, he was a killer who had shot his own father under mysterious circumstances.

Willing her teeth not to chatter, she said, "Why are you here? State your business and be gone."

"First things first." He reached to the piecrust table beside him. "I brought you a gift."

He tossed something underhand, and she caught it by reflex. Startled, she found herself holding a stalk of lush purple flowers, each one the size of her fist. "Orchids?"

"I thought you might like them. That variety is native to India."

Portia had seen such blooms growing in the jungle, the plants clinging to the branches of trees. He couldn't possibly have known of her love for them. Yet none of her other suitors had bothered to consider her likes and dislikes. They brought her English roses and French bonbons and expected her to launch into rhapsodies of gratitude.

It wouldn't happen now, either.

She dropped the stalk on a nearby table. In a tone heavy with sarcasm, she said, "You cannot really think to dazzle me with flowers, my lord."

"One can always hope." Grinning, he looked down at the orange and black striped fur beneath his feet. "So this is the famous tigerskin rug." With languid fingers, he stroked the feline's head, its glass eyes staring and its sharp-toothed mouth open in a perpetual snarl. "I understand you shot the beast yourself. Will you tell me about it?"

The request startled Portia. Where had he learned of that? Did he really have acute hearing as he'd claimed at the Duke of Albright's ball? No, the account she had told to Mrs. Beardsley and the others must have reached his ears through gossip.

She would not permit him to turn this invasion of her privacy into a social visit. "I've no interest in chitchat. I'm ill, that's why I stayed home tonight."

"You appear in the pink of health to me." His gaze sweeping over her, he went on, "If I may add, you look extremely fetching. What is that garment you're wearing?"

"A sari. Now that's enough questions. You may call on me at a more appropriate time and place."

"And be refused admittance once more?" He shook his head. "Come, come, Miss Crompton. We both know that were I to depart now, I'd never have the slightest chance of seeing you alone again. You've made it devilishly difficult to get within a dozen yards of you."

"So you'll break into my chamber and hold me hostage?" she snapped in frustration. "Is *that* supposed to inspire my trust in you?"

For a long moment Ratcliffe stared at her, his expression dark and unreadable. A sense of foreboding crept like cold fingers down her spine. She knew so little about him. He might be volatile, hot-tempered, even unhinged. If she drove him to fury, he could overpower her in a flash.

He abruptly broke his promise to remain seated. Rising to his feet, he seemed to crowd the dimly lit bedroom with his menacing presence. He slid his hand inside the front of his coat.

Portia took an involuntary step backward. Her muscles tensed and her heart pounded. God help her, if he had a pistol . . .

But he merely withdrew her key from inside his coat, went to the door and unlocked it. He returned to his chair and resumed his relaxed posture. "Go on, then," he said. "If you're so terrified of me, you may as well flee."

Half of her itched to do just that. The other half—the prideful half—balked at another display of spineless panic.

How neatly Ratcliffe had maneuvered her. By unlocking the door, he had made flight the act of a coward.

"If you're discovered here," she said coldly, "my reputation will be ruined. No doubt that's your intention, to force me into marriage."

He shook his head. "I've already told you, I merely came to talk. There didn't seem to be any other way to catch you alone."

Her lips compressed. She could hardly throw him out on his ear when he had the advantage of superior physical power. It might be best to let him have his say. Perhaps then she could convince him to go.

"Answer one question truthfully," she said. "If you refuse, there is no chance of me believing anything else you have to say."

"Did I kill my father?" Though steel touched his tone, Ratcliffe kept his gaze focused on her. "The answer is yes, though it was a tragic accident. I won't discuss the matter any further—not with you or with anyone else."

The shadows in his eyes intrigued Portia. She sensed secrets there that she longed to probe. Was he telling the truth? If so, what exactly had happened? Had he been cleaning a pistol and it had gone off? Was it a hunting mishap? Or perhaps a stray shot in the dark at a burglar?

Sympathy tugged at her, but she resisted its allure.

She must not allow any weakening of her defenses. For all she knew, he could be lying through his teeth. The incident could have occurred just as the Duke of Albright believed, that Ratcliffe had murdered his father in order to gain his inheritance.

"That wasn't my question," she said.

He lifted one dark brow inquiringly, but made no reply. The only sounds were the soft ticking of the ormolu clock on the mantel and a spattering of raindrops against the windowpanes.

Uneasy with the silence, she asked, "I would like to know, would you be pursuing me if I were penniless—if I didn't have the largest dowry of any of the debutantes?"

"An interesting question. I applaud your directness."

"A simple no or yes will suffice."

"Then no . . . *and* yes. I'll admit, your marriage portion is what first drew you to my attention."

"So you came uninvited to Albright's ball for the sole purpose of cozening me."

He frowned, clearly annoyed to have his stratagem exposed. "If you choose to regard it that way. However, matters changed once we met. That's the *yes* in answer to your question. I *would* pursue you, Portia, no matter what your circumstances. Because you fascinate me."

He spoke in the smooth, deep tone of a man experienced in luring women. She should correct his forwardness in using her name, yet there were other, more important issues at stake. "Never mind the flattery. The truth is all that matters to me."

"I'll grant you both." He leaned forward with his elbows resting on his knees. "I came to that ball expecting to meet a giggly girl with air for brains. Instead I found a spirited woman who is more than able to match wits with me. From that moment onward, I've been determined to make you mine."

Despite her mistrust of him, her pulse leaped. The feeling was nothing more than an instinctive reaction to an attractive man, she assured herself. Arun owned her heart. Arun, whose kindness and chivalry put this scoundrel to shame.

Crossing her arms, she glared at Ratcliffe. "To be quite frank, my lord, I can see no benefit to allowing your courtship. For title and status, I certainly can do better than a viscount with a wicked reputation."

His jaw tightened, and she feared for a moment that she'd driven him over the edge. "Albright," he snapped.

She almost blurted out that the duke was merely a friend, not a suitor. But if she could use Albright to convince Ratcliffe he had no chance . . . "You saw us together today at the lending library," she said. "I thought that was you, hiding behind the shelves."

The dangerous look faded, and she wondered if she had imagined it. Once again, his eyes were unfathomable, making her intensely curious about the secrets behind those too-handsome features.

Much to her surprise, a slow grin banished his moody expression. He looked exactly like the devil-may-care rogue she had met at the duke's ball. "That's what you've reduced me to," he said. "A lonely wretch skulking in the shadows, hoping to catch a glimpse of your beauty."

Unexpected laughter bubbled up inside her. His teasing somehow eased her inner tension, and she found herself sinking cautiously onto a chair a short distance from him. "A wretch, yes, you are that. But I very much doubt you're lonely."

"I am, indeed, every moment we're apart."

Heaven help her, he was charming. He must have women falling at his feet. "Enough of your nonsense. If you're so determined to make conversation, then tell me about yourself."

"I find *you* far more interesting—"

"No. It's my home and I'll set the rules. I should like to know why you believe yourself worthy to be my suitor. Tell me about your family, your interests, how you live your life."

Colin felt his mouth go dry. He seldom discussed private matters even with his friends. It was easier to keep things light, to guard those certain events best kept hidden from the world.

Unfortunately, Portia Crompton was far less susceptible to glib talk than any woman of his acquaintance. God, she was gorgeous, even in her self-righteousness. The gold sari clung to her curves like a second skin and tendrils of curly chestnut hair had sprung loose from her topknot. He wanted nothing more than to haul her over to the bed and kiss her senseless, to touch her and stroke her until she lay purring in his arms. Unfortunately, such a rapscallion approach was guaranteed to win her ire.

She sat primly on the straight-backed chair, her skeptical expression trained on him. Clearly, she was waiting for him to reveal his redeeming qualities—*if* he possessed any, her look seemed to say.

He cleared his throat. "I own an estate in Kent, some five thousand acres of entailed farmland. My mother lives there, too. I have a younger sister, Elizabeth, who's married to a Scotsman and lives in Edinburgh. She has three children, two boys and a girl."

Portia didn't need to know that Elizabeth had deliberately chosen a husband who would take her far away from their childhood home. Colin hadn't seen her in more than five years. She hadn't even returned for their father's funeral three years ago, although to be fair, she had been recovering from childbirth at the time.

"You make yourself sound like the typical country

gentleman," Portia said. "However, I understand you're deeply in debt because of your gambling."

Colin struggled to keep the vexation from his face. Did she hold no topics sacred? "The subject of my finances is best left to your father."

"You haven't my permission to speak to Papa about anything," she countered. "And let me make one fact clear: I'll never wed a man who would squander my dowry on dice and cards."

It came as no surprise that she had her mind made up about him. He considered spilling his guts, but that would mean breaking a vow, and he wasn't yet so desperate. So he pacified her with a half-truth. "You have my promise that I'll never again set foot in a gaming hell."

She gave him a withering look. "If you think to bamboozle me, Lord Ratcliffe, we've nothing more to discuss."

"Then perhaps you'll talk about this." Determined to shift the heat off himself, Colin reached down between the cushions and withdrew the miniature he had tucked there. He had a burning need to know the identity of the man whose image she clearly held dear.

Portia sucked in an audible breath. She gripped the sides of the chair. Her big blue eyes fastened on the little oval painting, then swung to him. "Where did you get that?"

"When I came in, I saw it lying on your pillow."

She surged to her feet and marched toward him, the bangles on her arms jingling musically. "It doesn't belong to you. Give it back to me at once."

Colin sprang up, too. "First tell me who he is."

"A friend."

She made a grab for the miniature, but he held it high out of her reach. "He must have a name."

"Arun," she ground out. "Now hand it over to me. You've no right to come in here and touch my things."

The panic on her face intrigued Colin. What importance could a young, handsome native man have to her? A man whose picture she would keep in her bedchamber? The most probable answer made Colin livid. "He must be more than a friend. Was he your lover while you lived in India?"

"No!"

She made another futile attempt to snatch the miniature out of his hand, her bosom brushing against him. The chance to slide his arm around her proved too delicious to resist. Colin clasped her close, keenly aware of the curves barely concealed by thin gold silk.

"I don't believe you," he said. "While you blistered me for my sins, it would appear you yourself are no angel."

Pressing her palms to his chest, she pushed hard. "Release me at once!"

"Only when you tell me the truth about him."

"I *am* telling you the truth."

She struggled against his grip, but Colin had no intention of letting her go. His loins had an instantaneous reaction to her sinuous movements. Again, he was sorely tempted to carry her across the room to the four-poster bed. Bending closer, he murmured, "Stay still. Unless you wish me to forget what little gentlemanly restraint I have."

Gasping, she reared back at once, drawing her upper body as far away from him as possible. Desperation blazed in her eyes. "All right, blast you. I *love* Arun. When I return to India, we're going to be married."

Stunned, he stared into her flushed features. He could see every individual black lash that lined her clear blue eyes. She wasn't lying. She planned to do the unthinkable. It suddenly made sense to him why she was dressed in the sari, why she had that ridiculous red dot on her forehead and the armful of bangles.

She was pretending to be Arun's bride.

Tossing the miniature onto the chair, he grasped hold of her shoulders. "Do your parents know this?" Seeing the flash of guilt on her face, he answered for her. "Of course they don't. You've let everyone believe you're available for marriage. But you've never had any intention of choosing an Englishman for a husband."

She lifted her chin. "No. So you see, you'll never win me over. You might as well leave."

Colin was still trying to get his mind around the rashness of her plan. "You can't marry a native. You'll be shunned, not just here, but in India, too."

"It's my decision. There's no one in society I care about, anyway."

"Your father will cut you off without a penny. How will you live?" She had no idea what it was like to be poor. But Colin knew all too well.

"Arun is the son of a maharajah. I'll live in luxury in a palace."

The news that his rival was a prince irritated him more than it ought. "You can't have thought this through. You're giving up everything, your life, your country, your family. Once you act on this foolishness, there'll be no turning back."

She glanced away for a moment, then raised her chin in resolute stubbornness. "My mind is made up. I won't be dissuaded. And . . . and I would appreciate it if you wouldn't tell anyone."

"So now I'm your trusted confidant? There's a turnaround."

"You give me no other choice—oh!"

A knocking on the door startled both of them. Instantly, Colin released her, holding his finger to his lips. Portia frantically shooed him toward the balcony.

Damn it, he was not through speaking to her. He had no intention of giving up his suit. She had to realize the sheer idiocy of her plan—if only because he needed a rich wife and she was far too wealthy a prize to relinquish.

Perhaps if he waited outside for a bit, the visitor would go away. He doubted Portia would betray his presence, especially considering the volatile secret he now knew about her.

But he had taken only one step toward the balcony when the passageway door swung open. Two girls in white nightgowns burst into the bedchamber.

CHAPTER 4

Portia seldom saw her sisters speechless. But she did now.

Blythe had entered first, of course. As the youngest, she considered it her right to do as she pleased, even if it meant invading a bedroom without an invitation. Spying the man standing beside Portia, she stopped short and stared.

Lindsey, the middle sister and the tallest of the three, barreled straight into Blythe. For once they didn't squabble over who had caused the collision. They were too busy ogling Lord Ratcliffe.

Portia longed to sink into the floor. She bitterly regretted inducing him to unlock the door. Had he not done so, she would have had the chance to hide him from sight. How in the world was she to explain his presence here?

Blythe recovered first. Short and curvaceous, she patted her coppery hair, which was tied up in rags to create the wavy curls that came naturally to her sisters. Of the three, she looked the most like their mother. "I couldn't sleep. Linds and I were going down to the drawing room to fetch a deck of cards when we heard voices."

"More specifically, a *man's* voice," Lindsey corrected. Always a stickler for rules, she frowned accusingly at Portia while eyeing her sari. "Why are you dressed like that? And who is *he*?"

Portia was keenly aware of how damning the scene must look. She decided it was best to ignore the question about her garb. "This is Viscount Ratcliffe. Lord Ratcliffe, my sisters, Blythe and Lindsey."

As if they were in a ballroom, Lord Ratcliffe bowed deeply from the waist. "It's a pleasure to meet you both. I can see that beauty is a family trait."

Blythe giggled like a seasoned coquette instead of the barely fifteen-year-old schoolgirl she was. "How generous of you to say so, my lord, since we're hardly dressed for company."

"Ratcliffe?" Lindsey muttered, pulling the edges of her nightgown close around her neck. "I should like to know why *he's* in your bedchamber."

"He came to . . . to give me something." Portia cast about for an excuse, then snatched up the stalk of orchids from the table. "This."

Blythe clasped her hands to the bosom of her nightdress. "Oh, famous. They're *beautiful*. Exactly like the ones Patel used to fetch from the jungle."

Lindsey looked unimpressed. "They should have been delivered at a more suitable time and place."

"I've already told Lord Ratcliffe exactly that," Portia said. "He oughtn't to have come here. He needs to leave at once."

"As you wish," he said in a suspiciously meek tone. "Oh, but I seem to have dropped my pocket watch."

He casually sauntered back to the fireplace to pick up the gold-framed miniature of Arun, half-hidden by the arm of the chair. Her sisters fell for the ruse, much to Portia's relief. Although they knew about Arun, they—like her parents—believed she had put the youthful indiscretion behind her. They had no inkling of her plan to return to India and become his bride.

In the next breath, Portia realized that Ratcliffe was

heading toward the balcony door with the miniature hidden in the palm of his hand.

Alarmed, she went flying after him. "I'll see him out," she told her sisters over her shoulder.

She caught up to him as he opened the door. In her haste, she brushed against him. The feel of his hard-muscled form caused a tingling rush of awareness in her. Portia rubbed her arms, wishing she could blame the irksome reaction on the chilly air.

Glancing at her sisters to make sure they couldn't overhear, she whispered, "The miniature. I want it back."

A calculating smile touched his lips. "I'm sure you do. However, I don't stand a chance of winning your heart if you're mooning over another man."

"You don't stand a chance regardless." Though he towered over her, she stood her ground, thrusting out her hand. "Now give it to me at once."

"You look as if you'd like to claw my eyes out. Pray remember it wouldn't be wise to create a scene in front of your sisters."

He was right. She didn't want Lindsey and Blythe to witness her wrestling him for the miniature. Besides, if they saw the painting, they would discover that Arun remained a shining part of her future.

Ratcliffe lifted her hand to his mouth, and the warm brush of his lips tickled her skin. It set off a scandalous heat in the depths of her body. "Forget about him," he murmured, his voice deep, soft, velvety. "Dream of me tonight."

Shaken by his audacity, Portia yanked her hand free and stepped back in an instinctive effort to put distance between them. As she did so, he tucked the miniature in an inner pocket of his coat, then strode out onto the night-darkened balcony. He grasped hold of the stone railing, vaulted over the side, and vanished from sight.

She flew to the balcony. "Wait," she cried out.

But he was already a dark shadow at the bottom of the rose trellis. He turned, gave her a jaunty wave, then went loping off into the gloom of the garden, where the trees soon hid him from sight.

Her tongue brimmed with unladylike curses. Blast him, blast him to *hell*. Dream of him? She would sooner dream of the devil himself!

A panicky thought displaced her fury. He alone knew her secret; he alone had the proof of her devotion to Arun. If Ratcliffe tried to blackmail her, threatened to tell her parents . . .

She realized that Blythe stood beside her, peering out into the darkness. "Is *that* how Lord Ratcliffe reached your bedchamber, by climbing up the trellis?" she asked in awe. "How very romantic! Why, it's like something out of a storybook."

"It's appalling, that's what," Lindsey said, marching over to join them. She pulled them both back inside, then shut the balcony door with a decisive bang. "Had we not arrived when we did, he might have murdered our sister in her bed."

"Oh, bah," Blythe said with a wave of her hand. "You always think the worst of people."

"*I* have the good sense to be cautious. And I've heard talk about Lord Ratcliffe from the servants, that he shot his own father in cold blood." Lindsey gripped Portia's arm and gazed searchingly at her. "Do you suppose he had a pistol just now?"

"No! Of course not." Portia didn't want to give her sister any more fodder for suspicion. "He . . . he wishes only to court me. For my dowry, of course."

"How can you be certain? I shall report the matter to Papa the instant he arrives home."

"And then Papa will make Lord Ratcliffe wed you,"

Blythe added. Clasping her hands to her bosom, she sighed. "He's so handsome and dashing, only think how the other ladies will envy you!"

Portia rolled her eyes, then turned to Lindsey. "Do you see what will happen if you tell? I'll be forced into marriage. And Ratcliffe is a scoundrel—he would make a deplorable husband. So you must both promise me you'll keep silent."

Her sisters glanced at each other, Lindsey clearly troubled and Blythe just as clearly disappointed. Much to Portia's relief, however, they both nodded. At least she knew she could trust *them*.

Needing time to think, she shooed them out of the bedchamber. Then she paced to the fireplace and used the poker to brutally stir the coals, causing the flames to hiss and dance. The action failed to calm her volatile mood.

Now that Ratcliffe had stolen the miniature from right under her nose, he had her in his power. He could threaten to go to her father with the evidence of her duplicity. He could claim the picture had fallen out of her reticule, that he had coaxed her into telling him the truth, that she planned to return to India at the end of the Season. Her parents would be furious, heartbroken, and, worst of all, disappointed in her. They would keep her under lock and key until she married an English lord according to their wishes.

The alternative would be to submit to Ratcliffe's blackmail and accept *him* as her husband. Either way, she would lose Arun forever.

Despair washed over her. What was she to do now? In one fell swoop, Ratcliffe had ruined everything. Unless . . .

Her mind working feverishly, Portia set down the poker and straightened her shoulders. Unless she could figure out a way to steal the miniature back from him.

* * *

By breakfast the next day, Portia had settled on a plan. It was risky, it was dangerous, but it just might work. The only trouble was, the scheme would be difficult to manage without help—and she needed more than Kasi's assistance this time. So after much agonized reflection, Portia had decided to take Lindsey into her confidence.

Her sister was shocked to learn that Portia intended to leave England and marry Arun. She had argued vehemently against it. But regardless of her disapproval, she did agree that Portia needed to retrieve the miniature and had offered several sound suggestions on how to do so.

Now, they sat at the breakfast table with their parents. Always tardy, Blythe had not yet come downstairs to join them. At one end of the white-draped table, Edith Crompton spread orange marmalade on her toast, while at the other end, George Crompton sat reading the newspaper as a footman discreetly removed the china dish containing the remains of his kippers and eggs.

The scenario was so familiar that a lump formed in Portia's throat. For as far back as she could remember, the family had always eaten breakfast together. Of course in India, they would have been feasting on mangoes and bananas with *naan,* and the air would have been scorching hot, with a *punka* turning overhead, the fan operated by a native boy sitting on the other side of the wall.

Yet she couldn't deny that the present moment had a certain heartfelt coziness, too, with a fire blazing in the hearth and the watery English sunlight trickling past the tall blue draperies.

You're giving up everything, your life, your country, your family. Once you act on this foolishness, there'll be no turning back.

Using her fork, Portia stabbed a strawberry on her plate. Ratcliffe had had no right to express any opinions on her actions. She knew her own mind, and if she wished to wed a chimney sweep and live in a hovel, it was no concern of his. He was a scoundrel who only wanted her dowry—

"Darling, did you hear me?"

Portia started, realizing her mother was staring at her. "I'm sorry, I must have been woolgathering."

"I was just saying that seventeen gentlemen asked after you yesterday evening. Seventeen!" A satisfied smile on her face, Mrs. Crompton addressed her husband. "Mr. Crompton, didn't I tell you Portia would be an unqualified success?"

Stout and balding, George Crompton looked every inch the prosperous businessman in his dark coat and white cravat. A pair of reading glasses was perched on the end of his nose. He groped for his coffee cup without looking up from his newspaper. "I'm sure you're right, my dear."

"Of course I'm right. And Portia, you've had nearly twenty bouquets delivered already this morning. Everyone was terribly concerned when I told them you were indisposed."

"Thank you, Mama. My cold is ever so much better today."

Portia had made a miraculous recovery because she needed to attend Lord Turnbuckle's ball tonight. At Lindsey's suggestion, she had already sent Kasi to Ratcliffe's town house with a note inviting him to a rendezvous in Turnbuckle's garden. Ratcliffe would take the bait, she was sure of it. The knave would believe he had achieved his purpose, to make her cowed by his treachery and ready to do his bidding.

Little did he know how sorely he'd underestimated her.

"Are you quite certain you're well?" Her mother peered closely at Portia. "You're looking a bit flushed."

"It's the flush of good health," Lindsey said, giving Portia a meaningful glance. "She's adjusting very nicely to the climate of England. After all, this is where she belongs."

Portia ignored the jab. "I assure you, Mama, I feel perfectly fine."

"I'm pleased to hear it," Mrs. Crompton said, taking another slice of toast from the platter offered by a white-wigged footman. "I shouldn't like for you to cancel your drive with Albright this afternoon."

"My drive? Oh . . . I'd nearly forgotten." Dismayed, Portia recalled that several days ago—a lifetime ago—she had agreed to a carriage ride with the Duke of Albright. So much for her hope to spend the afternoon finalizing every aspect of the plan with her sister.

Mrs. Crompton slathered butter on her toast. "How could you possibly forget? The duke is more attentive than any of your other suitors. And certainly the richest and most important as well."

Portia blinked. "The duke isn't my suitor. He's merely a friend, a protector."

"Is that what you think?" Mrs. Crompton laughed indulgently. "Why, a man of his stature would never bother himself with a young lady unless he had an eye on matrimony. Isn't that so, Mr. Crompton?"

George Crompton tore his gaze from the newspaper long enough to give Portia a fond smile. "Quite. I understand the fellow is nearly as wealthy as the Regent. It would please me greatly to see you betrothed to the duke, rather than one of those other greedy pups."

Portia couldn't speak. Her gaze flew from him to her mother, who was beaming proudly. Was it true? Had she misread the duke's kindness toward her? Dear God, she must have.

She wanted to protest that the duke was more than

twice her age, that she viewed him as a paternal figure, not a potential husband. But her parents looked so delighted that the words lodged in her throat.

Everyone was gazing at her expectantly. "I . . . I don't know what to say," she hedged.

"You need only smile and look pretty," her mother advised. "If you'll make every effort to be agreeable, darling, you'll be a duchess by autumn."

Portia regretted the coddled eggs that lay sourly in her stomach. She glanced to her sister for support, but Lindsey merely gave her a wry look of concern. Clearly, she, too, considered the duke a more suitable husband than the son of a maharajah. Portia couldn't be angry at her sister. After all, Lindsey only wanted her to remain in England with the family.

But Portia had never felt more alone, and she suddenly longed for reassurance that she was doing the right thing. If only she had received a letter from Arun . . .

A footman entered the breakfast room and approached Portia's father. "A visitor to see you, sir."

George Crompton rattled the newspaper impatiently. "I don't take callers during breakfast."

"I'm sorry, but he asked specifically for you to be notified of his presence at once."

Ratcliffe. It has to be Ratcliffe.

Alarm spurred Portia to sit up straight. Gripping the arms of her chair, she watched as her father picked up a small pasteboard card from the silver salver held by the footman. Frantic thoughts tumbled through her mind. Ratcliffe had lost no time in approaching her father to ask for her hand in marriage. Papa would refuse on her behalf, of course; he and Mama wanted her to wed the Duke of Albright. Then, out of spite, Ratcliffe would reveal her secret plan to elope with Arun.

Oh, why hadn't the viscount come to her first? She

had expected him to threaten exposure in exchange for her hand in marriage. She had anticipated having the chance to outwit him . . .

Her father rose. "I'll see him in my study."

"*No.*"

Without conscious decision, she was pushing back her chair, shooting to her feet, hurrying to her father's side. The footman jumped back to give her space. Seeing everyone looking strangely at her, she gathered her composure. "You really should finish your coffee, Papa. Whoever it is can wait."

And then Portia could go and eject Ratcliffe from the house.

Her father frowned distractedly. He was looking at her mother, as if trying to convey a covert message—perhaps that their daughter had suddenly gone mad. "It's quite all right," he told Portia, patting her on the arm. "I'm through here."

"But you can't go yet," she blurted out. "Because . . ." Her mind went blank of excuses.

"Good morning, everyone." Blythe's cheerful voice came from the doorway. "I hope you don't mind that I invited someone for breakfast. He was waiting in the foyer for you, Papa."

Portia spun around to see her sister glide into the room. Blythe was dressed in pale green, her hair a mass of perfect auburn ringlets. Her hazel eyes sparkled with mischief, causing Portia's heart to jump into her throat. Oh, she was going to *murder* her sister. It would be just like her to bring the viscount here . . .

But the elderly man who shuffled into the doorway was no one familiar.

Thin and stooped, he wore an ill-fitting brown coat and old-fashioned knee breeches with buckled shoes. His bushy brows matched the untidy mass of white hair on his head. He turned a battered top hat in his gnarled hands. With his deferential manner, he brought to mind a tutor or perhaps a scholar.

The breath left Portia in a long whoosh. How foolish of her. Of course Ratcliffe wouldn't have played his hand so swiftly. He was far more likely to toy with her as a cat teases a mouse.

Then she noticed her mother staring at the visitor with an oddly intense look. The impression vanished in an instant as Mrs. Crompton addressed her youngest daughter, who stood at the buffet table, loading a plate with eggs and sausages. "Blythe, dear," she said in a firm tone.

"Yes, Mama?"

"I'll see you in my boudoir at once."

"But I'm hungry—"

"Immediately."

Pouting, Blythe defiantly took her plate and sashayed out of the breakfast room. Portia hadn't the least sympathy that Blythe would face a scolding for her impetuous invitation. Not after the scare she had given to Portia.

Rising, Edith Crompton rounded the table and glided toward the stranger. "Sir, you must be eager to conduct your business with my husband. You may talk in the study."

"Yes, ma'am."

He slid a longing glance at the array of delicacies on the buffet, then followed George Crompton out of the breakfast room. Mrs. Crompton departed right after them, followed by Lindsey.

Left alone at the table, Portia mulled over her mother's rudeness. She couldn't imagine what business he had with Papa, but that was no reason to refuse the man sustenance. Before they had moved to London, all English guests, no matter how humble, had been invited to dine with the family. That had been the informal way of life she had known growing up near Bombay.

But here, the aristocracy had strict rules about mingling with the lower classes. They kept themselves sequestered as if they were more godlike than human. It made her all the more determined to return to the freedom of India.

Edith stood at the window of her boudoir, peering through the lace undercurtain that kept the room dim and private. The streets around the square teemed with carriages and horsemen, while ladies and gentlemen strolled the tidy green jewel of the park. It was a sight she had craved to see during all those wretched years in India. She had dreamed of residing in a stately home like this one, of acquiring the vast wealth that would enable her to shed her common roots at last and take a place in the elite society that ruled England.

But today, ambition foundered beneath a stormy sea of anxiety.

She had ordered Blythe here for a scolding. That task had been completed swiftly; then she had sent her youngest daughter away, for once without a care for her saucy behavior. The poor girl didn't know the reprimand had been only a pretext. Edith's true reason for coming up here was to keep watch at the window.

She was just beginning to fidget when a movement far below caught her attention. Their visitor was trudging down the front steps. He hadn't stayed more than fifteen minutes.

She gripped the curtain, heedless of the fragile lace shredding under the pressure of her fingernails. How had Percy Thornton learned of their arrival in England?

She had recognized him at once. His hair had gone

completely white and his face now had a webwork of wrinkles, but he was the same man who had once made her feel stupid and slow. He had been the estate manager then, responsible for keeping the books and paying the wages. She had resented his patronizing manner, the way he looked down on those he considered less intelligent than himself.

She was the clever one now. As much as she would have liked to flaunt that fact in his face, she hoped and prayed he hadn't recognized her.

Feverishly, she studied Thornton's progress down the foot pavement. He didn't look like a successful blackmailer; there was no spring in his step or gloating grin on his face. Nevertheless, she watched until he vanished around a corner. Then she hurried to the door, intending to confront her husband.

George was already marching down the corridor toward her. The grimness on his weathered face could have been worry or just his usual grumpiness, she couldn't tell.

"I knew you'd want a full report," he said gruffly. "So I came straight up here."

Edith glanced up and down the passageway to make sure no maids were lurking nearby, listening as servants often did. Taking him by the sleeve, she yanked him into the boudoir. She closed the door and leaned her back against it, grasping the handle to keep her hands from shaking. "Hush, someone will hear you."

"There's no one nearby."

"Nevertheless, we must be extremely careful. So tell me, why on earth did Percy Thornton come here?"

George shrugged. "To catch up on old times, what else?"

Fraught with frustration, Edith itched to take hold of

his shoulders and shake him. "And? What did he say? What did *you* say? Does he know—"

"He knows nothing. He inquired after my health, that's all. And he asked about my experiences in India. It was naught more than a courtesy visit."

"I find that hard to believe. He must have wanted *something*."

George hesitated, then said, "I believe he was hoping for a pension. So I wrote him a bank draft for fifty guineas."

"You did *what*?" Edith lunged at her husband, seizing hold of his lapels. "How idiotic can you be? You'll rouse his suspicions. Don't you realize that if you give him money, he'll keep coming round for more?"

Her attack made his face darken. Jerking himself free, George slammed his fist onto the dressing table. The glass bottles rattled and clashed, but he took no notice. "This is precisely why I never wanted to return to England. We should have stayed in India where no one would ever ask questions."

Edith realized she had pushed him too far. In a conciliatory tone, she said, "I'm sorry, I shouldn't have shouted. And you know full well why we had to come to London. It was for the sake of the girls."

"Was it?" he asked sharply. "Or did we really come here for you? So that you could finally play the lady?"

Edith was too canny to deny it; he knew her too well. "Be that as it may, Portia should be our main concern. She nearly disgraced herself once already. You wouldn't want anything to ruin her chance at making an excellent marriage, now would you?"

As she'd hoped, George's anger crumbled at the mention of their eldest daughter. Portia had always been his favorite, the apple of his eye. She was the one he had taken for rides in the *palka-ghari* every Sunday, the one who had accompanied him on his business trips to the maharajah's palace. If not for George, she would never have met that dark-skinned boy, the one who had enticed her into an indiscretion. Edith shuddered to remember the shock of finding them together, kissing and whispering in the darkness of the verandah. It had taken swift action to avert a ruinous scandal, all because George had indulged Portia with far too much freedom.

Thank God it was all over now.

Edith's only consolation was that her husband still suffered guilt for his mistake. It had given her the ammunition to force him to move back to England.

Heaving a sigh, he ran his fingers through the sparse brown hairs on the top of his balding head. "You're right, we must concentrate on what's best for her. But are you quite sure she favors Albright?"

George might be a shrewd businessman, but he had no notion of how to arrange marriages. "Of course—what girl wouldn't wish to become a duchess? She'll have a perfect life, and our first grandson will be the heir to a dukedom. So long as *you* make certain Thornton won't cause any trouble for us."

"He's nothing," George assured her. "No one would take the word of that old pensioner over mine. I'll make certain of it."

Edith smiled. Oh, how she loved wealth and the power it brought. And with Portia a duchess, no one would ever again dare to close their door to her. She would let nothing—and no one—stand in the way of her daughter's marriage to the Duke of Albright.

CHAPTER 5

As the open landau entered the gates to Hyde Park, Portia tilted her head back to bask in the sunlight. The warm rays felt wonderful after several weeks of rain and gloomy skies. She breathed in the aromas of damp earth and new green foliage, so fresh and different from the smells of her youth. If it wasn't so improper, she would have shed her bonnet and let the breeze flutter through her hair.

"Enjoying the balmy weather?" the Duke of Albright asked from beside her.

She turned to see him smiling at her, his white-gloved hands wrapped around the silver knob of his walking stick. The duke was the epitome of elegance in a charcoal-gray coat and black trousers, with a dazzling white cravat at his throat. A top hat covered his silvering dark hair.

It shook her anew to think of him as her suitor. Especially since being with him like this reminded her of the leisurely drives she'd taken with her father in India. Perhaps her parents were reading too much into Albright's attentiveness. Perhaps, like her, he was interested only in passing the time with a pleasant companion. Because if he had no need of her rich dowry, why would he court a commoner when there were so many blue-blooded girls who would leap at the chance to wed a duke?

The answer didn't signify. It was too beautiful a day to fret about the future. If ever he made her an offer of marriage, she would simply find a gracious way to refuse him.

She returned the duke's fond smile. "It's a lovely afternoon, indeed. Is it often so warm here in the spring?"

"I'm afraid today is something of an anomaly for April," he said wryly. "That is why nearly all of London seems to be out on Rotten Row enjoying the fine weather."

A coachman in blue livery sat on the high perch ahead of them, directing the landau toward a broad sandy avenue where carriages and horsemen abounded. The aristocrats were out in full force, dressed in their finery, to see and be seen. No one had better equipage than the duke, she decided, from the silver crest on the polished black door to the two footmen like statues standing at the rear. A set of perfectly matched grays pranced in front, hooves clopping and harness jingling.

"Rotten Row," she repeated. "That's such an odd name for so pretty a place."

"Many years ago, this road was used by the king to travel from St. James's Palace to Kensington Palace. It was known as *La Route du Roi*. Since the good people of England are famous for their mispronunciation of French, it became known as Rotten Row."

Laughing at the story, she caught a glimpse of the waters of the Serpentine. Children sailed toy boats along the edge, while their nannies gossiped on benches. "Oh, look at the ducks, Your Grace. There, among the reeds. Do you suppose we could stop?"

"If it pleases you, certainly."

He gave a brisk order to the coachman, who guided the landau onto the grassy verge. One of the footmen hastened to open the half-door and let down the step. The duke went out ahead of her, turning to offer his gloved hand to her in polite assistance.

As he did so, she spied two familiar faces in the stream of carriages. It was Mrs. Beardsley and her daughter Frances, the breeze blowing their magnificently feathered bonnets. Both women glared at Portia, only to smile obsequiously as the duke tipped his hat to them. Aware that he was the most eligible bachelor in the ton, Portia couldn't deny a sense of petty satisfaction as she took hold of his arm.

If only they knew how little she wanted him as a husband.

She rested the handle of her parasol on her shoulder, resisting the urge to twirl it. The frilly white umbrella was a bothersome accessory, but Mama had been firm. Portia was not to let her skin become brown from the sun as she had done in India.

Chatting amiably, they set off down the path that led to the river. When they arrived at the edge of the Serpentine, she laughed in delight. A large russet duck glided through the water while five bits of yellow fuzz paddled after it.

Enchanted, she crouched down on the bank, wishing she could cuddle them in her hands. "It's a mother and her babies."

"So it is," the duke said indulgently, leaning on his walking stick and smiling at her. "Mind you don't dirty your gown, though."

Portia longed to kick off her shoes and wade into the murky water, the better to see the ducks. Only the duke's fastidious nature forestalled her. He would be aghast at such uninhibited behavior. He comported himself with perfect manners—unlike another nobleman she knew.

Viscount Ratcliffe would have applauded her. And then he would have splashed into the water himself.

The thought irritated her. They were not at *all* alike. He was a scoundrel who would invade a lady's bedchamber and steal whatever he pleased. She scoured the man from her mind, unwilling to let even the thought of him spoil her day.

But fate intervened.

By ghastly coincidence, Lord Ratcliffe appeared on the path alongside the river. He was a fair distance away, strolling toward her, a woman clinging to his arm.

They appeared to be deep in conversation.

Portia forgot all about the ducks. She scrambled to her feet, only marginally aware of Albright rescuing her parasol as it slipped from her shoulder. Her attention was glued to Ratcliffe and his companion.

The woman wore a gown of vivid gold gauze that clung to her lush curves. She was half turned so that her overflowing bosom pressed against Ratcliffe's arm. Loosely styled hair in a brassy shade of red draped one bare shoulder. She looked like a lady—yet not.

Who was she?

Portia knew the exact moment Ratcliffe spied her. He paused almost imperceptibly. Even from a distance, she could feel the force of his scrutiny. His gaze moved over her azure-blue gown with its demure bodice, lingering there a moment. Her skin suddenly felt flushed, as if she'd been lying under the hot Indian sun rather than standing in the cool shade of an English oak.

The duke's hand tightened on her arm. His face had gone hard and cold. "Ratcliffe. What a blight upon a beautiful day."

She asked the question that gnawed at her. "Do you know the woman with him?"

"His cyprian, no doubt."

"Cyprian?"

"His paramour. Suffice it to say, she is the sort of tawdry female he prefers." Albright patted her hand. "But never mind, my dear. You are much too innocent to know of such sordid matters."

Portia's insides churned with dark emotions. Shock, because she had never imagined that Ratcliffe would be so bold as to walk in public with his mistress. Anger, because he had courted *her* the previous evening while the very next day sought the company of a fallen woman. And curiosity, because she couldn't help wondering what exactly they did together behind closed doors.

The duke made no move to escort Portia back to the landau. His hand firm around her upper arm in a proprietary manner, he watched the approaching couple with narrowed eyes, almost as if he relished a confrontation. He was always the consummate gentleman. How could he not be mindful of the gossip if Portia were to be seen with the scandalous pair?

She herself was anxious to leave, though not because of any potential disgrace. Rather, she feared Ratcliffe might mention the note she had sent him that morning, asking him to meet her at midnight in the garden at Lord Turnbuckle's ball. She couldn't risk exposure of her plot to retrieve the miniature of Arun.

"We must go at once," she murmured. "I cannot associate with those two."

The duke gave a start as if he had been so intent, he had forgotten her presence. "You're quite right, of course," he said, handing her the parasol. "We should return to the landau lest his presence taint you."

His presence—not the woman's?

As they started back up the path, Portia sensed a revulsion in the duke that went beyond mere dislike. It was evident in his tightened lips and wrathful steps. She hastened to keep pace with his strides. "Why do you hate Lord Ratcliffe?"

"His behavior offends me. There is much you don't know about the rogue."

"I know you believe he murdered his father."

"There can be no question of his guilt."

"But he was never convicted in a court of law. Were you particular friends with his father—or with someone else in his family? Did you hear something that wasn't told to the judge about circumstances of the death?"

The duke scowled, clearly displeased that she would question his verdict. "The subject is not for your tender ears. However, if you wish further proof of Ratcliffe's wicked nature, then know this—he also keeps his mother confined at his country estate."

"Confined?" Portia asked in astonished confusion. "Do you mean . . . locked up?"

"Perhaps not in so literal a sense. But he refuses Lady Ratcliffe permission to come to London, to enjoy the simple pleasures of visiting her dearest friends and going to the shops. So you can see how he ill-treats the women in his life. You would be well advised to avoid him."

The news about his mother deeply disturbed Portia. Was he truly so cruel? Although she disapproved of his low morals, he didn't strike her as having a cold, heartless nature. Was the duke mistaken in his information? Or had she herself been too dazzled by Ratcliffe's charm to recognize the depths of his depravity?

She glanced back, but a stand of boxwoods hid him from her view. She certainly *would* avoid him, but not because the duke commanded it. Rather, it would be extremely foolish to associate with a rakehell like Ratcliffe. He could entrap her in a compromising situation. Especially now that he had the miniature in his possession.

But all that would soon change.

Tonight.

* * *

"The place looks deserted," Lindsey whispered. "The viscount must have taken the bait."

Portia huddled with her sister in the shadows of a plane tree. A gust of wind stirred the leaves, making her grateful for the warm cloak that covered her revealing gown. The night had turned cold and blustery, the mild weather of the afternoon now only a distant memory.

Across the street, Lord Ratcliffe's residence loomed at the end of a row of narrow town houses. The darkened windows revealed no sign of life. Ratcliffe must have gone to the appointed rendezvous.

So why did she feel a prickly sense of foreboding? All evening, she'd had the jittery sense of being watched. It didn't make sense because her plan thus far had gone off without a hitch.

She had attended Lord Turnbuckle's ball, dutifully dancing with a number of eligible gentlemen, including the duke. At a quarter past eleven, she had gone to her parents and pleaded a headache, convincing them to remain behind to enjoy the festivities while the coachman took her home. Little did they know, she had slipped out a side door and escaped around the corner, where Lindsey was waiting inside a hired cab along with the necessary change of clothing. Portia had slithered hastily out of her fancy ball gown while the cab drove them to this shabby section on the outskirts of Mayfair.

"I certainly do hope he's gone," she murmured. "I'd feel more confident if I'd actually seen him at Lord Turnbuckle's house."

"He wouldn't have been invited," Lindsey said with a sniff. "But if the rat could sneak into your bedchamber, you can be certain he'll also find a way to slip into the garden to meet you."

Lindsey was right. Ratcliffe needed Portia's dowry, and he would seize any chance to catch her alone and charm her into marriage. While he waited there in vain, however, she intended to invade his home and search for the stolen miniature.

Lindsey was consulting her pocket watch, angling the face to the dim light of the moon. "He's supposed to be there at midnight. That's precisely nine minutes from now, so there's no time to waste. Come, let's find a way inside."

"What?" Alarmed, Portia grabbed her sister's arm to drag her back into the shadows. "You're not going in with me. We agreed you're to wait in the cab." The hired hack was parked out of sight at the far end of the block.

"*You* agreed, not me. *I* would never commit myself to any such craven act."

"This isn't a game, Linds. I'm handling the matter myself. And that's that."

Lindsey's pouting expression was visible through the darkness. "I shan't hide myself away while you brave all manner of danger. Do you think me a coward, to flee at the merest hint of peril?"

Portia's agitation faded beneath a rush of fond humor. It was no wonder her sister relished this act of skullduggery—she read far too many adventure stories. It was partly Portia's fault for always fetching her the latest books from the lending library.

Gently, she rubbed her sister's hands. "Of course you're not a coward. It's only that I've already embroiled you in my troubles far more than I ought."

"Yes, and just so you know, I won't be a party to your scheme to marry Arun," Lindsey declared, sabotaging their brief closeness by pulling away. "You shouldn't have kept his miniature in the first place. Then Ratcliffe wouldn't have been in a position to steal it."

Portia parted her lips in a defensive retort, then decided that, given the present circumstances, it might be wiser to placate her sister. "Yes, well, be that as it may, there *is* something you can do to assist me."

"What's that? Do you want me to pick the lock?"

"No!" How in the world did her sister know of such things, anyway? "It would be helpful to have someone cry an alarm if the viscount returns home unexpectedly. If you wait on the side street, you can observe both the front and the back doors."

Lindsey made a grumbly noise in her throat. "I'll be the lookout, if I must. Don't worry, the villain won't get past me." She took a step away, then turned back, fishing in her reticule before pressing something into Portia's hand. "Here, you might need this more than I."

In consternation, Portia found herself grasping a dainty pistol that fit easily into her palm. "Where did you get a gun?"

But her sister already had crept off into the gloom. In her dark clothing, Lindsey blended so well with the shadows that she might have been mistaken for part of the shrubbery. Her sister had a truly astonishing knack for subterfuge, Portia realized.

Now if only she herself could do as well.

She stepped out from under the tree to examine the pistol by the faint light of the moon. In India she had handled guns for hunting, although nothing quite so small as this one. After assuring herself it wouldn't go off by accident, she gingerly secreted the pistol in the pocket of her cloak. She couldn't imagine pointing the weapon at Lord Ratcliffe, let alone firing it, but at least it made her feel marginally safer.

Taking a deep breath, she glanced up and down the deserted street before heading toward the mews behind the row of attached houses. According to their plan, it would be safest for her to make her entry out of sight of any passersby.

The stench of dung permeated the alley. There were stables back here where the genteel residents kept their horses, and sleeping grooms that she had no wish to awaken. The dense darkness forced her to proceed carefully lest she trip and fall. When she found the gate and gave it a push, the hinges squeaked loudly.

She froze in place, half expecting someone to throw up a window sash and yell, *"Stop, thief!"*

But the only sounds were the sleepy twittering of a bird in one of the trees and the bark of a dog in the distance.

She slipped into a tiny garden that smelled of roses and refuse. Going down the graveled path, she winced several times as the flimsy dancing slippers provided scant protection from the stones. A small porch led to the back door. There, she cupped her eyes and peered through a window to see a long dark passageway lined with black lumps of furniture.

Very carefully, she tried the door handle. Locked.

Pursing her lips, she moved down the narrow width of the house, checking all the back windows. To her frustration, they were secured as well.

Blast, perhaps she ought to have had Lindsey try to pick the lock, after all—if indeed she really had acquired such a skill. But Portia disliked involving her sister in this act of burglary any more than she had already done.

That left one unpleasant course of action. She would have to break the glass.

The noise might bring a servant running if any were awake at this late hour. Reasoning that it was better to take a chance on brazening her way inside than to be caught red-handed, Portia rapped hard on the back door.

Her palms felt cold and damp inside her kidskin gloves. Any servants were probably fast asleep in the attic bedchambers. Nevertheless, she forced herself to wait a few minutes to see if anyone responded to her knock.

Conscious of the time ticking away, she shifted from one foot to the other while rubbing her arms beneath the cloak in an effort to stay warm.

How long would Ratcliffe wait at the rendezvous before he grew impatient with her absence? At that point, would he suspect something and come straight back here? Or would he go and seek out the comforting arms of his mistress?

Portia clenched her teeth at the memory of him strolling in Hyde Park with that red-haired strumpet. What a wicked charlatan he was, to declare his fascination for Portia while he continued to consort with women of ill repute!

And what about him banishing his mother to his estate? No decent gentleman would treat a parent so callously. In so many ways, the man was beyond the pale.

Buoyed by righteous anger, Portia stepped down to the garden in search of a rock to break the window. She found a better missile at the base of the porch. It was a small iron boot scraper the length of her hand. Straightening up, she was startled by the glow of an approaching light inside the house.

The handle rattled and the door swung open. The breath froze in her throat. Holding up a lantern in one meaty paw, an ogre stood glowering at her.

CHAPTER 6

The flickering flame shone upon a face so ugly that only innate good manners stopped Portia from gasping. He had a bulbous, misshapen nose beneath sunken eyes and shaggy black brows. A number of hideous scars crisscrossed his skin, including the left side of his head where only half an ear remained. The coarse dark clothing that covered his massively muscled form marked him as a servant.

"Who the devil are ye?" he demanded. "An' why are ye stealin' the master's goods?"

Portia realized she still held the boot scraper. It was imperative that he not view her as a thief.

She forced a pleasant smile. "Were I a burglar, I wouldn't have knocked," she said in a reasonable tone. "I only picked this up because . . . because I didn't know who would answer the door and I thought I might need a weapon to defend myself."

"Humph. Mayhap ye meant to clobber the wee maidservant what answered yer knock. Don't suppose ye reckoned on me."

"I assure you, sir, you're mistaken." Her heart thumping, Portia slowly set down the boot scraper while keeping a close watch on him. Bless Lindsey for giving her the pistol. Its slight but comforting weight rested against her hip. Mounting the steps to the porch, she reminded herself of the role she and her sister had planned. "This *is* Lord Ratcliffe's house, is it not? I was sent here by him."

One bushy eyebrow lifted. "Eh?"

"I left his lordship's company only a few moments ago. He asked me to await him in his bedchamber."

"Ye? Ye're a lady."

A wealth of suspicion layered his gruff tone. Belatedly she wondered if she ought to have adopted the speech of the lower class. But time had been too short to study the nuances of an accent that she hadn't grown up hearing. Better this man should think her a gentlewoman fallen on hard times, reduced to being one of the viscount's doxies.

She let the cloak fall slightly open so he could glimpse her form-fitting gown, the one that Lindsey had brought to her. "I *was* raised a lady, although those times are long past. Now, will you kindly show me to his lordship's private chambers? If you refuse, you'll be thwarting his wishes."

The ogre continued to block the doorway. He glanced past her, peering into the night. "Where is the master? Why didn't he come with ye?"

"He wanted to finish up a card game with his friends, so he sent me ahead to prepare myself for him."

She had only a vague idea of what preparation a night of passion might entail, but she was desperate to make the ogre cease his questions. Although it was hardly the same circumstances, her own father never discussed private female concerns. The slightest reference to such matters would cause him to disappear into his study or to bury himself in his newspaper.

To her vast relief, the ploy worked and the servant stepped back, albeit still radiating grumpy distrust.

"Follow me, then. An' next time the master best warn me 'bout any visitors."

He clomped down the corridor toward the front of the house, holding the lantern high to light the way. Portia scurried in his wake. Despite her nervous anticipation, she noticed that the place had a shabby air of neglect. There was no fresh scent of beeswax or gleam of polish on the chairs and tables. The marble floor looked scuffed and dull. Even the wallpaper was peeling in places.

Grasping her skirts, she hastened to keep pace with the ogre, who turned at the newel post and marched up a narrow staircase, his shovel-sized feet taking the steps two at a time. Elation filled her. What had seemed so hopeless the previous night now lay within her grasp. She had breached Ratcliffe's defenses and had the chance to reclaim the evidence of her regard for Arun.

On the landing, they passed the gilt-framed portrait of a beautiful, dark-haired lady with a spaniel resting at her feet. Her aqua gown was in an old-fashioned style of some three decades in the past. Her smiling face radiated a sparkling vitality, as if she had trouble keeping herself seated sedately in the chair.

Was she the viscount's mother, Lady Ratcliffe? Portia didn't dare press her luck by asking unnecessary questions.

The ogre shoved open a door in the upstairs corridor and preceded her into the room. Muttering under his breath about the extra work, he set down the lamp on a table and stomped to the hearth, where the banked embers glowed faintly. He hurled coal from the hob onto the ashes, then jabbed around with the poker until the fire bit back with flaming orange teeth.

"Thank you for your kindness," Portia said, aware of the precious minutes ticking away. "But it really isn't necessary. I can see to my own comforts."

"Master'd 'ave me 'ead if I left ye in the cold and dark." He grabbed a beeswax taper and held the wick to the lamp, before jamming it back into a pewter candlestick, which he ungraciously left on a table. "An' don't bother pokin' through the master's things. All the gold's been locked up."

She swallowed a pithy retort and strove to look guiltless. Little could he guess, she had no interest in the usual valuables.

With one final glower, the manservant departed from the room, closing the door with an unnecessary bang.

Portia hastened to put her ear to the wooden panel. She listened until the tramp of his heavy footsteps disappeared down the stairs. Only then did she turn to survey her surroundings.

The meager light illuminated a chamber adorned with the threadbare elegance of the previous century. The colors were blue and gold, with velvet draperies covering the tall windows and age-darkened landscape paintings hanging on the walls. A faint spicy aroma hung in the cool air.

Ratcliffe's scent.

Beneath the cloak, a shiver riffled over her skin. Again, she had that unnerving sense of being watched, as if his spirit lingered in the deep shadows.

Nonsense. The bedchamber was deserted because the wicked viscount had been lured away to Turnbuckle's garden. Right now, he would be waiting for her to slip out of the ballroom and join him. Perhaps he was pacing, planning how best to use his charm to talk her into marriage. Hoping for the prize of her dowry, he would tarry there for a good while before he realized she had reneged on the tryst.

He might not even know he'd been deliberately duped until he returned here. By then, she would be long gone.

And he would be faced with the maddening knowledge that she had been right here in his private quarters, that he had missed the perfect opportunity for seduction.

Averting her gaze from the four-poster bed that dominated the room, she spied a wingback chair by the marble fireplace. A stack of books sat on a nearby table, a pair of spectacles resting on the topmost one.

She had to laugh at the incongruous image of him wearing the eyeglasses. Ratcliffe was certainly no scholar. In truth, she couldn't begin to guess what a man of his indecent character might be reading.

She held up the candle and scanned the titles. *The Gentleman Farmer* by Henry Home. *The Gardener's and Botanist's Dictionary* by Philip Miller. *Horse-Hoeing Husbandry* by Jethro Tull.

Portia blinked. Ratcliffe—studying techniques of agriculture? Perhaps he had made a muddle of his estate and was looking for ways to squeeze out every last bit of revenue. She could think of no other explanation for his interest.

Then the book on the bottom caught her attention. Her pulse sped up a notch. Now here was something more suited to him: the *Kama Sutra*.

Years ago in India, she had overheard a group of ladies whispering about the scandalous book, which one of them had confiscated from a servant and then burned. Portia had asked Arun about the work, and in dismay he'd warned her it was improper reading for an unmarried girl.

She had been curious about it ever since.

On a whim, Portia pulled out the tome. The text was in Hindi; she could read it tolerably well but surely Ratcliffe could not. Then her puzzlement vanished as she leafed through the pages and spied the illustrations. Now there was the likely source of his attention.

Her eyes widened at the explicit drawings of couples engaged in all manner of intimate relations. A blush suffused her from head to foot, yet she couldn't stop staring. Who would have thought there were so many different ways a man and a woman could join their bodies? And did they really enjoy it? She couldn't imagine herself doing such intensely personal acts with Arun. The whole business seemed more embarrassing than pleasurable.

Until she thought of Ratcliffe.

Her gaze went to the four-poster bed where pillows lined the headboard and hangings of midnight blue velvet formed an intimate bower. Heat seared her veins, pooling in her nether regions. She could see Ratcliffe lounging naked between the sheets, and herself clasped in his arms while they kissed and caressed . . .

A strong gust rattled the windowpanes, startling Portia back to her senses.

Mortified, she clapped the book shut. She shoved it to the bottom of the stack and stepped back, flushed and breathless. What was wrong with her, that she could think of that rogue in so unseemly a manner? It must be the effect of viewing those drawings, of catching a glimpse into the tantalizing secrets of the bedchamber.

Overly warm, she unfastened the merino cloak and tossed it onto the bed. The ticking clock on the mantelpiece showed the hour as a quarter past midnight. She had wasted enough valuable time.

The candlestick in hand, she looked around to determine the most likely places where he might have put the miniature. She hastened to a small writing desk and examined the contents of the cubbyholes and the single drawer. But there was only a sheaf of paper, quill pens and an inkpot, a glob of red sealing wax. A nearby cabinet held crystal decanters of liquor and a collection of glasses.

She made her way around the bedchamber, searching every drawer, every box, every receptacle, to no avail. Frustration nagged at her as she considered where he might have put her property. The manservant had mentioned safeguarding the gold. Suppose Ratcliffe had locked the miniature in a safe?

She stood stock-still by the bedside table. But no, that didn't make sense. Ratcliffe would not have expected her to be so brazen as to break into his house. Surely he would have left the miniature somewhere close at hand.

Perhaps in his dressing room?

Of course. Upon his return home the previous night, he might have carelessly tossed it down on a table.

Whirling around, she headed toward the shadowed doorway in a corner of the bedchamber. The white-painted panel stood open to a yawning, pitch-dark hole. Inexplicably, the fine hairs at the back of her neck prickled. Scorning her foolish fears, she forced herself to move forward, only to halt with a gasp.

Something moved within the well of absolute blackness. A tall menacing shape entered the doorway.

Her heart gave a sickening jolt of recognition.

Lord Ratcliffe settled one broad shoulder against the doorframe. The half-smile on his mouth was at odds with the dangerous intensity of his eyes. "Looking for something, Miss Crompton?"

CHAPTER 7

Portia's feet felt rooted to the rug. She could scarcely believe her eyes. Ratcliffe was dressed for the evening in a tailored dark coat and knee breeches, a white cravat at his throat. At the ball, she had danced with a score of gentlemen clad just like him.

But none of them had looked so intimidating. None of them had made her pulse race with alarm—and something darker. None of them had watched her with the hungry acuity of a predator.

Dear God, how had he discovered her deception so swiftly?

"You're supposed to be in Turnbuckle's garden," she said hoarsely.

"Or so you hoped." His smile deepened with mockery. "You almost convinced me of your sincerity in that note you sent. But being suspicious by nature, I doubted you'd wish to be alone with me again. So I asked a favor of Turnbuckle."

With a sinking sensation, she remembered meeting the jovial earl who was of an age with Ratcliffe. Numbly, she stated, "You know his lordship, then."

"We were good friends at Eton. He allowed me to wait in an antechamber during the ball so I could keep an eye on you, to see if you truly meant to meet me in the garden. When I saw you leave early, I surmised your intention and took a shortcut straight back here."

So she had been right to sense someone watching her all evening. From the start, her plan had been doomed. Then another thought appalled her even more. Ratcliffe must have been in the dressing room the entire time, observing her search, waiting, biding his time.

Had he seen her looking through his copy of the *Kama Sutra*?

She moistened her lips. "You must think yourself exceedingly clever to have caught me, my lord. I imagine even the ogre was playacting."

"The ogre?" His fleeting frown cleared, and Ratcliffe chuckled. "Oh, you mean Orson Tudge. Yes, he did as I instructed. I told him not to let you in too easily lest you become suspicious."

"Does that mean he's more gracious to your other women callers?" Portia clamped her lips shut. She hadn't intended to sound so shrewish. She had no interest in his mistresses. He could have a thousand of them for all she cared.

Ratcliffe looked genuinely amused. "Pray don't take offense. Tudge is never gracious to anyone. But he's loyal to a fault. He and I share a long history."

Which meant that if she screamed, the ogre wouldn't come running to her aid. He would turn a deaf ear to whatever transpired in the master's bedchamber. And it was doubtful her sister would hear anything outside with the windows shut tightly.

Portia was on her own.

She drew a sharp breath as Ratcliffe moved abruptly. He stepped out of the dressing room and walked to the door of the bedchamber, blocking her only escape route. He placed his hands on his hips, his coat pushed back to reveal a leanly muscled form beneath the gentlemanly trappings of charcoal-gray waistcoat and white shirt.

"We seem to have a penchant for meeting in bedchambers," he said, a hint of flirtatiousness entering his tone. "Tell me, what shall I do with you now?"

A disturbing warmth flared to life deep inside her. It radiated throughout her body until her knees felt on the verge of buckling. The involuntary reaction was shocking in its intensity, nay, even in its existence. How could she feel even the slightest attraction to this scoundrel?

It wasn't violence she feared from Ratcliffe. It was seduction.

Out of the corner of her eye, she could see her cloak lying on his bed. She edged toward it, anxious for the protection of the hidden pistol. "You'll let me go, that's what. After you've given me the miniature, of course. It belongs to me and I want it back."

"All in good time." His voice lowered a notch, becoming velvety smooth. "First, though, you and I should use this opportunity to get to know each other better."

His gaze flitted to her gauzy scarlet gown with its indecently low neckline. Her skin tingled and she crossed her arms, hoping the gloom hid the atrocious effect he had on her. It had been Lindsey's idea for her to pose as a fallen woman in case any servants questioned her presence in the house. Heaven only knew where her sister had procured such a vulgar garment. But now Portia fervently wished she had refused to wear it.

"Yes, do let's talk," she said, desperate to forestall his lecherous intentions. "You may begin by explaining to me why you keep your mother confined to your estate."

Her accusation had the desired effect. He took a step toward her, his face darkening and his charm vanishing. "Who told you that? Let me guess. Albright."

"Yes. He said you won't permit Lady Ratcliffe to come

to London. That you purposely keep her from her dearest friends and her favorite pastimes."

He made a dismissing gesture. "My mother enjoys many friends and amusements in the country. So you shouldn't believe everything people tell you."

"The duke seems to have particular knowledge of your family. Are he and your mother acquainted?"

"Everyone in society is acquainted to some degree or another. And Albright is a master at twisting the facts to suit his own purposes."

Ratcliffe hadn't really answered her question, Portia noted. It was too dim in the bedchamber to read the nuances of his expression, yet she had the distinct impression he was hiding something. "Is that your mother's portrait I saw on the staircase landing?"

Ratcliffe glanced over his shoulder at the door, as if he could peer through it. "Yes. It was painted shortly after my parents were married." He started forward and she retreated in alarm, the backs of her legs bumping into the bed. But he merely walked to a stool, propped up one foot, and regarded her gravely. "I must say, I'm concerned that you consider Albright so trustworthy."

Incredulous, she laughed. "How ridiculous for you to cast aspersions on him. You're the one with the wicked reputation."

"He isn't all that he seems, Portia. Take it as a word of caution, that's all."

He had his own purpose in trying to make her doubt the duke. Ratcliffe wanted to win her—and her dowry— for himself. Yet she also remembered Albright's attitude toward him, a loathing that implied a personal connection. "If the two of you have quarreled in the past, then tell me the nature of your disagreement. Perhaps that will convince me."

"There's nothing to tell."

"Then I see no reason to credit your vague warnings." She decided it was time to put a firm end to his marital aspirations. "For that matter, I'll tell you exactly why I prefer the duke to you. He's extremely wealthy, which means *he* isn't chasing after my money. Nor does *he* consort with sordid women behind my back."

His eyes narrowed. "You're referring to Hannah Wilton, the woman with me in Hyde Park today."

Hannah. So the woman had a name.

Portia considered herself a tolerant person, yet the thought of that flame-haired floozy hanging on his arm made her livid. "Quite," she said icily. "Although if you choose to spend your time with filthy whores, it is of little importance to me."

Turning away, she grabbed for her cloak. Just like that, he was standing beside her. He tossed the garment back down on the bed and took hold of her shoulders, bringing her around to face him. His cold expression revealed no hint of the charming rogue.

"Hannah and I were close at one time," he said sharply. "For that reason, I will not tolerate hearing her belittled by a pampered young miss. She's a kindhearted woman who was forced into the service of men by dire circumstance. You should be grateful that your wealth has insulated you from being reduced to her position."

The blood rushed into Portia's face. Pampered young miss? Kindhearted woman? She was furious with him for comparing her so unfavorably with his ex-mistress, and a little ashamed as well, for it had never occurred to her to consider the woman's background.

She focused on the anger, tilting her head back to glare at him. "If you aren't seeing her any longer, then why were you out walking with her?"

He hesitated, then dropped his hands to his sides and stepped back. "Hannah is in a spot of trouble. The details don't matter, but she asked for my help."

"What sort of trouble?"

"She was tossed out of the house where she had worked for a number of years. Beyond that, it isn't a topic that any decent young lady should know about."

His secretiveness frustrated Portia. The candlelight played over his face, casting stark shadows over his chiseled features. There was so much about himself that he kept hidden from her. Or perhaps it was just her own mulish curiosity that refused to quit.

"Tell me, anyway," she said. "I don't care a fig for false propriety."

"If you must know, she's with child." He held up his hand. "And lest you accuse *me* of abandonment, let me assure you, the baby cannot possibly be mine. She and I parted ways nearly a year ago."

Her mind whirling, Portia leaned against the bedpost. *A baby.* She remembered the malicious whispers in India when the daughter of an English merchant became pregnant out of wedlock. There had been a hasty marriage and an infant boy born five months later. Even though the shame had lingered, the close-knit family had weathered the storm together.

Now Portia could see how lucky that girl had been. "Does Hannah have no relatives?"

"None that will acknowledge her."

"Shouldn't she seek help from the baby's father, then?"

His mouth twisted, and he looked away. "Unfortunately, he could be any one of a number of gentlemen."

Portia was struck by the sordidness of the men of society using a lower-class female for their own gratification, then abandoning her to her fate. She had never before considered the consequences to the woman—or to the children that might result from an illicit union. In truth, she had hardly been aware that such women even existed because the topic wasn't considered fit for the ears of ladies.

A distasteful notion occurred to her. What if the father of Hannah's child was one of the gentlemen who had flocked around Portia, seeking to win her hand? She wouldn't be able to look at any of them again without wondering. They were a high-and-mighty lot who had never been required to take responsibility for their actions.

She took a step toward Ratcliffe. "Well, then? Did *you* help her?"

"I've seen to the matter."

His answer was too evasive, and she mistrusted his word, anyway. "But where is she? Does she have food? A roof over her head? And who will take care of her when her baby is born?"

"Enough questions. I've said too much already." His authoritative voice softened, taking on a silky quality. "Besides, we've strayed far from the topic of you and I."

He had that look in his eyes again, the one that reminded her they were all alone in his bedchamber. The one that made her blood beat faster. The one that proved that when it came to the gentlemen of society, Lord Ratcliffe himself was the most notorious of the lot.

"There is no 'you and I.' There never was and there never will be." She snatched up her cloak again and swirled it over her shoulders, her fingers fumbling with the clasp. "And since you refuse to hand over the miniature, there is no point to me staying here a moment longer."

He stepped closer, crowding her against the bedpost. "You can't expect me to let you walk out of here just like that. We aren't finished talking."

His nearness made her breathless. She leaned as far back as possible to avoid touching him. Even so, she could feel the heat of his body, smell the intoxicating scent of him. "Perhaps you aren't finished, but I certainly am."

"At least hear me out, if you will. You've chastised me several times for wanting your dowry. But you've never once asked me what *I* have to offer *you*."

"The miniature returned in exchange for my hand in marriage, is that it? Well, the answer is no. I won't stoop to your blackmail."

"Never mind the blasted miniature." His hands settled on her shoulders, kneading the tense muscles through the fabric of the cloak. "I can give you something far better. It's something you won't find with Arun or Albright or any other man."

"Trouble, that's what. Trouble is all you've ever given me."

He threw back his head and laughed, and the effect held her transfixed. The enjoyment on his sinfully handsome face gave her a rush of pleasure, reminding her of the fascinating man she had first met more than a fortnight ago before she had learned of his wicked reputation. On that occasion, he had seen Mrs. Beardsley's nasty treatment of Portia, and he had lobbed a strawberry in retaliation. Though his weapon had been unconventional, she had viewed him as her knight in shining armor, if only for a brief time.

His smile mellowed into an expression of devastating appeal. His palm cupped the underside of her jaw, his thumb playing lightly with the corner of her mouth. "What I can give you, Portia, is this: passion beyond your wildest dreams."

Her mouth went dry. Her heart was pounding so rapidly he surely must hear it. She couldn't believe his boldness, not only in what he said, but also in the way he was touching her mouth. That one simple caress caused eddies of sensation throughout her body. It made her want to lift up on tiptoes and press her lips to his.

That would be madness. Sheer, utter madness.

The temptation was so strong, she turned her face away to break the contact. "Conceited cad. You've no right to speak to me so crudely."

"Under ordinary circumstances, I would agree. But you're a bit more knowledgeable than most innocent ladies." He glanced meaningfully at the fireplace. "I saw you looking at my books, one in particular. Then you stared at my bed for quite a while. I can't help but wonder what exactly you were thinking about."

A wild blush burned her cheeks. He had been watching her from the concealment of the dressing room. He had seen her paging through the *Kama Sutra*. Dear God, if he were to guess even half of her unladylike fantasies . . .

Horrified, she tried to push him away. "I was thinking about how much I despise you. Now let me go."

He ignored her request. Instead, she found herself being clasped more securely in his arms. He held her flush against him while his hands moved in soothing patterns over her back. "Forgive me," he said softly. "I shouldn't tease you. I keep forgetting just how young you are."

Portia went still, partly because she recognized the futility of struggling against his iron strength, and partly because she was captivated by the novelty of his embrace. She stood stiffly, her head turned to the side, her cheek pressed to the smooth fabric of his coat as the scent and feel of him flooded her senses.

His fingers found her chin and tipped up her face. He was all seriousness now, his face devoid of its usual rakish smile. His shadowy features had a curiously tender aspect that intrigued her.

"Passion is nothing to be feared," he murmured. "It all begins with a kiss."

Bending closer, he captured her mouth. His action shouldn't have caught her by surprise, yet it did. Without thinking, she closed her eyes and lifted her lips to the thrilling pressure of his. When his tongue entered her mouth, she gasped and tried to draw back, but his arms tightened, keeping her locked to him as he tasted deeply of her.

The experience was not at all like the warm, affectionate peck she had shared with Arun. Ratcliffe's kiss was hot and erotic, and she reacted to it with stunning fervor. Her body melted like wax beneath the flame of a candle, ready to be shaped by his skilled hands. She had never guessed a man's touch could arouse such a powerful yearning inside her.

Of their own accord, her palms slid over his coat to explore the heated skin of his neck. The strands of his hair felt coarse yet silky, and she indulged the desire to tangle her fingers there. He seemed to take that as an incentive to deepen the kiss, plundering her mouth until he filled her with his taste. His large hands roved up and down her back, following the contour of her curves. Bliss infused her body until she found herself moving against him in shameless delight, making small pleading sounds in her throat.

No wonder he had such a scandalous reputation. He knew exactly how to keep a woman enthralled. It was folly to let herself fall under his spell like this, but the pull of pleasure was too great to resist. And surely no harm could come of a mere kiss.

Even as the hazy thought flitted through her mind, Portia had the sensation of falling, of being guided downward onto the bed. Then the heavy weight of his body settled over hers without breaking the heated contact of their mouths. The shock of his intentions struck the fog from her dazzled senses.

Ratcliffe wanted more than just a kiss. He meant to seduce her, right here, right now.

She jerked her head to the side and squirmed in his grasp. "Stop, my lord! You can't do this. You mustn't."

Denied her mouth, he kissed her throat, and her cloak fell open when he unfastened the clasp. "Don't fight your feelings. And call me Colin . . . I want to hear you say it."

Colin. She was momentarily distracted to remember that Ratcliffe possessed such an ordinary name.

She shook her head. "I hardly know you. I—oh!"

The moistness of his tongue traced the skin along her low-cut bodice, sending shivers of sensation down to her core. His hand cupped her fullness. "You've nothing to fear from me," he murmured. "I only want to taste you, that's all."

Nothing to fear?

The gauzy gown provided scant protection from his assault, and the sight of his dark head bent over her breasts sparked a fire of longing and alarm in her. What was she doing, lying with him on his bed? As much as she craved the feel of his lips on her skin and the stroking of his hands on her body, the prospect of surrendering her virtue to this scoundrel released a monsoon of panic in her.

He had no intention of stopping. Not while he had the prize within his grasp. And once he'd dishonored her, he would have the perfect tool to force her into marriage.

She must never allow that to happen.

Driven by desperation, she reached down and groped for the lump in the pocket of her cloak. Her trembling fingers wrenched the pistol free. She jammed the small barrel into his ribs.

"Get off me at once, or by heaven, I'll shoot you."

CHAPTER 8

Colin swam up from a dark pool of passion. Lifting his head, he saw Portia glowering up at him. For a moment he couldn't comprehend her frown. He was too taken by her aura of eroticism, the dark brown hair so soft and tumbled, the eyes so blue and long-lashed, the breasts so perfectly formed. He was keenly aware of her lush body beneath him as his blood-starved brain strove to decipher her harsh words. She was pressing a small round object to his side.

A pistol?

Reality returned with a jolt. Where the devil had she found the weapon? She must have had it secreted in her cloak—because she damn sure couldn't have hidden it in that form-fitting gown.

For the first time in his life, he was struck speechless. No woman had ever drawn a gun on him. They usually begged him to continue, rather than commanded him to stop.

"You heard me," Portia said sharply. "Move quickly now. This pistol may be small, but it's deadly at this range."

By God, she meant it. She would put a bullet through him if he didn't obey. The realization was as galling as it was startling.

Bracing his hands on the mattress, he thrust himself

from her. The weapon she pointed at him was a tiny pistol, almost a toy, but she was right—it could kill at this short distance as easily as a rifle at twenty paces.

A plethora of emotions bombarded Colin. His forced capitulation to her demand left him mortified and insulted. He was frustrated by his unslaked desire, angry with himself for taking the kiss further than he'd planned, and irked with her for threatening him. It was enough to make his temper snap.

"Have you gone mad? Give me that gun."

He lunged for the pistol, catching her off guard as she was scrambling from the bed.

"No!" she cried, twisting herself away from him.

He caught her by the wrist and tried to pry the pistol free from her taut fingers. For a moment they struggled, and he managed to turn her to face him, keeping the barrel pointed away from him. She was stronger than she looked. On some distant level, he was appalled at himself for wrestling with a lady, but he wasn't about to let her continue to threaten his life, either.

Uttering a choked cry, she gave a sudden violent lurch, breaking his hold on her. A shot exploded.

Colin saw the flash and a puff of smoke, felt a sharp sting along his upper arm. The shock of it sent him stumbling backward to crash into the escritoire. Blinking, he looked down to see a neat furrow torn in his sleeve.

An instant later, it burned like hellfire.

The stink of gunpowder gave him a dizzying jolt. It sent him rushing back to a dark place, to another room where his father lay in a pool of blood. The horror of that memory made him sway on his feet.

Her eyes wide, Portia dropped the spent pistol and clapped her hands to her mouth. "Oh, my heavens! Are you hurt?"

Banishing the past, he sucked a breath through his teeth. "I'll live, I'm sure. Much to your sorrow."

Anxious to examine the wound, he gingerly tugged at his fashionably tight coat, and she hastened to help him remove it. "I didn't mean to pull the trigger," she said, looking shaken. "I just wanted you to stay away from me."

"Never mind. No doubt I deserved it."

The throbbing pain had banished every vestige of lust in him, allowing him to see his disreputable actions more clearly. That is, until she pushed him into a chair and bent over him, removing his silver cuff link and rolling up his sleeve.

Her cloak had fallen to the floor by the bed. He had a magnificent view of her breasts, mounded above her revealing red bodice. He could see right down into that tantalizing valley where he wanted to bury his face and breathe deeply of her scent—

"Argh!" He bit off an involuntary curse as she thrust a folded handkerchief over the bleeding wound and pressed hard. "Must you be so brutal?"

"Must you stare at my bosom?"

He snatched the cloth out of her hand and applied it in a more cautious manner. "I can't imagine what else I am to look at when you're flaunting it right in front of me."

"I'm not flaunting anything." Stepping back, she crossed her arms in a futile attempt to hide her charms. "I'm trying to help you. Not that you've shown the slightest appreciation."

"I don't appreciate the fact that you shot me."

"Lecher! It's your own fault for trying to seduce me."

She glared at him, and he glared back. Any retort he might have uttered died on his tongue as someone rapped hard on the door. Before he could even move, the door burst open.

A woman in a flowing green dressing gown scurried

into the bedchamber, her hair caught in a long red braid down her back. Her exquisite features were drawn with worry.

Colin suppressed a groan. God help him, here was a complication he didn't need.

"I heard gunfire," she said breathlessly, glancing from him to Portia, then back again. "Oh, my stars! Have you been injured, my lord? Shall I summon a doctor?"

"No. Go back to your chamber at once."

"Wait," Portia said, countermanding his order. Her eyes narrowed, she marched toward the woman. "You're Hannah Wilton, aren't you? I saw you walking with Lord Ratcliffe in Hyde Park."

"Yes, miss, I recognize you, too." Dipping a curtsy, Hannah gazed askance at Portia's skimpy gown, as if trying to work out why she was in his bedchamber. "You're Miss Crompton. His lordship mentioned your name."

Portia arched a skeptical eyebrow at Colin. "Oh? And just what did he say—"

Another arrival interrupted her, much to Colin's relief. The last thing he wanted was any conversation between his former mistress and the woman he intended to coax into marriage.

Orson Tudge stomped into the bedchamber. "Wot's goin' on in 'ere?" he asked. "I 'eard a gun go off. Woke me up all the way down in the basement."

"It was nothing," Colin snapped. "Return to bed, both of you."

But Tudge was staring from the dainty pistol lying on the floor to Colin, who was still sitting down while holding the compress over his upper arm. "So the little lady shot ye, eh?" He cast a rather admiring look at Portia.

She gave a crisp nod. "I did, indeed. He tried to force me into his bed."

Colin bit back a retort that she had encouraged him

by melting in his arms. But no gentleman kissed and told, and despite her low opinion of him, he possessed at least a modicum of honor.

Much to his annoyance, Tudge chortled. "Lemme 'ave a look at the damage." He tramped closer, pushed Colin's hand away, and pulled off the handkerchief. "A right fine furrow. But t'ain't near as bad as when Westbrook shot you in that duel last year."

"He'd never have succeeded had not my pistol misfired," Colin said, gritting his teeth as Tudge poked at the wound. He waved the servant away. "That's enough of your fussing."

Hannah was hovering, too. "You should pour some whiskey on it," she advised. "My father was in the army and that is what he would have done."

"I believe I saw some right here," Portia said, hurrying to a cabinet and withdrawing a chipped crystal decanter. She brought it over, along with a glass.

Hannah gave her a sidelong look of startlement. She must be wondering how a refined young lady like Portia knew her way around his bedchamber, Colin thought blackly. Hannah didn't know about Portia's search for the miniature. He would have to come up with an explanation, lest she think Portia had come to his bedchamber for a liaison gone awry.

Good God, how had he landed himself in such a royal mess?

A searing pain penetrated his arm. He sucked in a breath as Portia poured a trickle of liquor over the injury while Hannah held a washbasin beneath his arm to catch the drips.

"Cease and desist," he growled, tired of being treated like a complete sapskull who had no say in his own treatment. "It's a waste of good Irish whiskey. Pour me a glass instead."

No one listened to him.

"Have you any basilicum ointment, Mr. Tudge?" Portia asked. "It will help prevent infection. And fetch some bandages, too, if you will."

As Tudge went to do her bidding, he was nearly bowled over by a tall, pretty girl who came running into the bedchamber. A black cloak flapped like the wings of a crow around her dark gown. Colin was taken aback to realize she was Portia's middle sister, Lindsey, whom he had met the previous night in Portia's bedchamber.

What the devil was she doing here?

Remembering his manners, he attempted to stand up, saw spots swirl in his vision, and promptly sat back down. It was aggravating since he'd hardly lost enough blood to fill a thimble.

Well, perhaps several large thimbles.

"What's happened?" she cried out. "I heard a shot downstairs and came as quickly as I could."

"Downstairs?" Portia asked. "You were supposed to be outside."

"I was searching his lordship's study. It didn't make any sense for me to stand out in the cold, doing nothing."

"'Ow'd ye get in?" Tudge asked with a lowering frown. "Place is locked up tight as a drum."

"I used a hairpin to spring the back latch," Lindsey said. "You really ought to invest in iron bolts. Now, what is going on here?" She pushed everyone aside and planted herself squarely in front of Colin, her hands on her hips. "Did you harm my sister, Ratcliffe? Because if you touched one hair on her head, I shall summon the Watch and have you hauled off at once to Bow Street Station."

"It should be obvious who has come to harm here," he said testily. "And I don't appreciate having a crowd in my bedchamber. It's the middle of the night and I command all of you to depart."

Tudge immediately ducked out of the room. Hannah also glided toward the door, but Portia stopped her. "Before you go, I would like a word with you. If you'll sit down, please."

Hannah flashed a cautious glance at Colin. "I—I couldn't."

"You're exactly right," he concurred. "Go on off to bed."

"Nonsense, this will only require a few moments of your time," Portia said, taking Hannah by the arm and leading her to one of the overstuffed chairs by the fire.

"Who is *she*?" Lindsey hissed to her sister. "What's going on?"

"I'll explain later," Portia said, shushing her with a wave of her hand. She picked up her cloak and put it on, covering that delectable gown before going to sit opposite Hannah. "Forgive me for being blunt, but Lord Ratcliffe told me about your situation. However, he neglected to mention you were staying here under his roof."

"There was no need for you to know," Colin snapped, surly from the throbbing in his arm. "And there still isn't. So run along now. I won't have you badgering my servants."

"Your servant?"

"Quite. She's my new housekeeper."

"Ah," Portia said, giving him a long, inscrutable stare that made Colin want to shift in his seat like a naughty schoolboy. Of course, she probably believed the employment was merely a ruse for him to keep a handy woman available for his lecherous pleasures.

"I feared this might happen," Hannah said in a miserable tone, her fingers twisting the folds of her dressing gown. "I told his lordship it wasn't fitting for one of my ilk to stay in his house, that people of consequence will find out, and the gossip won't bode well for a gentleman about to be married."

As if she'd been poked by a pin, Portia sat up straight. "He isn't getting married—at least not to me."

"Oh! I do beg your pardon, miss." Hannah looked as if she didn't quite know what to believe. "But regardless, I don't wish to be a burden. I—I'll depart at first light, if that's all right. I'd go straightaway, but it's dark and there are footpads—"

"You misunderstand me." Portia leaned forward to lay her hand over Hannah's nervous fingers. "I won't allow you to do anything to endanger yourself or your unborn child. You'll stay right here—so long as Ratcliffe gives his solemn vow not to make undue demands on you."

Livid at the implication that he'd force himself on a pregnant woman, Colin jumped to his feet. He willed away a brief dizziness and stalked toward Portia. "I haven't given you permission to issue orders in this house," he said. "Nor have you the right to make any stipulations in regard to my—"

"Stop, villain!" Lindsey rushed in between him and Portia. In her hand, she brandished a small pocket knife. "Keep your distance from my sister."

Colin went stock-still. "Good God, have you lost all sanity?"

"Lindsey!" Portia popped up from the chair to seize her sister's arm. "For heaven's sake, Lord Ratcliffe isn't threatening me, at least not anymore. Now, put that knife away at once and go wait out in the corridor."

"But he might—"

"*Go.*"

To Colin's relief, Lindsey dropped the blade into her reticule. She scooped up the toy pistol and walked out of the bedchamber, scowling at him over her shoulder as if he were the devil incarnate. Like her sister, she was a bossy little baggage. But at least Miss Lindsey Crompton knew when to bow to authority.

Unlike Portia.

He stalked over to pour himself a double splash of whiskey. "A bloodthirsty lot, you and your family," he muttered.

"If you don't like us, then pray stay out of our lives," Portia said tartly before returning her attention to Hannah. "Now, I should like to have a look at the room you've been given. If it's up in the attic as I suspect, you must move at once to this floor. It cannot be good for you to be climbing too many steps in your delicate condition."

Colin almost choked on a swallow of liquor. Coughing, he couldn't manage to voice a protest as the two women left his bedchamber. By the time he could breathe normally again, Tudge had come bustling back, armed with linen and ointments. He bullied Colin into sitting down and having his arm bandaged.

Colin could hear the faint buzz of female conversation far down the passageway. But no matter how he strained his ears, he couldn't make out their words. It jolted him that Portia would even speak to a fallen woman, let alone see to her comfort. Any other well-bred lady would have given Hannah the cut direct, pretending she didn't even exist.

Portia had to have an ulterior purpose. But for the life of him, he couldn't figure out what it could be. Her abrupt about-face made him extremely uneasy. Nothing good could come of her asking questions of his former mistress.

Nothing good at all.

CHAPTER 9

The next day, Portia entered the nearly deserted ball-room in her house to see her sisters taking a dancing lesson. Sunlight poured through the soaring windows, shining over the polished parquet floor and brightening the plaster medallions that decorated the pale yellow walls. As usual, Lindsey and Blythe were squabbling over who was to play the male role as they prepared to practice a reel.

"You're taller so you should do it," Blythe said with a toss of her coppery curls. "It would look quite ridiculous for a petite girl like me to take the lead."

"You're younger," Lindsey argued. "*I'm* going into society next spring, so *I* need more practice as a lady than you do."

Their dancing master, Mr. Bartholomew Horton, looked as if he wanted to tear out the remainder of his sparse sandy hair. He was a prissy, middle-aged man in a curry-brown coat, dark knee breeches, and old-fashioned buckled shoes. Plagued by allergies, he alternately swabbed at his red nose with an oversized handkerchief and pleaded with them to get on with the lesson.

The woman seated at the pianoforte rose gracefully from her bench and glided toward them. Miss Agnes Underhill wore a modest gown of gray serge with long sleeves and a high neck that emphasized her sallow features. A plain white cap tied beneath her chin covered her salt-and-pepper chignon. She had been hired shortly after the Cromptons' arrival in England and charged with the task of teaching the sisters all the myriad rules of polite society.

She ended the battle with a clap of her hands. "This nonsense must stop at once. Bickering is most unbecoming of a lady. You will take turns, as you always do. Miss Blythe, you will play the gentleman for the first dance, then it will be Miss Lindsey's turn."

As Miss Underhill headed back to the pianoforte, Blythe stuck her tongue out at the older woman. Portia swallowed a laugh. Having herself been subjected to Miss Underhill's rigorous guidance for nearly a year, she could understand her sister's irritation.

But today, she hoped to utilize Miss Underhill's close connections to society. The woman hailed from a proud noble family that traced its ancestry back to the Conqueror himself, as she was fond of reminding the girls. Over the centuries the ancestral wealth had been lost, putting Miss Underhill in the heinous straits of needing to earn an income. Yet as poor as she might be, her blue blood made her welcome in the finest households.

Portia reflected on their contrasting situations. If not for her father's vast riches, she would be sent around back to the tradesmen's entrance. That ironic thought served as a caution against adopting the haughtiness of the haute ton.

She strolled to the pianoforte and stood beside it. "If you like, I'll turn the pages for you."

Miss Underhill glanced up, her bony fingers moving over the ivory keys without missing a beat. "Why, thank you. But shouldn't you be out making calls with Mrs. Crompton?"

Portia spent most afternoons in one noble household or another, chatting over tea and cakes with the ladies and parrying the fawning attentiveness of their purse-poor sons. Her mother was in her glory, but Portia found it all exceedingly tiresome.

"Mama isn't quite ready yet." She paused, striving for a casual air. "I've been hoping for a chance to ask you about something. Whenever you have a free moment, that is."

"You may speak now. I am quite competent enough on the pianoforte to play and hold a conversation at the same time."

Portia had expected her to say as much, since Miss Underhill took great pride in her genteel achievements. "I've been meeting so many of the nobility that it's set my mind awhirl. I was hoping you could enlighten me about several of the families."

Tilting her capped head up, Miss Underhill gave her a severe look. "If you are seeking tittle-tattle, may I remind you that would be most improper." She nodded at the sheaf of music on the stand. "Now, mind your duty, Miss Crompton."

"Oh." Portia hastened to turn over the page. "I'm not asking for gossip, only the facts as you know them. It's difficult for an outsider like me to remember everything I need to know."

That admission, too, was calculated to encourage Miss Underhill's sense of superiority.

"Indeed," Miss Underhill said, taking the bait. "About whom in particular are you inquiring?"

"I'm wondering about Viscount Ratcliffe and his family."

Her fingers paused almost imperceptibly on the keys as her lips formed a prim line. "He is a rake of the worst ilk. You must take care never to be seen in his company."

To avoid Miss Underhill's sharp eyes, Portia pretended to watch Mr. Horton correct her sisters over a missed step in the dance. The aging woman would keel over in a swoon if she knew the truth—that only the previous evening Portia had been in Ratcliffe's private chambers and had lain beneath him on his bed while he kissed her senseless. Even in the light of day, she could still feel the dark, scorching intensity of it.

And she cringed to recall the aftermath, when she had shot him in the arm. It had happened so fast, Portia still wasn't certain if her finger had slipped on the trigger, or if she had deliberately pulled it. Odd that, for she was no stranger to firearms, had even bagged a tiger in India, for heaven's sake. But her mind had been rattled by that kiss, her poise shaken by the fear that Ratcliffe intended to steal her virtue. When he had grabbed for the pistol, she had panicked.

What if she had killed him? Only a scant few inches to the left, and the bullet would have penetrated his heart. The horrifying notion had haunted her ever since.

Devilish man, she thought angrily. It was ridiculous for her to feel even a shred of remorse. He had brought trouble down on himself by his own arrogant actions.

Miss Underhill's censorious voice called her back to the present. "Lord Ratcliffe was tried in court for the murder of his father. That should be sufficient proof of his despicable nature."

"But he was acquitted, was he not? What was his defense?"

"He claimed to have been cleaning his dueling pistol when it went off. The death was pronounced an accident due to the lack of evidence to the contrary."

The news jolted Portia. She immediately noted the eerie parallel between the two shootings. Right after he'd been hit, Ratcliffe had looked pale and grim, more so than the flesh wound had warranted. Had last night's mishap reminded him of another pistol going off by accident, resulting in his father's death?

She could not begin to imagine how terrible that incident must have been. And because of his disreputable character, people in society still held him to blame. But she herself wasn't so certain. It made her all the more determined to uncover the facts of the case.

At Miss Underhill's nod, she turned over another page of music. "If the court has absolved him, then we should accept the verdict. Besides, I find it difficult to credit that any gentleman could purposely do something so monstrous."

"You are being willful and obtuse today," Miss Underhill scolded, her fingers flying over the keys during a lively section. "It is a blessing that you have attracted the attention of the Duke of Albright. Not only will it be a brilliant match for you, he will keep you safe from scoundrels like Ratcliffe."

Portia's stomach churned. Why did everyone take it as a foregone conclusion that she would accept Albright's offer—*if* he made one? "Speaking of the duke, there seems to be bad blood between him and Ratcliffe's family. I'm sure it wouldn't be proper for me to ask His Grace about it."

"I should hope not! Nor should you question anyone else in society, lest you become known as a scandal-monger."

Miss Underhill needn't learn that Portia was already guilty of quizzing the duke. "But I can ask *you*, can't I? Have you knowledge of any particular incident in the past that might have caused this feud?"

Miss Underhill frowned thoughtfully down at the pianoforte. "Now that you mention it, I believe there *was* something. I heard my mother discussing it with her cousins quite a long time ago. I cannot recall exactly what it was, though . . ." She shook her head. "I was only a little girl then. I am nine-and-thirty now, so that would have been perhaps thirty years ago."

Portia hid her shock. She had assumed Miss Underhill to be closer to fifty years old at the very least. Perhaps laboring for a living caused a lady to age faster. It made Portia more keenly aware of the lucky stroke of fate that allowed her to live in luxury while other women struggled to make ends meet.

Women like Hannah Wilton, although Miss Underhill would be aghast to be placed in the same category as a ladybird.

"My mother has passed on," Miss Underhill was saying, concluding the piece with a flourish of her fingers over the keys, "but if you like, I can write to her cousin and see if perhaps she can enlighten you."

"Would you?" Thrilled by her unexpected success, Portia bent down and embraced the woman's bony figure. "Thank you so very much. I've been wondering, and it would set my mind at ease."

"You're welcome, my dear." Miss Underhill lost her starch for a moment and awkwardly hugged Portia back. For a moment, she looked younger and happier . . . almost pretty. Then she reverted to the vinegary old maid and chastised Portia for the public display of emotion. "That's quite enough gossiping. Run along now. Mrs. Crompton surely must be ready to depart."

Portia started toward the arched doorway. The thought of facing Mama brought on an attack of nerves. She had been on pins and needles since the previous evening, fearing her mother might discover her deceit in leaving the Earl of Turnbuckle's house under false pretenses. She had planned to return to the ball after leaving Ratcliffe's house and cover her tracks by taking the family coach home, but it had been too late to risk it. Besides, Ratcliffe had insisted upon escorting her and Lindsey home.

This morning, much to her relief, Mama had chattered away at breakfast about having shared a cozy tête-à-tête with the Duke of Albright. With that triumph foremost in her mind, she'd apparently never thought to question the coachman as to whether or not he had actually taken her daughter home early.

But she might still find out by belated mischance.

"Portia, wait!"

She turned back to see Lindsey hurrying toward her. In a gown of celery green, her long chestnut hair held back with a ribbon, she looked younger than seventeen. Her cheeks were flushed from dancing and her blue eyes bright with purpose. She looped arms with Portia. "I haven't had a chance to ask you what we're going to do next."

"Next?"

"You know, about the . . ." Glancing furtively over her shoulder, she pulled Portia out into the spacious corridor outside the ballroom and lowered her voice to a whisper. "The miniature. Since you couldn't find it in you-know-who's chambers, where else do you think he may have hidden it?"

Portia had lain awake at night wondering that very thing. It still incensed her that he had stolen her property and held it over her head like the sword of Damocles. "Perhaps in his safe or his desk or a hundred other places. However, he'll be on his guard now, so I won't go skulking around his house again. Nor will you."

"But what if we create a better diversion?" Lindsey leaned closer, her eyes alight with zeal. "Just listen, I have it all thought out. You can go with him on a drive, actually *go* this time, whilst I creep into his house and search the premises."

"No!" Portia's blood ran cold at the prospect of the scandal that would ensue if her sister were caught in an act of robbery. "Henceforth, you are to forget all about the miniature. Do you understand me?"

Lindsey scowled. "Just because you couldn't find it doesn't mean I won't. I'm a far better sleuth than you are. Remember the time Mama lost her reticule, and I found it in the *tikka-ghari*, stuck between the seat cushions, because no one else remembered she'd gone for a drive that morning? And what about when Blythe wanted to know who was leaving flowers on her pillow, and I sat in hiding for hours and hours, only to discover it was that rascal Harvey Stanhope?"

Portia smiled at the memory. Harvey had been the fifteen-year-old son of her father's shipping agent, and he had earned a sound thrashing for his romantic efforts. "The silly boy was smitten with the minx. She was only thirteen, but she'd been flirting shamelessly with him."

"Yes, well, as far as I'm concerned *she's* the silly one, always sighing over the gentlemen," Lindsey declared. "*I* have more important concerns on my mind. Now, I've been wrestling with the problem of how to open Ratcliffe's safe. I might be lucky enough to find the key in his desk, but—"

"For heaven's sake, didn't you hear me? You won't be looking in his desk or anywhere else." To emphasize the point, Portia took hold of Lindsey's shoulders and gave her a firm shake. "If I find out that you did, I'll tell Mama about the stash of adventure novels you have hidden under your bed."

"You wouldn't dare, because then I would tell her that *you* borrowed them from the lending library for me."

"And I will declare I had no idea they were so full of manly derring-do and swaggering nonsense unfit for a lady's eyes. In any event, she will make certain you never read one ever again."

Crossing her arms, Lindsey stuck out her lower lip. "Why are you being so mean? If that's all the thanks I receive for helping you last night—"

"You did help me, very much so," Portia conceded. "Although I have mixed feelings about the pistol. Where did you obtain it, anyway?"

"It's Mama's, of course."

"Mama's?"

"Yes, she keeps it in her bedside table for protection against thieves; I heard her tell her maid." Lindsey shrugged. "And don't worry, I put it back this morning while she was asleep."

"Good heavens." Portia was astonished to learn their mother kept a pistol, let alone that her sister had the bravado to steal it and then return it while their mother was in the room. Truly, Lindsey was becoming far too adept at subterfuge.

"There will be no more guns or knives," Portia said firmly. "And promise me you won't go anywhere near his lordship's house ever again." She held up her hand. "I'll have your sacred blood vow."

With obvious reluctance, Lindsey touched the tips of their fingers together according to the secret gesture they had devised as children, when they had been shut inside during the monsoon season with nothing else to do but dream and play.

"Oh, have it your way, then." She lowered her voice to a petulant whisper. "But it'll serve you right if Ratcliffe

presents that miniature to Papa—and tells him about
your plan to marry Arun. That might be the best thing,
anyway. At least then our family wouldn't be split asun-
der by your moving back to India."

Her head high, she flounced back into the ballroom to
finish the dancing lesson.

Portia released a long sigh. She wilted down onto one
of the gilded chairs that lined the opulent passageway. In
a distinctly unladylike pose, she leaned forward to rest
her chin in her hands.

Her mind dwelled on the troublesome realization of
how distressed Lindsey would be when Portia left England. She had been so wrapped up in her own secret
plans that it hadn't even occurred to her to consider the
effect on her sisters and her parents. What if she never
saw them again? Was her love for Arun strong enough to
sustain a permanent separation from her family?

It hadn't been strong enough to stop her from finding
pleasure in another man's arms.

The vivid memory of that kiss threatened to beguile
her again, but she pushed it away. Ratcliffe was a skilled
lover, that was all. He could probably coax a nun into
sinful acts. However, there was no substance to his passion because it lacked the vital essence of love.

But Arun felt true affection for her. Arun, with his
warm smile and gallant nature. She *would* return to India and be reunited with him. No one must be allowed to
dissuade her from that purpose.

She felt a sudden desperate emptiness that could only
be attributed to a longing to be back in the familiar surroundings of her childhood. Perhaps it was just that she
hadn't received a letter from Arun in ages. She craved to
read his thoughtful observations about life there. It was
frustrating that she would have to wait for weeks until
her old *ayah*, Kasi, had her next half-day off and could

make inquiries at the London docks. No doubt next time there would be two letters at once.

Buoyed by the thought, Portia rose to her feet. In the meantime, it would be prudent to unearth the truth about the feud between Albright and Ratcliffe. If she were to hold both suitors at bay, she needed as much knowledge as possible in her arsenal. With any luck, she might even uncover information to hold over Ratcliffe's head.

Wouldn't *that* be turning the tables?

She started purposefully down the corridor. There would be no twiddling her thumbs while Miss Underhill waited for a reply from her mother's aging cousin. Rather, Portia had another plan that she intended to implement at the first opportunity.

Her sister didn't know it, but all future sleuthing would be done by Portia herself.

A commotion out in the hall caught Colin's attention in his study. The upraised voices broke his concentration. He had spent the morning poring over the monthly report from his steward, immersed in a detailed description of the spring planting, and it was disconcerting to be yanked back to reality. At least for a time, he had managed to forget the dull soreness in his upper arm—and the woman who had caused it.

Grimacing, he removed his spectacles, tossing them down on the desk as he surged to his feet. He stalked out into the foyer to find Tudge face-to-face with a midget in the front doorway.

Well, perhaps it was more like face-to-chest, for Tudge towered over his adversary. The stranger's oily black hair had shed a snowstorm of dandruff onto the shoulders of his ill-fitting green coat. He clutched a sheaf of papers in his hand.

"I'll give these to his lordship and nobody else," the

man insisted, shaking the papers in Tudge's face. "I brung them all the way from Kent, I did."

"An' ye can take them all the way back, too," Tudge countered. "Now get out, ye little pipsqueak, afore I toss ye in the gutter like the rubbish ye is."

A dun collector. Colin should have surmised as much and remained in his study. But he couldn't dodge the unpaid bills forever.

He strode forward to address the visitor. "I am Lord Ratcliffe. You may hand the invoices to me."

The man did so, his small black eyes and twitchy nose reminding Colin of a rat sniffing for cheese. "An' what about me payment? I ain't leavin' without gold coins in me pocket."

"Ye'll leave quick enough," Tudge retorted, brandishing a ham-sized fist, "wid the help of an undercut to the jaw."

"That won't be necessary," Colin said. He addressed the bill collector. "Follow me into my study while I review these charges."

Five minutes later, he sent the odious little man on his way with a partial payment that caused a considerable lightening of his strongbox. It was money that had been meant to pay the crushing monthly cost of upkeep on his properties.

The bills lay scattered across the mahogany desk. In a fit of anger, he wadded them into a ball, which he hurled into the fire. Then he stood by the hearth, watching as the edges blackened and curled before being consumed by the hungry flames.

Once again, his mother had gone on a spending spree. He had hoped that by relegating her to the estate in Kent, he could better control her expenditures. Instead, it seemed she had imported a mantua-maker from London and ordered an entire new wardrobe. She had not asked his permission because she knew full well he would have forbidden the extravagance.

Going to the sideboard, he splashed brandy into a glass. He tossed back the drink, wincing as the motion caused a jab of pain in his arm. It reminded him of Portia ministering to the gunshot wound, inadvertently teasing him with a view of her breasts. Much to his chagrin, he found himself consumed as much by the fire of lust as by his cold-blooded objective of making a rich marriage.

He closed his eyes, recalling the exotic fragrance of her skin, a blend of cinnamon and something else, something as mysterious as the look in her beautiful blue eyes. And that kiss. She had been wild for him, rising on tiptoe as if she couldn't get enough of his mouth, abandoning her acerbic words for the sweetness of passion. He had intended only to coax her, to give her a taste of pleasure. But her swift, uninhibited response had made him lose his head. It was the only explanation he could fathom for pushing her down onto his bed.

Damn it, he knew better than to seduce a virgin. Even if she felt so perfect beneath him. Even if he couldn't resist the taste of her skin and the enticing curves of her body.

"Excuse me, your lordship."

Startled, he opened his eyes to see Hannah hovering in the doorway. She looked very different in the gray serge gown of a servant, a white cap hiding her red hair and a ruffled apron concealing all but a hint that she was breeding.

"Yes?" he barked.

"I have your luncheon ready in the dining room. Or would you care for a tray in here instead?"

"The dining room will do. In the future, ring the gong."

"I'm sorry . . . I didn't know."

Hannah went away, but not before he spied a flash of hurt in her eyes. Bloody hell. He shouldn't have snapped at her. Now she would think he was still angry about that long-ago betrayal, when her past misbehavior simply didn't matter to him anymore.

Hannah had been trying very hard to adjust to the new role of housekeeper. It wasn't her fault she had interrupted his fevered fantasy.

He was hungry all right, but not for food.

And not for any other woman but Miss Portia Crompton.

CHAPTER 10

In the garret where the servants slept, Portia cautiously opened one of the doors off the passageway. The dim little room with its narrow cot smelled strongly of sandalwood. A curl of smoke rose from the saucer of incense in front of a shrine to Shiva. There, a small stone statue depicted the Hindu god sitting in a meditative pose, his hands resting in the cradle of his crossed legs. Pansies scattered the bare plank floor in front of the shrine.

Kasi swayed in front of the figurine, singing softly in her native tongue. Her thin gray hair was drawn up in a knob, while a green sari covered her squat form.

Portia stepped inside and closed the door, anxiously turning the sealed letter in her hands until the *ayah* finished her song. "Kasi, did you not hear my knock?"

"I hear," the old woman said serenely. Picking up a porcelain pitcher, she poured a thin stream of milk over the flowers, an offering to the gods that Portia had seen her perform often back in India.

The familiar ritual made her momentarily forget her urgent errand. None of their other Indian servants had made the voyage to England. Her parents had consented to bring Kasi only because all three girls had begged and pleaded. Kasi had been a mother to them for more years than Portia could remember. The *ayah* had crooned to them when they were ill and coddled them after Papa's scoldings when they were naughty. Her loyalty to the family was fierce and unwavering.

"Should you be doing that here?" Portia asked dubiously. "The milk will curdle and smell."

"English do not understand," Kasi replied as she set down the pitcher. "Gods need food, too. And gifts to grant favors."

"Why are you praying in the middle of the day, anyway? I thought you did so only at dawn."

"I pray for you, missy. More prayers, more help."

Portia blinked in surprise. It seemed uncanny because she had come here to beg a favor of Kasi. "Help? Why would you think I needed help?"

"To find your karma, your destiny." Kasi shuffled forward to pat Portia's cheek with her leathery hand. The warm touch was as familiar and comforting as her singsong voice. "Shiva help you if I pray to him."

"You mean . . . my destiny with Arun?"

Without answering, the *ayah* took hold of Portia's hand, running her fingers over the palm, exploring it with her stubby forefinger and tracing the various lines. It was something she had done a number of times over the years, to Portia as well as to her sisters. When they were children, having their palms read had been pure entertainment, for Kasi would spin tales about all the wonderful things that lay in store for them in the future. At least she had until the day Mrs. Crompton had walked in on one of their sessions. Mama had denounced palmistry as heathen superstition and had forbidden Kasi to practice it.

Now, the *ayah* muttered to herself while bobbing her head. She kept rubbing the topmost line on Portia's palm, following it all the way to Portia's little finger.

"What is it? What do you see?"

"Fate give you one love, missy. He live here in England."

Ratcliffe's sinfully handsome face popped into her mind. Although two days had passed, the memory of his kiss was so vivid she felt a pulse of raw desire. It was the same response that plagued her thoughts by day and haunted her dreams at night.

Appalled, she grabbed hold of Kasi's arm. "That can't possibly be true. Arun is the man I love."

Kasi shrugged. "I tell what I see."

Portia stiffened. "Well, I won't listen to such rubbish. It's too dim in here to see my hand, anyway."

Those dark button eyes seemed to peer into Portia's soul. Then Kasi pressed her palms together and bowed deeply in a *salaam*. "Do not be angry, missy. I not speak of it again."

Portia compressed her lips. She was well aware that Kasi hadn't changed her convictions, only promised not to voice them. It irked her that the *ayah* would declare that Arun was not a part of her future.

A revelation struck Portia, one that had never occurred to her before but now seemed very possible. "You don't like that I've promised myself to a native prince, do you? Because I'm a foreigner and not of his caste."

"It not for me to say."

Kasi kept her eyes lowered, hiding her thoughts. That evasiveness confirmed Portia's deduction. Who would have guessed that all this time while Kasi had been going faithfully to the docks once a month to pick up Arun's letters, she disapproved of the association? Portia felt foolish for not realizing the truth before now. It made perfect sense because the Indians had a class system that was every bit as rigid as the English one.

And that would explain the palm reading, too. It

wasn't that Kasi was deliberately lying to her. Rather, the *ayah* had seen only what she had wanted to see.

Perversely reassured, Portia decided to let the subject pass. Kasi was faithful and trustworthy, and at the moment nothing else mattered.

"I need you to do something for me." She pressed the letter into Kasi's hand. "Please post this for me. It's already been franked. And take great care that no one sees you, for I wouldn't want anyone to connect the letter to me—especially not my parents."

"Yes, missy."

"Thank you so very much." Touched by the *ayah*'s loyalty, Portia enveloped her stout form in a hug. Kasi smelled of incense, a nostalgic reminder of Portia's childhood. Those happy memories lingered, making her smile as she left the attic room and closed the door.

"Portia? Is that you?"

She froze, her eyes widening at the sight of her mother gliding down the cramped passageway. Clad in a morning dress of white and green striped muslin, Edith Crompton wore a stylish bonnet over her dark russet hair. Her elegant appearance in the servants' quarters was as incongruous as seeing snow fall from the hot Indian sky. "Mama! Why have you come up here?"

"I could ask you the very same question."

"I—I was visiting Kasi, that's all."

Edith Crompton shook her head in disapproval. "Henceforth, you are not to do so. Proper young ladies do not mingle with the staff. You haven't the same leniency here as you had in India."

Under different circumstances, Portia might have argued that Kasi was almost a member of the family. But now she merely said, "Yes, Mama."

"We are due to call on Lord and Lady Madison shortly."

That critical hazel gaze examined Portia from head to toe. "It would behoove you to tidy your hair. And wear the straw bonnet with the blue ribbons. It will match the sprigged flowers in your gown quite nicely."

Portia refrained from heaving a sigh at the prospect of another afternoon spent making visits. She started toward the stairway, only to pause when her mother didn't follow. "Aren't you coming downstairs with me?"

"I wish to speak to Kasi myself. I will see you in the entrance hall in precisely ten minutes."

That dismissing tone brooked no more questions. Uneasy, Portia headed for the stairs, looking over her shoulder. She had the distinct impression that her mother had not ventured up here in search of her missing daughter, but for the sole purpose of seeing Kasi. But if Mama wanted some little task done, why had she not rung for the servant? Or sent a footman to summon Kasi downstairs? It didn't make sense, especially since Mama had become such a stickler for rules.

As she made her way down a narrow staircase to the opulent family quarters, a far greater concern swamped Portia. Heaven help her if Mama caught sight of that letter. She would confiscate it at once.

And then she would demand to know why Portia was writing to one Hannah Wilton, in care of the notorious Viscount Ratcliffe.

"Miss Crompton, you are looking exceptionally lovely tonight." Lord Wrayford bent over her gloved hand that evening, giving her a view of the bald spot at the back of his sandy hair.

"Thank you, my lord," Portia said with a polite smile.

They stood in the crowded foyer at the Drury Lane Theater. Along with the other patrons, they were slowly making their way toward their seats. While her parents paused to exchange greetings with several acquaintances, Wrayford had taken the opportunity to corner her.

It wasn't the first time he had done so. The purse-poor profligate had sought her out at every ball and rout. He spent most of the time ogling her bosom as he was doing now. The scrutiny of those pale blue eyes made her wish she had worn one of Miss Underhill's high-necked gowns, instead of the primrose silk with its fashionably low bodice.

Her mother and father had inched ahead, still chatting with their friends, not noticing that she'd fallen behind. "If you'll excuse me," she said, "I must catch up to my parents."

When she tried to extricate her hand, Wrayford held on tightly. "My dear Miss Crompton, we are forever meeting in a mob. I simply must have you all to myself. May I take you for a drive on the morrow? I should like for you to see my new yellow curricle."

The ardent expression on his florid face made her want to flee at once. Yet good manners dictated that she let him down easily. "That's very kind of you to offer, but—"

"You're too late," Ratcliffe said. "She's going for a drive with me."

The sound of that deep voice caused a tremor inside of Portia, shocking all of her senses awake. She turned to find her nemesis standing at her side, so near that she could feel the heat of his body and smell the spicy scent of his skin. Tall and strikingly handsome, Ratcliffe stood out in the masses of gentlemen and their ladies. The cocoa brown of his coat and the white of his cravat enhanced the swarthiness of his skin. And those lips . . . the mere memory of his kiss had the power to make her legs melt.

Wrayford scowled. "Ratcliffe. Didn't think you were welcome in polite society these days."

Ratcliffe's green eyes betrayed a mocking amusement. "They may bar me from their homes, but alas, not from a public theater."

With that, he took Portia's arm and drew her ahead into the swarm of patrons, leaving Wrayford behind. Her heart fluttered every time Ratcliffe brushed against her, which was often in this crush. She had to remind herself she had traded one fortune hunter for another.

"You certainly are *not* taking me for a drive," she whispered, so no one around them could overhear. "And I didn't need you to rescue me, either. I am quite capable of managing a persistent suitor."

"You'll hear no argument from me on that issue."

The dry humor in his tone brought a rush of heat to her cheeks. Of course he would say that after she'd shot him. "How is your arm?"

"The pain keeps me awake all night, tossing and turning." He glanced down at her horrified expression and gave her a grin of pure deviltry. "That was a jest, sweetheart. The wound is healing quite nicely. Which means it must be something else that makes me toss and turn."

With his voice so soft and silky, there was no mistaking his meaning. Especially when he caught her gaze and held it for a prolonged moment. The dark fire there made it clear that he, too, remembered their kiss and wanted more . . . much more.

He bent closer, murmuring into her ear, "Have I told you how ravishing you look tonight, Portia?"

His eyes flicked downward to caress her bosom, and she had an entirely different reaction than with Wrayford. This time, she felt as if she were smoldering under the heat of the sun. Her breath grew fast and shallow, making her light-headed. She had the mad desire to pull Ratcliffe into a closet—or anywhere they could be alone—so they could share another wild, passionate tryst.

She turned her gaze from him, staring straight ahead at the quail feather bobbing on a lady's bonnet. Gritting her teeth, she hissed, "Don't say things like that. And stop inflicting your presence on me. I've no wish to see you ever again."

"A difficult objective since I'm courting you."

In spite of her resolve, a thrill jolted her. She denied it at once, shooting him a fierce glare. "You are *not* courting me. I *forbid* it."

He chuckled, infuriatingly undaunted. "You may wish to compose yourself, darling. Your parents are looking this way."

She immediately schooled her features into an expression of well-bred disinterest. Mama mustn't suspect even a hint of the intimacy that had transpired with Ratcliffe. She would suffer an apoplexy if she knew he had visited Portia's bedchamber, and that Portia had done likewise to him.

She'd already had a close call with that letter to Hannah. Thankfully, Mama had not discovered it in Kasi's keeping, but Portia had an uneasy feeling her luck was bound to run out at some point.

Her parents stood waiting for her by the gilded entrance to the box seats. They made a pleasing couple, Papa the prosperous gentleman in his dark suit and white cravat, and Mama in rich amber satin with a gold circlet adorning her russet hair.

More and more, Portia disliked the notion of disappointing them when they wanted so much for her to be a success. She wouldn't let herself even think about how distraught they would be at the end of the Season when she proposed to return to India.

She summoned a smile. "Mama, Papa, I lost you in the crowd. Lord Ratcliffe was kind enough to escort me here."

"I encouraged your daughter to take advantage of my height by asking me to look for you."

Her mother gave him a cool nod. "We appreciate your assistance, my lord."

He bowed. "It was my pleasure, Mrs. Crompton. And you must be Mr. Crompton. I understand you're quite the phenomenon in the business world."

As the two men shook hands, George Crompton studied the younger man assessingly. "Some might say so. I seem to have a knack for trading in tea and spices."

"And you've the fastest fleet on the high seas. I recall seeing one of your ships myself when I stopped in Calcutta some seven or eight years ago."

Portia stared at Ratcliffe in astonishment. He'd never breathed a word of having visited India. "You—*what*—?"

He gave her that famous half-smile, the one that hinted at secrets beyond her imagining. "Many young gentlemen do a European tour. I preferred to see a bit more of the world."

"A wise choice," George Crompton said with an approving nod. "If you like, I'll show you around one of my ships when it comes into port."

"I'll hold you to that promise, sir."

"Excellent." His hearty smile vanished as he looked at his frowning wife. "Ahem, well, we must be off to our seats. Wouldn't want to be late and miss the opening scene."

"We are joining the Duke of Albright in his box," Mrs. Crompton pointedly told the viscount, taking hold of Portia's arm. "We mustn't keep His Grace waiting."

As they walked off, Portia had one last glimpse of

Ratcliffe. The charming courtier had vanished, and a cool mask now covered his features. There was something dangerous in his eyes, something that hadn't been there until her mother had mentioned the duke.

Something that gave Portia a cold shiver.

CHAPTER 11

"You can see the stage quite well from right here," the Duke of Albright said as he guided Portia to a gilt chair at the railing.

Ever the gentleman, he waited for her parents to take the two chairs to the rear before sitting down beside her. He was meticulously groomed in a coal-black coat with white satin knee breeches, clocked white stockings, and polished black shoes. In the few minutes since their arrival, he had been a model of courtesy, directing a footman to take their wraps, chatting with her parents, complimenting both Portia and her mother on their gowns.

Portia found his ministrations akin to curling up in a comforting chair by a warm fire. With the duke, she wasn't beset by a storm of emotional upheaval. She wasn't in a dither of frustration and anger and—yes—unladylike lust. She wasn't fretting about her own character flaw in succumbing to the spell of a scoundrel. She could relax and enjoy the evening out.

The well-appointed box enclosed the party in privacy while providing a sweeping view of the theater. Oil lamps flickered at intervals along the walls, painting the scene with a golden glow. The upper tiers, where the aristocrats sat, formed a semicircle around the stage. They looked down on the floor seats, which were a mass of humanity with people jostling to find a place to sit before the play commenced.

"I hope you will enjoy the performance of the esteemed Edmund Kean," the duke said.

The actor had taken London by storm, and Portia looked forward to seeing his much-praised portrayal of Shylock in *The Merchant of Venice*. "I must confess, although I've read a few of Mr. Shakespeare's plays, I've never actually seen one performed."

"Never? Yes, I suppose you would have had little occasion to experience sophisticated culture, growing up as you did in the remote reaches of the Empire."

His dismissive tone made her protest, "But you mustn't think I was deprived. India has all manner of fine art and literature, including heroic plays and epic poetry. And the sights are truly magnificent to behold—in Agra, there is a white marble mausoleum called the Taj Mahal—"

"I meant no offense, my dear. I'm sure it was all very beautiful." The duke reached over to pat her hand, and his cordial manner smoothed her ruffled feathers. "Now, are you familiar with the story we are about to see?"

"I'm afraid not."

"Then you must prepare yourself for a surprise in regard to one of the central characters."

"What do you mean?"

"You'll see soon enough."

Smiling, he would say no more, and curiosity filled her as the crimson curtain began a slow rise. The buzz of conversation died down to silence, except for a cough or two. She turned her attention to the actors on stage and quickly learned that the heroine of the play was a young heiress named Portia. Just like her, the fictitious Portia had to decide which of her many suitors to marry.

The duke glanced at her, seeming to enjoy her amusement as much as the play itself. He lent her a pair of gold opera glasses. As she lifted them to her eyes, however, her gaze fell on a box on the opposite side of the theater—and one of its occupants.

Ratcliffe.

He was sitting with a group of gentlemen and ladies. For someone who was ostracized, he certainly seemed comfortable with the ton. She recognized a few of them as members of the fast crowd, those who liked to gamble and drink and race their carriages, no matter what the danger to innocent pedestrians on the street. All of a sudden, he turned his head. He looked straight at her and smiled.

Blushing, she whipped her attention back to the stage. But the play went unnoticed, because her mind was once again preoccupied with thoughts of Ratcliffe. Instead of the actors, she saw that rakish quirk of his lips. Instead of the dialogue, she heard the murmur of his husky voice in her mind.

It must be something else entirely that makes me toss and turn.

She hadn't wanted to admit to him that she, too, had lain awake at night. One taste of his mouth had been like partaking of forbidden fruit. Ever since that moment, the deep slumber of the innocent had eluded her. She had lost the ability to find a comfortable position in her vast featherbed. And her restless imagination had developed an annoying tendency to run wild. While lying in the darkness of her chamber, she found herself spinning fantasies of Ratcliffe pressing her down into a nest of pillows, of him covering her with his strong body.

His naked body.

Not, of course, that she had ever viewed a man's entirely unclothed form—except in drawings of Greek and Roman sculptures.

And in Ratcliffe's copy of the *Kama Sutra*.

Abandoning the opera glasses, Portia groped for her fan and snapped it open. Thankfully, everyone was too engrossed in the play to notice her waving the fan at her flushed face. It was most aggravating, the effect he had on her. One would hope she'd have better sense than to moon over a man who had made an art out of seducing women.

Yet the mere thought of him rendered her breathless. Oh, those broad shoulders, the muscularity of his thighs in the form-fitting breeches, the naughty glint in his eyes. It was enough to give her a fit of the vapors . . .

With a blink, she realized that the curtain was coming down to thunderous applause. She dropped the fan in her lap and clapped along with everyone else.

"The play seemed rather short," she commented.

The duke gave her a quizzical look. "It's merely the interlude—the halfway point."

"Oh, I see," she said, feeling foolish.

"Portia, darling," her mother said from the chair to the rear, "your father and I are going to pay our respects to the Marchioness of Wargrave. Do pardon us, Your Grace."

The duke rose politely as they left. It was a ploy, Portia realized in mortification, to leave her alone with Albright. Didn't Mama realize how transparent she was being?

Albright extended his white-gloved hand to Portia. "Perhaps you would care to take a short stroll around the theater. You will wish to partake in a glass of lemonade, as well."

She hesitated. From the corner of her eye, she could see that Ratcliffe's seat was vacant. He must have gone out to the lobby, where she would be vulnerable to his approach. She had no wish to encounter him again, especially not in the company of the duke. Their hostility toward one another had all the makings of an embarrassing scene.

Here in the duke's private box, however, she was safe from being caught in the middle of any such confrontation. It wasn't cowardly, she assured herself. Rather, it was mature and responsible of her to avoid all contact with a rogue like Ratcliffe.

"Lemonade does sound refreshing," she said. "But I'm feeling a trifle unwell. Would you mind terribly if I stayed here rather than faced the crush of people?"

Something flickered in the duke's eyes, a faint displeasure that vanished so quickly she might have imagined it. With perfect civility, he bowed. "I will fetch you a glass, then. And if you like I will instruct the footman to stand outside and bar any visitors from entering."

"Yes!" She toned down her enthusiasm lest he guess that her illness was merely a pretext. "Thank you, that would be most thoughtful."

He departed, the door closed, and she was alone. Releasing a long sigh, Portia entertained herself by glancing around the theater. Many of the patrons had gone out, but a scattered few remained, conversing in groups. She couldn't see Ratcliffe anywhere.

Had he gone to the lobby? Or to visit someone else's box?

She picked up the opera glasses and slowly scanned the seats. Her gaze paused on the stout form of Mrs. Beardsley, encased in a hideous brown dress with too many ruffles. Her daughter, Frances, appeared to be making a cake of herself as usual, simpering with false shyness while clinging to the arm of a red-faced Henry Hockenhull.

Portia continued her search. Ratcliffe, thank heavens, was still nowhere to be seen. It was just as well. Let him turn his lecherous attentions elsewhere, on someone who welcomed them.

Just to be fair, though, she had to admit his character wasn't completely devoid of redemption. He had helped Hannah Wilton after she'd been turned out onto the street. He'd given her a place to live and an honest livelihood. Society would frown on him employing a courtesan, especially one who was breeding, but Portia thought it a kind and generous act.

Of course, that was only if he didn't have additional bedtime duties for Hannah to perform. The nagging possibility kept Portia from feeling overly charitable toward him. She didn't trust him not to take advantage of the poor mother-to-be. Soon, however, she would ascertain the truth. Portia's letter had been delivered to the woman earlier in the day, and she could scarcely wait for a reply—

Her leisurely perusal of the audience came to an abrupt halt. So did her heart.

Ratcliffe was climbing onto the railing of the box beside hers, balancing high above the floor. Several men down below gave a shout. A woman screamed.

Ratcliffe paid them no heed. He walked nimbly along the railing and leaped into Albright's box. Only then did he look down to give a jaunty wave like a performer in a circus.

Several cheers and huzzahs arose, along with laughter and the heightened buzz of conversation.

He took the seat beside Portia. A devilish light danced in his green eyes, as if he'd enjoyed showing off to an audience—without a thought for the damage to her reputation. "I see that Albright was careless enough to leave you all alone."

Sitting stiffly upright, she breathed deeply in an effort

to calm her turbulent emotions. "Have you gone mad? You could have killed yourself."

"It's encouraging to know you care whether I live or die."

"Care for *you*?" She turned to glare at him. "Your dead body lying on the seats down below would put a damper on everyone's evening. And I for one do not wish for the rest of the play to be canceled."

"Oh, you are cold, just like the fair Portia on stage, choosing her husband by whimsical trickery. It will be interesting to see if she gets her comeuppance in the second half."

Portia was too upset to engage in a polite discussion of Shakespeare's work—or to argue against the implied similarity to her own situation. "It was foolish of you to come here. The duke will be furious when he finds you sitting in his seat. No doubt someone is already hastening to report your idiotic behavior to him."

The warning proved no deterrent to Ratcliffe. He merely grinned and settled more comfortably into the chair. "I'd call my behavior practical. There's a rather imposing footman guarding the door. So this seemed the most expedient way to continue our conversation."

"There is nothing more to be said." She paused, curiosity overcoming her need to eject him. "Except for one thing. Why did you never tell me you'd visited India?"

"You never asked."

She gave him a withering look. "You must have known I would be interested. Did you only visit Calcutta?"

"Yes. It's quite the fascinating area, close to both the jungle and the hills with all the tea plantations."

She and her family had lived near Bombay, hundreds of miles across the country. "How long were you there?"

"Several months."

"Months?" The news startled her. "What could have possibly kept you there for so long?"

"I was seeing the sights. Exploring the countryside." A faint smile touched his lips. "Buying books."

The *Kama Sutra*.

Despite her resolve to remain unaffected, Portia blushed. To give herself something to do, she took up her fan again and snapped it open, only to close it as she realized the action might draw his attention to her overheated state. "You can't have learned to read Hindi in so short a time. It's a difficult language to master since it doesn't use the English alphabet."

He shrugged. "Perhaps for you. But I happen to have an affinity for foreign tongues."

What an arrogant jackass! "Foreign tongues in foreign ladies, no doubt. You were probably carrying on a liaison. That's what kept you in Calcutta."

He threw back his head and laughed. "Your low opinion wounds me, darling."

His amusement captivated her momentarily. It made her want to smile, too, when he needed to be blistered into going away. "Do not address me in so familiar a manner. And you really should leave before the duke returns with my lemonade."

Ratcliffe's good humor faded. "I see you've decided to disregard my warning about Albright."

"There is no reason for me to discourage his friendship. At least *he* isn't chasing after my wealth."

"You should know he has a fondness for intrigue and trickery. He amuses himself by playing the marionette, by making people dance on his strings."

"I am not his puppet," she flared. "His Grace has been the perfect gentleman. The only cunning schemer I know is *you*."

Ratcliffe took hold of her hand, his warmth penetrating the thin kid glove. For once, his face was absolutely serious. "Portia, listen to me. I'm telling you the truth. You don't know him as well as I do."

When he looked at her that way, his eyes so deep and green, she felt her defenses melting, letting in an element of doubt about the duke. But she wasn't a naïve schoolgirl to accept Ratcliffe at his word. Nor was she a feather-brained lady, easily gulled by a handsome face and smooth charm. "Then answer the question I've asked you before. Explain to me exactly what he's done to you."

Uttering a growl of frustration, he looked away from her. "I cannot. To do so would require me to break a confidence. And it is not my story to tell—"

His voice broke off. His eyes narrowed, he stared intently across the theater. "Good God," he muttered under his breath.

"Is something wrong?"

He surged to his feet. "Pray excuse me."

"Wait. Where are you going?"

But she was talking to the air. Ratcliffe had already leaped onto the railing and departed the way he'd arrived.

A few moments later, the duke came storming back, along with her parents. She had to explain to them what had happened, that yes, Lord Ratcliffe had entered her box in a most unorthodox manner, but that nothing untoward had happened. They had conversed in full view of enough members of the ton to satisfy even the strictest of moralists.

As she pleaded her case, Portia caught sight of Ratcliffe entering a box across the theater, just below the one he'd occupied with his friends. He went straight to a dark-haired female standing with several gentlemen. The woman was petite and slim, her fine figure enhanced by a gown in a brilliant shade of peacock blue. He pulled her aside as if his rights to her company superseded all others. They stood near the rear of the box with their heads together, apparently deep in conversation.

A burning lump smoldered inside Portia. Who was she? Another of Ratcliffe's mistresses? The nerve of him to come courting her, then rush off to join another female.

The woman was too far away to discern her features. Portia dared not pick up the opera glasses to take a closer look, not with the duke and her parents hovering nearby, dissecting Ratcliffe's rude behavior and lack of manners.

Then, just as the duke's party was settling down for the rise of the curtain, Ratcliffe took the woman by the arm and led her out of the box. Although Portia kept close watch for the remainder of the play, they never reappeared.

Colin allowed her to precede him through the front door. The house in Berkeley Square had to have cost a tidy sum, he noted bitterly, assessing the extravagant interior with its gilt chairs, fine paintings, and curving marble staircase. No doubt he would receive the invoice for its rental shortly. The thought made him livid.

They handed their wraps to a waiting footman. Then Colin ushered her into the drawing room, while another footman hurried ahead to light several branches of candles and to stir up the fire on the hearth. "Go," he ordered the servant. "And close the doors behind you."

He waited in the center of the plush rug until his command was obeyed. Only when they were alone did he pivot toward the woman who had seated herself on a striped chaise.

The sight of her after all these months stirred a powerful tide of emotion in him—resentment, anger, and yes, affection. Annoyed with himself for feeling even the slightest softening, he released the rigid restraint he had employed at the theater, when he had been determined not to cause a public scene.

"The truth now, Mother. Why have you come to London?"

Lady Ratcliffe looked up from arranging her peacock-blue skirt. Except for the fine lines around her green eyes, her features showed little sign of aging. Her hair was as dark and luxuriant as it was in the painting that hung in his house; he wondered if she used lamp blacking to conceal the gray seen in other women of nine-and-forty years.

"As I said at the theater, I've grown weary of the country," she said coolly. "All of my dearest friends are here for the Season. It isn't fair of you to expect me to languish in the backwaters of Kent for the rest of my life."

"You know precisely why you were to stay there. You agreed to the terms yourself."

"And I've abided by them for three long years." Her lips formed a pout. "Besides, my concession was made before I realized how dull it would be to count the sheep in the meadow and to have as my only entertainment the doddering old vicar for tea."

"Dull?" Rage surged in Colin, so strong he couldn't stand still. He stalked to the fireplace and brought his fist down on the mantel, rattling a china figurine of a shepherdess. "And you believe that's an adequate excuse for canceling out what you've done?"

Behind him, her skirts rustled as she rose to her feet and approached him. When she laid a gentle touch on his arm, he stiffened. "Please look at me, Colin, I beg of you."

He couldn't disregard that soft voice. It was the same voice that had read him stories as a young boy, the same voice that had sung him lullabies when he was ill. He reluctantly turned to face her.

"I'm truly sorry for all that's happened," she murmured, reaching up to touch his cheek. The faint, familiar scent of roses wafted to him. "How many times must I tell you so? If I could change the past, I would. I swear I would."

The tears swimming in her eyes almost did him in. The trouble was, he believed she spoke the truth. She really did feel remorse for her actions. But unfortunately, regret wasn't enough. It would never be enough.

He stepped away from her. "I want you to return to Kent in the morning. You know full well I haven't the funds to rent this pile."

"The lease covers half a year, and anyway, I wish to stay for the remainder of the Season."

"The lease is invalid without my signature."

She took hold of his hand and rubbed the back of it. "Please, Colin, don't be angry. My behavior will be exemplary, I promise you. Besides, I do so want to meet the heiress who has caught your interest. Miss Portia Crompton, I believe is her name."

He scowled, realizing that his mother must have witnessed his balancing act in the theater, then his conversation with Portia. "She's no concern of yours."

"Pish-posh. You're my only son, so of course your choice of a bride concerns me. And I must say, she appeared rather disapproving of you. I thought perhaps I could help in that respect—"

"No," he said sharply. "I won't brook any interference from you."

"But it's imperative that you marry her. She's the premier heiress of the season. We need her dowry."

"Yes, we do, don't we."

Rather than chide him for his sarcasm, his mother

merely pursed her lips. "*You*, then. As head of the family, you need her money. And there's no time to waste. Albright is courting her, too, and you mustn't let him walk off with such a prize."

Colin wanted to retort that Portia was far more than a trophy to be won. She had independent thoughts and deep convictions, along with a saucy manner that intrigued him. But how could he chastise his mother, when he, too, regarded Portia as a rich bank account?

"Albright won't win her," Colin said flatly. "I'll see to that."

He started to walk away when Lady Ratcliffe touched his arm. "And you'll let me stay, then?"

He shouldn't. It went against all rational judgment. Yet the hopeful pleading in her eyes did him in.

He inclined his head in a curt nod. "On one condition. I will have your solemn vow that you will behave yourself."

"Of course."

She didn't have to ask what he meant, he noted cynically. She knew her own weaknesses as well as he did.

Now, if only he could trust her promise.

CHAPTER 12

Portia and Kasi sat in the hired hack parked halfway down the street from Ratcliffe's house. The *ayah* had come as chaperone on a fictitious errand to the milliner's shop. It was a flimsy excuse, which was why Portia needed to hurry back home before her mother discovered her absence at breakfast and grew suspicious.

They had been waiting here for half an hour already.

Outside, a fine mist made the early morning cold and damp. Water droplets beaded on the grimy window of the cab. Anxiously, she peered out, watching the tall brick façade of the row house. Not so much as a blind twitched in the windows.

She wanted to go up to the porch and knock on the front door. But that hulking ogre, Orson Tudge, would likely answer. He would inform the viscount of her presence and then all of Portia's scheming would be for naught.

Of course, it might be for naught, anyway, if Hannah Wilton failed to heed the instructions in the letter Portia had sent two days ago. Belatedly, it had occurred to her that the former courtesan might never have had the benefit of schooling. Which meant she'd have had to have asked someone else to read the letter to her.

What if that person was Ratcliffe? He would likely forbid Hannah to come to this rendezvous.

Ratcliffe. The mere thought of him made Portia's heart beat faster. It was a ridiculous reaction, considering how much she loathed him. Was he at this very moment slumbering in his chamber? More to the point, was that woman from the theater in bed with him?

A hot blade of resentment twisted through Portia. She didn't care if he cavorted with anything in skirts. It was just that he had dumped her like a bit of Haymarket fluff the instant he'd caught sight of one of his paramours. And to think Portia had made excuses about his behavior to her parents and the duke!

A touch on her arm distracted her. Kasi shifted on her seat, her short legs not quite reaching the floor, a cloak swathing her stout form. Her black-currant eyes glinted from within the burnt-orange scarf that covered her thin gray hair. "Lady not come, missy. We go now, or *memsahib* be angry."

"Leave Mama to me." Not yet ready to give up, Portia studied the Indian woman. "I've been meaning to ask, what did Mama want with you, the day she came up to your chamber?"

Kasi hesitated, then looked down at her folded brown hands. "*Memsahib* wish to see my shrine. She tell me no more pray to false gods."

Portia had the nagging feeling there was more to the matter than Kasi let on. "But why? Did one of the other servants complain about the smell of incense? Or perhaps the sour milk?"

Kasi lifted her shoulders in a shrug. "I do not know."

The unfairness of it troubled Portia. Kasi always seemed so placid, even in the face of this new development. Was she unhappy living in England, so far from the land of her birth? "Well, you needn't fret about it," she said, patting the old woman's hands. "When I return to India, you can go with me. Arun and I will provide a home for you. And you'll be able to worship Shiva to your heart's content."

To her surprise, Kasi stubbornly shook her head. "London your home now, missy. I stay with you right here."

Portia was about to protest when a movement outside caught her eye. Someone trudged around the corner of Ratcliffe's house. The woman was wrapped in a dark hooded cloak, from which a few strands of brassy red hair escaped. She paused beneath the spreading branches of an oak tree and peered uncertainly toward the hired hack.

"There she is," Portia said in excitement.

She opened the cab door and beckoned. Hannah Wilton glanced nervously over her shoulder, and then hastened toward the vehicle. She ducked inside, accepting the aid of Portia's extended hand.

"Miss Crompton," she said by way of greeting, pushing back the hood to reveal a spill of brilliant hair. The voluminous cloak concealed all evidence of her pregnancy. Even in drab clothing, however, she was a strikingly beautiful woman, with high cheekbones, luminous skin, and ruby-red lips. "Forgive me for being so late. I had to wait until Mr. Tudge went down into the wine cellar."

"It's quite all right. You were able to read my letter, then."

Hannah gave a tight smile. "My father was a sergeant in the army. He and my mother never married, nor did he ever openly acknowledge me as his. However, he did arrange for my education."

Portia had the uneasy suspicion that she'd offended the woman. Odd that, for she had never before considered that a courtesan might harbor a sense of pride. "Well, you're here now and that's all that matters." Seeing Hannah flick a glance at her thickset companion,

Portia added, "This is Kasi, my *ayah*—my former nurse-maid. Let me say, she's entirely trustworthy."

Silently, Kasi flattened her palms together and bowed her head.

Hannah nodded in return, before shifting her attention back to Portia. "You said you wished to ask me a few questions. I haven't much time, so I will get straight to the point. His lordship and I ended our liaison nearly a year ago. There is nothing intimate between us anymore."

Portia fought against an awkward blush. Her etiquette lessons had not prepared her for how to respond to such a blunt comment. It was difficult enough to keep herself from imagining what the two of them had done together in bed. "Um . . . that isn't what I wanted to ask you."

"No?"

"I'm curious about how long you've known him. Were you . . . acquainted with him at the time of his father's death three years ago?"

"Only briefly. Lord Ratcliffe used to visit occasionally at the house where I worked. Eventually he set me up in my own place, with servants and a carriage."

Hannah exuded an air of sensuality, from the lush fullness of her lips to the knowing look in her eyes. In her company, Portia felt gauche and juvenile, uncomfortably aware of her own inexperience—and undeniably resentful of this woman who had satisfied his appetites. It was an irrational reaction, Portia knew, considering she had no intention of marrying the man.

She forced herself to focus on her purpose. "Do you know what happened to his father?"

Hannah shrugged. " 'Twas an accident with a gun, some of the other gentlemen said. But his lordship never talked to me about anything so personal."

"Have you ever heard him mention the Duke of Albright?"

Hannah's eyes widened, deep brown and unfathomable. "Albright? Why do you ask?"

Intrigued, Portia leaned forward. "You do know the name, then."

"Yes." Hannah turned her gaze out the window of the cab, whether to peer into the past or to avoid Portia's scrutiny, Portia couldn't tell. "Those two despise one another. His lordship has quarreled with His Grace."

"When? And what was the nature of their quarrel?"

"These are questions you should direct to Lord Ratcliffe himself."

"I have—and he won't tell me."

"Then neither should I speak of it." Her manner suddenly secretive, Hannah reached for the door handle. "I've gossiped more than I ought. It's a poor way to repay his lordship after all the help he's given me and my poor babe. Now, I mustn't tarry any longer, else my absence will be questioned."

Beset by frustration, Portia placed her hand over the woman's. She wanted to know something, even if it was none of her business. "At least tell me this: Why did Ratcliffe end his liaison with you?"

Hannah blinked. Her cheeks faintly flushed, she gave Portia a brittle smile. "He discovered me lying with another man. You see, it has never been my nature to wait alone for one man to come calling on me. Now, I really must get back to my work."

Shocked, Portia watched as Hannah pushed open the door and stepped out onto the foot pavement. Drawing the hood back up over her head, she hastened through the mist to the house. As she approached, a thick-chested man emerged onto the front porch.

It was the ogre. Orson Tudge.

Portia drew back out of sight behind the rain-streaked

glass of the cab window. She watched as Hannah spoke a few words to him; then he took her by the arm and led her into the row house. Thankfully, he didn't even glance at the hired hack parked down the street.

"We go now?" Kasi asked.

Portia gave a start of surprise. She had nearly forgotten the *ayah*'s presence beside her. "Yes, of course."

Reaching up, she knocked on the roof to signal to the driver to take them home. As the cab moved slowly away from Ratcliffe's house, she brooded about Hannah's evasiveness. The woman had seemed open and willing to talk until Albright's name had been mentioned. Was her abrupt change of heart due only to her loyalty to Ratcliffe?

Or was it something else?

Portia didn't know. But if she had learned nothing else, it was that Hannah Wilton knew more than she'd let on about the hostility between Ratcliffe and the duke.

"Mmm, how lovely these smell," Blythe said, bending over a bouquet of pink roses in the drawing room.

It was early afternoon the next day, and the three Crompton sisters had gathered together to attend to their sewing. Miss Underhill believed all ladies should devote an hour a day to the art of needlework. Portia wasn't required to attend their lessons any longer, given her busy social schedule. But on the rare occasions when she was free, as she was today, she enjoyed the company of her sisters as they embroidered handkerchiefs and undergarments.

Miss Underhill herself was absent. She had been called upstairs to help the housekeeper organize the linen closets. Blythe had immediately seized upon the opportunity to abandon her assigned work, leaving it in a tangle of threads and gauzy white fabric on her chair.

"You ought to sit down," Lindsey chided. "You'll be in trouble when Miss Underhill returns to check on your progress."

"But I loathe sewing," Blythe said, plucking out a rose and brushing the soft petals against her cheek. "It seems so pointless when we have servants to do such tasks for us. And who cares if we have embroidered chemises, anyway? It's not as if I'll be undressing in front of a man anytime soon."

At once, Portia saw herself slithering out of her chemise while Ratcliffe watched from his bed. In the midst of sewing a stitch, she accidentally pricked herself with the needle.

Annoyed, she sucked on her injured forefinger until the sting receded. "Honestly, Blythe, you shouldn't even be thinking about such matters yet."

"Why not? *You* were carrying on with that Hindu prince when you were my age."

Portia shared a cautionary glance with Lindsey. Blythe didn't know about Portia's secret plan to return to India.

"His name was Arun," Portia said. "As for 'carrying on,' I certainly wasn't doing anything immoral with him."

"Then why did Mama and Papa move us to England in such a rush, hmm?" In the pale green gown, Blythe looked older than her fifteen years—at least until she gave a childish toss of her flowing auburn hair. "Not that I mind, of course. I would far rather be in London than stuck in the backwaters of India, far from any decent shops."

"It's having close neighbors that I like," Lindsey said. "There's always someone to watch. Did you know that Mrs. Faraday picks her teeth in the privacy of her garden? And Lord Gilhearst . . . I wonder where he goes at precisely nine o'clock each morning?"

"To his club, perhaps." Portia welcomed the change in

topic from Arun. "Or to Tattersall's to look at the horses for sale. Or to the watchmaker or the tailor or any one of a number of places that gentlemen frequent."

"I think they're all going to buy flowers," Blythe said as she strolled to another table overflowing with bouquets. "It does seem the standard token to send to a lady he danced with the previous evening."

Portia had to concur. She had attended a ball at Lord and Lady Wortham's house until the wee hours, and her feet still ached from the hours of dancing. This morning, a torrent of gifts had begun arriving from the men who had vied for her attention. A team of servants had been kept busy accepting deliveries and arranging flowers in vases.

"Men." Lindsey snorted. "I can't imagine why they think a mere posy would influence how a lady regards them."

"Oh, I rather think it depends upon the posy," Blythe said. "Portia, do you hold any affection for the Honorable Henry Hockenhull? I hope not, because he's only sent you daisies."

Portia laughed. "Daisies are fine enough. And in his defense, he's a third son with very few coins to spare."

Blythe was reading the cards tucked into each vase of blooms. "The daffodils are from Lord Dunn. Pretty but a bit too prissy, I think. And this enormous bouquet of tulips is from the Duke of Albright, of course. He always manages to outdo all of your other suitors."

Portia kept silent. Increasingly, she felt uncomfortable showing any interest in the duke. She didn't know what the fuss was all about, anyway. He always treated her with the utmost courtesy. He never asked her for more than two dances at any ball. He had never made any improper advances toward her, either.

Unlike another man she knew.

Ratcliffe had flirted outrageously at every opportunity. He had pushed her onto his bed and kissed her madly. The mere memory of it threatened to suck her into a quagmire of longing.

"I suppose one *can* learn something about a man by the gifts he chooses," Lindsey said thoughtfully.

"Absolutely," Blythe agreed. "Take these pink roses from Lord Wrayford, for instance. They're beautiful, I'll grant, but rather clichéd, which suggests the gentleman himself is lackluster. Is that true, Portia?"

The man's sole interest was staring at her bosom. "Quite."

"And look at the other presents. Bonbons? Delicious, but dull. A handkerchief? How practical of a suitor to give a lady something with which to wipe her nose."

Lindsey looked up from her sewing, her mouth curled in droll humor. "What's worse, it's something else that Miss Underhill will expect Portia to embroider."

As the girls shared a laugh, Blythe went on. "The best flowers you've received aren't even here, Portia. Remember how Lord Ratcliffe climbed up to your bedchamber to deliver a stem of orchids to you? Now *that's* original."

A thrill skittered over Portia's skin. She did remember. Far too well. Even now, she couldn't walk through her room without thinking of him sitting in her chair by the fire, a wicked half-smile on his lips.

"Shhh," she said, glancing at the open doorway. "I don't want anyone to know about that."

"I expected him to call on you sometime," Blythe went on in a lowered tone, giving her a speculative look. "I wonder why he hasn't."

"Obviously you've forgotten, the scoundrel has been barred from polite society." Anxious to change the subject, Portia added, "So you've found fault with everything here. What sort of gifts *would* please you?"

Her sister took the distraction. "Diamonds," she declared, a mischievous glint in her hazel eyes. "Necklaces and bracelets and earbobs."

"A young lady must never accept jewelry from a man unless they are betrothed," Lindsey said in a fair imitation of Miss Underhill's severe voice.

"Oh, pooh. When *I* am a debutante, I intend to break all the rules." Blythe twirled around the drawing room, her skirts flying. "I'll waltz at my first ball. I'll dance more than twice with any man I like. I'll—oh!"

She came to an abrupt halt, narrowly avoiding a collision with a footman who had entered the drawing room.

The poker-faced servant was carrying a silver salver, on which rested a parcel no larger than a snuffbox. He advanced straight to Portia. "A delivery for you, Miss Crompton."

In the middle of a stitch, she nodded at the table across the room. "Pray set it down over there with the other things, please."

Blythe came hurrying over, snatching the little box from the tray and turning it over in her hands. "Who is it from? Oh, there doesn't seem to be a return address. May I open it, please? I do so enjoy unwrapping presents."

Portia smiled. "It's likely another handkerchief. But go ahead."

"Maybe it's jewelry. Maybe one of these buffoons has finally given you something interesting." Blythe gleefully tore at the paper and opened the box. Reaching inside, she lifted out a small object and frowned. "Why, look at this. Someone's sent you a miniature."

Portia's head shot up. From across the room, she recognized the distinctive filigreed gold frame.

Horror surged through her. Blythe would see the painting of Arun. She would want to know where it had come from. She might run to Mama with the news and there would be all sorts of sticky questions . . .

Uttering a choked cry, Portia threw down her sewing and leaped out of her chair. Too late.

Blythe had turned over the frame and was gazing down at the picture. "Oh, my! Now here's something novel—"

"Give me that." Portia snatched it out of her hands. Fingers trembling, she looked at the little oval frame, expecting to see Arun's familiar features.

Instead, she was flummoxed to find herself staring at a portrait of Ratcliffe. It must have been painted at least a decade in the past because his face had a more youthful look, his black hair was cut shorter, and his features had not yet gone hard and calculating.

Blast him! The scoundrel had replaced the painting of Arun with one of himself. She was too livid to feel even the slightest relief that her secret was safe.

"What's wrong with you?" Blythe said in an injured tone. "You told me I could open it."

Portia reined in her runaway fury. "I know. I'm sorry. I—I just couldn't believe anyone would be so bold as to send me a miniature of himself."

"Let me see," Lindsey said. Taking it, she studied it for a moment before handing it back to Portia. "Lord Ratcliffe. And to think we were just talking about what a depraved man he is."

"I knew he hadn't given up on you," Blythe crowed. "I just knew it."

"Oh, bah," Lindsey said. "Imagine, giving such a personal item as a gift. I've never heard of anything so conceited."

"I don't believe it's conceited at all," Blythe enthused. "I believe it's romantic and clever. Lord Ratcliffe wants Portia to think of him, and what better way than to send her a miniature of himself?"

What better way, indeed? Portia thought darkly as she jammed the miniature into her pocket. It gave her more reason than ever to despise him. She was incensed to know he had dared to get rid of Arun's picture. What had the rascal done with it?

Just what had he done with it?

CHAPTER 13

Colin was beginning to doubt himself. It was irritating because he seldom suffered qualms over his own actions. The nagging uncertainty he felt was about as welcome as a sore tooth.

Or a sore arm.

In his dressing room, he winced while donning his fashionably tight coat with the help of Tudge. "Good God, man. Have a care how hard you yank on that sleeve."

The manservant chuckled. "Ain't healed yet, eh? Who'd a thought ye'd be brung down by a mere slip of a girl."

"That slip of a girl is stronger than you think," Colin muttered.

Tudge didn't know Portia very well, or he wouldn't view her as weak. She had turned out to be a far more formidable woman than the naïve young girl Colin had envisioned at first. She wasn't easily charmed. She could match wits with him in a way no other female of his acquaintance had ever done. And he couldn't always predict her reactions. He had fallen far short on the business of the miniature.

At the least, he had expected to receive a scathing letter from her. At the most, he'd harbored the hope that she might come charging over here to his house to blister him in person—and then he would have another prime opportunity to romance her.

But in the past three days, there had been no communication from Portia. Not a word.

Her silence set him on edge. Perhaps he had made a mistake in sending her that miniature of himself. Perhaps she viewed his replacement of her dear Arun's picture as an unforgivable sacrilege.

Or perhaps she hadn't received the miniature at all. Maybe that dragon of a mother of hers had opened her daughter's mail and then tossed it into the rubbish bin.

That last possibility had spurred him into action. He had cooled his heels long enough. He had to talk to Portia. Tonight.

Adjusting the lapels on his dark brown coat, Colin strode to the pier glass. He wanted to look his best, but the sight of his reflection made him scowl. "This green waistcoat looks all wrong. And what the devil is this cravat you've tied for me?"

"A waterfall," Tudge replied, eyeing him proudly. "'Tis the latest rage among the toffs."

"It looks more like a puffed-up snowball." Colin ripped off the offending raiment and reached for a fresh strip of linen. "I should never have plucked you out of that sinking ship in Madagascar. You make a better pirate than you do a valet."

"Huh. Lemme do that." Tudge stood in front of Colin, his thick fingers deftly tying the new cravat. "Mebbe I shouldn't 'ave saved yer skin along the Barbary Coast, either. If I 'adn't known them pirates, ye'd've been fed to the sharks."

"Instead, I'll be fed to the sharks tonight."

He was going to a ball that would be attended by all the snooty hens of society who had been so quick to condemn him as his father's murderer. Always clucking gossip, they would be eager to revive the old scandal, especially now that his mother was back in their flock. He only hoped they had the manners to shutter their beaks in her presence.

"Off to lure Miss Crompton into yer clutches again, are ye?" A grin slashed across Tudge's scarred face. "No wonder ye're so jittery."

"I'm perfectly calm." Realizing his snappish words had failed to put a damper on Tudge's amusement, he added in a more reasonable tone, "I shan't wait around twiddling my thumbs while she's being courted by the Duke of Albright."

Glinting in the lamplight, a knife appeared in Tudge's hand. "Ye want I should waylay 'is coach, m'lord? 'Twould be a pleasure to slit 'is scrawny throat."

"For pity's sake, put your weapon away. You're not sailing under the Jolly Roger anymore. I'll handle Albright myself."

He couldn't fault Tudge for his loyalty. The man had been his boon companion on his world tour. Having left home the instant he'd reached his majority, funded by a small inheritance from a maiden aunt, Colin had spent four years on the high seas, traveling to Africa and India and China. He had absorbed the sights, collected exotic plants, and reveled in the freedom of answering to no one. When at last he had returned to England, a pauper again, all hell had broken loose at home.

Or rather, all hell had continued during his absence, and resolving the disagreements between his parents had once again fallen onto his shoulders. It was the same old drama, act seven hundred and forty-five, scene two thousand and one.

Would he have such a marriage with Portia? The uneasy thought made him break out in a cold sweat. He couldn't imagine how two people could live forever together in peace, especially when they were like tinder and flint, as he and Portia were.

It didn't matter, he reminded himself. He was only wedding her for her money. The lust he felt was merely an added bonus, ensuring them nights of vigorous love-making. Nothing else mattered.

At least he knew one sure method to melt her frosty regard. He had only to disrobe her, to stroke that beautiful body in all the right places, and she would be his willing slave. The fantasy invigorated him, yet an unsettling disquiet lingered. It was time he coaxed her into marriage, using any means possible.

Only then would he have the right to keep her all to himself. He wanted no other man to touch her, not her precious Arun, not all those toadying lordlings, and certainly not that viper Albright—

A knock sounded on the outer door, jolting him back to the present. Tudge went to answer it, and Colin followed, leaving the dressing room and entering his bed-chamber.

The door opened before Tudge was halfway there, and Hannah stepped inside. It was still rather startling to see her in the modest gray gown, the ruffled white apron concealing all but a hint of her pregnancy, rather than the scandalous garb of her past.

"I could have been dressing," he growled. "Next time, kindly wait until you're admitted."

She arched an eyebrow. "Forgive me, your lordship. Though if I may be permitted to point out, I've already seen everything you have to offer."

Her impudence rubbed him the wrong way. Then again, everything had rubbed him the wrong way tonight. Nevertheless, he was about to take her to task again when he spied the letter in her hands. "Is that for me?"

"Yes. It's just arrived."

He snatched it from her. Perhaps this was it. Perhaps Portia finally had written to him. He grabbed his gold-rimmed spectacles from the bedside table and shoved them on. His heart thumping, he tore the letter open.

As abruptly as his hopes had arisen, they crashed to pieces. He was staring down at another bill. This one for a diamond tiara ordered by his mother.

"Damn!" Crumpling the paper, he hurled it onto the bed. For good measure, he slapped the mahogany bedpost. "Damn, damn, *damn*."

His palm stinging, he turned to see Tudge and Hannah standing side by side, their heads together. They made an incongruous couple, Tudge with his scarred face and missing ear, and Hannah with her sensual beauty beneath a prim white mobcap.

"Master's a bit tetchy tonight," the manservant was telling her. " 'E's goin' to see 'is little miss."

"Oh? I'd been wondering if he'd lost interest in Miss Crompton. Considering his present mood, I'm thinking perhaps it might be best for her if he did."

Colin wanted to retort that he was standing right there and they could cease their infernal gossiping. But expedience made him swallow his ill humor.

"I need a woman's opinion," he told Hannah. "What do you think of this waistcoat? Would I look better in a gold pinstripe?"

Portia had just finished dancing a reel with the Honorable Henry Hockenhull when she spied Lord Ratcliffe.

She came to an abrupt halt. Much to her frustration, the brief glimpse of him was blocked by the clusters of guests leaving the dance floor. Surely he was a figment of her imagination. He wouldn't have been invited, not to a ball given by Lady Jersey, one of the grandes dames of society. Not when so many of the ton still believed he had murdered his own father.

"Are you feeling faint?" Mr. Hockenhull asked, his gloved hand cupping her elbow as if she were a delicate butterfly. "Did the dance overtax you, Miss Crompton?"

She dragged her attention back to her partner. His freckled features were taut with worry beneath a boyish thatch of auburn hair. "Certainly not," she murmured, while covertly trying to look over his shoulder at the area where Ratcliffe—or his twin—had been walking through the crowd. "I enjoyed it very much."

"May I fetch you a glass of punch? Or champagne perhaps?"

"Thank you, but no. I'm perfectly fine, truly I am. And you needn't escort me back to my mother. I can see my next partner right over there."

Portia nodded vaguely toward the entryway, and while he turned his head to peer in that direction, she slipped away into the throng of guests. She garnered a few curious looks, no doubt due to her solitary status. It was a cardinal rule that young ladies were to be taken back to their guardians at the end of each dance. Portia had only a few minutes until the next set, which she had promised to the Duke of Albright.

But she could not ignore the curiosity burning inside of her.

To discourage conversation, she kept her gaze modestly lowered so as not to meet anyone's eye. She didn't quite understand her sense of urgency. She ought to be avoiding Ratcliffe. After receiving the miniature in the mail, she had vowed not to give that scoundrel the satisfaction of a response. Why bother when it was highly doubtful that he would tell her what he had done with the painting of Arun. Besides, if she ignored him, he might lose interest and leave her be.

Yet he was here tonight. That one brief sighting had raised the specter of his presence—if indeed she wasn't mistaken. She would rather ascertain the truth right now than wait on pins and needles for him to approach her.

Several guests moved, and her heart fluttered like hummingbird wings. By heaven, it *was* Ratcliffe.

He was strolling through the throngs of aristocrats, a petite lady clinging to his arm. His dark hair gleamed in the glow of the candles. He looked breathtakingly handsome in a mahogany brown coat, a gold pinstriped waistcoat, and buff breeches.

He bent down to say something to the lady with him. She smiled up at him, her manner coquettish. Slim and beautiful in a gown of midnight blue, she had a swanlike neck and upswept black hair crowned by a diamond tiara.

A nasty jolt of recognition struck Portia. It was the woman from the theater. The one who had made him leave Portia and go rushing off to her side.

Her lips tightened. So his current paramour was a member of society, was she? Had the rascal come to this ball tonight not to court Portia, but to flirt with that . . . that female?

As they drew nearer, the lady turned her head and, with uncanny accuracy, gazed straight at Portia. She murmured something to Ratcliffe, then left his company to glide in Portia's direction.

Portia stood glued to the floor. Guests swirled around her, but if any of them spoke, the roaring in her ears blocked it out. Why would one of his mistresses seek her out? Did the woman intend to warn her off Ratcliffe? Would she cause a scene right in the middle of the ballroom while all the ton watched?

Portia ordered herself to walk away. But the ability to move had deserted her. There was something vaguely familiar about that exquisitely lovely face, something she couldn't quite place.

The lady stopped in front of her, her gaze politely assessing, as if she were memorizing every detail of Portia, from her Grecian-styled hair down to the embroidered hem of her pale pink gown. From close up, the woman was older than she had looked from a distance, with fine lines around her green eyes and mouth, and an unmistakable maturity to her patrician face.

"Do pardon my boldness," she said in a throaty voice, offering a slender, gloved hand. "You are Miss Crompton, I believe."

Portia hesitated, then reluctantly touched the woman's hand. Why hadn't she provided her own name? And why did Portia feel so tongue-tied in her presence? "Yes . . . I . . ."

A faint amusement curved those ruby lips. "You must be wondering who I am, why a perfect stranger would waylay you like this. I cannot say that I blame you for looking apprehensive."

At that moment, Ratcliffe appeared at her side. He gave the woman a hard stare that was part irritation and part fondness.

He snagged two glasses of champagne from a passing footman and handed one to each lady. "Stop teasing the poor girl, and allow me to make a proper introduction. Mother, this is Miss Portia Crompton. Portia, pray meet my meddlesome mother, Lady Ratcliffe."

His mother. He had abandoned Portia at the theater in order to visit with *his mother.*

Sipping the champagne, Portia felt such a lifting of relief, she almost laughed out loud. No wonder Lady Ratcliffe looked familiar; she was the young, vivacious woman in the painting on Ratcliffe's staircase. The resemblance to her son was subtle but apparent in the high cheekbones, the sensual shape of the mouth, the deep green of the eyes.

A sobering memory entered Portia's mind. The Duke of Albright had claimed that Ratcliffe kept his mother confined to his estate, that he'd refused her permission to come to London. Ratcliffe, on the other hand, had insisted that his mother preferred the country life. It was unsettling to discover that the duke either had been mistaken or had lied to Portia.

"I am hardly meddlesome," Lady Ratcliffe said, affording her son a mock glare. "Rather, it seems only right for me to meet the girl who has so captivated your attention. And he does speak highly of you, Miss Crompton."

Ratcliffe quirked an eyebrow as if to make light of her comment. "You've only just arrived in town, Mother. We've barely had a chance to speak at all." He turned his gaze on Portia, and his warm scrutiny stirred shivers that congregated in her inner depths. His eyes seemed to convey the message that he'd thought of little else but her since their last meeting.

In a determined effort to ignore him, she focused her attention on his mother. "Forgive me for looking so puzzled earlier, my lady. I must confess I never anticipated meeting you. Lord Ratcliffe has mentioned that you spend most of your time in Kent."

"I've leased a home in Berkeley Square for the Season, so that I might visit my friends here. Perhaps you would do me the kindness of joining me for tea soon. It would be quite pleasant for the two of us to have a cozy chat."

The invitation made Portia acutely uncomfortable. It seemed rather fast of Lady Ratcliffe to expect a tête-à-tête with Portia when there was no betrothal on the horizon. Was she merely anxious to see her profligate son settle down and marry? Or had Ratcliffe told his mother a Banbury tale about the closeness of their relationship?

As she took a fizzy swallow from her glass, another thought occurred to her. As unsuitable as it might seem on the surface, the visit might be a brilliant opportunity to uncover the truth about the feud between Ratcliffe and Albright. Portia would have to be very circumspect in her questioning so as not to offend Lady Ratcliffe, yet so much could be learned. "Thank you, my lady, I'd consider it an honor—"

"No," Ratcliffe stated, scowling from her to his mother. "It wouldn't be appropriate in the least."

Lady Ratcliffe gave a tinkling laugh. "Since when have you cared about the proprieties, my dear boy?" Reaching up, she patted his cheek as if she were proud of his rakish reputation. "Now, I hear the orchestra tuning their instruments. Do ask Miss Crompton to stand up with you for the next dance."

He flashed his mother a sardonic look before he dutifully bowed to Portia. "May I have the honor?"

Portia's breath caught at the image of them waltzing over the dance floor, their bodies so close she could feel his heat . . .

She took a step backward on the pretext of setting her empty glass on a table. "I'm sorry," she said with a firm shake of her head. "It's the supper dance, and I've promised it to the Duke of Albright."

Lady Ratcliffe's mouth twisted in a secretive smirk. "Never mind Albright. I'll be happy to have a word with him on your behalf."

CHAPTER 14

Portia found herself being whisked through the crowd of guests against her will. Or *was* it against her will?

Ratcliffe's hand rested at the small of her back, propelling her forward with subtle power. His touch seemed shockingly intimate against the gauze of her gown, as if his fingers rested right on her bare skin. As if he were branding her as his before all the nobility.

A trio of older ladies stood watching, muttering among themselves. Another gray-haired matron lifted her jeweled lorgnette in a cold scrutiny, her thin lips curled in disdain. The stooped-shouldered gentleman with her frowned, then turned his back in a cut direct.

Ratcliffe seemed oblivious to it all. He nodded to a few acquaintances, his expression unperturbed even when there was no reciprocal greeting.

Portia felt a peculiar immunity to the stares, as well. Perhaps it was the champagne she'd drunk, but a giddy excitement seemed to cushion her from all censure. It was as if she and Ratcliffe were enclosed in a golden bubble where nothing from the outside world could affect them.

As they passed through an arched doorway, she noticed they were heading away from the dance floor. "The lines are forming," she murmured. "We need to take our places."

"I'd rather be alone with you."

His husky words gave her a pleasurable shiver. A part of her brain scolded her for being so reckless. The voice in her head sounded so much like Miss Underhill that Portia ignored its dire warning. What could happen in a house full of people?

Except perhaps a stolen kiss in a quiet corner.

Anticipation sizzled through her, but she immediately squelched it. No, she mustn't allow Ratcliffe even that much liberty. Yet she rather enjoyed matching wits with him. Especially now when she was fairly bursting with recriminations to throw in his face.

He guided her past several groups of guests in the entrance hall and down a passageway where she caught a glimpse of gentlemen and ladies playing cards in a drawing room, then a second chamber from which the smell of cigar smoke wafted.

In another moment, they were walking down a deserted corridor. He sent her ahead of him through a doorway and into a sitting room decorated with an Egyptian motif. An oil lamp on a table cast flickering shadows over the alabaster statues, a large painting of the pyramids, and numerous chairs with carved scarabs on the backs.

She stopped beside a closed stone sarcophagus and ran her fingers over the cold granite. "I do hope there isn't a mummy in here."

Ratcliffe didn't answer. The click of the door closing brought Portia whirling around. The sight of him striding purposefully toward her stirred a measure of alarm in her. She didn't want to be *this* alone with him.

"Shouldn't you leave the door open?"

"No one saw us come in, so it hardly matters."

"It *does* matter," she objected. "If we're discovered here without a chaperone, my reputation will be ruined. Or perhaps that's your intention."

As she attempted to step past him on her way to the door, Ratcliffe took hold of her shoulders and brought her to a stop. "I simply don't want anyone to overhear us," he said, his gaze intent on her. "I wanted to ask you—did you receive my gift?"

The reminder snapped her fully to her senses. "The miniature? Unfortunately, yes. And may I add, I do not appreciate your replacing Arun's picture with your own."

The faint tension in Ratcliffe's face melted away. He gave her a brash smile. "As the Bard said, all's fair in love and war. I was rather hoping you'd sleep with it under your pillow."

She had hidden the little oval in her bedside table. He didn't need to know that several times she'd given in to the temptation to study the image of him as a young man, and had wondered what he'd been like then.

She pulled back and crossed her arms. "Very amusing. Now what have you done with Arun's picture? If you've destroyed it, I vow I will never forgive you."

"There's no need to fret. It's still safe and sound."

"I'm not *fretting*. I'm ordering you to return my stolen property."

"All in good time. We'll see if you still want it when I'm through courting you."

His arrogance raked at her nerves. She wanted to shake him hard and see the tiny painting fall out of his pocket. She would do it, too, if she truly believed he had secreted it on his person.

Where could he have put it?

Needing an outlet for her pent-up frustration, she paced to the unlit fireplace. "Conceited oaf. What are you doing here, anyway? I thought you were shunned by society. Or are you hiding behind your mother's skirts?"

His gaze turned frosty. "She invited me as her escort

tonight. Lady Jersey could hardly protest the arrangement."

"Your mother seems to be a very pleasant lady. Why have you barred her from coming to London before now?"

"I've told you before, I've done no such thing. She stayed in Kent of her own accord."

Was it just a trick of the lamplight, or did something secretive flicker in his gaze?

Then she forgot the question as he crossed to her in several quick steps. Drawing her close, he circled his arms around her waist to hold her flush against him. Her body thrilled to the awareness of his muscular strength. The brief anger in his expression had faded beneath an alluring sensual darkness.

"I didn't bring you here to quarrel, Portia," he said, his voice lowering to a deep, rasping murmur. "I was hoping we might find something better to do with our time."

Her heart was beating so fast, he must surely feel it. This was what kept her awake at night, this irrepressible longing to be held in his arms again. She ached to savor every moment of it, to rest her cheek on his chest and breathe in his scent, to run her fingers through his thick black hair. In token resistance, she whispered, "Let me go."

"That isn't what you want. What you want is me—every bit as much as I want you." As he stroked her cheek, his impassioned tone stirred a shivery warmth that penetrated to the core of her. "You've driven me mad these past weeks. I can think of no other woman but you, Portia."

He brought his mouth down onto hers. The contact was deliciously arousing, firm and commanding. His tongue traced the seam of her lips, enticing her into opening to his exploration. The glorious experience of being kissed by Ratcliffe was a real-life dream that enveloped her entire body. From head to toe, every part of her felt a hot wash of yearning. It was an elixir to her heart to know that he'd been as obsessed with her as she'd been with him. Surrendering to the need inside herself, she arched on tiptoes and wrapped her arms around his neck.

Had she been of sound mind, Portia could have come up with a dozen reasons why he was all wrong for her, why she ought to run as far and as fast as possible. But at the moment, she didn't want to think, she only wanted to feel, to enjoy the pleasure of his touch.

And touch her he did. His fingers adored the smooth skin of her throat, and then moved downward to worship at the shrine of her bosom. The deep kiss went on and on, and somehow—she couldn't identify when—he loosened the back of her gown, enough to allow his hand to slide into her bodice. He pushed aside the linen chemise and worked his way inside her corset to cup her naked flesh, his thumb playing with the tip. The shocking intimacy wrested a gasp from her.

She tilted her head back, intending to order him to stop, but instead found herself uttering little whimpers of delight. When her knees threatened to buckle, he tightened his arm around her waist. He continued his magical assault on her breasts, giving equal attention to each one. Then he did something even more wicked. Reaching down, he slipped his hand underneath her skirts and up her stockinged leg.

Even through the haze of her arousal, she realized the danger of his action. "No . . . you mustn't . . ."

"I mean you no harm, darling," he murmured, his face in shadow. "I swear it on my life. I want only your happiness."

He silenced any further protest with an impassioned kiss. But his mouth held only a small portion of her attention. The rest of her perception was focused on the progress of his fingers along her inner thigh. She was scandalized and intrigued, fevered and breathless, unsure of what to expect, yet eager for it all the same.

Brushing past garters and petticoats, he found her most private place. She moaned under the stunning bliss of his touch. Ratcliffe pressed his lips to her throat, her name emerging from him in a long groan. He moved his finger in light circles that seemed equal parts torture and pleasure, causing her to squirm against him in a quest for relief.

Yet as maddening as it was, she didn't want him to stop. Mindless with need, she clutched the smooth lapels of his evening coat in an instinctive effort to keep him close. She craved what he was doing so much that she feared she might die if he ceased. His exploration became deeper, sliding into her slick folds and rhythmically stroking her. His every caress caused a hot throb of sensation deep inside her. Never had she dreamed that a man's touch could wrest such a powerful reaction from her body. It was almost too much to bear.

"Ratcliffe, please, oh, please . . . I want . . ."

"Damn," he swore, his breath heating her throat. "Damn it to *hell*."

She heard him through a mist of passion, only dimly registering the torment in his voice. Then she was caught up in her own swelling desire, uttering tiny gasps of desperation, writhing against his hand. All at once, a powerful surge of pleasure poured through her. She cried out, and he swallowed the sound with another kiss, his fingers continuing to caress her until the last sensations died away.

In the idyllic aftermath, she clung limply to him, trying to catch her breath. Her face was tucked in the lee of his neck, her mind unable to think beyond the wonder he had introduced to her. Nothing in her experience had prepared her for such an extravagance of feelings.

He abruptly removed his hand from beneath her skirts. Lifting her head, she opened her eyes to look at him. The taut expression on his face was almost a grimace. He was breathing hard, and even in her innocence she realized his own appetites had not been satisfied.

She reached up to touch his face. "Ratcliffe . . ."

He seized hold of her hand and brought it to his lips. His eyes glittered in the shadows. "Marry me, Portia. Marry me, and we can do that as often as you like."

Astonishment and fervor vied within her. For an instant, she found herself swaying toward him, enthralled by the prospect of endless lovemaking. Already the splendor had faded, leaving her hungering for another taste of that extraordinary pleasure.

Then the cold meaning behind his words slapped her. This had all been a ploy. Ratcliffe didn't love her. He had used his expertise to coax a response from her body; he had offered rapture as an enticement to marriage, nothing more. He had done so for the sole purpose of securing her dowry.

And she had fallen for his trick.

She shook her head, wanting to deny the creeping horror that left her chilled. "Dear God," she whispered, "what have I done?"

"You've done no wrong." Ratcliffe bent his head and lightly kissed her brow. "You've only seen how very perfect we are together."

His overconfident manner filled her with fury. She gave him a mighty shove, sending him staggering backward. "Dastard! I'm not marrying you."

He eyed her warily while running his fingers through his hair. "You needn't answer me now. At least take a few days to consider my proposal."

"I've done all the considering I need to do. The answer is *no*."

His lips tightened, but he took a step toward her, his hand held out in supplication. "Portia," he murmured, "you're a passionate woman. But I want you to know the act isn't always so gratifying. Not every man has the skill to bring you to ecstasy."

Her cheeks burned. Ratcliffe had known exactly what to do, how to use his mouth and hands to arouse a carnal ache in her. He'd had years of practice with all of his courtesans and mistresses. How easily she had been duped into believing he might actually care for her.

A lump formed in her throat. It was sickening to realize she'd hoped that his interest in her had been spurred by affection. That, deep down, she had wanted him to like her for herself.

Not for her money.

Aware of her disheveled state, she tugged up her bodice. "So you expect me to choose a husband on the basis of his bedroom skills. Do you really think me such a featherbrain?"

He frowned quizzically. "Of course not. You're a beautiful, clever woman. I merely thought to demonstrate the happiness you'd find in our marriage."

His callousness enraged her. "You care nothing for my happiness. You broke the rules of gentlemanly behavior. You cold-bloodedly plotted this seduction. You even had the gall to execute your scheme at a party with all of society present."

The faint lilt of music drifted to her ears. Remembering the aristocrats she would have to face, Portia caught her breath in a ragged sob. All she wanted to do was to burrow under the covers of her bed. She wanted to hide from the fact that she'd betrayed Arun by behaving like a wanton with another man.

That was one sin she couldn't blame on Ratcliffe.

Tears stung her eyes. He started toward her, but she froze him with a look. "Stay away from me."

"You'll need help restoring your appearance."

He nodded at a gilt-framed mirror, and the sight of her reflection appalled her. Her hair was mussed, her bodice sagged, and her skirt was wrinkled. She looked like a woman who had been thoroughly compromised.

How could she have been so foolish?

Blinking hard, she turned her back on Ratcliffe and savagely straightened her gown. "Blast you! You're nothing but a worthless rake. I wouldn't marry you to save my life."

He made no reply, and Portia was glad. She was too distraught to engage him in further conversation. To be in the same room as him was intolerable. But she couldn't leave now, not while she resembled a two-penny whore.

After a moment, she felt his hands at her back, deftly fastening the row of tiny pearl buttons. His touch was impersonal, and even in the midst of her anger and anguish, she wanted him to slide his arms around her, to whisper sweet nothings in her ear. It confounded her, this power he wielded over her.

As she took one last look at herself in the mirror, she caught sight of Ratcliffe standing behind her in the shadows. The grave look on his face tugged at her heart, but that weakness, she bitterly acknowledged, was her fatal flaw. And it only reaffirmed the necessity of staying far away from the scoundrel in the future.

CHAPTER 15

"I must say, I'm appalled that Viscount Ratcliffe dared to show his face in public yesterday evening," Mrs. Beardsley said.

Sitting with a group of aristocratic ladies in the gold drawing room, Portia had been dreading this moment. It was inevitable that Ratcliffe would become the subject of conversation because all four of the visitors had one trait in common: They loved to gossip.

She and Mama had been readying themselves to leave on an afternoon of social calls when the Duchess of Milbourne had arrived. While the horse-faced elderly woman had enthroned herself on a chaise by the hearth, white-haired Lady Grantham had been admitted, followed shortly thereafter by plump Mrs. Beardsley and her bird-witted daughter, Miss Frances Beardsley.

Edith Crompton had been delighted to play hostess to such stellar members of the ton, pouring tea from a silver pot and enlisting Portia to deliver the dainty china cups. Now, Mrs. Crompton flashed Portia a keen stare that warned her to remain silent.

"I'm afraid my daughter and I know very little about Lord Ratcliffe," Mrs. Crompton said smoothly, offering the stout woman another slice of poppy cake from a silver tray. "Perhaps you'll tell us more, so we will know the necessity of avoiding him in the future."

Her voice held the perfect note of maternal concern, but Portia knew her mother well enough to detect a trace of stiffness in her manner. She hadn't forgiven Portia for abandoning the Duke of Albright for the supper dance. Or for being spotted leaving the ballroom in the company of the notorious Viscount Ratcliffe. Although Portia had managed to convince her mother that nothing untoward had happened, she knew she would be watched more closely henceforth.

Little did her mother realize, Portia welcomed the vigilance. The events of the previous evening only proved that she couldn't trust herself around Ratcliffe. There was a sensual weakness inside her that he knew exactly how to exploit. She loathed him for using such dishonorable means to entice her into marriage, and yet at the same time, she couldn't stop thinking about that wonderful, euphoric moment. She had slept fitfully, dreaming of his hands on her body and awakening with the longing to experience it all again. The wickedness of her desire was a constant torment.

How could she have responded to him with such utter abandon when she loved Arun?

"Ratcliffe is a gambler and a rake," the Duchess of Milbourne said with a sniff of her long nose. "Why, he's had to sell all of his unentailed land in order to pay off his debts."

"I have it on excellent authority that he began gambling when he was still at Eton," Mrs. Beardsley added. "My son Geoffrey was a form below him, and he said Ratcliffe was the leader of the libertines."

Lady Grantham harrumphed, setting her teacup down with a clatter. "Let us not forget his worst sin. Ratcliffe murdered his own father. Shot him in cold blood when he refused to pay the boy's gaming markers."

Frances Beardsley uttered a squeak of horror. Dressed in pale pink ruffles, she resembled a china doll as she looked straight at Portia. "How monstrous! *I* would never be seen with such a man."

Everyone turned to look at Portia.

Her mother quickly said, "Nor would any of us had we all known the extent of his crimes."

Portia felt compelled to speak out. Although she despised Ratcliffe—for very different reasons than these biddies—she also disliked injustice. "I thought the courts had exonerated him."

The Duchess of Milbourne pursed her lips. "Of course he was declared innocent. One can hardly expect a peer of the realm to go to the gallows, lest it give the common people ideas. Why, the next thing we'd know, the masses would be setting up a guillotine and making us all surrender our necks."

A collective shudder coursed through all the noble ladies. The biggest nightmare of the aristocrats was that they would suffer the same fate as their counterparts in France some twenty-five years earlier.

Lady Grantham shook her head. "Poor Lady Ratcliffe. How I do pity her, losing her husband under such terrible circumstances, and at the hand of her own son."

"It is beyond my understanding how she could ever forgive him," Mrs. Beardsley added. "One can only imagine how difficult it must have been for her. Why, she's been unable to face the ton these past three years."

"That's dreadful," Edith Crompton commiserated. "I'm afraid I didn't have the pleasure of an introduction, but she appeared to be a most lovely woman."

"Lillian is quite beautiful, always has been." The Duchess of Milbourne leaned forward, her gnarled hands clutching her cane. "If I dare say so, she was once a bit racy herself. Over the years there have been rumors of her illicit affairs."

Affairs? The news troubled Portia, although she took it with a grain of salt. Gossip was hardly a reliable source of the truth.

"Then perhaps it is little wonder that her son turned out as despicable as he did," Mrs. Beardsley pronounced, while her daughter nodded vigorously in agreement, setting her blond curls to bouncing.

Lady Grantham tut-tutted. "Dear me, do you remember that scandal involving Lillian and Albright? It quite set London on its ear."

Portia froze with her teacup halfway to her lips. This must be what Miss Underhill recalled her mother discussing a long time ago. Portia could not remain silent, no matter how much her own mother might scold her later. "Scandal?" she asked. "What do you mean?"

The Duchess of Milbourne bared her teeth in a caricature of a smile. "Never fear, my girl, Albright did no wrong. Rather, it was Lady Ratcliffe who was at fault. You see, long before you were born, he—"

She stopped in mid-sentence as a white-wigged footman entered the drawing room. The servant bowed to Mrs. Crompton and presented a silver tray to her. When Portia's mother picked up the pasteboard card that lay upon it, her eyes widened.

"Well! This is most remarkable. Lady Ratcliffe herself has come to call." She looked to the duchess as the senior woman present. "Shall I be home, Your Grace?"

"Most certainly."

"Then do send her ladyship up at once, Higgens."

Portia felt an agonizing stab of disappointment. She

had been about to learn the truth at last, but now cruel fate had intervened. Proper etiquette prevented even these ladies from spreading malicious talk in the presence of their subject.

Curse their good manners!

Then she wondered why Lady Ratcliffe had come here at all. Had Ratcliffe put her up to it? Did he think that his mother could smooth troubled waters? Dear heavens, had he confessed to her exactly what he had done last night?

Portia battled the rise of a hot blush. She must remain cool and aloof—and make certain that the viscountess did not corner her for a private chat.

A moment later, Lady Ratcliffe glided into the drawing room. Slender as a girl in deep green silk, she wore a feathered bonnet on her elegantly upswept black hair. She greeted each lady cordially, exchanging pleasantries and gracing Portia with an especially warm smile before sitting in a chair right beside hers.

Portia found it difficult to meet those astute green eyes. It was too embarrassing to wonder how much Lady Ratcliffe knew. Besides, she sensed a shrewd intelligence in the older woman that somehow made her uneasy.

Lady Ratcliffe accepted a cup of tea from Mrs. Crompton. Very soon it became clear exactly where her son had inherited his charm.

"Your home is exceptionally lovely," she told Portia's mother. "You simply must give me the name of your linen draper, so that I might choose some of these pretty fabrics for myself."

Edith Crompton preened. "Why, thank you, my lady, I'd be honored to do so."

Lady Ratcliffe turned her attention to the duchess. "My dear Henrietta, I do regret that we had so little chance to speak yesterday evening, what with the crush of people. After so much time rusticating in the country, I'm looking forward to hearing all the latest *on-dits*. From all of you ladies."

She extended her smile to include Lady Grantham, Mrs. Beardsley, and Frances Beardsley. "Now, what is this I hear about Turnbuckle mending his wicked ways by marrying Oglethorpe's daughter? Colin never breathed a word of it to me, but how like a man to overlook the significance of such an event."

The ladies launched into a spirited discussion of the marital matches that had been made in the past few years. Quietly observing, Portia couldn't help but notice how deftly Lady Ratcliffe controlled the conversation, asking questions at the right moment, offering witty commentary to draw laughter, and introducing a new name whenever there was a lull. The older woman made no attempt to speak directly to Portia, much to her relief. She was almost beginning to relax, thinking she'd been mistaken about the purpose of the visit, when Lady Ratcliffe rose to her feet and addressed Mrs. Crompton.

"Pray forgive me, but I have an appointment I simply must keep. Perhaps your daughter wouldn't mind seeing me to the door?"

Portia froze, her fingers stiff around the saucer. She could think of no gracious way to refuse such a simple request.

Nor, apparently, could her mother. "As you wish, my lady. May I say, we've enjoyed your visit very much."

Portia set down her empty cup on a table. As she accompanied Lady Ratcliffe out of the drawing room, she glimpsed the other women eyeing them with avid speculation. No doubt they, too, would take their leave soon, anxious to be the first to pass along news of the visit. By nightfall, the rumor mill would be abuzz with reports that Ratcliffe's mother was making a blatant effort to negotiate a match between her son and the premier heiress of the Season.

They headed down a high-ceilinged corridor decorated with gilt chairs and landscape paintings. Portia wanted to walk fast, but forced herself to match steps with Lady Ratcliffe's measured pace.

"Perhaps it is no surprise, Miss Crompton, to learn that I came here hoping to speak to you alone."

"I'm afraid I haven't much time. I must return to my other visitors."

"Surely you can spare a few moments." The viscountess took Portia's hand and patted the back of it. "I understand from my son that the two of you quarreled yesterday evening. On the way home, Ratcliffe seemed quite distraught about it."

Distraught? Portia nearly choked on a lump of suppressed anger. What a cartful of nonsense. If he was upset at all, it was because his dastardly plot had failed.

Then she noted how closely Lady Ratcliffe was watching her, and realized the woman was fishing for information. In that moment she saw her mistake. Ratcliffe hadn't confessed everything, after all. His mother was merely making guesses as to why he'd been in a sulk.

"I can't imagine why he would be troubled," Portia said coolly. "It was nothing of significance—at least not to me."

"I see. Well, I do want you to feel that you can come to me with any concerns you might have about Colin. After all, I know him better than anyone."

Once again, Portia felt Lady Ratcliffe was being rather fast in presuming a closeness with her. Yet couldn't two play that game? "Then perhaps you won't mind telling me why he and the Duke of Albright dislike one another so much. I've gathered it has something to do with you."

For the barest moment, Lady Ratcliffe looked startled. She blinked those long-lashed green eyes, so similar to her son's eyes it was uncanny. Giving Portia an assessing look, she laughed with genuine amusement. "Forgive me for being surprised. The incident happened thirty years ago. However, I'm sure the old trolls back there would be more than happy to dig it out of the cave of ancient history."

"I'd prefer to hear about it from you, my lady."

"Then so you shall. Take me somewhere private, and I'll tell you the whole dismal story."

Her heart thumping, Portia led the way down the curving sweep of the grand staircase and into a small antechamber off the entrance hall. She took care to hide her excitement because she didn't want Lady Ratcliffe to wonder why Portia was so interested in finding out the truth.

Portia acknowledged her own growing need to understand Ratcliffe. She had speculated on the subject so much, it had become something of an obsession.

Lady Ratcliffe seemed disinclined to sit. She strolled through the antechamber, touching knickknacks with her elegantly gloved hand. "It all started when I was about your age," she said, glancing over her shoulder at Portia, who had also remained standing in deference to her guest. "It was my first Season, and I was having a wonderful time dancing at balls and flirting with all the eligible gentlemen. If it doesn't seem vainglorious, may I say I was the foremost debutante of the year."

Portia could believe it. Lady Ratcliffe exuded a vivacity of spirit, which, along with her beauty, would have attracted men in droves. And an unsettling suspicion told her where this was heading. "Was the Duke of Albright one of your suitors?"

"Yes, he was new to society himself, having just gained

the title at the same time as he finished his schoolwork. Within days, he fell madly in love with me . . ." She paused, then added contritely, "Oh, my dear, I am sorry. I understand he's now courting you, and I mean no offense."

The situation did make Portia feel awkward, but not because she cared a fig about Albright's past loves. It was simply odd to think that the duke had paid his addresses to both of them. "I could never be offended by your honesty, my lady."

"Well, then, let me say that a number of gentlemen vied for my hand in marriage, including Albright and Roger—Colin's father. Eventually I bowed to the wishes of my parents and chose Albright as my betrothed."

Portia was so taken aback, she sank down onto the nearest chair. "You were to *marry* him?"

"Yes, I agreed to the match even though I couldn't bring myself to return his professions of love."

Lady Ratcliffe gazed out the window, the filtered light illuminating an expression of tragic sorrow on her fine features. Portia found herself wondering if the woman had deliberately assumed a pose designed to elicit sympathy. Then she instantly felt guilty for being uncharitable when she hadn't yet heard the entire tale.

"But . . . you didn't wed him. What happened?"

"Though my heart was aching, I went through with all the preparations. It wasn't until the very day of the wedding, as I was being garbed in my bridal raiment, that I realized the terrible mistake I was making. It was Roger I loved, not Albright. Yet even then I convinced myself that it was too late, that I must go through with the ceremony, or cause terrible dishonor to my family."

"And to the duke," Portia added.

"Oh, please be assured his happiness weighed heavily on my mind, as well. And truly, I was firm in my resolve as I reached St. George's Church. I was prepared to make the ultimate sacrifice. I even walked down the aisle on the arm of my father. But then"—she smiled wistfully into the distance—"then as I stood waiting for the nuptials to begin, Roger appeared at the back of the church. Oh, he was such a fine-looking buck and so very bold. He came marching down the aisle, swept me off my feet, and carried me away to Gretna Green."

And left Albright standing at the altar. With all the ton watching.

Aghast, Portia imagined the scene in her mind. It would have been a dreadful humiliation to any man, especially one who had as much pride as the duke. And if Albright had truly loved Lady Ratcliffe, then his heart must have been broken. Yet Lady Ratcliffe had made no mention of the pain she had caused him. Probably because she had been too wrapped up in her own romantic adventure.

At least now Portia could understand the loathing exhibited by the duke. "Albright must have transferred his anger at you to your son."

Her face grave, Lady Ratcliffe nodded. "So it would seem. I've expressed my apologies to him several times. But I do fear he will never forgive me."

As the viscountess took her leave, Portia was stricken by a troublesome thought. Was *she* like Lady Ratcliffe?

The similarity of their situations disturbed Portia. She had promised herself to a decent, admirable man. Then she had forgotten him the instant she'd met a handsome rake. She had allowed Ratcliffe to sweep her off her feet. And in the doing, she had betrayed Arun.

Edith Crompton tried not to be obvious about watching the doorway. But even as she chatted amiably with her aristocratic guests, she was fuming inside. How dare Lady Ratcliffe whisk Portia away like that. The woman must be attempting to arrange a match for her wastrel son.

Edith had no intention of allowing Portia to wed a mere viscount. Especially one who had earned the censure of all the ladies present. They had made their low opinion of him quite clear, and Edith was keenly aware of how swiftly a female could fall from grace. It could take only a single misstep, and the previous evening Portia had already pressed her luck by going off alone with that handsome rakehell.

The girl had a wayward streak that had first manifested itself with that native boy back in India. She was strong-willed and rebellious, but Edith had no intention of suffering such disobedient behavior from her ever again.

"We have decided your home will be the perfect setting," the Duchess of Milbourne said.

Edith realized the haughty old woman was addressing her. And she hadn't the foggiest notion as to the drift of the conversation. Cautiously, she said, "Indeed, Your Grace?"

Clutching the knob of her cane, the duchess gave an imperious nod. "Lord and Lady Dearborn usually host the annual masquerade ball. However, Annabel has fallen ill with the ague, and thusly we have determined that you and Mr. Crompton should take over the duty this year."

"We simply must have a masquerade," Lady Grantham said with a bob of her white curls. "Why, it is a tradition of every Season!"

Edith's heart pounded. They were asking *her* to sponsor a ball? She could scarcely believe her ears. This moment was the very pinnacle of social acceptance she had longed for as a girl here in England, when she had been a nobody staring enviously at the privileged nobility. That dream had sustained her all those dreadful years in India, too, when George had accumulated their riches and she had struggled to convince him to return to London.

Hiding her elation, she formed her lips into a gracious smile. "Why, I would be honored."

"Since it is a masquerade, you won't be expected to make any introductions," Mrs. Beardsley explained, brushing a cake crumb from her massive bosom. "That is why you are so admirably suited to the task."

"What Mama means," Frances Beardsley added guilelessly, "is that, well, you know so few people in society."

Edith's euphoria drained away at once. It took a herculean effort to keep a pleasant look pasted on her face. Just like that, they had knocked her back down to the common masses with the reminder that she had not been born a lady.

They were all looking at her, the Duchess of Milbourne, Lady Grantham, Mrs. Beardsley, and her odious blond daughter.

Edith rallied her strength of will. She would never allow them to glimpse her shredded pride. The time would soon come when Portia would marry the Duke of Albright, and then Edith would have an indisputable position in their exalted ranks. No one, especially not Lord Ratcliffe, must interfere with that objective.

Picking up the silver pot, she smiled amiably. "More tea?"

CHAPTER 16

Colin had been reduced to spying on Portia again. He sat
on a park bench where he could keep watch on her
house. His old brown nag cropped a nearby patch of grass.

He wasn't accustomed to rising so early, at least not
here in London. He seldom felt the chill of the morning
mist or saw the servants out shining the door brass. But
for the past three nights he'd slept only fitfully, awaking
at dawn with a hunger that had him growling at Tudge
and snapping at Hannah.

His appetite had little to do with food and everything
to do with Miss Portia Crompton. Each night he'd tossed
and turned, filled with the memory of kissing her sweet
mouth, of caressing her beautiful breasts, and touching
her moist heat. It had been intoxicating, the pleasure he'd
taken in building her arousal to a fever pitch.

Lying alone in his bed each night, he had relived her
cries of ecstasy again and again. Knowing he was the
first man to bring her to the summit had been a triumph—
and an unbearable torment, as well. Stroking himself
brought only temporary relief, not the bone-deep satisfaction he craved. He felt no inclination to visit a bawdy
house, either. It was Portia he desired, Portia he craved.
He wanted to lose himself inside her, flesh to flesh, to
share with her the closeness of full-fledged lovemaking.

Instead, his dissolute actions had driven her away from him.

You're nothing but a worthless rake. I wouldn't marry you to save my life.

Haunted by her censure, Colin shifted position on the hard bench. He took full blame for what had happened. It had been wrong of him to treat her like a bit of Haymarket fluff. Never before had he attempted to corrupt an innocent girl. Despite his reputation, he had enough gentlemanly scruples to confine his trysts to more experienced women. But from the moment he'd taken Portia in his arms, he'd been doomed. The temptation had been too powerful to resist.

Now she had refused to see him. She had returned his letters unopened. She had walked away from him at a party. He'd lost all his carefully laid groundwork and was back to the barren beginning: hiding in bushes and peering around corners, hoping to catch her alone and unguarded. He couldn't give up on her—he wouldn't. Certainly, he still needed her money to pay his mounting bills. Yet there was no denying that Portia had become more than just a bank account to him. His pride had taken a dive out the window, and he didn't even care.

For the first time in his life, his knack for charming the fairer sex had failed him. Portia had opposed him at every turn because she fancied herself in love with the son of a maharajah. He would never forget the look of horror on her face when she'd returned to her senses. Nor could he erase from his mind her guilt-stricken words.

Dear God, what have I done?

Scowling, he leaned forward to rest his elbows on his knees. The utter foolishness of her plan befuddled him. By running off to India and marrying a native, she would be shunned by her family, her friends, her acquaintances.

Did she think he could just stand by and allow her to ruin herself?

Then he caught himself. *He* had nearly ruined her. If anyone had walked in on them three nights ago, Portia would have been condemned along with him. He had abandoned all decency in subjecting an innocent young lady to such intimacy. It was little wonder she had been shocked and traumatized, for no one would have warned her of how utterly enthralling the act could be.

Nevertheless, given half a chance he would do it again. It didn't matter if his soul was cast into the blackest depths of hell. Nothing would satisfy him but the feel of Portia lying naked beneath him, panting and moaning. And this time, he would have his pleasure, too . . .

A movement at her house snapped him out of his sensual trance. Two women had walked out the front door and onto the pillared porch. They were bundled up in bonnets and cloaks, making it difficult to establish their identities. Squinting, he recognized Portia and her middle sister, Lindsey.

He surged to his feet, his legs stiff from the damp chill. Untying the chestnut mare, he started after the women, not wanting to draw attention to himself by mounting. He followed them at a circumspect distance, watching as they rounded a corner and vanished. If they were going on a walk, perhaps to Hyde Park, he might have a chance to approach them.

Leading the horse, he quickened his steps. When he caught sight of them again, they had stopped on the side street. Portia gave Lindsey a brief hug. Then, much to his surprise, she left her sister standing on the curbstone while she hailed a hackney coach and clambered inside.

Alone.

Colin swung onto his swaybacked mount. The old mare trudged along placidly, and he was forced to dig in his heels to increase her speed to a canter. Making a detour to avoid encountering Lindsey, he pulled his beaver hat down low, the better to disguise himself. Not for the world would he allow that nosy girl to intercept him—or to cry out a warning to Portia.

In his haste, he nearly ran down a stout maidservant walking a pug. With an apologetic tip of his hat, he rode onward. He kept the hired hack in sight, riding fast until he achieved a comfortable distance. Then he slowed to a walk, keeping pace with the enclosed black coach as it maneuvered through the crowded streets.

It was highly unusual for a young lady of privilege to set out on her own. At this early hour, she wouldn't be going to call on anyone respectable. And if she was heading for the shops, why was she alone? At the very least, why had she brought no servant to carry her packages?

Colin could only surmise that her purpose was clandestine. If not, she would have taken the family coach. A maid and a footman would have accompanied her. And Lindsey would not have left the house with her, making it appear to their parents as if the sisters were going on a walk together.

Yes, Portia was up to no good. Just where the devil was she going?

His mood grew progressively grimmer as the hired hack left the elegant streets of Mayfair and headed toward the Strand. She could have no justifiable reason for visiting an area that dealt in commerce and industry. The traffic here was denser, with drays hauling kegs of beer or piles of merchandise, workmen riding the omnibus, and tradesmen going about their business. Costers hawked their wares on street corners, selling all manner of foodstuffs from hot meat pies to pickled whelks. The shops catered to the middle classes, bakeries and greengrocers and secondhand clothing stores.

A stiff breeze carried the fishy odor of the river. After a time, he could see the spire of St. Paul's Cathedral jutting into the cloudy sky. They were nearing Blackfriars now, hardly a place for any decent young woman to venture.

In a shadowed alleyway, a drunkard lay sprawled beside an empty bottle of gin. Strings of laundry hung between the grimy buildings. A burst of loud laughter came from a public house. Here and there, a slattern stood soliciting customers. Several of them blew kisses to him, lifting their ragged skirts to show off their wares.

Scowling, Colin narrowed the gap between himself and the hack. With her privileged upbringing, Portia could have no notion of the evils that might befall her in the stews of London. He did, though, and kept a sharp eye out for ruffians. A band of them could easily overpower the hunched old cabman and take her hostage. Of course, Colin would plunge in with fists flying, but she didn't know that. And there was always the possibility that one of them might have a pistol. If she were shot in the mayhem of a fight . . .

His gut churned. He wanted to ride ahead, to force the hack to turn around and take her straight home. Reluctantly, he rejected the action. Portia likely would oppose his command, and this was hardly the place for a gentleman and a lady to stand in the middle of the street and quarrel. Besides, he wanted to find out where she was heading.

And then once he had her safe, by God, he would blister her hide.

To avoid attracting attention in the seedy neighborhood, Portia kept as far from the windows as possible. The task was a challenge. The cab jolted and swayed over the cobblestones, jostling her from side to side. She hung onto the frayed strap with one hand, using her other hand to press a handkerchief to her nose, for the smells of damp musty leather and stale cigar smoke permeated the interior.

This public vehicle was a far cry from her family's well-sprung coach with its plush velvet cushions and sparkling clean windows. Nothing short of desperate determination could have induced her to set out alone on this errand.

Tension knotted her stomach. She prayed her absence had not been discovered. Lindsey had made a solemn vow to remain in hiding until Portia returned, letting everyone believe they were out on a walk. If Mama discovered otherwise . . .

There was no need to worry, Portia reminded herself. Edith Crompton had taken ill with a headache during the night and remained abed, with Kasi waiting on her hand and foot. She'd been resting with a cold cloth on her brow when Portia had departed.

There would never be a better opportunity.

Unfortunately, traffic on the main streets had been heavy, and the trip was taking longer than she'd anticipated. She opened her reticule and checked her pocket watch. The dainty gold hands indicated she had been riding in this cramped vehicle for more than an hour already.

Uneasily, she wondered if the coachman might be leading her astray. Her imagination offered up a scenario in which he was in cahoots with a band of thieves and was at this very moment driving her to their lair. Perhaps he did that all the time, waited until he picked up a vulnerable female passenger and then took her deep into the stews of London, never to be seen again.

Shivering, she scooted closer to the door and peered

through the smeared window. To her vast relief, a forest of masts pierced the skyline. The cramped tenements had given way to clusters of brick warehouses and small office buildings.

Men scurried to and fro, hefting heavy crates or rolling casks down gangways. Sailors swabbed down the deck of a huge merchant ship. A workman moved along the railing, pausing now and then to pound in a nail with his hammer.

She watched all the activity in wide-eyed fascination. It had always been a treat for her to accompany her father to the docks in Bombay. There, the workers had been dark-skinned Hindus and the burning hot sun had replaced the overcast sky, but otherwise, the hustle and bustle was much the same.

Did any of these ships belong to her father? Luckily, he hadn't mentioned any new arrivals before disappearing into his study after breakfast. Nor had he spoken of visiting the docks to check on cargoes. It was a blessing not to have to worry about running into him here.

And now that she'd arrived, matters would go smoothly. It would take only a few minutes to conduct her business. Then she could return home again with no one the wiser.

Her emotions had been in such turmoil of late, she couldn't bear to wait until Kasi had her next half-day off. Portia had to know right now if Arun had written any letters.

She closed her eyes, calling up the memory of their last meeting. Under the guise of an errand, she had joined him in the bazaar the morning before her father's ship had set sail for England.

The rendezvous had been planned as a chance encounter. They'd stood side by side in a booth, pretending to examine the colorful saris on the display table.

A lump tightened her throat, and she'd scarcely noticed the swirl of native shoppers and the cacophony of voices.

"Promise me you'll write," she'd whispered, sliding her hand over his, entwining their fingers atop a pile of silk garments. "Please, I must be certain you won't forget me."

"I will send you many letters, my dear Portia," Arun vowed in his musical voice. "And you, too, must not forget me, either. You must take this as a token of my love. It will help you remember."

He pressed the miniature of himself into her palm. While she blinked away tears, he purchased a sari for her in a deep marigold color, waiting gravely while the shopkeeper wrapped it in brown paper. Then Arun had presented that to her, as well. She had looked up at him, memorizing every aspect of his dear features . . .

Opening her eyes inside the cab, Portia realized with a knell of dismay that she could no longer conjure Arun in her mind. The previous evening, the same awful event had happened. When she had tried to picture him, his image had grown somewhat hazy. Was the dimple on the right side of his face—or the left? Did his black hair cover the tips of his ears—or was it cut shorter? If only she had the miniature, she could have checked every detail.

In its absence, she craved a letter from Arun as a reminder of the boy who had been her dearest friend for many years—the man she loved with all her heart. She wanted a tangible token that would prompt her to think of *him* while falling asleep at night. Not Ratcliffe.

Ratcliffe.

Portia had been steadfast in her determination to shut him from her thoughts, but before she could slam the door on those memories, a slew of vivid impressions rushed out to entice her. His laughing green eyes. The sinful quirk of his lips. The hard strength of his body as he held her close.

And oh, sweet heaven, his hands on her bosom, beneath her skirts, between her legs. A powerful wave of desire swept away all her good intentions, and she found herself flushed with yearning again, aching for the pleasure of his touch . . .

The coach jerked to a stop. She drew several shaky breaths in an effort to compose herself. Blast the man! He was a cad of the worst ilk. His disrespectful treatment of her only proved him to be the most ungentlemanly of gentlemen.

Fuming, she climbed out and fished in her reticule for a coin. Handing the stoop-shouldered man half a guinea, she instructed him to wait for her return. Then she started toward the soot-blackened brick building in front of her. The structure had a squalid appearance from the sagging lintel of the door to the cracked windows and peeling paint.

Upon her arrival in London the previous year, Portia had made arrangements for her overseas mail to be delivered here. Kasi had accompanied her on that occasion, and ever since had collected the mail once a month. Mr. Brindley, the shipping agent, had been wary at the prospect of dealing with a woman, at least until Portia had made it well worth his while.

In a matter of moments she would have her hands on Arun's letter, the one that had failed to arrive a few weeks ago. Surely it had come on one of the many ships that entered port daily. By reading Arun's words, by smelling the faint sandalwood scent that clung to the paper, she would recall all the nuances of his kind and chivalrous nature. She would reassure herself that he was the perfect husband.

Not a scoundrel who tried to win her by using the most unscrupulous of methods. Who thought nothing of preying upon a young lady's virtue. Who had the audacity to introduce her to intimacies that should be known only to a wedded wife.

Caught up in her brooding thoughts, Portia failed to sense impending danger. As she approached the door, a small dark form rushed at her from around the corner. She caught the whiff of a fetid odor, saw the flash of a dirty face in the instant before the midget thief grabbed her reticule.

She cried out and attempted to fend him off, but it was too late. The strings of the purse broke under a hard tug. The robber turned and ran, taking the coins that were supposed to pay for Arun's letter.

Portia acted on pure instinct. Lifting her skirts, she plunged after him in pursuit. "Stop, thief!"

With the noise from the docks, no one paid any heed. The felon darted toward the narrow lane, heading for a warren of tenement buildings.

The grizzled old coachman sat blinking in befuddlement atop the hackney. He made a creaky move to climb down, but his lack of speed rendered him useless as a rescuer.

Then she glimpsed a gentleman tying up an old nag a short distance behind the coach. "Help!" she called. "Help me, sir!"

As the criminal attempted to dash across the street, the man reached out and seized him by the scruff of his neck.

She hastened toward them, her heart pounding and her mind awash with thankfulness. It was only upon nearing the pair that she noticed two facts in quick succession.

Firstly, the robber was not a midget, as she'd initially

assumed. Beneath the filth on his face and the ragged garments that hung from his skinny form, he was a boy of perhaps eight or nine.

Secondly, the hero who had made the swift capture was none other than Viscount Ratcliffe.

CHAPTER 17

The shock of his presence slowed her steps. In stark contrast to his tattered prisoner, Ratcliffe was the essence of masculine grooming in a tiered greatcoat, tasseled Hessian boots, and a beaver hat. He held one arm extended, from which dangled the wriggling youngster.

All of her gratitude vanished under an avalanche of insight. Ratcliffe's sudden manifestation could be no coincidence.

"You!" she accused on reaching them. "What are you doing here? Did you follow me?"

"And lucky for you that I did." He turned his attention to his sullen captive. "Hand over the goods, lad."

"Nay!"

"Do it quickly now. Or by God, I'll make you sorry you were ever born."

The urchin angled a suspicious scowl up at Ratcliffe, then slowly stuck out his grubby paw.

Portia took the reticule, its weight reassuring her that the contents were intact. The broken cord dangled uselessly, so she tucked the purse into an inner pocket of her cloak. Then she bent down to take a closer look at the boy. He gazed back with defiant blue eyes that were ringed with what looked like years of accumulated dirt. The mistrust he radiated unexpectedly touched her heart.

"What is your name?" she asked.

"Bane."

"Bane?"

"Aye, me mum said oi were a bane an' a pain."

Good heavens. "Where is your mother? Does she live nearby?"

"She be dead," he said in a matter-of-fact tone. "'Twere a fever wot took 'er."

"Have you a father? Or any other family?"

Glowering, he gave a quick shake of his head and offered nothing more, as if he regretted admitting so much.

His plight appalled Portia. She vacillated between wanting to empty the contents of her reticule into his dirty hands and realizing that she shouldn't reward his thievery. "You oughtn't steal what doesn't belong to you, Bane," she chided. "If you had asked politely, I would have been happy to give you a coin."

Ratcliffe stood watching, one eyebrow cocked. "I'm sure he'll remember that little lesson in manners while he's rotting in Newgate."

The statement set off a wild panic in Bane. He redoubled his efforts to get free, wriggling and kicking to no avail. "Lemme go. *Lemme go.*"

Horrified, Portia hastened to reassure him. "Do calm down. I promise, you won't be sent to prison." To Ratcliffe, she snapped, "I have no intention of prosecuting him. He's merely a child. I won't let him be locked up with hardened criminals."

"Shall I release him, then, so he can rob someone else?"

"Yes . . . *no.* Well, he won't turn to stealing if he has funds of his own." She reached into her reticule, intending to give Bane enough to purchase a hot meal. A month's worth of hot meals, if he were prudent.

Ratcliffe stopped her. "Thieves don't deserve handouts. He should work for his pay."

This elicited another futile struggle from Bane. "Oi ain't goin' t' no work'ouse!"

"Not the workhouse." Ratcliffe produced a coin, which he waved in front of Bane. The boy's eyes followed it avidly. "Guard my mount while the lady and I conduct our business. If you—and the horse—are still here when we return, you'll have earned your wages."

He released his hold on the boy. Rubbing the back of his neck, Bane gazed askance at Ratcliffe, then at the ancient brown horse that was cropping a skimpy patch of grass. For a moment, Bane looked as if he might take off running. Then he edged toward the horse and stationed himself by the wooden post where the reins were tied, looking small and defenseless beside the great beast.

Ratcliffe took hold of Portia's arm, steering her toward the shipping office. She bit her lip, glancing over her shoulder. "Is your mount very spirited? Will he kick or bite?"

"*She* is as placid as a lamb."

"Humph. Was it truly necessary to frighten Bane so badly?"

"If he's ever to better himself, then he needs to learn the value of hard work."

She blinked at Ratcliffe in surprise. It was odd to hear such sensible talk from a dissolute like him. Her mind shifted back to Bane. It broke her heart to imagine the child all alone in the world. "What will happen to him when we leave? He's too young to survive on his own."

"Children do it all the time in London. In India, too."

Portia often had seen street children in Bombay as well as here, and to her shame she'd seldom spared a thought for their welfare beyond giving them a few coins. "I can't leave him to his own devices. Where is this workhouse you mentioned? Perhaps he should go there."

"Certainly, if you'd like him to subsist on gruel and beatings. You might as well put him in prison."

How did Ratcliffe know so much when she herself had never even heard of such a place? "Then we should take him to an orphanage."

"*We* will do no such thing," Ratcliffe said as they reached the door. "Now, enough talk of that pint-sized pickpocket. Isn't it time you told me why we're here?"

The memory of her purpose came rushing back. Heaven help her, she didn't want Ratcliffe discovering where she picked up her letters from Arun. The rogue might abscond with them as he'd absconded with the miniature.

She dug in her heels. "As you said, there is no *we*. I have business to conduct. You will wait right out here. Or better yet, mount your horse and go away."

"No. You've already proven yourself vulnerable to attack. I'm not leaving your side until you're safely home."

He meant every word, Portia realized in dismay. His implacable features showed no willingness to negotiate. The moment she went inside, he intended to follow her to Mr. Brindley's office. Ratcliffe was bound to find out the truth, so she might as well tell him now rather than risk a quarrel in front of the shipping agent.

"You leave me little choice, then," she said stiffly. "But first I'll have your promise that you won't interfere in any way."

Those green eyes studied her consideringly. "With one exception. If you're planning to purchase a ticket back to India, I will not let you do it."

Was *that* what he thought? And what gave him the right to dictate how she lived her life, anyway? "You mistake my purpose. I'm merely checking to see if any letters have arrived from India."

She reached for the door handle, but Ratcliffe put out his arm to block her. "Letters. You mean from your beloved Arun. I'd wondered how you were managing to correspond with him."

Portia resented the disapproval in his tone. She raised her chin and coolly met his gaze. His nearness stirred erotic memories that she fought to control. "Yes. He *is* my beloved. He's good and honorable in ways you could never understand."

"Tell me this: If he's so gallant, why hasn't he come to England? Why has he made no attempt to reunite the two of you?"

The question startled her. "Because . . . he can't. The maharajah—his father—has forbidden Arun to marry me. Just as my parents have done to me."

Ratcliffe moved so swiftly, she had no time to react. He trapped her against the hard brick of the building, his arms like prison bars on either side of her. The intoxicating scent of him threatened to make her swoon.

He bent his head close so that his warm breath fanned her face. "Let me tell you very plainly, Portia—if you and I were separated by an ocean, I'd move heaven and earth to be with you again. I wouldn't let the devil himself stop me from claiming you as mine. And I'd kill any man who dared to touch you."

On that thrilling declaration, he kissed her. The pressure of his mouth was hard and forceful, a feast to her starved senses, and she craved every morsel of it. All the reasons he was wrong for her faded to nothing, for Ratcliffe tasted too delicious to resist. The feel of his hard body consumed her with passion. With a moan, she succumbed to the temptation to wind her arms around him and return his kiss. It seemed impossible that something so wonderful could be a sin, impossible for their closeness to be anything short of perfection.

All too soon, he drew back. She opened her eyes to see him breathing hard, his gaze intent on her. He tenderly ran his thumb over her lips. "Stubborn little minx. I'm the right man for you, not Arun. Give me half a chance and I'll prove it to you."

A tempest of emotions swirled inside her. Ratcliffe had done it again. He had used his charm to bedazzle her, and she had fallen for his ploy. Worse, the gossamer chains of his spell still held her captive. She loved the pressure of his body against hers, the way his touch caused a melting warmth in her depths.

She struggled to understand the powerful desire he could stir in her with one caress, one look, one kiss. It mattered little to her that they were standing outside where passersby might see them. Her inexplicable infatuation with him could have no basis in trust and friendship, yet its influence over her seemed boundless.

Baffled and frustrated, she gave Ratcliffe a shove. "I despise you," she said fiercely. "Please, just stay away from me."

He backed off, letting her grasp the handle and swing open the door. Fueled by the need to escape from him, she went marching down the dimly lit corridor. On either side lay rooms where clerks labored over small wooden desks, recording the inventories of ships' cargoes.

Ratcliffe's heavy footsteps sounded right behind her, but Portia decided to pretend he wasn't there. She would regard him as nothing more than a pesky fly. In a few moments, she'd return to the hackney cab and hopefully never see the scoundrel again.

She rapped on a closed door at the rear of the building. A moment later, a short man swung open the wooden panel. With his luxurious moustache, abundant brown hair, and dark beady eyes, he brought to mind a bushy squirrel.

"Good morning, Mr. Brindley. I hope you can spare a moment of your time."

He peered over the gold-rimmed spectacles that rested on the tip of his nose. "Miss Crompton? Oh, fiddle, this is a surprise, indeed." Snatching his nut-brown coat from a hook on the wall, he threw it on, all the while staring curiously over her shoulder at her companion.

"This is Ratcliffe," she ground out, purposely leaving off his title to keep the introductions as short as possible. "Ratcliffe, Mr. Brindley."

"I'm her fiancé," Ratcliffe added.

Portia's jaw dropped at the blatant lie. Then she clamped her teeth shut to hold back a furious denial. If she protested the statement, it would only raise questions in Mr. Brindley's mind as to why she was out unchaperoned with a man who was unrelated to her. Mr. Brindley might then refuse to collect her mail on the grounds that she was an unchaste woman.

The shipping agent gave Ratcliffe's proffered hand a hearty shake. "A pleasure, sir, truly a pleasure. I'm afraid my office is in a bit of a whirl today, what with all the ships that have arrived this week. Will you sit down?" He indicated two straight-backed chairs in front of his paper-strewn desk.

"Gladly," Ratcliffe said.

He put his hand on Portia's elbow as if to guide her to a chair, but she impatiently stepped away while keeping her gaze on the agent. "I'm sorry, we can't stay more than a moment. I wondered if you might have collected any mail for me."

"Mail. Hmm." Mr. Brindley went to a wall of cubbyholes. Adjusting his spectacles, he bent down to read the names inscribed on each compartment. Many of the boxes were stuffed with letters. He stopped before an empty one, stuck his hand inside it and felt around, then straightened up to face her. "I'm afraid there's nothing."

"Nothing at all?" Distressed, Portia glanced at the blizzard of papers on his desk. "Are you quite certain? Perhaps my letters haven't yet been filed."

Mr. Brindley shook his head emphatically. "Oh, no, miss, I have strict methods when dealing with the post, indeed I do. The very moment it arrives, I file it away in its proper place." An arrested look crossed his squirrelly features. "Er, wasn't it India that you receive your letters from? Bombay to be precise?"

"Yes. Are you expecting a ship anytime soon?"

Mr. Brindley frowned in reply, then turned to Ratcliffe. "If I may have a word with you in private, sir?"

"Certainly. We can talk in the corridor."

Portia watched in disbelief as the two men walked past her. As if she didn't exist.

She rushed into the doorway to block their exit. Incensed that Mr. Brindley would defer to Ratcliffe over her, she snapped, "Excuse me. If there is anything to be said, you will say it directly to me."

Mr. Brindley shifted uncomfortably from one foot to the other. He slid a glance at Ratcliffe, who gave him a crisp nod. "Go ahead," Ratcliffe said. "Else my darling betrothed will pester you into giving up all your secrets."

"Er, hmm. Yes, well, it is just that . . . I've heard reports from several ship captains about certain troubles in Bombay."

"Troubles?" Pricked by foreboding, Portia took a step closer to him. "What do you mean?"

The agent gave her a grim, apologetic look. "Pray forgive me for being the bearer of bad tidings, miss. But I'm afraid there's been a cholera epidemic. It's wiped out more than half the population of the city."

* * *

Water drenched Colin as he kept Bane confined in the tin bathtub by the hearth in the kitchen. The little fiend howled and thrashed and squirmed. Hannah was as wet as Colin. Kneeling on the other side of the tub, she attempted to scrub away the accumulated grime, lathering her hands with soap and rubbing his skinny limbs.

"Ow! 'Elp, somebody! Oi'm dyin'!"

"Stop the melodrama," Colin growled, turning his head to the side to avoid another splash of dirty bathwater. "If you're to live in my house, you'll follow my rules of cleanliness."

It had taken considerable persuasion to convince Bane to accompany Colin home. The boy had seen little reason in his sorry life to trust adults. But in the end, the promise of a hot meat pie every day and a warm corner in which to sleep had won him over. Now, however, he appeared to have changed his mind.

Colin held on to Bane in grim determination. As irksome as the task was, he welcomed the distraction. It kept him from brooding about that scene with Portia.

For as long as he lived, he would never forget the paleness of her face, the disbelief, then her horror over Arun's likely fate. She had been frozen, unable to move until Colin had slipped an arm around her and escorted her outside. Only then had tears spilled unchecked down her cheeks. He'd held her close, dabbed her face with his handkerchief, while murmuring any nonsense that might make her feel better.

"You can't know for certain that he's gone," he'd said. *"Perhaps he survived."*

"He must be dead," she'd whispered. *"That explains why I haven't received a letter from him in nearly two months. It all makes sense now."*

"Maybe he was only taken ill. He might need time to recover."

His words of succor failed to penetrate the vastness of her grief. She seemed almost unaware of his presence until he helped her into the hackney cab. Then she turned those shimmery blue eyes on him and asked, "Now will you give me back his miniature?"

Her mournful request made him feel lower than a worm. Under the circumstances, his deceit seemed more cruel than clever. "You have it in your possession already," he'd admitted gruffly. "It's right beneath the painting of me. I never removed it from the frame."

Soap suds splashed his face, yanking Colin back to the present. He blinked away the stinging bubbles to see Hannah doing her valiant best to wash the boy's hair. "Ungrateful pipsqueak," she chided. "I should take a brush to your backside."

She dunked his head under the water to rinse off the soap. Upon surfacing, Bane spluttered and coughed. "Argh. 'Tis nasty!"

In spite of his dark mood, Colin grinned. Bane looked like a drowned rat. A very scrawny rat. "Keep your mouth shut next time, and you won't swallow water."

"Won't be no next time. Ow!" He tried to shy away as Hannah set to work scouring his grimy face. "Ow, me eyes!"

"Close them," Hannah said tartly. "Or do I need to wash out your brain, as well?"

"What on earth is going on in here?"

The sound of his mother's voice caught Colin's attention. He looked up to see her standing in the doorway. Wearing a copper gown with a matching pelisse, a stylish bonnet framing her face, she radiated an elegance at odds with the disorder in the kitchen.

Orson Tudge hovered behind her. He lifted his massive shoulders as if to say he'd tried his best to show her to the drawing room.

Colin firmed his jaw. He knew full well how difficult it could be to make his mother behave. She also had a knack for visiting at the most inconvenient times.

He rose to his feet, grabbing a linen towel to blot his damp clothing. His shirt was plastered to him and his breeches looked as if he'd had an accident on the way to the privy. "Hello, Mother. If you'd warned me you were coming, I'd have been dressed properly."

She scarcely glanced at him. Her sharp eyes raked the scene in front of the hearth, Bane in the tub and Hannah kneeling beside him, gripping his thin shoulders to keep him from bolting.

Lady Ratcliffe raised a haughty eyebrow. "Who is that boy?"

"My new tiger." He could tell she wanted to lecture him on his poor choice of servants, so he signaled his valet into the room and then bent down to address Bane. "This is Mr. Tudge. I'd advise you to obey him because he used to be a pirate."

Bane ceased thrashing at once. Water dripping from his tangled hair, he gazed up wide-eyed at Tudge. "A—a pirate?"

"Aye, matey," Tudge said, settling down to take Colin's place alongside the tub. "If'n ye don't settle down, I'll skewer ye wid me cutlass."

Bane sat frozen, staring at Tudge with a look that was part awe, part apprehension.

"Well, damn," Colin muttered under his breath. If he'd known the man would have such a miraculous effect, he'd have summoned Tudge at once.

He tossed down the towel and joined his mother in

the doorway. "If you wish any refreshment, it'll have to be sherry. My servants are busy at the moment."

As they went down the corridor toward the front of the town house, Lady Ratcliffe pursed her mouth in distaste. "Where did you hire such a motley staff? Your valet is a former pirate, the boy is a hooligan, and that woman . . . she's in the family way, if I'm not mistaken."

"Never mind them. I'd rather you get to the point and tell me why you're here. And if it's going to take a while, I'd like to change out of these wet clothes first."

She waved away his untidy state. "I would prefer not to wait. Now, since you've offered, I would appreciate a glass of brandy."

He gave her a pointed stare. His mother never imbibed anything stronger than sherry or champagne except in times of distress. The last time he'd seen her drink brandy was right after his father's death. What the devil was weighing on her mind now?

God spare him, he didn't want to know.

He steered her into his study, where he kept a row of decanters on a sideboard. Filling two crystal glasses, he handed one to her. She sipped at it daintily while strolling around his desk, running a gloved fingertip over the account book that lay open to show columns of figures.

"You always were clever at mathematics," she said. "I'm afraid I don't have much of a head for numbers myself."

Ominous commentary, Colin judged.

He took a bracing swallow and watched her through narrowed eyes. "So tell me, Mother. What have you done this time?"

"Done?" she repeated on a little tinkling laugh. "I can't imagine what you mean."

"I very much doubt that you came here to chitchat

about the estate's accounts. Unless, of course, you're in need of funds again."

She pouted, blinking those long black lashes at him. "And if I am? Please, darling, promise you won't be angry with me."

"Tell me the amount," he said coldly.

"It's a trifling sum, hardly enough to sneeze at."

"How much?"

She hemmed and hawed before finally admitting, "Five hundred guineas."

"What?" Choking on her gall, Colin flung down his glass and seized her by the shoulders. "You've taken up gaming again, haven't you?"

"It was merely a private wager among friends."

Anger rushed through him. Thinking of the improvements he could have made to the estate with that amount of money made him sick. Only with effort could he keep himself from shouting at her. "By God," he bit out, "don't try to pretend this is nothing. You swore me a solemn vow that you'd never again risk another farthing on the turn of a card."

Tears glossed her eyes. "It was only the once," she said in a small voice. "I didn't wish to appear a pinchpenny. A lady has her pride, too, you know."

As a child, he'd been frightened to hear the loud quarrels between his parents behind closed doors that invariably ended in his mother weeping. Now he had a better understanding of them. Struggling to hold his temper in check, he enunciated every word. "To whom do you owe this money?"

"Why should it matter?" she countered with a little shrug of her shoulders.

"It matters when I'm the one paying your markers."

She flung up her chin, eyeing him defiantly. "All right, then. If you must know . . . it's Albright."

A tide of fury rolled over Colin, so powerful that a red mist blurred his vision. "My God! What the devil were you thinking?"

To keep himself from raking her over the coals, he stalked to the window and stared unseeing into the garden. He couldn't blame it all on his mother. Albright had been plotting her downfall for years—and Colin's as well. This was precisely the sort of devious swindle in which the duke specialized.

After a moment, Lady Ratcliffe tentatively touched his arm. "Darling, there is only one thing to be done. You must marry Miss Crompton."

That was the one thing he couldn't do. Portia needed time to overcome her grief. Seeing her in such anguish had made him realize how badly he'd underestimated her attachment to that Indian prince of hers. And how little by comparison she cared for Colin.

The incident had opened his eyes to one daunting truth. He wanted her to adore *him* like that. He craved it with all his soul. But it wouldn't happen now, at least not anytime in the near future.

And especially not if he married her for her money.

CHAPTER 18

One morning a fortnight later, a tapping on the door disturbed Portia in her bedchamber. She was curled up in a chair by the hearth, a book open in her lap, although her attempt at reading Miss Austen's latest novel had met with little success. It wasn't the fault of the author. Rather, Portia had been too preoccupied to comprehend the words printed on the pages.

She frowned at the door. If she pretended not to hear, then perhaps the visitor would go away. She could think of no one she wanted to see, not her sisters, not her parents, and certainly not any servants bearing gifts from unwanted suitors.

The shock of Arun's death had been dulled by the passage of time. At first it had been a sharp, unbearable agony. To escape the round of social events, she had pretended illness for several days until her family's baffled concern for her welfare had prodded her out of bed.

Mama had wanted her help in planning the upcoming masquerade ball they were hosting, but Lindsey—the only one who knew the true source of Portia's malaise—had offered to write out the invitations in her stead. Portia had resumed her other daily activities, visiting the nobility and attending various parties, though without her usual high spirits.

A part of her wanted to believe what Ratcliffe had suggested, that Arun might have fallen ill and needed time to recover before writing again. But in her heart, she knew the futility of such a hope. She had witnessed the horrors of other such epidemics in India. And Arun had been the sort of faithful, dependable person who, even in the throes of dire sickness, would have roused himself enough to send a scrawled note. Because he wouldn't have wanted her to worry.

Tears welled in her eyes, but she blinked them away. It was best to face the truth. He was gone. And denied the objective of returning to India at the end of the Season, Portia found herself drifting like a ship without a rudder.

The rapping came again, louder than before. Again, she ignored it.

But this time, the door opened. Miss Underhill peered inside, her sallow features showing a startled look above the gray serge of her high-necked gown. "Oh! Forgive the intrusion, Miss Crompton. I assumed you were in your dressing room."

Portia summoned a polite smile. "I'm sorry, I must have been absorbed in my reading."

Miss Underhill didn't challenge the fib. A rare smile lighting her usually stern face, she walked into the bedchamber and clapped her hands. "Come, you must make haste. You've a very important visitor waiting downstairs."

"I'd rather not see anyone just now." Portia had come to treasure the mornings before the hustle and bustle of afternoon visits, and she guarded her free time jealously. "Anyway, isn't it too early for callers?"

"This is a most special personage. His Grace of Albright."

Portia frowned, trying to think back to her most recent

conversations with the duke. "Why is he here? I don't recall agreeing to go on a drive with him."

"Pray, don't be churlish. You've been so cross of late, it's a wonder you have any suitors left at all." Miss Underhill removed the book from Portia's lap and placed it on a nearby table. "You should know, the duke has spoken privately with your father in his study just now. And that can only mean one thing."

Portia's mind worked sluggishly. "What?"

"Silly goose. If you can't guess, you'll find out soon enough. Stand up now so I can tidy your gown."

It was easier to comply than to resist. Portia dutifully rose to her feet and allowed the older woman to brush at her skirts and straighten a bit of lace by her bodice. She patted Portia's hair, twisting several curls around her forefinger and then setting them into place. All the while, she chattered in an untypically exuberant manner.

"It is quite auspicious that just an hour ago, I received a reply from my mother's cousin."

She paused expectantly, as if Portia should know what she meant. "And?" Portia prompted.

"If you'll recall, you asked me to write to her on your behalf. You wanted to know why there was bad blood between the duke and Lord Ratcliffe."

"Oh . . . of course." That concern seemed ages old, as if it had happened in another lifetime. Portia had not allowed herself to think of Ratcliffe these past two weeks. It had seemed disloyal to Arun, especially in light of her guilt over those passionate encounters. Now, she had a clear memory of Ratcliffe holding her close, wiping her tears, murmuring words of comfort. And she felt a sudden aching need to feel his strong arms around her again.

"It seems," Miss Underhill went on, as she gave the gown one last tug, "that the duke was once betrothed to Lord Ratcliffe's mother. She left him standing at the altar in front of all the ton, whilst she eloped to Gretna Green with the present viscount's father. As you might well imagine, it caused quite a scandal back in my mother's day."

Portia had heard the story straight from Lady Ratcliffe. Odd how important it had been to her at one time. Instead, she found herself wondering what had happened to Ratcliffe. Why had he ignored her of late? Had he given up on courting her? He must have, for he had made no attempt to contact her since that day at the docks.

A sense of loss settled over her, keen yet somehow different from the grief she'd felt for Arun. She missed Ratcliffe's wit and charm, the excitement his presence evoked in her. A part of her yearned to feel alive again, instead of being trapped in a gray colorless world. Yet she must never again delude herself into believing he cared for her. The cold hard truth was that he'd only wanted her dowry.

And Bane . . . she had been so distraught over Arun that she'd gone off in the hackney cab without assuring herself of the boy's welfare. The memory of his dirty little face haunted her. She hoped that Ratcliffe had had the decency to spare him a coin or two.

Portia continued to brood about Ratcliffe as she and Miss Underhill headed downstairs to the reception rooms. She only marginally noticed her sisters peeking out the doorway of the morning room, whispering and giggling.

Then her mother appeared behind them, shooing the girls back inside before hurrying out to meet Portia. At a dismissing flick of Mrs. Crompton's fingers, Miss Underhill vanished into the morning room, too.

Mrs. Crompton's face was flushed with excitement. "Whatever took you so long?" she whispered, critically examining Portia's hair and gown. "The duke has been waiting for more than ten minutes. You must go to him at once. And remember, under no circumstances are you to turn down his offer."

She gave Portia a little push into the drawing room. Preoccupied, she found herself walking into the cavernous chamber with its tall gold draperies and its numerous chairs and tables. His offer?

Of *marriage*?

Reality struck her like a splash of cold water. She faltered to a stop just inside the doorway, seized by the panicked urge to turn around and flee. But the duke was coming forward to greet her, bowing over her hand and then leading her to a chaise by the white marble fireplace. He looked as distinguished as ever in a charcoal-gray coat with a diamond stickpin glinting in his cravat.

Without releasing her hand, he seated himself right beside her. The soft kidskin of his glove rubbed soothingly over her stiff, bare fingers. "My dear Miss Crompton," he said, gazing deeply into her eyes. "It has been an honor these past weeks to enjoy the company of such a lovely young lady as yourself. You must permit me to express how very much I've come to hold you in the highest esteem."

Silver threaded his well-groomed brown hair. Fine lines radiated from the corners of his pale blue eyes. He had always reminded her of a father, not a husband.

Desperate to stave him off, she murmured, "I'm no different from any other girl. Truly, I'm not."

He smiled approvingly. "Modesty becomes you, my dear. It is an admirable quality in a lady—and a wife." His voice grew husky, his eyes intense. "I have received the blessing of your father to ask you a very important question. Pray know that your answer will most certainly affect my future happiness. Miss Crompton—Portia—will you do me the great honor of becoming my wife?"

Her mouth went completely dry. She saw a startling image of him speaking similar words to Lady Ratcliffe so many years ago. What more did she know of his past? And what did he know of hers? "I—I hardly know what to say. This is so sudden."

His eyes narrowed slightly. "Pray don't regard me as one of the profligates who have tagged at your heels. My affection is solely for you, my dear, and not for any monetary gain. That is why, as a token of my sincerity, I am prepared to refuse your dowry in its entirety."

His declaration stunned her. Surely this proved Ratcliffe was wrong about the duke. Albright wasn't a cunning schemer, for only a man of high principles would turn down such a vast sum of money.

Ratcliffe himself would never do such a noble act. He had made it plain from the start that he had courted her only because of her wealth. He had proven himself a cad time and time again.

Burying the bitter thought, Portia looked at the duke with new eyes. The warmth in his gaze revealed a true fondness for her, and the realization was a balm to her battered spirits. Despite the difference in their ages, the duke reminded her of Arun in many ways. Both men were chivalrous, kind, and steady in character.

Perhaps it was time for her to behave in a mature and responsible manner. To leave her childish dreams of romance behind. All of her plans for the future had shifted irrevocably. She had no reason to return to India anymore. And if she were to remain in England, why not wed Albright? He was a pleasant companion, a man who made her feel safe and protected. The marriage would thrill her parents, who wanted her to achieve the pinnacle of society. And there would be no mad emotional upheaval as she'd experienced with Ratcliffe.

Oh, Ratcliffe . . . but no, she mustn't think of him ever again. His interest in her had been based on selfish financial gain. He was a part of her past, not her future.

Taking a deep breath, she spoke the words that would seal her destiny. "I'm honored, Your Grace. And I'm very happy to accept you."

Three days later, Portia strolled through the family ballroom on her father's arm, her mother at his other side. The scene before her was rather curious, for the occasion was their masquerade ball. Instead of the usual fashionable garb, the ton had turned out in costumes of all sorts, from knights and friars to queens and milkmaids. There had been no receiving line, nor any names announced, since that would have defeated the purpose of trying to guess who was who.

"A most absurd business," Mr. Crompton muttered, tugging at the sword that kept getting twisted in the striped pantaloons of his medieval king's attire. He had drawn the line at wearing a mask, and his face reflected exasperation. "How the devil are we to know who's who?"

"Hush," Mrs. Crompton hissed. Dressed as Marie Antoinette in a towering white wig and panniered gold gown, she wore a black-and-white domino that covered the top half of her face. "And do smile at our guests, George. This should be the happiest of occasions, the finest hour of our lives."

Agitation stirred in the pit of Portia's stomach, but she attributed it to nerves. Tonight, the Duke of Albright would formally announce their betrothal. At his request, she had dressed as the Roman goddess Diana, so that he might easily recognize her in the crowd.

Accordingly, the soft white folds of a toga left one of her shoulders bare, and a filigreed gold diadem glinted in her upswept chestnut curls. She peered through the eyeholes of a demimask. Against her back rested a leather quiver of arrows, though she'd opted against carrying a longbow, which would have proven awkward while dancing.

She was determined to make the duke proud—and to overcome the lethargy that had plagued her of late. In six weeks' time, she would be a duchess, for Albright wanted their wedding to be a big splash at the end of the Season. The newly exalted position would give her the power to help her family and to ensure good marriages for her sisters. Gossips like Mrs. Beardsley would never again dare to question the Crompton family's status at the peak of society.

And once she embarked upon her new life, certain memories would be vanquished forever. She wouldn't think of Ratcliffe at odd moments, like now, when she caught herself searching for his tall form among all the gypsies and princes and military officers. Although he hadn't been invited, such a trifling obstacle would mean nothing to a rogue like him.

She acknowledged her disappointment when she didn't spy him anywhere in the swirling throng of guests. Although they often had struck sparks off one another, there had also been laughter and witticisms and a peculiar sort of kinship between them.

But he had made no attempt to see her since that day at the docks. In retrospect, it seemed highly unusual that he hadn't taken advantage of her grief in an effort to press his own suit. Instead, he had held her close while she'd dampened his coat with her tears . . .

"Diana the Huntress?"

A Roman senator stood before her, a circlet of laurel leaves adorning his silvered dark hair. Despite his half-mask, she recognized his proud demeanor at once.

"Your Grace." Portia dipped a curtsy. She thanked the

heavens for the domino that helped to conceal her blush. How awful if he were to guess she had been thinking about Ratcliffe.

The duke exchanged courtesies with her parents, and then requested her permission for the first dance, which she had no choice but to grant. "Come, my dear," he said, offering his arm. "Let all those present envy me for dancing with the loveliest goddess in the room."

The effusive compliment made her smile, renewing her determination to enjoy the evening. By prior agreement between the duke and her parents, the announcement would not be made until everyone was seated for the midnight supper. With resolute gaiety, Portia joined the line of dancers assembling on the floor. Albright was an excellent dancer, and she soon found herself taking pleasure in the familiar steps and the lilting music of the orchestra.

Throughout the evening, a number of swains approached to secure her company for upcoming sets. It wasn't terribly difficult to discern their identities. She recognized the Honorable Henry Hockenhull as a court jester, his auburn hair covered by a drooping harlequin's hat. Lord Wrayford was an Egyptian pharaoh complete with gold paper crown that nearly tumbled off every time he tilted his head down to ogle her bosom. The gangly Marquess of Dunn made an incongruous Robin Hood, complete with doublet and green tights.

Several of her partners made oblique comments on Albright's preference for her company. Apparently, word of their betrothal was an open secret in the ton, though whether people were merely guessing or whether the duke had dropped a discreet word in the ears of the right gossips, Portia didn't know. She deftly deflected all attempts to fish for the truth, but the process grew increasingly wearisome.

After bandying words with yet another purse-poor second son—or was he a third?—she escaped upstairs to her bedchamber for a moment of quiet. She removed her domino and rubbed the bridge of her nose, where the half-mask had left red marks. Sinking onto the edge of a chair, she rested her aching feet on the tigerskin rug. It brought a poignant reminder of the time when Ratcliffe had sat right here, his long lean fingers stroking the tiger's head. He had climbed up the trellis to bring her that stem of orchids. How charming he had been, how very witty and handsome.

Portia released a long sigh. It was useless to think about him anymore. Clearly, he had given up on her. She must focus her mind on the duke and their upcoming nuptials.

The ormolu clock on the mantelpiece ticked a steady reminder of her impending duty. It was half an hour before midnight, nearly time for the supper dance and the big announcement that would set the course for the rest of her life. A part of her dreaded standing before the crowds of nobility, accepting their good wishes, pretending to be happy when all she really wanted was to be left alone.

With a sigh, Portia forced herself up from the chair. There was no point in donning her domino again since everyone would soon know her identity. Abandoning the quiver of arrows, too, she tidied her hair in front of a mirror and then trudged out of the bedchamber, only to stop in surprise.

In the dimly lit corridor, a masked man stood waiting for her.

Her heart leaped with instant recognition. *Ratcliffe*. No other gentleman of her acquaintance had that tall, cocky stance. Nor had any other guest garbed himself as a pirate. A billowy white shirt covered his broad chest and a red scarf was tied at his throat. Black knee-high boots and tight buckskin breeches defined his long, muscular legs.

Removing his mask, Ratcliffe tucked it into his waistband. His face wore the brash smile that never failed to stir heat in her depths.

It was working spectacularly at the moment.

"You!" she snapped, in an effort to deny his effect on her. "What are you doing up on this floor? You weren't even invited to the ball."

He ignored her words as his avid gaze made a slow survey of her from head to toe. "My God, Portia, I'd nearly forgotten how beautiful you are."

His deep husky voice awakened all of her senses. She drank in the vivid details of his face, the green of his eyes, and the strong angles of his jaw and cheekbones. "Why are you here?" she repeated.

"I had to see you." His face intent, he strolled toward her. "Where can we talk in private?"

"Nowhere. Now please leave here at once, or I'll have one of the footmen toss you out on your ear."

"I'm asking for a few minutes of your time, that's all."

She braced herself for his attempt to manhandle her back into her bedchamber. Heaven help her if he tried to kiss her again. Perhaps he would press her down onto the bed and lift her skirts. The very thought sparked an onrush of molten desire.

But oddly, Ratcliffe didn't take advantage of her nearby bedroom. He slipped his arm through hers and tugged her down the corridor in the opposite direction from the grand staircase. She glanced over her shoulder at the emptiness of the passageway. With every step, the lilt of music and the buzz of voices seemed fainter.

She tried in vain to shake off his hold. "This is absurd. I must return to the ball at once."

"So you can be there when Albright announces your betrothal?" His lips thinned, Ratcliffe shook his head in disgust. "I want to know why you've agreed to marry him despite my warnings. You owe me an explanation."

"I owe you nothing! What gives you the right to come into my home uninvited and make such demands on me?"

"This does."

He pulled her close, took her head in his hands, and kissed her. Too transfixed to resist, Portia could only stand there with her hands on his chest while his mouth plundered hers. Awareness of him poured like heated honey through her body, bathing her in the sweet joy of desire. It made her feel vibrantly alive for the first time in weeks.

Succumbing to temptation, she moved her palms over his thin shirt, reveling in the feel of his hard muscles. He groaned in response and cupped her bottom, lifting her to his loins. For one radiant moment, the scantiness of their costumes revealed the distinct shape of his male anatomy, and she moved her hips in instinctive curiosity. With a muffled curse, he broke off the embrace and held her at arm's length.

The heaviness of his breathing disturbed the quiet air. "Tell me," he muttered, "do you respond so passionately to Albright?"

Crashing back to earth, she wanted to lash out at Ratcliffe for causing the wild emotional disruption that good sense warned her to avoid. "Cad! What matters to me in a husband are kindness, chivalry, and respectfulness. You lack all of those qualities."

Ratcliffe growled in exasperation. Then he took a deep breath and smoothed back her hair with a gentle hand. "Portia, please listen to me. You must see the truth. He's marrying you because he knows how much *I* want you."

"You?" she scoffed. "I haven't even seen you for the

past few weeks. So why would he think you were still pursuing me?"

"Believe me, he knows."

She remembered the darkness of hatred on the duke's face whenever he encountered Ratcliffe. Yet wasn't that understandable given the way Ratcliffe's mother had abandoned him at the altar? "I don't doubt the duke despises you and your family. He certainly has every reason to do so. But I've seen no evidence of him taking action against you—other than these unfounded suspicions of yours."

Ratcliffe eyed her measuringly. "Then I'll tell you the proof. But not here, where someone might happen upon us."

Taking hold of her upper arm, he accompanied her down a little-used back staircase. He seemed to know his way around her house with unerring instinct. Intrigued, she had only a moment to wonder at his familiarity as they walked down a darkened corridor and through a door that led outside.

There, he grasped her hand and drew her deep into the shadows of the garden. The sound of a waltz drifted from the open windows of the ballroom. Decorative lanterns hung from some of the trees, and a few costumed couples strolled the lighted pathways. Avoiding exposure, Ratcliffe made straight for the stone wall at the rear of the property.

Instinct made Portia wary. She ought to speak up, to dig in her heels and insist upon returning to the ball. Yet the feel of their intertwined fingers, the strength of his presence, filled her with an irresistible excitement. She had a few minutes' reprieve before the supper dance would begin. What harm could come from listening to whatever he had to say?

Taking a swift look around, as if to make sure there

were no observers, Ratcliffe opened the gate. He slipped his arm around her waist and drew her out into the gloom of the mews. The stamp and snort of a horse called her attention to the black outline of a coach at the end of the alley.

Uneasiness prickled over her skin, especially when Ratcliffe urged her in that direction. She reminded herself there were many vehicles parked around the neighborhood, waiting for the ball to end.

Nevertheless, she twisted away from him and stepped back against the stone wall. "That's quite far enough. No one will hear us here, so give me your proof."

He stepped very close, an ebony shadow blocking out the faint starlight. "First I'll have your vow not to speak of this to a soul, aside from the people directly involved."

She hesitated, reluctant to make promises about the unknown. But curiosity got the better of her. "As you wish."

"Let me start by correcting a falsehood I've told you," he said. "I suggested that Hannah's infant could have been fathered by any one of a number of gentlemen. In actuality, the child is Albright's."

The statement hit Portia like a jab to the ribs. Certain she must have misunderstood Ratcliffe, she stared up at him in utter disbelief, trying to make out his features in the darkness. "What?"

"You heard me. It's the truth, I swear it on my father's grave." His fingers gently kneaded her shoulders as if to soften the blow of his words. "Hannah was my mistress for a time—I'd taken her away from the brothel where we met and set her up in her own household so that she was mine exclusively. Then one day I called on her unexpectedly and found Albright warming her bed. He'd deliberately set out to woo her away from me with jewels and pretty compliments."

Portia remembered Hannah's cagey response as to why she and Ratcliffe had ended their liaison. *He discovered me lying with another man.*

Yet Hannah hadn't named the duke. To attribute such reprehensible behavior to Albright seemed impossible, the direct opposite of the gentleman Portia knew.

She shook her head. "I . . . I cannot believe it."

"Hannah will corroborate the story if I ask her. Albright kept her as his own mistress until he cast her out for the sin of conceiving his child. He threatened to kill her if she told anyone."

Portia leaned her head back against the stone wall. Her mind whirled. *Was* it possible? The duke had always behaved toward her with the utmost gentility. Yet the incident would explain so much—such as why Ratcliffe regarded Albright with such loathing. Dear God, it made her ill to think of any man being so callous as to abandon his own baby.

Ratcliffe took hold of her arm. "I cannot allow you to marry him, Portia. I *won't* allow it. I hope you can understand that."

Wrapped up in her troubled thoughts, she didn't realize his intentions until it was too late. He propelled her the short distance to the waiting coach, yanked open the door, and half lifted her inside.

CHAPTER 19

Portia found herself dumped unceremoniously into the pitch-dark interior of the vehicle. Landing on a cushioned seat, she heard the door shut, followed by the click of a turning key.

With a cry of disbelief, she groped for the handle, only to discover it wouldn't budge. Ratcliffe had locked her in. He was abducting her!

She pounded on the door. "Blast you, Ratcliffe! Open this door at once. Let me go!"

There was no answer, nor had she expected one. The abrupt rocking of the coach told her they were moving. She cupped her hands to peer out the window, then realized that blacking had been applied to the outside of the pane. There was no hope of signaling for help from a passing vehicle.

Dear God, what was she to do? Her parents would be looking for her by now. The duke would be waiting for her in the ballroom to join him for the supper dance. At the very least, she wanted the chance to ask him about Hannah Wilton and judge by his reaction whether or not Ratcliffe had spoken the truth.

Behind her, a rustling noise caught her attention.

Portia whirled around, her heart pounding. She tried

to discern movement in the absolute blackness. "Is someone there?"

A sleepy little voice replied, "Who're ye?"

There was something very familiar about that childish Cockney accent. But surely not. Wondering if she might have knocked her head on entering the coach, she ventured, "Bane?"

"Aye . . . who be ye?"

"It's Miss Crompton. The lady whose purse you filched that day at the docks." Astonishment rose to the fore as Portia struggled to sort out an explanation for his presence here. "Has Lord Ratcliffe abducted you, too?"

"Ab . . . wot?"

"Abducted. Stolen you away." She scooted closer, straining to see him. It was impossible to distinguish anything through the gloom. "Oh, I do wish I had the means to light a lamp."

"There be a tinderbox, miss. Right 'ere 'neath the seat. Found it when oi was lookin' fer a place t' 'ide."

Portia heard him moving around, then a metallic rattle sounded as he opened the container. A moment later, he struck the two pieces of flint together and a shower of sparks revealed his presence. It took him several tries before a tiny flame started in the pile of tinder.

Swiftly, she patted the walls and found a lamp fastened to one overhead corner. She moved aside the glass chimney to access the candle, then touched the wick to the tinder. At last a pale glow illuminated the interior of the coach, showing Bane nestled in a blanket on the seat across from her.

He looked considerably cleaner than the last time she'd seen him. The accumulated grime was gone from his face. In place of his ragged clothing, he wore a smart little suit of blue livery.

Mystified, she asked, "What did you mean just now

when you said you were looking for a place to hide? Were you concealing yourself from his lordship?"

"Aye, mum. 'E tole me t' stay wid Mr. Tudge. But oi jest couldn't." Bane leaned forward, his blue eyes as big as the gold buttons on his coat. "Mr. Tudge be a *pirate*."

"A pirate?"

Bane nodded vigorously. " 'E captured ships an' kilt folks wid 'is sword. 'Twas the master wot saved 'im from a life o' crime."

Her confusion began to clear, replaced by a stunned realization. "The master? Are you saying . . . you're now *living* with Lord Ratcliffe?"

Bane proudly thrust out his skinny chest. "Oi be 'is tiger. Oi runs errands and oi 'olds the 'orse wherever the master goes. 'E pays me tuppence a week."

So Ratcliffe hadn't abandoned Bane, after all. He hadn't fobbed him off with a handout, either. Instead, he had taken the grubby little street urchin under his wing. He had scrubbed him spotless, given him new clothing and a post where he could earn a wage.

Ratcliffe had done the same for Orson Tudge, if Bane could be believed, and for Hannah Wilton—even though he knew she was carrying the child of his enemy.

Portia drew in a shaky breath. Was it possible she'd been blind to his true character? That he was more than just a dissolute profligate? The notion was too much to absorb, so she concentrated on Bane. "You ran away, then. Rather than remain home with Mr. Tudge, you hid yourself in this coach. And you fell asleep here."

"Aye." Bane eyed her warily. "Ye won't tattle on me, will ye, miss?"

He looked so woebegone at the prospect, she had to restrain the impulse to hug him close. "No, of course not. Only tell me, do you know where his lordship is taking me?"

Bane shrugged. "Dunno. But oi 'eard 'im say t' Miss 'Annah not t' expect 'im back fer three or four days."

Days!

Aghast, Portia sank back against the cushions. By tomorrow, her reputation would be in shreds. If *days* passed, she would be a complete disgrace to her parents, and her sisters would be tainted by her infamy, as well. In all likelihood, the ton would spread malicious rumors that she'd run off with Ratcliffe of her own accord.

And the duke would endure the humiliation of being abandoned by yet another bride. Though perhaps he deserved that and more after his ill treatment of Hannah and his unborn child.

Now that Portia had had time to adjust to the news, she could think more clearly. She could see that only Ratcliffe's version of events made all the pieces of the puzzle fit. Albright had every reason to hate Lady Ratcliffe and her family. But Portia had never quite been able to grasp why Ratcliffe despised the duke in equal measure.

Unless the duke had exacted revenge against Ratcliffe in the matter of stealing his mistress.

She shivered, chilled by the possibility that she'd been a pawn in a dastardly chess match played by the duke. Her thoughts ranged back to the first time she'd encountered Albright at the start of the Season. It was the same night she had met Ratcliffe. Upon their introduction, the duke had spared her scarcely a glance. It struck her now that he had begun courting her only *after* he'd observed Ratcliffe's interest in her.

Her gaze fell on Bane and her heart melted. Asleep again, he lay curled on his side, his eyes closed, his breathing steady. How astonishing to know that Ratcliffe had given the boy a home.

Despite the lulling sway of the coach, Portia felt wide awake. She wrapped herself in a blanket to ward off the

cold evening air and spent a long time mulling over all
that had happened, contemplating her future, and decid-
ing what to do. Only when she was satisfied with her
appraisal of the situation did she finally close her eyes
and drift off to sleep.

Early morning light bathed the lush hills of Kent as Colin drove past the pair of stone pillars that marked the
entrance to his estate. He waved to the gatekeeper, an
ancient codger who had held the position since the time
of Colin's grandfather. The old man lifted a gnarled hand
and then shuffled forward to close the gate again.

Holding the reins in his gloved hands, Colin sat
hunched in the coachman's box. His breath fogged the
chilly air. The nighttime cold had settled into his bones
even though he had donned a greatcoat over his pirate's
costume. In preparation for the long drive, he'd slept all
the previous afternoon. Yet his eyes felt scratchy and his
limbs were stiff. It had required great concentration to
traverse the dark country roads that were lit only by
moonlight and the feeble glow of the twin headlamps.

As he directed the team of horses down the long curving drive, he waited for the usual uplifting of his spirits
that always occurred upon reaching his estate. There
was usually the pleasure of seeing the planted fields of
hops and barley in the distance, the satisfaction of viewing his orchards of apple and pear trees. Instead, he
could only brood about Portia, as he'd done all night.

He had expected her to pound on the roof of the coach,
to shout or even curse him from time to time. He'd been
prepared for her to enact some clever ruse in order to
convince him to release her.

But Portia hadn't made a peep after that one initial
outburst, and her silence worried him. Had he been too
harsh with her? Had she bumped her head when he'd

pushed her into the coach? Or was she otherwise indisposed? For all he knew, traveling over rutted roads for so many hours might have made her ill. One of his aunts had seldom journeyed to London because of the misery she'd endured en route.

For most of the trip, he had been plagued by the image of Portia in such a wretched state. All of his planned strategies would be for naught if she had fallen sick. Or if she'd been injured. Not to mention, he'd have a hard time forgiving himself for putting her through any pain or discomfort.

He urged the team faster. The ten minutes it took to reach the final turn seemed more like ten hours. Then the ivy-covered stone house appeared around a bend in the road. Sunlight touched the mullioned windows, making them wink like diamonds.

Anxious to see his prisoner, Colin reined the horses to a halt near the pillared entryway. He had purposely not sent a note ahead to warn the staff of his visit. That way, there might be a chance to coax Portia into the house with a minimum of fuss.

At least he hoped so.

As he leaped down from the coachman's box, a groom came running from the stables to hold the horses. Luckily, no one inside the mansion seemed to have noticed his arrival.

Colin dug in the pocket of his greatcoat. Finding the ring of keys, he inserted one in the lock and prepared himself to do battle. If he knew Portia, she wouldn't submissively accept her fate. She might well come at him with fists flying.

Cautiously, he opened the door. A guttering candle cast a pale glow over the interior. Awake, Portia sat on one side of the coach, looking like a goddess in that white tunic with the gold diadem crowning her deliciously mussed chestnut hair. For a moment, he was awash in a fantasy in which she threw her arms around him and praised him for saving her from the duke.

Instead, she gazed coolly at him, her hands folded in her lap. She was not smiling.

Nevertheless, relief poured through him. She appeared well and unharmed, so at least he could lay those worries to rest. "Good morning, Portia. You must be wondering where we are—"

He broke off his words, startled by something moving inside the heap of blankets across from her. A boy sat up, rubbing his eyes and yawning.

Disbelieving, he stared. "Bane?"

Spying Colin, the lad uttered a squawk and dove back into his nest. Colin reached inside and snatched off the covering. "What the devil are you doing here?"

"Er . . ."

"He was afraid to remain with Tudge," Portia said. "Tudge is a pirate, you see. Though I cannot imagine why he would feel any safer with *you*."

Bloody hell. At the moment, Colin could have cheerfully made Bane walk the plank himself. His presence threatened to put a huge wrinkle in the fabric of Colin's carefully laid plans.

"I'll have a word with you later." Giving the boy one last frown, he returned his attention to Portia and struggled for a semblance of his much-vaunted charm. "Welcome to Willow Bend. I'm sure you'll want some refreshment after your journey."

He offered his hand to her, and she accepted his assistance in stepping out of the coach. At least he wouldn't have to carry her inside, kicking and screaming, past all the servants. But her pursed lips warned him that she wouldn't fall willingly into his embrace. She must be furious at him for abducting her. By God, he had to make her realize that he'd acted for her own good, that she would have been miserable married to Albright.

The stooped old butler was descending the broad steps, walking slowly due to his arthritic knees. More ancient than the gatekeeper, he wore the same formal black garb that Colin remembered from childhood. A smile wreathed his wrinkled face. "Your lordship! This is indeed a most delightful surprise."

"Good morning, Thurgood. Pray ask Mrs. Hodge to prepare the Queen's Bedchamber for Miss Crompton. She'll want a breakfast tray, as well."

"As will Bane," Portia added, placing a protective hand on the boy's shoulder.

Bane looked decidedly rumpled. The tails of his shirt hung loose from his coat and his brown hair was tousled, with tufts sticking out every which way. His head tilted back, he stared agog at the sprawling mansion.

"He'll eat in the kitchen," Colin said. "Thurgood, if you'll be kind enough to show him the way."

Thurgood made a creaky bow, revealing a shiny bald pate that was rimmed with wisps of white hair. "Very good, my lord."

When Bane made no move to follow, the butler took hold of the boy's hand and led him up the steps. Bane didn't seem to mind the servant's sluggish progress. He was too busy ogling the house with its surrounding gardens and stands of willow trees. It occurred to Colin that Bane had never been out of the city before. Having a taste of country life might do him good—so long as he didn't interfere with Colin's purpose here.

He noticed Portia frowning at Thurgood. In a low tone, she said, "He's rather old to still be on staff. Oughtn't you give the man a stipend so he can retire?"

"I've tried. He's refused." Intent on resuming control

of the situation, Colin took hold of her arm. "I'll escort you to your chamber now. You'll want to freshen up."

"Yes, thank you."

Her brief response put him on edge. As they headed for the house, he wished feverishly for the ability to see into her mind. Where was her fighting spirit, her fury at being abducted? Had a miracle happened and she'd finally decided to believe his accusations about Albright? Or was her calm demeanor merely a ruse to entice Colin into lowering his guard so that she could escape?

The last scenario had to be it.

He had no intention of letting her go. Not while there was a chance that Albright and her parents might conspire to cover up her mysterious disappearance. They could put out the story that she'd fallen ill at the costume ball. They could reaffirm her betrothal to the duke. People might whisper among themselves, but no one would dare shun Albright or his bride-to-be. And Portia would find herself bound forever to a man whose sole purpose was to use her for revenge.

Grimly, Colin ushered her through the echoing entryway and up the curving staircase. The only sound was the scuffing of their shoes on the marble steps. Her continued silence grated on his nerves, but he was determined not to start a quarrel. Better to let her recover from the journey first so they could talk later with clear heads.

Upstairs, he showed Portia into the bedchamber directly across from his. The blue and white décor was a legacy of his grandparents, before the family had lost its money. Now he wished he'd warned the staff to prepare the room. To keep off the dust, white cloth draped most of the furniture. The place looked sadly neglected, old and outdated.

Striding to the windows, he drew open the tall draperies to let in the sunshine. Then he took out his ring of keys. Portia had been studying the landscape painting above the fireplace, but the jingling sound made her whirl to face him.

She frowned first at the keys, then at him. "It isn't necessary to lock me up again. I've no intention of running away."

"Perhaps not. But I can't take the risk."

"There *is* no risk." Walking to him, she placed her hand on his arm. "Ratcliffe, listen to me. I've had ample time to reflect during the ride here. I can see now that you must have told me the truth about Hannah. Why else would you despise the duke the way you do?"

Why else, indeed? He could give Portia a host of other reasons. But those were things he didn't want her to know.

Besides, he could scarcely think while she was standing so close. He wanted to drag her to the four-poster bed and make passionate love to her until the beast in his loins had been sated.

The trouble was, that would only bolster her view of him as a worthless rake. "I very much doubt you've changed your mind about me based on one incident."

"You're right, it was more than that." Stepping back, she crossed her arms and regarded him intently. "It was Bane who made me realize the truth."

"Bane?"

"Yes, you took a poor street urchin into your home when others would have left him to starve on the street. You did the same for Hannah, giving her a position in your household. And for Orson Tudge, too, it would seem. I have to wonder, why have you hidden this philanthropic side of yourself?"

"I needed servants. It was easier than dealing with an agency."

She huffed in disbelief. "Then what about Thurgood? As his employer, you could force him into retirement. But you haven't. You've allowed an old man to have a purpose in his life. And I greatly admire you for that."

Her praise made him exceedingly uncomfortable. Enough so that he threw away all logic and caution.

He walked away from her, then turned back. "Save your admiration. The truth is, I abducted you in order to achieve your ruin. Now you have no choice but to wed me."

Portia merely raised an eyebrow. "Oh? And what makes you think my father will give you my dowry in such a case? He may well cut me off without a penny."

Colin brushed off the possibility. Although having the funds certainly would make his life easier, he was willing to take the risk of losing it in order to have Portia in his bed. "Your parents will be so anxious to cover up the scandal they'll pretend to be happy with the marriage."

"Perhaps. But how, pray tell, do you intend to force me to speak my vows to you?"

"Coercion won't be necessary. You'll do it or your reputation will be damaged beyond repair."

"And it will all be fixed by marrying a known philanderer?" Smiling, she shook her head. "I'm afraid your plan is for naught, my lord. I won't be bullied into marriage to you or to any other man, especially one who will squander my dowry at the gaming tables. In fact, you've done me a great service."

He fought the urge to haul her up into his arms and show her the prime benefit of marriage to him. "What the devil does that mean?"

Strolling to a covered chair, she twitched off the dust cloth, then sat down as if settling in for a long visit. "I've never cared much for society. It was my parents who wanted me to marry Albright. By ruining me, you've allowed me to escape that gilded cage. Now I'm free to go anywhere, even back to India if I choose."

Her words hit Colin like a sharp jab to his abdomen. He'd thought that upon Arun's death, she would have put that foolish idea out of her mind. "Don't be absurd. There are cholera epidemics—and vicious tigers. And even if you survive all that, how would you support yourself? As you said, your parents will cut you off without a penny."

"I'll work as a governess. English families often advertise for help in the newspaper there."

"You can't be serious. You've no notion what it's like to be poor, unable to pay your bills." But Colin knew. He knew far too well.

"Then I'll learn. I've saved more than enough of my pin money to pay for the voyage." Infuriatingly serene, she gazed up at him. "So you see, my lord, I shan't run away from here. Rather, I owe you my thanks."

CHAPTER 20

Two hours later, Portia stepped out of her bedchamber and paused in the dimly lit corridor. A troop of maids had delivered fresh clothing, hot water for a bath, and a tray of breakfast. It had been a relief to discard that preposterous toga and to soak away the travel dust. The pale green gown she wore fit remarkably well, and she could only surmise that Ratcliffe had sent the garments ahead from London.

He had planned the abduction well—except for his arrogant assumption that she would fall like a goose into his matrimonial trap. Apparently, he hadn't counted on her discovering that he possessed a sense of integrity underneath all that masculine bluster.

She needed such weapons at her disposal because it was only a matter of time before he attempted to seduce her. A rush of heat permeated her body, sparking a reminder of the rapture she had found in his arms. Now that he had ruined her in the eyes of society, would she allow him to do so in truth? Would she have the strength to resist him—did she even *want* to resist him?

Pushing the questions away, Portia glanced up and down the deserted passageway. One of the closed doors must lead to Ratcliffe's chambers. After staying awake driving the coach throughout the night, surely he must be asleep. That should give her a fair bit of time in which to satisfy her curiosity. She burned to discover more about his past, to speak to those who had known him since childhood, and to clear up the mysteries about the man behind the charming façade.

She picked a direction at random and headed down the corridor, peeking into open doors here and there. The house had a certain appeal to its shabby elegance, from the pale yellow painted walls with their shell-shaped sconces to the graceful columns placed at intervals along the passageway. Unfortunately, while gazing up at the arched ceiling, she nearly tripped when a hole in the carpet runner caught the heel of her shoe.

The place had been allowed to fall into sad disrepair. Quite likely because Ratcliffe had gambled away the profits from the estate. Why would a man be so foolish with his money? Especially one who clearly cared for his people and felt a duty to provide for them?

The passageway ended at the landing of a staircase. There, a mullioned window looked out on a lush garden. Unlatching the casement, she pushed open the glass and rested her forearms on the stone sill. Birdsong drifted from a nearby stand of willow trees. Beyond the garden, thick hedgerows formed natural fences for the patchwork of fields. A refreshing breeze carried the scent of the outdoors.

As a sense of contentment crept over her, Portia sighed. How odd to realize that she'd remained in the city ever since her family had moved to England the previous year. Until now, not once had she ventured outside of London. Although vastly different from India, the countryside here made her miss the wide-open rural settings where she had gone on drives with her father.

Papa. The thought of him brought a troubling reminder of her present situation. At first, he and Mama must have been furious when she had failed to appear at the midnight supper. They would have placated the duke while discreetly dispatching a servant in search of her. How swiftly their anger must have changed to alarm when she was nowhere to be found. Did they believe she had run away of her own accord? Or did they guess the truth?

Dear heaven, she wanted desperately to reassure them. She couldn't bear the thought of her parents and sisters frantic with worry. But what could she do? Thus far, Ratcliffe's servants seemed to be extremely loyal to him, and he surely would have given them instructions not to post any letters for her. It was a matter she intended to take up with him at the very first opportunity.

In the meantime, she distracted herself by focusing on her surroundings. She wondered if Ratcliffe had ever stood at this window, if he'd ever felt a swell of pride at the sight of his land. It seemed incredible that anyone would choose to stay in the crowded city when he owned such a piece of paradise as this.

The approach of shuffling footsteps caught her attention. She turned to see Thurgood coming down the passageway. The butler's face had an amazing number of wrinkles, bringing to mind a withered apple.

He bent in a respectful bow, and she fancied she could hear his bones creak. "May I be of assistance, miss?"

"Yes, thank you." Turning to shut the window, she decided to seize this excellent opportunity to ask questions. "I was wondering about Bane, the boy who came with me. Is he still in the kitchen?"

"He ate a hearty meal and then went out to the stable yard." A twinkle in his rheumy blue eyes, Thurgood added, "The little tyke didn't trust our groom. He insisted upon seeing for himself that the master's horses were brushed and well fed."

Portia smiled at the news. "Bane has taken his duties

to heart, it would seem. Thurgood, would you mind giving me a tour of the rooms downstairs?"

He placed a white-gloved hand over his lapel. "I am completely at your disposal, Miss Crompton. His lordship was most specific on the matter."

How odd that the butler didn't question her presence here without a chaperone. What exactly had Ratcliffe told him? Perhaps Thurgood was so dedicated to his master that it had never occurred to him to doubt Ratcliffe's judgment in bringing an unmarried lady to the estate.

She pursed her lips. Maybe he brought his mistresses here all the time. Was that how the servants saw her, as just another light-skirt?

Curse him, that had better not be the case!

As they descended the stairs, she moderated her pace in order to accommodate his slow progress. "Have you served the family for a long time?"

"Going on seventy years. Under the present viscount's grandfather, I started out as a spit boy in the kitchen."

"A what?"

"It was my task to turn the haunch of meat over the hearth. From there, I advanced to footman and thence to my present position."

As they reached the bottom of the stairs, Portia searched for a tactful way to broach the subject that had nagged at her since first meeting Ratcliffe. "I understand his lordship's father died three years ago in a terrible accident. Did it happen here?"

Thurgood nodded mournfully. "Indeed so."

"I don't wish to be intrusive, but it would be helpful for me to understand all the particulars. Were you present at the time?"

"Yes, it was very late in the evening, so I and the rest of the household staff had already retired. A footman slept in the kitchen in case one of the family rang for service during the night. He awakened me, and when I went upstairs . . . his lordship was lying on the floor of the library in a pool of blood . . . with Lady Ratcliffe weeping at his side. He had been shot." Tears pooled in the old man's eyes and a decided slump dragged down his shoulders. "Master Colin . . . or rather, the present Lord Ratcliffe, bade me send for a doctor at once. Alas, by the time help arrived, it was too late."

Horrified both at the account and her own stirring up of memories, Portia murmured, "Pray forgive me. I didn't mean to upset you."

"It's quite all right." Thurgood pulled a large handkerchief out of his pocket and blew his nose. "As his lordship's betrothed, it is only proper that you would have questions."

His betrothed?

Portia's spine stiffened. So *that* was the Banbury tale Ratcliffe had told his servants. It made her situation only marginally more respectable. And if his entire staff was as faithful as Thurgood, they would not question her presence here. Yet that wasn't sufficient reason to excuse Ratcliffe's deception.

She steeled herself to probe deeper. "The courts proved that the present Lord Ratcliffe's pistol went off by accident. However, rumors in society persist that he murdered his father. They say he did it because he is a gambler and he wanted to gain his inheritance."

Thurgood reared back as if slapped. "Vile gossips, all of them. Please, Miss Crompton, you must not heed those who have no knowledge of what really happened. The poor lad was in a terrible state of agitation that night. Never in my life have I seen him so distraught."

The butler's certainty gave her pause. He was utterly convinced of Ratcliffe's innocence in the matter, and not simply out of blind loyalty, she judged. For herself, she shuddered at the thought of Ratcliffe's shock and horror that night. Any man who went out of his way to help servants as he did would never deliberately shoot his own father in cold blood. How he must blame himself, though! It was little wonder he became snappish whenever anyone mentioned the incident.

"That is precisely the way I thought things had happened," she assured Thurgood. "I appreciate your eyewitness account. It makes me all the more determined to correct those who would vilify him."

The affirmation wove a sort of friendship between them, and as the old butler took her on a tour of the house, he regaled her with stories of times past. He told her tales of Ratcliffe's many escapades as a boy that soon had her laughing. Apparently Ratcliffe had had a penchant for sliding down the banister and had done so once during a ball, knocking a portly earl completely off his feet. On another occasion, he had tossed acorns out of the nursery window during a garden party. The poor guests had been baffled since the nearest oak trees were some distance away. It had been Thurgood who'd realized the truth while serving and had gone upstairs to administer a sound paddling.

The tour ended on the ground floor, when Thurgood escorted her to an enormous conservatory. He indicated a wrought-iron table by a bench inside a stone grotto. "Perhaps you would like for me to bring tea to you here."

"Yes, thank you, that would be wonderful."

Transfixed, she stood in the doorway, scarcely noticing his departure. Sunlight poured through the glass walls and bathed an array of exotic flora. Palm trees brushed the glass ceiling that towered two stories high. Lush vegetation gave the air an earthy aroma, and orchid plants nestled in the crooks of tree branches here and there, spilling their colorful flowers.

She stroked the large purple petals of one bloom, leaning closer to inhale its faint scent. At last the mystery had been solved as to where Ratcliffe had procured that stem of orchids on the night when he'd invaded her bedchamber. He must have sent a messenger here to fetch it. How remarkable that he had gone to such trouble to please her.

Following a winding stone pathway, she wandered through the conservatory. The place was fertile and green, the air deliciously warm, bringing back memories of the jungles of her youth. She half expected a tiger to come bursting out of the undergrowth.

The click of a door opening snapped her attention to the glass wall straight ahead. Ratcliffe rounded a stand of thick shrubbery. His purposeful strides came to a halt as their gazes met. Her heart thumped wildly against her rib cage. For one long moment, they stared at each other like a predator encountering prey. Then he prowled toward her.

He had discarded his pirate's garb in favor of tan breeches and work boots. His white shirt lay open at the throat, and he wore no coat or cravat. Several strands of black hair dipped low on his forehead. Portia ached to brush them back, to run her fingers into their thick softness.

Worse, she wanted to kiss him—and more.

The powerful force of his attraction made her quiver. For self-preservation, she buried the reaction beneath a cool demeanor. "I've been hoping to speak to you, my lord. I'd presumed you were asleep."

"There's always too much to be done here." He made a vague gesture toward the outside, then braced his hand on the thick trunk of a palm tree. The action stretched his shirt over the contours of his muscles. "You wished to tell me something?"

Blinking, she pulled her gaze from his chest and found him studying her intently. What must he be thinking, now that his plot to force her into marriage had been thwarted? Did he regret abducting her in the hopes of securing her dowry? His manner was curiously aloof, as if she were an uninvited guest. And if he intended to seduce her, he certainly didn't seem inclined to haul her into the bushes right here and now.

To her shame, Portia craved for him to do just that.

She drew a shuddery breath. "It's about my family," she said. "They must be very distressed. I'd like to notify them that I haven't been murdered by brigands."

"I've already sent a message to your father. He should have received it by post this morning."

"I see." Perversely irked at the way Ratcliffe had seized control of her life, she took a step toward him. "You've had the decency to name yourself as my abductor, I hope."

"Of course. There was little point in hiding my identity when your father would have guessed it, anyway. Because something tells me your sister Lindsey will confess to our meetings."

"The Duke of Albright will guess, as well. And if he's as resolute in his hatred as you say, then he should be arriving here very soon to rescue me."

Not that she wanted him to do so, Portia added to herself. In truth, the thought of Albright riding up the drive made her stomach clench. How horrible of him to abandon Hannah and their child. And then to threaten to kill the poor woman! If Portia never saw him again, it would be too soon.

"Your parents aren't likely to have informed Albright of your disappearance," Ratcliffe said with a decisive shake of his head. "Remember, they don't know how badly he wants to thwart me. So they will have told him yesterday evening that you fell ill, for fear he would spurn you for being ruined."

Crossing her arms, Portia paced the stone pathway. Ratcliffe was right, of course. Mama would have perjured herself in a court of law in order to preserve the alliance with the duke. "Then my father will surely come. And he'll bring a band of armed men to arrest you."

Ratcliffe didn't look alarmed in the least. "He's far more likely to set forth on the Great North Road. You see, in my letter I led him to believe we'd eloped to Gretna Green."

He'd certainly thought of everything. She had heard tales of couples running off to the closest village over the border because their families had opposed their union. Unlike England, where the law required banns to be read in church for three weeks ahead of the wedding, in Scotland there were no restrictions to prevent a man and woman from being wed immediately. Ratcliffe's own parents had gone there after Lady Ratcliffe had left Albright standing at the altar.

As much as Portia disliked the notion of her father being sent on a wild-goose chase, it was a relief not to have to worry about rescuers bursting in on them at any moment. Her fate was sealed, it would seem. Unless she returned to London posthaste, she would be a pariah in the eyes of society. Her absence could be concealed only for a short time. The servants would whisper to their counterparts in other households, and in turn, they would relay the news to their employers. Already the reports of her disappearance might be spreading like wildfire.

Portia searched herself for regrets. Ratcliffe had set her free from society's constraints, albeit inadvertently. And yet . . . did she truly wish to leave England and her family? Could she face the very real possibility of never seeing them again? Of never again seeing Ratcliffe, either?

That last thought shook her more than it ought. How ludicrous, when he had orchestrated her ruination!

Thurgood arrived with the tea tray, placing it on the iron table inside the shallow stone grotto. On impulse, she asked Ratcliffe, "Will you join me?"

He hesitated, eyeing her guardedly before nodding. "It would be my pleasure."

They sat side by side on the stone bench. A fountain burbled musically in the background, the water flowing from a vase held by a boy carved in white marble. Portia made a conscious decision to set aside her uncertain future for the moment. Why not enjoy the day and forget about tomorrow?

While waiting for Thurgood to return with another teacup, she asked, "Where did all these plants come from? Does Lady Ratcliffe enjoy gardening?"

"My mother?" Ratcliffe threw back his head and laughed. "Her idea of gardening is to arrange cut roses in a vase. No, my grandfather imported the palm trees from Egypt some fifty years ago. The rest of this wilderness is my doing, I'm afraid. I collected most of these specimens on my journeys to Africa and India."

Nothing could have startled Portia more. "You?"

"It was rather an adventure, one might say." A self-deprecating smile quirked his lips. "I hired guides to take me into the jungles and forests. We gathered cuttings and uprooted plants, then I arranged for their shipment to England. Quite a few didn't survive the transport, but the hardiest of the lot are what you see here."

Armed with that startling information, she looked out over the lush green foliage, seeing it all with new eyes. She had assumed his stop in India had been filled with all manner of illicit activities, loose women, gambling, drunkenness. "But . . . why? I mean, it's very beautiful, but I never imagined—"

"That I would have the slightest interest in cultivation?" Looking noticeably uncomfortable, he leaned forward and clasped his hands together, resting his forearms on his knees. "You shouldn't think much of it, really. It's nothing more than a hobby. Some travelers purchase cheap souvenirs that end up in an attic, collecting dust. I thought it might be more useful to gather plants."

A mere pastime? The verdant vegetation in the conservatory belied his offhand statement. For all its wild appearance, the foliage appeared to be well tended. "You must have a team of gardeners."

Ratcliffe shrugged, gazing out at the conservatory, then giving her a sidelong glance. "Actually . . . I employ only one. I do a fair bit of the labor myself. On visits here, you see. And . . . in between supervising the farms on the estate, of course."

Her eyebrows lifted. He was always such a smooth talker. She'd never known him to sound so halting, as if the words were being wrested from him by force. Portia's mind leaped back to the books on agriculture that she'd seen in his bedchamber. At the time, she'd thought he was searching for ways to wring every last bit of revenue from his estate. But the truth was, Ratcliffe *enjoyed* working with plants.

For the first time, she noticed the tiny smudges of dirt on his shirt, the clump of mud clinging to the sole of his boot. The strength of his body, the sun-burnished quality of his skin, gave further evidence to corroborate his love of outdoor activities. She wanted to laugh in delight. The profligate rake, whom mothers warned their daughters to avoid, actually preferred digging in the soil and coaxing seedlings to grow.

Portia felt as if she'd been granted a glimpse into the secrets of his soul. It was the precise opposite of the man he presented to the world, the one whose only interests were selfish amusements. In the space of one day, she had learned of his generosity toward those less fortunate than himself. And now of his dedication to nature.

What other mysteries did he hide?

He was still gazing out at the conservatory, as if to avoid meeting her eyes. Judging by his rarely seen discomfiture, she suspected he regretted revealing as much as he had. A tender softness grew in her heart, radiating outward until it encompassed her entire being.

Without conscious thought, she placed her hand on his forearm, absorbing the heat and hardness of his flesh through the sleeve of his shirt. "You've accomplished a truly marvelous feat here. It reminds me so very much of the jungles of India."

He looked over, his gaze searching hers. "Do you really think so?"

"Absolutely. When I first walked in, it was uncanny, almost like stepping into another world."

"Yes, that's exactly what I was hoping to achieve."

His face was alight with fervor, his eyes very green and animated. Mingling with the earthy scents all around them, his faint spicy scent lured her. Then his dark lashes lowered slightly, and she sensed a shift in him to a keen awareness of their proximity. They sat beside each other on the bench, their bodies touching. He turned his arm so that their fingers were intertwined, his thumb rubbing idly across the palm of her hand.

The moment became charged with sensuality. Deep within her, desire throbbed to vivid life. She could feel the mad rush of blood in her veins, the melting away of her inhibitions. A beautiful hunger filled her, the need to feel his bare flesh pressed to hers. The yearning grew so great it emerged from her in a beseeching sigh.

His lips parted slightly. He bent his head closer, so that his warm breath fanned her face. Lifting his hand, he tenderly brushed the backs of his fingers over her cheek. "Portia . . . my love . . ."

The sound of someone clearing his throat made them spring apart. Thurgood shuffled forward with the second cup, beaming at the two of them like a doting grandfather. "Will you require anything further of me?" he asked.

A blush suffused Portia from head to toe. She could scarcely meet the old butler's eyes, let alone voice a coherent reply.

Luckily, Ratcliffe had no such trouble. Apparently, he could turn off his own feelings like a spigot. His face a cool mask, he gave the servant a nod. "That will be all, thank you."

As Thurgood left the conservatory, Portia covered her discomfiture by reaching for the silver teapot. Somehow, she managed to pour the hot liquid into their cups without spilling a drop. The butler's untimely entry had broken the spell, leaving her awash in a sea of frustration.

Ratcliffe seemed disinclined to romance her again. Stirring milk into his tea, he began speaking in a casual tone about his plans for the estate. As if the interlude had never happened, he told her about the crops raised by his tenants, and his own idea for growing exotic spices in an old disused greenhouse on the grounds. Portia smiled and nodded at intervals, though her thoughts remained wrapped up in the wondrous memory of what he'd said to her.

My love.

By the stars, what had he meant by that? Was it merely an endearment that he murmured to all of his women? Or had he truly fallen in love with her?

The second possibility left her breathless. It was astonishing to contemplate that Ratcliffe might harbor deep feelings for her beyond physical desire and his wish to claim her dowry. She warned herself not to make too much of the statement. Despite her inexperience, she had the sense to know that men spoke sweet nothings in the heat of passion. Especially a man who had a history of luring women into sin.

And yet the unguarded tenderness in Ratcliffe's voice, the ardent look in his eyes, seemed to preclude any trick designed to entrap her. Now, more than ever, she wanted to see inside his mind, to view his private thoughts and to learn all of his secrets. She burned to know the truth—though there was one question she was too much the coward to ask him.

What exactly had he meant?

CHAPTER 21

Colin paced the confines of his bedchamber. At the wall of windows, he pushed back the green brocade draperies to peer out into the night. The moon had not yet risen above the horizon, but he needed no light to discern the contours of his property. He knew every hill and valley, every field and hedgerow. His fierce pride in the land had its roots in his childhood, when he had wandered and explored at will.

Yet he would give it all away to have Portia in his bed.

His plan to seduce her had gone seriously awry. By now, they should have been naked between the sheets, coupling with unbridled passion. He had imagined it for so long, had been so certain of his persuasive abilities in winning her over, that her reaction to the abduction had been a slap of cold reality.

I won't be bullied into marriage to you or to any other man, especially one who will squander my dowry at the gaming tables. In fact, you've done me a great service.

Yes, she would travel to India and labor the rest of her life as a lowly governess rather than wed him. She scorned him that much. Then she had thanked him—*thanked him*—for releasing her from her gilded cage.

With a curse, he let go of the draperies and stomped to the closed door. He stood there glowering at it, as he'd

done several times since eating the evening meal alone
in the formal dining room. Miss Crompton was feeling
ill, Thurgood had informed him. She had requested a
tray in her chamber.

Ill, like hell. She was avoiding him, that's what. He
hadn't seen her since that interlude in the conservatory,
when he had come within a hairbreadth of revealing just
how besotted he was with her.

My love.

What brainless stupidity had induced him to utter
those words? He wasn't one to spout sappy sentiments
just to get underneath a woman's skirts. Thankfully, the
butler's interruption had saved Colin from making an
even bigger fool of himself.

But the damage had been done. Portia had become
quiet and distant, regarding him as she might an escapee
from Bedlam. It was a clear indication that she was appalled by the prospect of him falling in love with her.

Not, of course, that he *was* in love. Rather, he was
suffering from an acute case of unremitting lust. There
could be nothing more to it. Nothing at all.

Turning on his heel, he stalked to a sideboard and
poured himself a brandy. He took a bracing swallow,
welcoming the burn in his throat as a distraction. Her
bedchamber lay only a few steps across the passageway.
He ought to go straight over there and demand his due. It
wouldn't take much effort to awaken her desires since
she was an amazingly sensual woman.

He put the brakes on another feverish fantasy. Seducing her was out of the question. She had stated in no uncertain terms that she would never wed a gambler and a
reprobate. Which put them at an impasse since he was
not at liberty to disavow her of those notions.

And now she intended to set out for foreign shores
without him. *That* was all his rash ruination of her had

accomplished. It had ensured he would never see her again. He took another long drink of brandy. Damn his folly. Surely he could have found a better way to stop her from marrying Albright—

A hesitant tapping echoed through the room. His attention jerked to the door. Portia?

Colin threw down his glass and knocked over a chair in his haste to get there. Taking half a second to compose himself, he swung open the dark wood panel. Then his gaze dropped.

Bane hovered in the shadows of the passageway. Hair tousled, he wore a wrinkled linen nightshirt that trailed down to his bare feet.

"What the devil are you doing here?"

The boy hung his head, seemingly fascinated by the sight of his toes digging into the carpet. "Dunno."

Colin looked up and down the gloomy corridor. "How did you even know which room was mine?"

"Mr. Thurgood tole me t' count six doors from there." He pointed toward the darkened staircase used by the servants.

"I see. Well, then. Was there something you needed?"

By way of answer, Bane lifted his thin shoulders in a shrug. He sniffled a little, then scrubbed his nose across his sleeve.

Good God, was the boy crying? Flummoxed, Colin stood there in something of a fix, wondering what to do.

The door directly across the corridor opened. Portia emerged in the ivory satin nightdress that he had purchased for her. The one that clung lovingly to her shapely curves. The one he had imagined himself stripping off her, inch by slow inch.

And holy God, her hair was loose. It flowed in a rich, dark brown mass down her back. One lock had fallen forward to curl around her breasts.

"I heard voices," she said, looking from him to Bane. "What's wrong?"

His mouth was too dry to form words. Nevertheless, Colin managed to snap, "Nothing. Go back to bed."

With me.

Oblivious to him—and his fantasies—she hastened to Bane and crouched down, the gown pooling around her feet. She placed her hands on his shoulders, gazing straight into his face. "What's the matter, darling? Have you had a nightmare?"

Bane gave a little nod. "'Twas pirates," he mumbled. "They was goin' t' slice me throat, then toss me t' the sharks."

Colin relaxed. "Well, now you're awake and you know it didn't happen."

Portia flashed a glare up at him, then addressed the boy again. "You poor dear. I'm sure it all seemed very real. I would hate very much to have an awful dream like that."

She gathered him into her arms. Bane stood there stiffly for a moment, then buried his face in her neck. Cuddling him close, she cooed and stroked his hair.

Standing forgotten in the doorway, Colin scowled down at them. *He* wanted to be the one clasped to her lush bosom, damn it. How pathetic was that, envying a frightened little boy?

"Was your room too dark?" Portia asked. "Perhaps you'd like to have a candle. I'm sure his lordship wouldn't mind."

Bane gave a quick, wordless nod.

She looked up at Colin, sending him a warning not to disagree. "Then you shall have one. And his lordship and I will walk you back upstairs."

She vanished into her bedchamber and returned a moment later with a lighted taper in a pewter holder. Meanwhile, Colin fetched another from his room, for they would need illumination to find their way back through the darkened house.

Portia held Bane's hand, and Colin found himself doing likewise on the boy's other side. As they headed down the corridor, his full awareness was captivated by her. How had she known what to do to calm Bane's fears?

Another question eclipsed that one. Did she have any notion of the torture Colin endured in her presence? With every breath, he could smell the light feminine fragrance of her skin. With every glance, he found himself eyeing the fullness of her breasts and the curve of her hips. He sternly reminded himself that he had no right to take her virginity. No right to get her with child.

Because she would never marry him.

The truth of that left him moody and frustrated. Damn it, he needed to take a plunge in cold water. Maybe after he saw her back to her chamber, he'd head down to the nearest stream. A brisk swim ought to cool his loins and restore his equilibrium.

He released Bane's small hand so they could go single file up the narrow flight of stairs that led to the servants' quarters in the attic. Bane led them to his tiny room under the eaves of the house. He scrambled into the narrow iron bedstead while Portia put the candle on a nearby table and then arranged the blankets securely around him. Her hair swinging loose, she bent down and pressed a kiss to his brow.

Colin watched them obsessively. A strange pang struck him—the keen wish to see her tuck their own child into bed.

It would never happen.

To deny the wrench in his chest, he sought asylum in lust. He wondered what she would do if he came up from behind and pulled her flush against him, while his hands cupped her breasts. The erotic image was so powerful, he was startled when she touched his arm and motioned him out of the room. Glancing back, he saw that Bane was curled up beneath the covers, his eyes already closed.

The house was silent as they made their way back downstairs. Carrying the candle, he preceded her down the flight of stairs. As they walked down the corridor lined with bedchambers, the casement clock down in the entrance hall bonged ten times in a distant, mournful echo.

He halted in between her chamber and his. She was so gorgeously feminine, it took a supreme effort of willpower to keep his hands to himself. "Thank you for the assistance," he said gruffly. "I confess, I didn't know what to do with Bane."

"I was happy to help. I was merely in bed reading."

He had an instant vision of her in *his* bed. She wouldn't have the time—or the inclination—to read if he was lying there with her.

They stared at each other. An enigmatic expression on her face, she made no move to return to her bedchamber, just stood watching him. He tried not to stare as she sank her teeth into her lower lip. She looked uncertain, as if something weighed on her mind.

He certainly had something on *his* mind—something that placed her virginity in grave peril.

Why the devil didn't she go? Damn it, could she not sense the danger of lingering in his presence? They were both barely clad, and modesty alone should have sent her scuttling for cover.

Colin forced himself to bow. "Well, then. I'll bid you good night."

He stalked toward his door. Without warning, she darted after him, blocking his passage. She slid her hands up his chest and inside the collar of his shirt, her fingers caressing the hot flesh of his neck. In a throaty voice, she murmured, "Please, Ratcliffe. Won't you . . . invite me in?"

He nearly dropped the candle. All the blood left his brain on a downward race to his groin. She was too naïve to realize what could happen. "No. That's hardly prudent." Curse it, he sounded like a maiden aunt. But he didn't dare speak otherwise. "It'll lead to . . . things you shouldn't know about."

She took a deep breath as if for courage. Then she smiled up at him from beneath the screen of her lashes. "I certainly hope so."

Her provocative manner nearly did him in. It took an effort to make his tongue work. "My God, Portia. You don't know what you're saying."

"I know what I want. And what I want is you."

When she ran her fingertip over his lips, Colin promptly forgot all the reasons why he had no right to seduce an innocent who had refused his offer of marriage. The torment of the past hours and days and weeks went up in smoke. By God, she was granting him a dream come true. In return, he would give her a night to remember.

He caught her hand and brushed a kiss to the back. "Then come inside at once, my lady."

CHAPTER 22

Portia felt a bone-deep tremor of excitement. The fervency in his eyes revealed that he did still desire her, after all. She had been so afraid Ratcliffe would spurn her, so worried he would reject the decision that she had arrived at only after much intense reflection.

She had lied to him about being in bed reading. Instead, she had been pacing her chamber, trying to decide how best to approach him. Then fate had awarded her the perfect opportunity in the form of hearing Bane and Ratcliffe outside in the corridor.

In the eyes of society, she was about to engage in the most wicked of sins. Yet what difference did that make now that she was ruined, anyway? In the end, she had come to the conclusion that by letting this moment slip away, she would spend the rest of her life regretting it. And because she couldn't imagine ever sharing such intimacy with any other man, tonight was her one chance, quite possibly her only chance to experience life to the fullest.

Ratcliffe slid his arm around her. Their hips brushed as he thrust open the door and drew her inside. As he bent down to place the candle on the nearest table, she had the swift impression of a spacious chamber with a cozy fire in the hearth. Its flickering light played over the greens and creams of the furnishings.

The lock in the door clicked as he turned the key.

Then Ratcliffe turned to her and the world fell away. She didn't know if he reached for her first or if she lunged at him, but all of a sudden they were in each other's arms, their lips joined in a deep, drowning kiss. The feel of his mouth, the strength of his body, made her delirious with need. His ardor was a powerful aphrodisiac, a reassurance that he desired her as desperately as she did him.

The kiss went on forever, and rather than ease her hunger, it honed it. His hands roved over her back, moving up and down, from her breasts to her hips, as if he could not get enough of her. She experienced that same greed herself as she slid her fingers over his chest and arms, and into the rough silk of his hair.

Dimly, she knew that her feelings for Ratcliffe transcended desire. Until this moment, she had not realized just how lonely she'd been these past weeks without him. He made her feel complete, as if a piece of herself had been missing and now she had become whole. That remarkable revelation only enriched the powerful emotions he evoked in her.

He lifted his head, his breathing harsh. A crooked smile quirking his mouth, he traced his fingers over the swollen dampness of her lips. "We must slow down . . . or this will be over inside of a few minutes."

Portia arched on tiptoes, relishing the slide of her body against his. "I don't care if it's fast. As long as we do it."

Chuckling, he caught her hips and held her still. "You'll like it better slower. Trust me."

She *did* trust him. Utterly and completely. How

amazing was that, when for so long she had considered him a blight upon her life?

"Then be slow if you must," she said slyly. "Just be quick about it."

"Minx." He cradled her face in his hands, gently brushing his thumbs over her cheeks. His humor gradually died away and he gazed at her as if she were the answer to his dreams. She ached to be all that—and more. She wanted to be his wife.

The impossible thought caused a sharp pain in the region of her heart. If only Ratcliffe could be a man of integrity, a man whose honor was beyond reproach. If only he were not a gambler and a rogue . . . but she wouldn't think about all that now. None of those flaws mattered tonight. All she wanted from him was an introduction to the mysteries of the flesh. And at the tenderness in his eyes, her last lingering doubts dissolved.

"You are so very beautiful," he murmured. "I want to see all of you."

As his fingers unfastened the buttons at her bodice, he bent his head to kiss every inch of skin he exposed. The whisper of his warm breath caused a tremor in her legs, requiring her to grip his broad shoulders for support. Under a slight push of his hands, the gown slithered into a puddle on the floor. She shivered from the coolness of the air against her bare flesh, and an unexpected shyness came over her. Unable to bear his scrutiny, she buried her face in his throat.

He tipped her chin up, forcing her to meet his gaze. "You must never be afraid of me, Portia. You have my promise, I'll never harm you by design."

He was right; any regrets she would suffer in the weeks and months to come would be her own doing. "I'm not afraid."

"Then what are you thinking?"

"It's just . . ." Looking into his gorgeous green eyes, she drew an unsteady breath. How could she dare to express the powerful emotions in her heart? "I never want this night to end."

"Nor do I."

He pulled her close in another deep kiss that erased all of her inhibitions. There was something incredibly erotic in the feel of his clothing against her bare skin, as if every part of her had become infinitely sensitive and receptive to his touch.

His hands spanned her waist, and he walked her backward toward the bed. Once there, he pressed her down until Portia found herself sitting on the mattress. When she made a move to scoot farther onto the bed, to give him room to join her, Ratcliffe held her in place, positioning her arms behind her.

"Lean back," he said huskily. "Let me look at you."

She did as he instructed, propping herself back on her hands. It felt utterly decadent to perch on the edge of the bed without the means to cover her breasts. Under his dark, hooded gaze, she felt like a gift for his pleasure— and her own. The heat he roused in her had become a molten pool of longing, and she didn't know how much more of this torment she could bear.

He knelt before her and ran his hands lightly over her feet and ankles, caressing an upward path over her calves and knees. The fire burned hotter, and she held her breath in fevered anticipation. To her frustration, he skimmed past the juncture of her thighs and continued upward to circle her breasts, lightly plying the tips. Leaning closer, he suckled her, first one side and then the other. She moaned, loving what he was doing yet aching for him to shift his attention lower. How many times had she relived that rapturous moment in her memory, how many times had she longed to experience it again?

"Ratcliffe . . ."

She reached for him, but he backed off, shaking his head. "Not yet," he said hoarsely. "I'm far from through with you."

"Please . . . I want . . ." She bit her lip, bound by lady-like strictures from giving voice to her indecent desires.

"You want this."

His warm palm slid downward over her flat belly, then at last his forefinger slid into her moist center. A pulse of pleasure rolled through her, causing her hips to move of their own volition. "Yes . . . oh, yes . . ."

Tilting her head back, she parted her legs to welcome the indulgence of his caress. He stroked her with a thoroughness that brought all of her senses to vivid life. Everything in her became fixated on the demands of her most feminine part. As the sensations grew more torturous, she found herself panting, begging, melting bonelessly back onto the bed.

All at once, he removed his hand, and when she would have protested, he bent his dark head to her privates. The shock of his action wrested a gasp from her. But at the first swirling lick of his tongue, all of her objections fell away in a swift descent into madness. She felt immersed in a delight so scandalous it took her breath away, sending her on a headlong plunge into waves of bliss.

As the rapture gradually faded, leaving her limp and happy, she returned to the awareness that Ratcliffe stood beside the bed, wrestling with the cuff link on one of his sleeves. From his glowering expression, it occurred to her that his needs had yet to be satisfied.

Blushing at her own selfishness, she said, "May I help?"

"The cursed thing is stuck."

"Let me see."

He held out his arm, and she quickly worked the silver link loose from its mooring. She made short work of the one on his other sleeve, then helped him push off the shirt. As he tossed it to the floor, Portia slid her palms up the hard planes of his chest, marveling at the strength of his muscles, the breadth of his shoulders, the tapering perfection of his torso. It wasn't so uncommon to see a shirtless man in India, but none of them had ever moved her to awe as Ratcliffe did. His skin was taut and sprinkled with dark hair that arrowed downward into the waistband of his breeches.

Dear heaven, she couldn't bring herself to look lower.

With a quivery sigh, Portia glanced up only to find him staring down at her, his eyes dark and rich with promise. Taking hold of her hands, he placed them on the placket of his breeches. "I'll need your assistance here, as well."

After a moment's hesitation, she applied herself to the task of opening each button. The telltale bulge there made her breath catch, and her fingers became clumsy, brushing against him more than once.

He made a tortured sound in his chest. Pushing her hands aside, he freed himself from the confinement of cloth, giving Portia her first view of a man in full arousal. The sight filled her with mingled awe and alarm, for it seemed impossible that they could ever be joined.

"Touch me."

His rasping command sounded torn from him. He wrapped her fingers around him, and she marveled at the velvety hardness of his flesh. As she explored him, the muscles in his groin contracted. On a daring impulse, she leaned closer and kissed him as he had kissed her. Groaning, he tangled his hands into her hair in wordless encouragement. His unashamed pleasure gratified her, stirring the rise of her own passion again as well.

"Enough."

Abruptly, he caught hold of her and pressed her down onto the bed, covering her with his body. A tremor coursed through his powerful form and he looked deeply in her eyes. "My God," he murmured in a reverent tone. "What you do to me . . ."

The hunger in his voice inspired a tremendous rush of sentiment in her, and she tenderly ran her fingertips over his face. "My dearest Ratcliffe . . ."

Their mouths melded again with a wild urgency, so full of feeling she wanted to weep from the joy of it. Nothing had ever felt so right as his weight upon her. He sipped from her lips, then his mouth trailed down to the hollow of her throat and to her breasts. Desire kindled in her, much richer and deeper this time, for the closeness of their bodies gave the moment an even greater significance. She was keenly aware of him, hard and hot against her thigh, and then he was parting her legs, pushing inside of her. The sting of his entry caught her by surprise, and when she gasped, he soothed her with a swift conciliatory kiss.

"Forgive me. Are you . . . in pain?"

His intense gaze searched hers. He was breathing hard, holding himself very still. The discomfort melted into a glorious sense of fullness, and she arched her hips, the better to feel him. "Oh . . . it's *heaven*."

The light of passion flared in his eyes, and he began to move inside of her, each plunge delivering a bolt of pleasure to her senses. She wrapped her arms and legs around him in an effort to bring him ever closer. Hearts beating as one, they found a shared rhythm that carried them deeper and deeper into the frantic throes of passion.

With exquisite control, he whispered encouragements

in her ear, kissing her until a liquid heat suffused her entire body. The rising tension took her on a wild ride to the pinnacle. Only as she shuddered and cried out in the maelstrom of release did he join her there, groaning her name on one final thrust.

They clung to each other in the aftermath, drawing in long gasps of air. As her wildly hammering heartbeat returned to normal, Portia floated in a haze of pure happiness. After a time, he shifted position so that they lay side by side. He gathered her close and kissed her brow while she settled her head onto the hard pillow of his shoulder.

Snuggling closer, she sighed. "I never knew . . . never *dreamed* . . . how wonderful it would be. Is it always like that?"

"It is with you."

Colin knew the answer was inadequate. The trouble was, he couldn't quite express in words the magnitude of what they had just shared because it had knocked him off kilter. He'd had more than his fair share of trysts with loose women. His bodily appetites had been slaked many times over the years. But now, those episodes paled in comparison to his union with Portia—because he had never before realized the difference between mere coupling and making love.

It was a stunning revelation for a man of nine-and-twenty to make. Especially one who had prided himself on his sexual prowess.

He held Portia close, marveling at the perfect peace he felt in her arms. She had a wit that made him laugh, a spirit that kept him on his toes, and a strength that both frustrated and fascinated him. If truth be told, he didn't ever want to move from this spot beside her. They could carry him away in a casket fifty years from now, and he would have died a happy man.

Portia was idly exploring his torso as if to acquaint herself with every aspect of his body. Her fingers met the scar on his upper arm where she had shot him. Uttering a mournful cry, she lifted herself up to lean over and plant a soft kiss there. "I'd forgotten all about this. I could have killed you!"

At her stricken expression, he tried not to grin. "I'm glad you've finally realized that."

"Oh, do stop. You *know* I never meant for that pistol to go off."

"I don't know any such thing. At the time, you held me in utter contempt."

Did she still? Her indictment against him just that morning had been scathing. In her view, he was nothing more than a rake and a scapegrace, and to a degree, she was right. He had sown his wild oats for a long time, so why *should* she believe him when he said he was ready to set down roots?

Her lips curved in a come-hither smile. She draped herself over him, her legs entwining with his. "I confess, my contempt was merely a mask. Even back then, I was desperate to hide my desire for you, my lord."

He sucked in a breath. It was too soon, all of his strength had been drained, yet he felt an undeniable stirring in his loins. "Indeed?"

"Yes. From the moment we met, I've wanted you." She moved her hips lightly against him. "Oh, Ratcliffe, for so long I've been yearning to be with you like this."

His chest contracted. He'd fantasized for weeks about hearing her say just that. But now it wasn't enough, damn it. He wanted her to say she'd been pining in love with him. Because *he* had been pining. It was a shock to face that truth: He was in love with Portia.

Hopelessly, madly, completely in love with the one

woman who, in her own words, refused to be bullied into marriage.

Hiding his quandary, he pressed a kiss to her brow. "It's about time you addressed me by my given name."

"Colin . . . but do you really mind Ratcliffe so very much?" Her hand crept downward, exploring him with bold curiosity. "I've grown rather fond of the name."

He released a groan. "You can call me Robin Hood or even Maid Marian so long as you keep touching me like that."

Her smile was that of a siren who has just learned the extent of her powers. "Does that mean we can do it again?"

"As often as you like."

He cradled her face in his hands and kissed her long and deep. Then he devoted himself to teaching her all the myriad ways they could arouse each other. It resulted in an orgy of pleasure that left them both blissfully exhausted.

Much later, the fire on the hearth had died down, and she lay sleeping in his arms. Colin stared into the darkness and wondered if she'd considered the possible consequences of their lovemaking. He had always taken care not to sire any offspring. His women had all had their tricks for avoiding pregnancy. But Portia had taken no such precautions. And when he thought of her growing large with his child, a primal ache gripped his gut. By God, he would never allow his son or daughter to grow up without him as a father.

He almost hoped she had conceived because then she would have to wed him, whether she liked it or not. Let her put that damned dowry in trust for their children, for all he cared. It had been nothing but a thorn in his side, and somehow he would find a way to shore up his finances without it.

Now that he'd made the decision, he couldn't wait to tell her. Yet he had to wait.

Peering down at her through the shadows, he felt shaken by a powerful surge of love. Not for the world would he disturb her much-needed rest. They could talk in the morning, and maybe, after the spectacular night they'd shared, she would finally see the advantages of marrying him.

On that hopeful thought, he closed his eyes and slipped into a deep slumber. But when he awakened after dawn, she was gone.

CHAPTER 23

Portia unlatched the front door and slipped out of the house. It was early, so there were no servants about yet, except perhaps in the kitchen. She might have been the only person in the world.

Pausing on the porch, she took a deep breath of brisk morning air. The stone column felt cool to her bare fingertips. She had been in such a dreamlike state while dressing that she had forgotten her gloves. It was a wonder she'd remembered to don shoes and stockings.

After descending the short flight of steps, she followed the curve of the drive until it disappeared around a bend near a stand of willow trees. There she stood looking over the hilly landscape. A flock of starlings swooped and swirled against a blue sky dotted with fluffy white clouds. Only a few sounds disturbed the silence: the twittering of a bird, the baaing of a sheep somewhere in the distance, the whisper of the breeze through the leaves.

The peaceful setting served as a reminder that all was right with the world. Nothing had changed but herself.

A short while ago, she had awakened in Ratcliffe's bed. Cloaked in shadow, he had been sprawled on his back sound asleep, his arm thrown over his head. The sight of his nude body had riveted her. How she had wanted to kiss him, to enjoy the pleasure of his embrace one more time. But after driving the coach all night on their journey here, he needed his sleep. And she dared not dally past dawn for fear a servant might discover them in bed together.

The very thought made her blush. In the light of day, it was a bit shocking to face the fact that she had willingly offered herself to a man. And not just any man, but the notorious Lord Ratcliffe.

Yet how very different he was from the scandalous rogue he presented to the world. The snobs of society couldn't guess—nor would they have cared—that he had gone out of his way to help Bane and Hannah and other servants. Or that he had such a keen interest in the care and cultivation of his land.

And the most amazing secret of all was that he possessed the principles of a true gentleman. He would not have forced her into his bed—even though he'd had her at his mercy. Thank heavens she'd mustered the courage to approach him, for otherwise their marvelous night together would never have happened.

And she would not have been forever transformed.

The difference in her went far beyond the physical loss of her innocence. To be sure, a slight soreness lingered and her reputation lay in tatters. Yet in her heart, she had gained so very much. Intimacy with Ratcliffe had left her feeling enriched and blessed, as if her eyes had been opened and her childhood left behind. Now she could see clearly that her feelings for Arun had been the infatuation of a young girl. At last she had learned the difference between mere affection and womanly love.

Ratcliffe would be the perfect husband, the man of her dreams—if only he could curb his profligate nature.

She kicked a piece of gravel with her toe, sending it

sailing into the underbrush. Curse him for romancing so many women. And curse him twice for being a gambler!

Her arms swinging, Portia continued down the drive. Her burst of anger died a quick death as another thought occurred to her. Perhaps she should be praising his flaws, not denouncing them. Because if he hadn't had those weaknesses, in all likelihood he would have already settled down and married another woman. And he wouldn't have been in need of funds. Which meant he wouldn't have approached Portia with the intention of gaining her dowry.

She laughed aloud at her convoluted reasoning. No, she wouldn't waste time wishing Ratcliffe's past could be changed. Rather, she should concentrate on the goodness in him, the true character that few people bothered to see. If he could be persuaded to stay out of London and away from the gaming tables, then perhaps he could mend his wicked ways.

Who better than a wife to hold him close and encourage him?

Portia came to a complete stop in the middle of the drive. Drawing a shaky breath, she found herself enthralled by the notion of devoting the rest of her life to him. How wonderful it would be to live here in the country, to raise a family, to grow old together.

To have every night be as superb as the one they had just shared.

Desire began a slow burn inside her. Ratcliffe hadn't spoken words of love, she reminded herself. But he had held her in a cherishing manner, whispering endearments in her ears. If only they could nurture their closeness, perhaps love would soon follow. She had to at least give him that chance.

Without conscious thought, she found herself turning

back toward the house, a lightness in her steps. How foolish she had been to leave Ratcliffe's bed. Every moment with him was a precious gift that must not be squandered. If her father had gone off to Scotland yesterday, then it might be several more days before he found her here. In the meantime, she and Ratcliffe could be together. She wanted to know about every aspect of his life, to see the estate, to wander through his house, arm in arm.

Did couples make love in the middle of the day? What was to stop them from stealing into a deserted room, locking the door, and engaging in a clandestine bout of pleasure? *Oh, heaven.* She would have to raise that wicked notion with Ratcliffe at the first opportunity.

The distant sound of an approaching carriage shattered her fantasy. The quiet was broken by the clatter of wheels and the thudding of horse hooves. Curious, she glanced over her shoulder, but the trees masked the oncoming visitor from view. It was too early for any of the local gentry to call, unless there was some sort of an emergency.

Or . . . what if it was her father? What if he hadn't fallen for the ruse, after all?

A sudden chill made her shiver. *No.* She mustn't let herself panic. It was more likely an acquaintance of Ratcliffe's, someone who had found out about his arrival yesterday.

Nevertheless, Portia picked up her skirts and darted toward the house. It wouldn't do for her to be seen here, not even by a neighbor. Sticky questions would arise as to why a lady was staying under Ratcliffe's roof without the benefit of a chaperone. And unfortunately, there was nowhere to hide out here on the wide graveled drive. The house was as close as the nearest concealment of trees.

She stumbled over a rut in the road and nearly fell. Catching her balance, she hastened toward the front porch without looking back again. She was almost there when a fine black coach drew up alongside her.

A liveried coachman sat atop the high seat. Her gaze flashed to the silver insignia on the door.

Her steps faltered to a stop. The world seemed to tilt on its axis. Her heart thumped so hard it nearly made her swoon. Uttering a cry of denial, she made a mad dash for the stairs.

A commotion came from behind her, running footsteps. A hand clamped around her upper arm and yanked her to an enforced halt. Turning, she found herself gazing into a familiar stern face. His aristocratic features filled her with revulsion.

The Duke of Albright.

He leaned on his silver-topped walking stick, his pale blue eyes raking her with contempt. "So you *are* here, just as I suspected," he snapped without greeting. "Where is Ratcliffe?"

Not for the world would she betray him. "He's gone. He's out riding. I'm all alone." She struggled futilely against his iron grip. "Now unhand me at once."

A stout man hurried up behind him.

"Papa!" she cried.

Her father appeared haggard, with deep lines in his face, his thinning brown hair rumpled as if he'd combed his fingers through it innumerable times. He embraced her briefly, then stepped back to look her over as if checking for injury. Tears brimmed in his eyes. "Thank God! Oh, thank God you're safe."

"Please tell the duke to release me. He has no right to hold me like . . . like a criminal."

George Crompton glanced at Albright, then slowly

shook his head. "I'm afraid we daren't trust you, darling. You might run back to that scoundrel. We're here to escort you home."

Run back? Did they think she had come here willingly with him? Of course, that letter Ratcliffe had written to her father claimed they were eloping to Gretna Green. Her mind worked feverishly. She mustn't reveal the truth. If they knew Ratcliffe had abducted her, it would only give them further grievance against him.

"Let's get her into the coach," Albright instructed her father. "The sooner we're away from here, the better."

"You take her," her father said, grimly removing his coat and rolling up his sleeves. "I intend to find Lord Ratcliffe and teach him not to touch my daughter."

"No!" Portia cried out. Nothing could be worse than the two men she loved battling each other. For that matter, she feared Ratcliffe would be too honorable to defend himself. "You mustn't! I won't have you fighting."

"Nor will I," said the duke. "I intend to take care of Ratcliffe myself later."

Scowling, George Crompton flexed his fists. "It's my responsibility and I won't shirk it."

Desperate to ward off violence, she said urgently, "Please, Papa, I won't get into the coach without you, I swear I won't. If you truly wish me to go home, you'll have to come right now, too."

Agony tore at her heart. The last thing she wanted was to leave here. But what else was she to do? How was she to escape the inevitable? By fleeing upstairs, by seeking Ratcliffe's help, she would be endangering him, as well.

Her father released a furious breath. "As you wish, then. I'll leave this rat's nest for now."

Guided by the duke, Portia moved on leaden feet. Every step felt as if she were progressing toward the galows. All of her hopes and dreams had been shattered to bits. Her happiness of only moments ago had turned into a nightmare. She wanted to cry and rail and fight, yet she dared not.

"What the devil—Portia!"

The sound of Ratcliffe's voice made her heart leap. She whirled around to see him standing in the open doorway of the house, wearing only a shirt and breeches.

Fury hardened his face. He came charging down the steps of the porch, and her heart leaped with joy.

And in the next moment, with terror.

Releasing her, Albright used both hands to grip his walking stick like a cudgel. He kept the weapon hidden behind her skirts so Ratcliffe wouldn't see it.

Realizing his intent, she moved to shove him off balance.

Too late.

The duke surged forward and swung the cane. The silver knob struck the side of Ratcliffe's head.

Ratcliffe staggered backward, then dropped like a stone.

She was smuggled into the house through the mews.

The coach had been driven straight into the stables. To thwart any nosy neighbors, her father wrapped a cloak around Portia, pulling up the hood and instructing her to keep her face down while they walked through the garden. The duke followed close behind as they went up a back staircase to the morning room, where her mother and sisters were waiting.

Lindsey and Blythe fell upon Portia with glad cries, hugging and kissing her. She craved their comfort, but they were swiftly shooed away by their mother. "Run along, girls. You've seen her now, and you'll have a chance to visit later."

With much grumbling complaints, they trudged out of the room. George Crompton shut the door after them, then went to pour two cups of coffee from the silver pot on the sideboard, respectfully offering one to the duke.

Edith Crompton embraced her eldest daughter, enveloping her in the scent of lilac. Portia clung to her, wanting to weep, but she had no tears left, not after the buckets she had shed on the long drive home.

How she ached to pour out her fears to Mama. What had happened to Ratcliffe? How badly had he been injured?

But her mother wouldn't offer sympathy. Her father hadn't understood, either, when Portia had begged him to turn back so she could check on Ratcliffe. Instead, he and the duke had each guarded a door of the coach. She had been their prisoner, and for that cruelty she would never forgive her father.

When her mother pulled back, any happiness she might have felt at Portia's safe return had vanished. Her lips were pinched and censure narrowed her hazel eyes. "Well! We have been worried to the point of illness. What have you to say for yourself?"

"I'm sorry, Mama."

Portia spoke by rote without really meaning the words. She felt drained and empty, unable to fight any longer. She sank wearily into the nearest chair, propping her elbow on the arm. All she wanted was to retreat to her chamber.

No! All she wanted was Ratcliffe. She needed him desperately. Dear God, was he dead?

Her mind rejected the horror of that possibility. It couldn't be true. It had only been a knock on the head, and surely he would recover. Yet over and over, she found herself reliving the moment of seeing him fall, trying to discern if he'd been dealt a mortal blow.

"We cannot thank you enough, Your Grace," Mrs. Crompton said, curtsying to the duke. "To have offered your assistance so swiftly, and under such horrendous circumstances . . . we will remain forever in your debt."

"I must concur," Mr. Crompton added, placing an arm around his wife. "I would never have found Portia so swiftly without your aid. We owe you our undying gratitude."

Mrs. Crompton pressed her palms together in supplication. "And may I add, we implore you not to think too poorly of our wayward daughter. She knew not what she was doing, to put herself into the company of that vile rascal."

Leaning on his silver-topped cane, Albright regarded them gravely. He looked as dapper as ever in his charcoal-gray coat, the ubiquitous diamond stickpin in his cravat. His composed appearance betrayed no hint of remorse that he might have just murdered a man.

"It certainly has been a regrettable turn of events," he stated. "However, I must take a portion of the guilt upon myself. I knew the sort of scoundrel Ratcliffe was, and I should have guarded Portia against his villainy."

How smooth he was, how oily and snakelike, Portia thought scornfully. She angled her head away, staring at a blue porcelain vase of yellow roses. The sight of him sickened her. She just wanted him to go away. Then she would never have to see his loathsome face again.

"You are indeed the soul of kindness," her mother gushed. "How can we ever repay you?"

"It was no great deed on my part," the duke replied. "After all, I've a duty to protect her good name since she is to be my wife."

That last statement penetrated the lethargy that weighed on Portia. Turning back, she stared at him in utter shock.

What was he saying? That her ruination didn't matter to him? That he was not ending their betrothal?

"I'm sure you'll agree to the necessity of my leaving at once to obtain a special license," he went on to her parents. "In light of this scandal, the marriage must be performed as swiftly as possible. Then my stature will silence all the gossips."

Her mother clasped her hands to her bosom. "Oh, Your Grace, you are indeed a knight in shining armor. It is so magnanimous of you to—"

"No!" Portia surged to her feet. The others turned to stare at her. On the long ride home, she had attempted to denounce the duke, but her father had sternly ordered her to be quiet. So she had spent the time fuming in silence, and now all of her bottled-up anger broke free of restraint.

She stepped rapidly toward her mother. "I won't marry him. Not now or ever. Mama, he hit Ratcliffe on the head with his cane. It was a coward's blow, too. He hid his weapon behind my skirts until Ratcliffe came close enough to strike." Her voice broke, but she forced herself to go on. "He might have killed Ratcliffe. Then they pushed me into the coach without even checking to see if he was alive . . ."

"Is this true?" Mrs. Crompton asked, frowning from the duke to her husband.

"Indeed so," Mr. Crompton said grimly. "However, His Grace had little choice in the matter. The viscount was running straight toward us. God knows, the churl might have seized Portia and done harm to her."

"He most certainly would not have," Portia flared. "It was the duke he was going after. The two of them have been enemies for years. His Grace has never forgiven Lady Ratcliffe for spurning him at the altar."

Albright's face turned rigid, but he said nothing.

"Well!" Mrs. Crompton declared. "I'm sure if Lord Ratcliffe is dead, he deserved it for his contemptible actions. Perhaps he has finally received his just due for killing his own father."

"He didn't kill his father. He was exonerated in court. And it's the duke who deserves your contempt." She swung toward Albright. "Tell them, Your Grace. Tell them how you fathered Hannah Wilton's baby and then tossed her out into the street. You also threatened to kill her if she tried to expose you as a cad."

The duke neither denied or confirmed it. His face might have been carved from marble. His stony silence confirmed his perfidy.

Her father shot a frown at Albright. "What's this all about?"

"Hannah Wilton?" Mrs. Crompton asked in bewilderment. "Who in heaven's name is she?"

"His former mistress," Portia said. "And he stole her away from Ratcliffe, as well."

With a gasp, Mrs. Crompton came bustling toward her. "That's quite enough, young lady. I'm astonished at you, making such sordid accusations when the duke has been your savior today. You should not even know of such matters, let alone speak of them."

"It's all true. And I won't have such a cruel, heartless man for a husband. It's Ratcliffe I intend to wed." She held back a sob. *If* he was alive. *If* he still wanted her after all the trouble she'd brought down on him. *If* he loved her . . .

Her mother caught Portia by the arm. "Silence! You will not say another word!"

"Nor will I speak my vows to the duke, Mama. And there's nothing you can do to force me."

"Hush! You *will* show His Grace the proper respect." An angry red flush crept up her neck and into her cheeks.

She glanced wildly at Albright, then at her husband. "George! Will you allow her to be so insolent? Come here and chastise your daughter at once."

Mr. Crompton looked rather troubled. He trudged forward to stand in front of Portia. But any hope she might have had for his support ended when he spoke.

"Go to your chamber, child," he said heavily. "You'll stay there until you've realized the value of obedience."

CHAPTER 24

Portia couldn't sit still. For the umpteenth time, she went to the window and surveyed the darkened garden. Lights winked in neighboring residences. By looking down, she could see a faint glow from the windows of her own house, too.

Every few minutes, she glanced at the ormolu clock on the fireplace mantel. It was past nine o'clock. The gold hands had been creeping around the dial at an agonizingly slow pace.

Two hours had passed since Kasi had delivered a supper tray, along with the whispered news that Portia's parents had remained in the house for the evening, rather than attend any social events. The old *ayah* had provided sympathy and a shoulder on which to cry, but little more.

James, a young, freckle-faced footman, had stood waiting in the doorway for the servant. Portia had pleaded with him to summon her sisters, but he had refused, citing strict orders from her parents. Once he and Kasi left, he had locked the door again. When Portia knelt down and peered through the keyhole, she could glimpse him standing guard out in the corridor.

Little did her jailers realize, however, there was a crack in their defenses. The door to the balcony had not been secured. If Ratcliffe had once managed to climb down the rose trellis, then by heaven so could she.

But it was too early to make her move yet. She didn't dare risk being spotted by a servant or a neighbor or one of her parents. As nerve-racking as it might be, Portia had decided to wait until after midnight to make her escape.

Meanwhile, she had been roaming aimlessly through her bedchamber. Now, she went to the bedside table, opened the bottom drawer, and found the oval miniature that lay hidden beneath some books and papers.

A lump in her throat, she gazed down at the image of Ratcliffe. Her fingers moved lovingly over the tiny painting. He had been depicted at a younger age, his face not yet marked by maturity. But that devilish glint in his eyes brought a smile to her lips.

He had placed his image over Arun's, and she had left it there. It seemed the appropriate thing to do. After all, Arun was her past, Ratcliffe would be her future.

Or at least she prayed so.

Holding the miniature to her breast, Portia recalled the night when she had come out of her dressing room to see Ratcliffe lounging in the chair by the fire. How cocky he had been, how very handsome and charming. He had brought her a stem of orchid blossoms. At the time, she hadn't realized the unique quality of his gift. Who would have thought he had collected the plant himself in the jungles of India, brought it back to England, and coaxed it into bloom in his own conservatory? Back then, there had been so many things about him that she hadn't known, so much about his capacity for compassion and tenderness.

Her body still ached pleasantly from the residual effects of their night together. Only twenty-four hours ago, she had been in his arms, rejoicing in the warmth of his embrace and the passion of his kisses. The closeness they had shared had brought her a greater happiness than she had ever dreamed possible. Then in one felling blow, it had ended.

Dear God, where was Ratcliffe at this moment? Lying unconscious in his bed—or dead?

Shuddering, Portia ordered herself not to assume the worst. He would recover, he *must* recover. And in the meantime, she intended to find her way back to his estate, by mail coach or hired carriage.

She went into the dressing room and added the miniature to the small bundle of her belongings. It contained a change of clothing, the meager amount of money she could find, and several small pieces of jewelry to use for barter. The rest of her things were just that—things. She would suffer no qualms about leaving behind a wardrobe full of fancy ball gowns and other costly personal items. None of it mattered to her anymore, not if it came at the expense of love.

Her thoughts ranged back to Ratcliffe's manor house. What must the servants think of her abrupt disappearance? And what about Bane? How frightened he must have been to see Ratcliffe injured. Hopefully, Thurgood had taken the boy under his wing and soothed his distress.

The sound of voices came from out in the corridor. Hurrying to the door, she bent down to listen through the keyhole. That feminine tone had to belong to Blythe. She was talking excitedly to James, although Portia couldn't quite make out their words.

Then all fell silent again. No key rattled in the lock. James must have refused her entry.

Discouraged, Portia prowled back and forth in front of her bed. How she would have loved to have seen her sister! Although Blythe was a flighty fifteen-year-old, at least she would have offered a friendly listening ear so that Portia would not feel so all alone. And Portia would have had the chance to hug her sister good-bye.

Her heart ached. Mama and Papa surely would denounce her for fleeing to Ratcliffe. It might be weeks, even months, before she could see her sisters again. She only hoped that her parents would eventually realize the value of welcoming Ratcliffe as her husband. Despite his shady reputation, he was a peer, after all. And perhaps his mother would assist in smoothing things over with society . . .

Another noise outside in the corridor caught her attention. She spun around, staring. Was it Blythe again? Had she succeeded in persuading James, after all?

The door opened, and to Portia's surprise, Lindsey slipped into the bedchamber. Her chestnut hair hung in a long braid down her back. Clad in a dark blue night robe, her sister scanned the corridor one last time before closing the door.

Portia hastened to give her a quick, heartfelt embrace. "What are you doing here? James said he had orders not to let you or Blythe into my room."

Lindsey's blue eyes danced with mischief. "I borrowed the master key from Papa's desk. As for James, well, Blythe asked him to hurry and catch a mouse that's running loose in her chamber. Which should take him quite a while since the mouse doesn't exist!"

Portia laughed. "How clever of her—of you both."

"Surely you didn't think we'd forgotten you, I hope." Grabbing Portia's hand, she led her to a chair by the fire, then perched on a nearby footstool. "Now tell me all that's happened. Lord Ratcliffe abducted you, didn't he? Mama was afraid you'd run away with him of your own accord, but I knew that couldn't possibly be true."

"Yes, he did induce me to go with him." Biting her

lip, Portia glanced at the door. If James wasn't standing on guard, then maybe she should leave right now. Except for the fact that her parents might catch her in the act . . .

She returned her attention to her sister. "You mustn't think ill of Ratcliffe. There's so much you don't know about him. It's a long story, but suffice it to say, my feelings toward him have utterly changed. I'm in love with him now and I'm determined to marry him."

Lindsey recoiled. "What do you mean? He's a rake and a gambler."

"He's so much more than just that. Oh, Linds, he's truly a wonderful man." Quickly, she outlined his kindness toward his servants, his keen interest in horticulture, and his refusal to seduce her—without mentioning that she herself had taken the first step. Their night together was a precious secret that belonged to no one else but her and Ratcliffe. "Then this morning . . . it was so dreadful. I was out for a walk when Papa and the duke arrived to bring me home. When Ratcliffe tried to stop them, the duke knocked him over the head with his walking stick. Ratcliffe fell down . . . and . . . oh, dear God, I don't know what's happened to him."

The despair in her overflowed, and she buried her face in her hands.

Lindsey rubbed a soothing hand over Portia's back. "I never did like that prissy old duke," she declared. "When you seemed to favor the match, well, I didn't want to disparage him too much. But I always suspected there was something sneaky about him. In truth, it's no wonder . . ."

Portia lifted her head. "Yes?"

"It's no wonder you prefer Lord Ratcliffe. I'll concede, he *is* exceedingly handsome."

From the way her sister avoided her gaze, Portia had the feeling that wasn't what she had meant to say. "Please, at least give him a chance. Do try to see there's more to him than meets the eye."

"I'm trying, truly I am." Frowning, Lindsey gripped Portia's hands. "Are you certain, absolutely certain, that he'll make you a good husband?"

"Yes. And I've already thought things through. If I can convince him to live on his estate and avoid the city, he won't have much opportunity to gamble."

"I hope you're right."

"I know I'm right." Portia drew a shaky breath. She didn't want to admit aloud that Ratcliffe had yet to declare his love for her. Did he want to wed her for herself or for her dowry? She desperately needed to find out the truth. "I'm leaving tonight, Linds. I have to make certain he's well. Somehow I must find a way to return to his estate in Kent."

Lindsey sprang to her feet. Seizing the fireplace poker, she stirred the burning coals in the hearth. Then she swung back to face Portia. "There's something you should know. It's the real reason I came in here to see you."

An ominous quality to her tone lifted the fine hairs at the back of Portia's neck. "Tell me."

"A little while ago, Mama and Papa were talking in his study. They didn't know I was out in the corridor, listening." She sat down again and took Portia's hands in hers. "You'll be happy to know your beloved Ratcliffe is very much alive. He's come back to London. But . . . he's challenged the Duke of Albright to a duel."

Peering out the window of the hackney cab, Portia watched as the pitch blackness of night lightened to indigo. Veins of pink and orange slowly appeared in the deep blue depths of the sky. She gripped her gloved fingers, her every nerve strung as taut as a bow.

The duel was to take place at dawn. Would she reach Hampstead Heath in time to stop the madness?

Nothing thus far had gone her way. First, she'd had the very devil of a time convincing Lindsey to return to her chamber and leave matters to Portia. Then, upon tiptoeing out on her balcony just after midnight, she had been dismayed to hear the low drone of her parents' voices in the room below hers. She'd been forced to cool her heels and wait.

It had been past two by the time they'd gone to bed and she could climb down the rose trellis to freedom. Then she had walked—or rather, run—the long blocks to Ratcliffe's town house on the outskirts of Mayfair. She had banged on the door for what seemed like hours before finally awakening Hannah Wilton. To Portia's consternation, Ratcliffe and Orson Tudge had already set out for Hampstead Heath, a location north of the city favored by duelers since such matches were prohibited.

It had taken another precious half an hour to locate a cabbie who was willing to drive the long distance in the middle of the night. Unluckily, though, the cab was drawn by the slowest nag in all of London. Which was why Portia sat on the edge of her seat as the cramped houses of the city gave way to open land and small hamlets nestled in misty valleys.

Ratcliffe had survived the duke's attack, praise God. She wanted urgently to see him, to convince him not to risk his life. Closing her eyes, she whispered a frantic prayer that she would not be too late.

At last the cab jerked to a stop on the edge of a clearing. Scrambling out, she spied a copse of trees straight ahead where several carriages were parked, one group on one side, another group on the other. Portia tossed a few coins to the driver and bade him wait. Picking up her skirts, she darted across the dewy grass to join the small party of people. The stout man in the black top hat was clearly a doctor, judging by the brown satchel he held.

The dim morning light shone on the silvering hair of the duke. He was approached by a youngish man who looked vaguely familiar, his broad form clad in a leaf-green coat and buff breeches. She recognized him as the Earl of Turnbuckle, a friend of Ratcliffe's.

Turnbuckle held out an open case from which Albright removed a long-barreled pistol. Then the earl returned to the other party, half hidden by several carriages. As he did so, another man stepped into view and her heart leaped in wild joy.

Ratcliffe.

Slowing to a walk, she drank in the sight of him. In a dark blue coat, buckskins, and knee-high boots, he looked ready for a morning ride in the park rather than a duel to the death. His attention was on the case that Turnbuckle proffered to him. Her happiness turned to revulsion as Ratcliffe took out the second pistol, pointed it away into the trees, and sighted down the long barrel.

She closed the distance between them—and received a jolt of surprise. Lady Ratcliffe came out from behind the screen of carriages and touched his arm, saying something to him. He gave a sharp, impatient shake of his head and strode away from her. His mother stood there, a slim tragic figure wrapped in a sea-foam-green cloak, the hood down to reveal her swanlike neck.

He headed toward a flat area of ground a short distance away. So did Albright.

Portia hastened to the carriages. "Ratcliffe, no!"

He spun around on his heel and stared at her. His steely glare pierced her. He voiced no greeting, his face betraying no sign of pleasure at her presence, no trace of the tender lover who had awakened all of her hopes and dreams. If anything, he appeared irked by her sudden appearance.

Under the close watch of their seconds—Turnbuckle for Ratcliffe, and an unknown gentleman for the duke— the two duelers stood back to back and then counted off ten paces apiece.

Lady Ratcliffe hastened to Portia. "Colin mustn't do this!" she said frantically. "He'll die and it will be all my fault!"

With that, she ran to the duke and seized hold of his arm. "Please don't punish my son. I'll pay the money back to you somehow, just as I did last time. I should never have gambled with you in the first place."

Portia had stepped forward, but the comment confused her for an instant. Lady Ratcliffe was a gambler? She owed money to Albright?

The duke shook her off so hard she stumbled backward. His second took hold of Lady Ratcliffe and guided her back to Portia.

The men had achieved their ten paces. They turned. The Earl of Turnbuckle stood nearby, ready to drop the white handkerchief as a signal to fire.

With a strangled cry, Portia dashed in between Albright and Ratcliffe. "Stop this nonsense at once. I won't allow it."

Ratcliffe stood with his dueling pistol pointed to the ground. His face grim, he said nothing, only nodded to Orson Tudge. At once, the beefy man marched forward to pull her off the field. She struggled to free herself, but it was like wrestling with a tree trunk.

"Ratcliffe, listen to me! This isn't necessary. I've ended my betrothal to the duke. I intend to marry *you*."

Ratcliffe had been watching the duke. But now his gaze flashed to her and at last she glimpsed a flare of intense emotion in him. In the same instant, she caught a movement out of the corner of her eye. Taking advantage of Ratcliffe's distraction, the duke was raising his arm to fire.

"No—" she screamed in warning.

Too late.

Two shots shattered the air. The duke's went off wildly, and he stumbled backward, clutching his chest. Blood bloomed on his pearl-gray coat as he fell awkwardly to the ground.

CHAPTER 25

A short distance away, Lady Ratcliffe stood frozen with her arm extended, a small pistol glinting in the early morning light. A sob escaped her, and she swayed on her feet.

Ratcliffe and the other men rushed to the duke. The doctor knelt beside him to assess the wound.

Gripped by horror, Portia sprang to Lady Ratcliffe and slid an arm around her to keep her from falling. The older woman dropped the spent pistol and clung to Portia, tremors rippling through her slender form.

While murmuring soothing words to Lady Ratcliffe, Portia watched in disbelief as the doctor shook his head and closed the duke's eyes. He was dead? Her mind resisted the truth of it.

In a daze, she drew Lady Ratcliffe away. The woman was weeping uncontrollably, and it would only be worse if she lingered near the body.

"Which is your carriage?" she asked.

For a moment, Lady Ratcliffe stared dully at her, her green eyes misted with tears. Then she pointed. "The last one."

Portia took her there and helped her inside while the coachman held the door. Unwilling to leave the distraught woman alone, she seated herself beside Lady Ratcliffe and offered her a folded handkerchief.

"Here, my lady. Dry your tears."

"It's all my fault. What have I done? Oh, what have I done?"

"You did what was necessary. The duke attempted an act of treachery. If not for you, he would have shot your son." The notion of what might have happened to Ratcliffe made Portia shiver. How close he had come to being the one lying cold on the ground!

Lady Ratcliffe wiped her eyes, then twisted the handkerchief between her fingers. As if speaking to herself, she whispered, "I should have known better than to let Albright draw me into that card game. If I hadn't owed him so much money . . ."

Gambling. She had been gambling with the duke.

Reminded of what Lady Ratcliffe had said in an attempt to stop the duel, Portia was appalled. Why would the viscountess be so foolish as to gamble with a man who hated her and her family? "How much did you lose to Albright?"

Lady Ratcliffe blinked at her. "Quite a lot. Colin was furious with me. You see, I—I'd sworn to stay away from the card tables. But I only wanted a bit of fun . . . there's nothing wrong with that. It wasn't fair of Colin to make me stay away from London for so long."

As the woman continued to justify her own wrongdoing, Portia's mind worked furiously. Lady Ratcliffe was a gambler. Had Ratcliffe needed the dowry in order to pay off his mother's illicit debts, rather than his own? Was it possible that Ratcliffe himself was not the wastrel people believed him to be? The revelation shook Portia to the core.

If that was the truth, why hadn't he told her so? Was it

ome sort of misguided gallantry on his part, a means of
rotecting his mother's reputation?

Portia eyed the dainty woman who sat crying pite-
usly. What would become of Lady Ratcliffe now? She
ad killed a peer of the realm. Surely there would be
onsequences . . .

The sound of approaching footsteps drew her atten-
ion. The door opened and Ratcliffe thrust his head in-
ide. He glanced at his mother, then looked at Portia.
Their gazes locked for one long eloquent moment. A
lepth of feeling seemed to leap across the small con-
ines of the coach. Then the intensity in his eyes faded to
bleak coldness.

Lady Ratcliffe groped for his hand. "Colin! I didn't
nean to kill him. Whatever am I to do?"

"You're to go straight back to your town house. Perhaps
Miss Crompton will be kind enough to escort you."

His formal use of her name caused a knell of alarm in
Portia. "Certainly. But where are you going?"

"I'll be leaving England," he stated grimly. "Quite
ossibly for a long time."

She gasped. "What?"

"I shot Albright to death. That is the story the seconds
ave agreed to tell. Mother, you were merely a by-
tander."

Lady Ratcliffe looked stricken. "But . . . my dear
oy . . ."

"You did nothing, is that quite clear?" She nodded
lowly, releasing his hand and sitting back to stare down
t her hands. He turned his stern gaze on Portia. "And
ou are to corroborate the tale. No one else is to know
vhat really transpired here today."

Portia was aghast. He intended to shoulder the blame
or his mother's act. He would flee to the Continent to

avoid being prosecuted for murder. Her spine stiffened at the injustice of it. "I most certainly will not repeat such a lie! No one will blame Lady Ratcliffe for firing her pistol. She did it to save your life!"

"That is not the way society will view matters. I won't have her involved in such a scandal."

"I'll explain it to everyone. I'll vouch for you—and for her!"

A wintry smile touched his lips. "No one will believe you. You'll be wasting your breath. I'm the one with the wild reputation, remember?"

The cynical truth in his words gave her pause. The self-righteous snobs of society had already tarred and feathered him. They viewed him as a worthless profligate. Everyone knew about the feud between Ratcliffe and Albright, so they would be quick to believe he had killed the duke in cold blood. No matter what they heard to the contrary.

Agonized by the notion of losing him, Portia lifted her hand to his face and stroked the vital warmth of his skin. She made a swift, heartfelt decision. "Then I'll go with you."

A muscle in his jaw clenched. He drew back sharply out of her reach. "No. I'm riding fast, and you'll slow me down."

His rejection hit her like a slap. Without further ado he slammed the door of the carriage and walked out of her life.

Colin lay on his back in the narrow bed, his arms folded behind his head. It made a better pillow than the flat one provided by the inn. Because a storm had blown in, he had been forced to take a room in Dover. No ships would risk crossing the channel until the morning at the very earliest.

Rain drummed against the window, and a damp chill seeped through cracks in the walls. If the nasty weather kept up tomorrow, he would be forced to go into hiding farther up the coast. He certainly couldn't remain here where he was a sitting duck for the Bow Street runners.

Cautiously, he fingered the lump nestled in his hair. He had the very devil of a headache. The cowardly blow had caught him off guard the other morning because he had been so livid at seeing Albright with his hand on Portia.

Now Albright was dead. And Colin was left with nothing more than a hollow sense of relief. The spider had devoted his life to playing sly tricks on Colin's family, but when he had extended his web to ensnare Portia, that had been the final straw. If his mother hadn't pulled the trigger, then Colin would have done so—gladly. Either way, the road to ruin led straight here to this rented room with its bare walls and dingy furnishings.

The law wouldn't look kindly on the murder of an exalted duke.

Colin stared up at the bare plank ceiling. The crashing of the surf and the howling of the wind should have lulled him to sleep. God knew, he was weary enough. In preparing for the duel the previous night, he had slept only an hour or two, and not much more the night before that—the night he had spent in Portia's arms.

Those golden hours had been burned into his memory. Nothing could have prepared him for the bond of closeness between them. The depth of his feelings for her had knocked him off kilter. Even now, when he knew it was impossible, he kept entertaining feverish, foolish hopes of a reunion.

I'll go with you.

She had no idea of what she was offering. All of her talk about traveling to India and becoming a governess had been just so much nonsense. Poverty was out of the realm of her experience. Having grown up in luxury, she would be miserable living on the run with him, without being able to set down roots or even knowing if they had the funds to purchase their next meal. And once the romantic haze wore off, their closeness would deteriorate into wretched squabbling—as had happened to his own parents.

Nevertheless, Colin found himself wishing he had hauled her out of the carriage and taken her up onto his horse. It had nearly killed him to close the door on her, his last memory the sight of her stricken expression. The pull of her magnetism kept luring his thoughts back to London. He fought the craving to abandon his flight and damn the consequences.

He shifted restlessly on the bed. The last thing he needed was to be alone with only his thoughts for company. He ought to go down to the tavern where at least there would be a few other lost souls hunched over their pints of ale. But it was too dangerous to show his face. Better he should stay out of sight so that fewer people could identify his presence.

The gray light slowly faded to black. Colin fell asleep. Sometime during the night, he was awakened by the faint rattle of a key in the lock. Snapping to awareness, he sat up, the covers falling away. He grabbed the primed pistol lying on the bedside table.

A party of men burst into the room. One held an oil lamp high.

Squinting against the brightness, Colin cursed.

One shot. Three men.

"Lay down your weapon, my lord, lest things go worse for you," stated the tall one with the lantern. "As a representative of the Crown, I am hereby arresting you for the murder of His Grace of Albright."

CHAPTER 26

Four days later, Portia marched up the stairs of an elegant town house in Berkeley Square. Her gloved fingers grasping the brass knocker, she rapped hard. A moment later, a white-wigged footman opened the door.

"I should like to speak to Lady Ratcliffe," she said.

"I'm afraid her ladyship is not receiving at the moment. You may, however, leave your card."

"No. Pray tell her that Miss Crompton is here to see her."

"That is quite impossible. You see, her instructions were very specific—"

Portia pushed past the startled servant and walked into the foyer. The high-ceilinged entry was decorated in delicate greens and yellows, and a crystal chandelier glinted in the sunlight streaming through the front windows. But the beauty of the place didn't interest her. She headed straight for the curving marble staircase.

The pompous footman leaped forward to block her passage. "You mayn't go up there, miss."

"Then fetch your mistress at once. And pray relay the message that if she refuses to see me, I will come in search of her."

The footman hastened up the stairs, casting glances back over his shoulder as if she were a lunatic. He wouldn't be far from wrong. At the moment, Portia felt in the grips of a mad fear that Ratcliffe would go to the gallows and she had no power to stop it.

Her soles scuffed on the marble floor as she paced back and forth in the foyer. She was lucky to have escaped her mother's watchful eyes this morning, for she had been kept a virtual prisoner in her house. After the duel, with Ratcliffe gone, she'd had no other choice but to return home. She had been lectured until her ears hurt. Her parents had been aghast over the death of the duke, and horrified she had been brazen enough to sneak out of the house and witness it. They blamed her for Ratcliffe challenging the duke. If she hadn't run off with the wicked viscount, they'd said, Albright would still be alive.

There was no point in correcting them by saying Ratcliffe had abducted her, not vice versa. None of that mattered anymore. They would never understand that the duke was not a saint on a pedestal. Nor would they ever realize Ratcliffe was innocent of murder.

Unless Portia was successful today.

Word of his arrest had spread like wildfire through the ton. Her mother had announced it triumphantly, and in private her sisters had been eloquent with sympathy for Portia. Both Lindsey and Blythe had promised to keep Mama distracted this morning, long enough for Portia to perform this vital errand.

The patter of footsteps drew her attention. Clad in a gown of diaphanous green gauze, Lady Ratcliffe glided down the curving staircase. Her mass of black hair had been drawn up to reveal her slender neck. On closer inspection, one could see dark circles under her eyes and her mouth had a pinched look.

She regarded Portia with a trace of hauteur. Except for the handkerchief in her hand, there was little sign of the weeping, broken woman she had been after the duel. "Miss Crompton. What an unexpected pleasure."

"My lady." Portia dipped the obligatory curtsy. "May we speak in private?"

"*May?* I was under the impression you had commanded my presence."

"Forgive me. It's a matter of great importance."

"Well, then. Follow me." Despite her acerbic tone, the viscountess led Portia down the corridor and into a morning room decorated in creams and yellows. The windows looked out on a rear garden where roses bloomed in profusion. The setting suited Lady Ratcliffe, so dainty and pretty and frivolous.

How deep did her beauty go? Portia would soon find out.

"Do sit down." Her hostess waved a hand at a yellow-striped chaise. "Shall I ring for tea?"

"No, that won't be necessary." Portia seated herself, then leaned forward, watching Lady Ratcliffe closely as she floated to a nearby chair. "I've come to talk to you about Ratcliffe . . . about Colin."

"He's in prison, of course." She waved the scrap of lace that masqueraded as a handkerchief. "Please be assured I have engaged a solicitor who is making every attempt to have the case dismissed."

"Have you told this man the truth about what really happened?"

Lady Ratcliffe avoided Portia's eyes. "There will be no need for that if it never comes to trial."

Portia bit back an indignant disagreement. But before launching into a tirade, she wanted to confirm something that had been nagging at her since the day of the duel. "Be that as it may, I came here to ask you a question. A very personal one. I am sorry in advance if it proves to be upsetting to you."

Lady Ratcliffe clutched the handkerchief to her bosom. "Upsetting? Nothing could cause me more distress than knowing that my only son is languishing behind bars."

Portia drew a steadying breath. "I need to know . . . was it you who killed your husband three years ago?"

Lady Ratcliffe's face turned paper white. Her bloodless lips parted. She sat very still, her wide green eyes conveying the terrible, guilty truth. "What? Why would you ask me such a thing?"

A rush of cold anger enveloped Portia. So her suspicions had been correct. Just as with the death of Albright, and with the gambling, Ratcliffe had been protecting his mother.

She curbed her emotions, keeping her voice soft but firm. "You *are* responsible. Pray don't deny it, my lady."

That patrician chin wobbled. "I can't imagine why you're making these awful accusations."

"Nor can I understand why you would allow your son to shoulder the blame for your own misdeed. A gun went off. But it wasn't Colin holding it. It was you."

Lady Ratcliffe seemed to shrink, her shoulders lowering, her chin dipping down like a child caught in a naughty act. "All right, then. But it was an accident. I swear it."

Portia felt no triumph at the admission. She only wanted to understand matters for Ratcliffe's sake. "Tell me what happened."

For a long moment, Lady Ratcliffe was silent, her head bowed. "I quarreled with my husband," she whispered. "Roger was angry because I'd lost a trifling sum at the card tables. It had happened a few times before, but this time he wouldn't cease scolding me. He called me . . . a millstone around his neck." A sob caught in her throat, and her fingernails dug into the arm of the chair, shredding the delicate silk. "Please understand my despair, Miss Crompton! I found one of my son's pistols . . . and held it to my bosom. I asked Roger if he would be happier if I ended my life. I swear to you, I didn't know the pistol was loaded. *I didn't.* When Roger tried to wrest it away from me, it went off . . . it was nothing but a horrid accident . . ."

Her voice faltered to a stop. She lapsed into wretched weeping, her beautiful face gone ugly with tears.

Portia wanted to despise her, but could summon only pity. Lady Ratcliffe was a weak woman. She relied on the men in her life to conceal her errors of judgment. She had never been held accountable for her own actions.

Portia intended to put an end to all that.

Colin had been given one of the better cells at Newgate Prison. Which simply meant that rather than share his stone-walled cubicle with several other inmates, he had rats for company instead. Over the past few days, he had trained one rodent to beg like a dog for the bits of dry bread left over from his meager breakfast.

At the moment, Colin was sitting on his pallet on the floor and holding out a crumb between his thumb and forefinger. The skinny gray creature perched on its hind feet, its whiskers and black snout quivering. Colin tossed the tidbit up in the air. The rat pounced on it, nibbled daintily, then ventured back for more.

The tramp of footsteps approached from far down the corridor, but Colin took little notice. The prison was seldom quiet. Guards came and went. Prisoners howled and banged their tin cups on the bars. Men snored loudly or laughed raucously at all hours of the night. At least the noise drowned out the maddening *drip-drip* of water somewhere nearby, the source of which he had been unable to discern.

His life had dwindled to this cramped stone cell. The damp chill had taken up residence in his bones, despite the blankets and a few other amenities his mother had provided through her solicitor. She herself had not been here to visit because Colin had forbidden it. Nothing would be more incongruous than to see his elegant mother in this stinking hellhole.

Taking the blame for Albright's death had been the only course of action open to him. His mother wouldn't survive one night in prison. Besides, he was every bit as guilty as she. He would have pulled the trigger himself had she not done so first.

The only regret he had suffered—still suffered—was losing Portia.

He pulverized the last morsel of bread. The rat scurried here and there, cleaning the bits from the slimy stone floor.

Colin clenched his jaw, struggling to keep the memories at bay. But a succession of vivid impressions branded him. The silken softness of her hair. Her joyous cries of ecstasy. The tender touch of her fingers on his face.

I'll go with you.

He buried his head in his hands. Thank God he'd had the stamina to refuse her imprudent offer. Had she been tucked in bed with him when the runners had come, they might have arrested her as an accomplice. The scandal would have kept her from ever showing her face in public again.

If his abduction of her hadn't already accomplished her ruin. And *if* she hadn't conceived on their night together.

In such a dire instance, what would happen to her and their child? The question made him half-mad with anxiety. He should never have given in to his base urges. He should have insisted on marriage first, even if it made him appear as prim and prissy as a maiden aunt. No one but he was responsible for her downfall.

The jingle of keys penetrated his self-mortifying stupor. The tramp of footsteps had stopped in front of his cell.

Colin jerked up his head. A husky guard with two missing front teeth was opening the iron-barred door. The pet rat made a dash for a tiny hole in the corner.

The guard stepped aside to let in a small, officious man wearing a sleek black coat with matching pantaloons. He was carrying a small satchel at his side. His nose twitched like the rat's, and his dark eyes betrayed distaste at the surroundings, as if he were afraid he might catch a disease by touching anything.

It was the solicitor who had been hired to handle the murder case. Thus far, the fellow had served as little more than a go-between for Colin and his mother. But at least the visit provided a break from his morbid thoughts.

He rose, his legs stiff. "Entwhistle."

"My lord." Entwhistle made a deep, formal bow. As he straightened, his narrow face broke into an unexpected grin. "I bring the happiest of tidings. You, my lord, are a free man!"

"What?"

"Indeed so. You have been cleared of all charges. I have the papers signed and sealed right here." He patted his black satchel. "It was handled quite properly by the magistrate."

Disbelieving, Colin stared. "How can the case be dropped? I shot the Duke of Albright in cold blood. Unless he's risen from the grave to dance in the streets."

Entwhistle laughed as if it were a brilliant jest. Then he coughed and cleared his throat. "The fact of the matter is, new evidence has come to light that proves irrefutably that you are not the guilty party. Indeed, I must admire you for your gentlemanly conduct in protecting Lady Ratcliffe from admitting her guilt."

Colin seized hold of the man's lapels. "What the hell? Are you saying my mother has been arrested for the murder?"

The attorney's eyes bugged out. "Oh, nay, my lord! She is perfectly safe and sound at her home. I saw her there myself only a few hours ago."

"I don't understand, then. Who have the authorities arrested?"

"Why, no one. The magistrate was persuaded that it was an unfortunate accident. Both seconds have corroborated the testimony, along with the doctor who attended the duke. So you see, all's well that ends well."

In shock, Colin released the man and stepped back. By damn, he really was free. He would never have expected Albright's second to have revealed the duke's dishonor. Yet he couldn't feel any triumph, not when society must be blaming his mother for Albright's death.

Instead he felt mired in guilt. God help him, he had broken the promise he had made to his father as he lay dying. Colin had vowed to watch over his mother, to shield and protect her with his own life.

And now he had failed.

One fact was certain. His mother would never have willingly volunteered the truth about her involvement in Albright's death. She was too delicate and ladylike to face the risk of being thrown into prison. But Colin could certainly guess the identity of the instigator.

CHAPTER 27

ord Ratcliffe, innocent of murder?" Mrs. Beardsley
onounced. "Upon my word, it is too much to believe."

"Surely the courts have made a mistake," her daugh-
r Frances said hopefully, blinking her china-blue eyes.

While the gossip swirled around her, Portia serenely
pped her tea. It took great concentration to keep from
owing her elation over Ratcliffe's release. The news
d broken only a short time ago, and the grand hens of
ciety had come flocking to the Cromptons' drawing
om—probably because they hoped to spark a reaction
om the debutante who had been involved with Rat-
iffe.

"More tea?" Mrs. Crompton asked with grim-faced
rtitude, offering the silver pot.

With a gnarled hand, the Duchess of Milbourne
aved her away. "There has been no mistake in the mat-
r," she told the disappointed Beardsleys. "I heard the
uth from Lillian herself. Apparently, her son shoul-
red the guilt in order to protect her good name."

"Will she go to the gallows?" white-haired Lady
rantham asked with a shudder. "Oh, my stars, I cannot
nagine it!"

"The magistrate has verified the word of the seconds,"
e duchess replied. "The incident was deemed an act of

treachery on the duke's part, so there will be no need f
a trial. At present, Lillian is packing to return to th
country." The elderly woman stared straight at Portia. '
seems Ratcliffe has ordered her to take up residence
the dower house on his estate."

Portia pretended interest in the lukewarm dregs of h
cup. Her mind worked feverishly. Ratcliffe was movin
his mother out of the main house? What did it mea
That he didn't want her interfering when he broug
home a wife?

She mustn't let herself hope. So much had happen
since the duel. To her, the night they'd shared had bour
them together forever. However, it might have mea
very little to Ratcliffe. After all, he had engaged in mar
such trysts. She may already have faded in his min
especially if he believed her father viewed him as to
scandal-ridden to deserve her dowry.

Did he love her—or not?

Mrs. Beardsley tut-tutted. "Poor Lady Ratcliffe, to
banished to the country."

Her daughter nodded vigorously, making her blo
curls bounce. "How cruel of his lordship to send h
away from all the shopping in the city. And to deny h
the company of the ton, as well!"

"Nonsense," the duchess said crisply, motioning i
periously for Mrs. Crompton to hand her a slice of pop
seed cake. "No matter what the circumstances, Lillian
responsible for Albright's death. I, for one, am pleas
she has had the good sense to retire from society on
and for all."

Her firm tone brooked no disagreement, and La
Grantham and Mrs. Crompton quickly murmured th
support. Portia bit back a smile to see the consternati
on the faces of their other two guests. Stout Mrs. Bear
sley looked as if she'd bitten into a lemon, while her pir

wned daughter Frances thrust out her lower lip in a
tulant pout.

Mrs. Beardsley harrumphed. "Well, this incident cer-
inly does not absolve Lord Ratcliffe of his many sins.
e remains a menace to the young ladies of society."

"I quite agree," said Frances, with a sly glance at Por-
a. "What do you think, Miss Crompton? You know
m better than the rest of us."

Portia let her teacup clatter down on the nearest table.
ie had heard quite enough of their small-minded cen-
ire. Despite her mother's warnings to stay silent, it was
me to state her opinion in no uncertain terms.

She looked at each woman in turn. "Ratcliffe de-
rves to be commended, rather than criticized. For too
ng he's been denigrated by those of you who know
thing of his admirable character. After having met
very bachelor in the ton, I can say without doubt he is
e finest gentleman of my acquaintance."

Her mother gasped. Lady Grantham's jaw dropped.
he Beardsleys stared agog.

The Duchess of Milbourne thumped her cane on the
ie carpet. "Well said, my girl! I myself must confess to
new admiration for the fellow. It is the mark of a true
entleman to protect his family from harm. Why, he
irkens back to my day, when men were not so slavishly
evoted to such silly matters as tying the perfect cravat!"

"Ahem."

The sound of a clearing throat drew Portia's attention
the doorway of the drawing room. Her father stood
ere. But that wasn't why her heart took flight. Beside
m, dressed to perfection in a topaz-brown coat and
ickskin breeches, was Ratcliffe.

olin followed Portia down the corridor. Gazing at the
vay of her hips, he was hard-pressed to remember the

source of his grievance with her. The gauzy blue gov
skimmed the curves of her perfect, womanly form. I
damn, he wanted to sweep her into his arms and car
her upstairs to the nearest bedchamber. Maybe in lov
making they could forget all their differences. And
could do his best to ensure that she devoted herself
him for the rest of their lives.

Not, of course, that he would dare any such brazen a
right here under the noses of her parents. He need
their approval, which was why he had sought out her f
ther rather than go straight to Portia. But that didn't st
Colin from fantasizing.

He burned to know why she had offered to go wi
him on his flight to the Continent. Was it lust—or love

He had caught only a few words spoken by that o
crone Duchess Milbourne. Something about men now
days being slavishly devoted to tying the perfect crava
Now he wished he'd had the opportunity to eavesdro
outside the doorway, because those biddies had to ha
come here to gossip about his discharge from prison. I
desperately wanted to know what—if anything—Port
had said in response to them. Had she informed them
her own role in securing his release?

The reminder of her interference irked him.

At the end of the ornate passageway, they entered
cozy sitting room. Portia waved him past her and clos
the door. When she turned to face him, her gaze w
guarded. Rather than throw herself into his arms, s
primly clasped her hands at her waist.

God help him, he could drown in those blue eyes
hers.

He expected her to ask why he'd been speaking to h
father. Instead, she merely said, "You're looking well
must say, I'm happy your name has been cleared at las

Her polite manner made him want to shake her. N

wanted to haul her close and kiss her senseless. But
st he had to set her straight. "My name was cleared at
e expense of my mother. You deliberately interfered
ainst my express wishes."

"Your *wishes* allowed Lady Ratcliffe to escape all
sponsibility for her actions. It was completely unfair to
u—to both of you."

Colin negated the judgment with a slash of his hand.
'hat's for me to decide, not you or anyone else. And
cause of you, she might have been thrown into prison."

Portia set her hands on her hips. "Well, she wasn't.
nce I persuaded her to do right by you, we went to
eak to each of the seconds and the doctor, too. It was a
mple matter to convince them all to tell the truth to the
thorities."

"And little wonder!" he snapped. "*They* haven't sworn
vow to protect her."

Frowning, Portia took a step toward him. "A vow?"

"To my father as he lay dying."

Ridden with guilt, Colin raked his fingers through his
ir, already regretting the admission. It was something
had never told anyone else. That moment was seared
to his memory—his father, lying on the floor in a pool
blood, barely able to talk, using his final breaths to
g the promise from Colin . . . to guard his mother
om all blame.

A hint of compassion softening her face, Portia stood
tching him. "So that's why you've been so tenacious
your protection of her. This isn't the first time you've
vered for your mother."

"What is that supposed to mean?"

"Don't pretend ignorance. I know about her gambling.
u've let people believe *you* are the profligate. But in
ality, *she* is the reason you haven't any money."

"A lady's reputation is more easily ruined than a man's."

"And there's also the fact that *she* killed your father-not you. It was a tragic accident."

The words hit Colin like a punch to the jaw. A plethora of emotions threatened to overwhelm him. To keep himself from raging like a lunatic, he strode away, then pivoted to face her. "My God! Have you exposed all this to the public, as well?"

"Certainly not. I've no vendetta against her. In truth, your sense of honor is to be applauded." She took another step toward him. "But surely you can see that I had to set you free. Or perhaps you would have preferred to hang?"

Her tart tone gave no clue to her real feelings. By God, why had she taken up his defense? Because she truly cared for him? Or merely in a quest for justice?

He took a deep breath. "You didn't need to sully her name in the process. I would have found a way to escape the gallows."

"I couldn't take that chance." Portia regarded him a moment, then lifted her chin. "After all, you owe me a wedding ring. We could hardly marry if you were behind bars."

His heart lurched. Good God, was *she* proposing to *him*? "What?"

"Everyone in society thinks we ran off together. They believe that's the only reason you and Albright dueled. Now, they're sure to be speculating over why you were speaking to Papa just now."

It was hardly the tender admission of love that he had hoped for. Portia wouldn't be marrying him out of heartfelt affection, but for protection against gossip.

That knowledge stuck in his gullet like a bitter pill. Yet he had no more pride left where she was concerned. Moonstruck calf that he was, he'd take her under any circumstances she offered.

He bowed stiffly. "Your father has left the decision up
) you. Since you're in agreement, I shall apply for the
)ecial license at once."

Watching him stride out of the sitting room, Portia sagged
)own onto the nearest chair. She and Ratcliffe were going
) be married. But he was acting out of a sense of duty
ather than love. And she mustn't forget that he still
eeded her dowry, too, to pay off his mother's debts. How
old he had been, how angry at Portia for interfering in
is life!

For a moment, when their eyes had first met in the
rawing room, she'd had reason to hope for an ardent
eunion. His keen gaze had been concentrated on her, as
' he were aware of no one else but her in the room. But
fter his formal greeting to the ladies, he had treated
ortia with a cool remoteness that left her more discour-
ged than ever.

Why had he not taken her into his arms? What had
appened to the passion they had shared on that one
vonderful night?

Portia forced herself up from the chair. She refused to
vallow in self-pity. Somehow, she must find a way to
vin his heart.

And he *did* have a heart. One had only to look at the
vay he helped those in his employ and his willingness to
rotect his own mother. Duchess Milbourne was right;
ery few gentlemen would suffer jail and possible execu-
on in order to hide the guilt of a loved one. Once they
vere wed, Portia would have the chance to make herself
ndispensable to Ratcliffe. Perhaps love given would en-
ourage love returned.

Yes. She had to keep faith in that possibility.

Heading down the passageway, she decided to slip
pstairs rather than return to their guests. It was too

daunting to think of facing all those nosy ladies wh[o]
would poke and prod, trying to find out what she an[d]
Ratcliffe had discussed. Besides, she burned to tell he[r]
sisters about the imminent marriage. Lindsey and Blyth[e]
could always be counted on to bolster her spirits. The[y]
would say that given half a chance, he was bound to fa[ll]
madly in love with her.

Turning the corner near the staircase, she glance[d]
down the corridor. And frowned.

Ratcliffe hadn't departed, after all. He stood talkin[g]
to a cinnamon-skinned man in flowing white trouser[s]
and a turquoise surcoat, a turban on his head. The visi[-]
tor's fingers winked with multicolored jewels.

Portia stared. Her heart lurched. *Impossible.*

Without conscious thought, she found herself runnin[g]
down the corridor. Stopping in front of him, she dran[k]
in his familiar features. Her lips parted in a disbelievin[g]
gasp.

"Arun?"

CHAPTER 28

The English ladies—with the exception of her glowering mother—were positively slavering over the appearance of an exotic prince in their midst. Or rather, a maharajah, for Arun's father had died months ago in the cholera epidemic.

"If I may be so bold," Mrs. Beardsley said, "what sort of title is maharajah?"

"It means king," Arun explained in his modest way. "It is a great honor for me to bear."

"Oooh," Frances Beardsley twittered. "Then your wife would be a queen!"

He gave Portia an unreadable look. "Yes, the maharani."

Arun was alive. The shock of it hadn't quite settled into her heart and mind. Instead of writing any more letters, he had traveled halfway around the globe to surprise her. Quite probably to tell her there was no longer any impediment to their marriage, at least from his family.

Portia didn't know whether to laugh or cry. Watching Arun chat with the ladies, entertaining them with stories about his private zoo of tigers and elephants in his white marble palace, filled her with an unimaginable joy. She loved listening to his musical voice; it brought back nostalgic memories of her childhood.

Yet she couldn't stop thinking about Ratcliffe.

His face had been stony, unsmiling. He had been standing right there as a witness while she had thrown her arms around Arun and wept with thanksgiving over his survival. Then, a few minutes later, when she had turned around to introduce him, Ratcliffe had vanished.

Just like that, he'd left without saying good-bye. Dear God, what must he have thought? It was easy to imagine. He would believe mistakenly that she preferred to wed Arun.

The thought was so wrenching that she rose abruptly to her feet. Arun stood up as well, his quizzical gaze on her.

Frances Beardsley batted her lashes at him. "Please don't leave just yet, Your Majesty. You haven't finished telling us about your pet monkey."

Arun flashed her his beautiful smile, all dazzling white teeth and warm brown eyes. Pressing his palms together, he bowed. "It is time I speak to Miss Crompton. Perhaps later we talk?"

Frances gave him a sappy smile. "You simply must come to visit me tomorrow. May he, Mama? Please?"

"Why, we would be honored to entertain royalty such as yourself," Mrs. Beardsley said, avidly eyeing his jewels, from the huge oval sapphire on his turban to the diamond and ruby brooch at his throat. "Perhaps dinner with a few select members of society?"

Arun bowed his acquiescence, then Portia escorted him across the corridor to the blue sitting room. She was torn between wanting to catch up on all the news with her old friend, and her pressing need to find Ratcliffe. Had he gone to apply for the special license? Surely he must have. To contemplate anything else was too alarming.

Arun sat down beside her on a chaise. "You are worried," he said, taking her hand in his. "I see it in your face."

What was she to say? She laced her fingers through his, reveling in his warmth. "I'm so glad you're alive, Arun. It's absolutely wonderful to see you again. You cannot imagine how much."

When she paused, he added gently, "Yet you love another man now. Lord Ratcliffe."

Portia bit her lip. Had she been so obvious? "Oh, Arun, I thought you were dead. I was heartbroken. And the more I came to know Ratcliffe, the more I fell in love with him. I don't know quite how it happened, but it did."

The corners of Arun's mouth turned downward, then he gave a slow nod. "The distance between us was too great. I should have defied my father's wishes and come after you. But I did not."

"Yet you *did* come to see me. So it is all *my* fault, not yours."

He gave a little laugh, smiling at her. "We will not blame ourselves, dear Portia. It is karma that has decided the direction of our lives. You have found a man who loves you deeply, and as your friend I am happy for you."

Her heart overflowed. Arun's charitable, forgiving nature was one of the things she'd always treasured about him. She clutched his smooth fingers, desperately needing his friendship. "I must confess, it is not quite a love match for Ratcliffe."

"No? But I am certain it is so. The eyes do not lie. The way he looked at you revealed all to me."

She shook her head, afraid to believe it. "I don't doubt he cares for me, at least a little. But that isn't love. In truth, it's my rich dowry he needs."

Arun drew back, steepling his hands together in a

contemplative pose. "Then it is my duty to help you uncover the truth. I know the very way to put your Ratcliffe to the test."

"I vow, I shall never recover from another day such as this one," Edith Crompton told her husband that evening, while brushing her hair with hard strokes. "Never as long as I live!"

George came to stand behind her in the boudoir. Their gazes clashed in the mirror. He looked infuriatingly content.

He bent down to kiss her neck. "Now, darling, it isn't the end of the world. Portia will be a viscountess. After speaking at length to Ratcliffe, I rather suspect they will be happy together."

Edith slammed down the hairbrush and swiveled on the stool to face him. "Happy! She was supposed to be the Duchess of Albright. Our grandson would have been duke someday."

A scowl deepened the wrinkles on his weathered brow. "Albright. I'd always had my doubts about the fellow. If I'd known that he'd tossed his pregnant mistress out into the street, or that he would act with such treachery in the duel, I'd never have let you talk me into approving the match." Walking back and forth, George shook his head in disgust. "Portia deserves far better than such a man, duke or not."

He had always favored their eldest, a fact that Edith had exploited on occasion. Getting nowhere now, she changed her attack. "Perhaps you would as soon have her wed that Hindu prince of hers. It was *you* who let him into this house, wasn't it?"

"Certainly. I saw no reason why our daughter shouldn't visit with an old friend."

"He's a filthy native, that's why! It's a wonder his presence didn't taint us in front of society. And right on the heels of that dreadful scandal when Portia ran off with Ratcliffe."

"Everything has turned out remarkably well," he said sternly. "Portia will marry Ratcliffe. The matter is settled. I will hear no more about it from you."

Edith knew from his reddened face that his temper was on the verge of exploding. Yet she couldn't resist one final dig. "Then I suppose *this* is what you had in mind when we came to London—Portia betrothed to a rogue who is beyond the pale!"

He slammed his palm down on the dressing table, making the bottles and jars rattle. "Enough! These ambitions are yours, not mine. If you cannot bide your tongue, we will all go straight back to India, and damn your infernal matchmaking!"

Edith compressed her lips. She had pushed him too far. Nothing made her quail more than to think of returning to that heathen land. It was here in the rarefied culture of England that she had always aspired to be, a respected member of society. She had craved it ever since she had been a girl laboring for a living, watching and learning, studying her betters, planning the day when she would become one of them. And she was not content to be just a hanger-on at the fringes, someone accepted only because of her money.

No, she wanted her daughters to take her to the very pinnacle of the ton.

Leashing her frustration, she peered into the mirror and plucked out a stray gray hair among her thick russet tresses. All was not lost. Portia may have made a less than illustrious choice, but there was still Lindsey and Blythe.

* * *

Just after luncheon the following day, Portia stood in the middle of her bedchamber and gripped a letter. A footman had just delivered it, and she had run straight up here to read the missive. Her disbelieving gaze skimmed the bold black script again:

My dear Portia,

In light of recent events, I must hereby grant you a release from your consent to our nuptials. Pray know that you will always have a place in my heart.

Ratcliffe

Her legs gave way and she sank onto the edge of the bed. Despair pervaded every part of her soul. Arun's plan had failed spectacularly. He had promised to call on Ratcliffe today and offer him a treasure trove of jewels worth far more than her dowry.

In exchange, Ratcliffe would have to agree to give up Portia. If he refused to do so, as Arun predicted, she would know that Ratcliffe loved her more than any amount of wealth.

But apparently he had accepted Arun's offer.

She squeezed her eyes shut to hold back a hot rush of tears. Dear God, she had allowed herself to hope. She had taken heart from Arun's confidence that Ratcliffe loved her dearly. She had gone to sleep with a smile on her face and awakened with eager anticipation.

Instead, Ratcliffe had chosen the jewels over her. And then he dared to write that she would always have a place in his heart.

Blast him!

In sudden anger, she dashed her tears away. All of

their closeness had been merely a sham—at least for him. After all they'd shared, did the coward think he could fob her off with a hastily scrawled note?

By heaven, she wouldn't allow it.

Standing in the open doorway of his town house, Colin scowled down at the street. He watched as Arun climbed into the gold-trimmed coach, the door held by a burly guard with a scimitar at his side. Two other men staggered under the weight of a massive trunk, which they hoisted into another coach behind the maharajah's. Their turbans and flowing turquoise-blue garments garnered attention from all the neighbors, several of whom stood unabashedly gawking on the foot pavement.

The damn fool had a bigger retinue than the Prince Regent himself.

Arun would be able to give Portia the life she deserved. With him, she would never want for anything, and her every whim would be fulfilled. And the damnable thing was, he seemed a decent enough chap, grave and polite even as he'd offered Colin a bloody fortune to relinquish Portia into his keeping.

Colin hadn't bothered to tell him about the letter he'd already written to her. Let the fool find out on his own that his bribe had been unnecessary.

He slammed the door shut and turned to see that his own three motley servants had gathered behind him in the foyer.

"Cor!" Bane said in awe, trotting to the window to press his nose to the glass. "Was all them jewels real?"

"Yes, and good riddance to them."

"But . . . who was that foreigner?" Hannah asked in confusion. She rested her hands on her pregnant belly, and Tudge had his arm around her waist. "Why did he bring you a huge trunk full of jewels?"

"He wanted to trade them for Portia. In exchange for her hand in marriage." Raking his fingers through his hair, Colin paced back and forth. He focused on rage as a means of keeping the powerful ache inside him at bay. "You can be damned sure I told him exactly where he could stick them."

"Ye might 'ave a predicament," Tudge commented.

"What the devil does that mean?"

Tudge exchanged a glance with Hannah, and there seemed to be a silent communication between them. The two of them had been rather close lately, doing little things for each other, Tudge carrying heavy pails of water for her, while she cooked his favorite dishes. Colin had even had to duck out of the kitchen one evening when he had happened upon them kissing. It was a pitiful day when his own romantic life paled beside that of his servants.

Hannah's eyes widened and she looked at Colin. "That letter, my lord. The one you had Mr. Tudge deliver to Miss Crompton's house a short while ago."

"Ye broke off yer engagement," Tudge added, as if Colin would have already forgotten the contents.

He had wrestled with his conscience for half the night. By the morning, he had come to the daunting, inescapable conclusion that he had no right to separate her from the man she loved. Arun was alive, he was here, and she had always intended to marry him. So Colin had forced himself to pen the note to Portia, releasing her from their betrothal.

He lapsed into a fantasy where she hastened here to tell him that he was wrong, that she loved him so much she couldn't bear to live without him. In the next moment, he cursed himself for a fool.

Realizing his servants were watching him expectantly, he snapped, "What about the blasted letter?"

"It's quite simple," Hannah said. "If Miss Crompton knew that man was intending to offer you jewels, she's sure to think you were *bribed* into ending the engagement."

The pain of that cut into him. Had Arun really told her he was coming here today with his infamous offer? What if he never revealed that Colin had refused the jewels? For the rest of her life, Portia would believe he had been bought off, rather than having performed a selfless act of sacrifice.

"Look!" Bane said, still peering out the window.

Paying the boy no heed, Colin slashed his hand downward. "Let her think what she will. It doesn't matter anymore."

"Bah," Hannah said. "Does she even know how much you love her?"

"An' don't deny ye do," Tudge added. "Ye been a grouch an' we ain't 'ad a moment o' peace around 'ere."

Damn it, they were right. He ought to go see Portia. He'd grovel at her feet if it meant winning her back. Because the prospect of losing her forever made him want to throw back his head and howl.

Bane tugged on Colin's coat. "Yer lordship."

"What is it?" he snapped.

By way of answer, the boy opened the front door. Portia stood on the stoop, her hand raised to knock.

Colin's heart thumped in powerful strokes. He stood frozen, certain he must be hallucinating. She was a vision of beauty, her dainty features accentuated by a straw bonnet with a ribbon tied beneath her chin, and her luscious curves hugged by a bronze-hued pelisse.

She glanced over her shoulder. "Was that Arun's coach I just saw driving off?"

Colin had to cudgel his brain into speaking. "Yes."

Her blue eyes grew enormous. "Then . . . you wrote

to me before you saw him. You didn't accept the jewels just now, did you?"

"Hell, no! Do you truly think I would take a bribe in exchange for you?"

"Of course not. I never wanted to think that at *all*."

Portia experienced a relief so vast it made her knees weak. He made her fears and worries seem so ridiculous. How could she have doubted him even for one instant?

She knew the answer to that. Because she was so afraid to find out that he didn't love her as tremendously and completely as she loved him.

Ratcliffe stared at her transfixed, his gaze naked with a yearning that took her breath away. How heartening to know he hadn't been paid off, after all. He must have relinquished her of his own accord—because he thought she preferred Arun.

She couldn't let him go on holding that mistaken impression.

Stepping forward, she placed her hand on his arm, taking pleasure in the strength of his muscles. "Invite me inside, Ratcliffe."

He seemed to snap out of his reverie. "As you wish."

He allowed her to pass, and she entered the foyer to find herself facing an audience. Hannah Wilton and Orson Tudge stood beaming, while Bane threw his arm around her. Pleased to see him looking so well, she hugged him tightly in return.

"You should offer to take her bonnet and wrap," Hannah said in a loud whisper.

"Oh." Bane scratched his mop of dark hair and looked up at her. "Er . . . may I take yer things, miss?"

"Why, thank you."

Ratcliffe helped her slip out of the pelisse, and the brush of his fingers sent frissons of excitement over her ‹in. She removed her bonnet and then patted her hair, ervous and wanting to look perfect. Then Ratcliffe hisked her down the corridor and into a rather shabby rawing room. He closed the door, and they stood star-ıg at each other.

He was so tall and handsome, so perfect in her eyes. It emed impossible that she had ever scorned him, im-ossible that she had once believed him to be an incor-gible rogue. Now he had become the most important erson in her life, and a rush of emotion squeezed her ıroat.

"Ratcliffe . . ."

"No," he said, holding up his hand. "Allow me to peak first. I've been a fool, Portia, the worst kind of ›ol. I was willing to concede to Arun's prior claim on ›u. But the truth is, I won't let you go so easily. I can't t you go. No other woman could ever make me feel ven half as happy as you do." He closed the distance etween them and took firm hold of her hands. "I love ›u so much."

The declaration fulfilled her most fervent dream. And ›t she couldn't let him off so easily. "That was a dread-ıl note you sent to me. You ought to have spoken to me ı person."

"Damn that letter! I was a coward, afraid to face the ain of seeing you again. But I intend to fight for you, ›rtia. Because I can't bear to lose you."

"You never lost me. I love you, too, Ratcliffe. With all y heart."

The awestruck look on his face filled her with an in-:edible joy. Then they were in each other's arms, kiss-ıg with a passion made all the sweeter by the strength f their devotion to each other. Nothing had ever felt as ght as this moment, knowing that he shared the depth f her feelings. She wanted to swoon from the bliss of it.

When at last she could speak again, Portia drew bac
slightly to trace her fingertip over his chiseled lips. Th
adoration in his green eyes answered all of her heartfel
hopes. "Henceforth," she murmured, "you'll no longe
be a menace to the ladies of society. I intend to mak
very certain of that."

"Minx." He spoke softly, his hands caressing her hip
in a way that promised carnal happiness. "And I intend t
make certain you never look at any other man but me."